Pearl became suddenly, acutely aware of how alone they were . . .

Not another person in the world knew they were there. She continued to drown in his gaze, her heart thudding in slow, heavy strokes.

The spark in his eyes flamed into something intense, though they held a question as well. Without stopping to think how inappropriate, how foolhardy, how—anything—this was, conscious only of her own need, Pearl tipped her face up for this kiss.

His lips lowered to hers, first to gently brush, then to explore, and finally to claim. She responded. His mouth on hers felt like heaven . . . like something she'd waited for all her life.

Books by Brenda Hiatt

ROGUE'S HONOR
SCANDALOUS VIRTUE
SHIP OF DREAMS

Coming Soon

A REBELLIOUS BRIDE

BRENDA HIATT

Rogue's Honor

AVON BOOKS

An Imprint of HarperCollinsPublishers

This is a work of fiction. Names, characters, places, and incidents are products of the author's imagination or are used fictitiously and are not to be construed as real. Any resemblance to actual events, locales, organizations, or persons, living or dead, is entirely coincidental.

AVON BOOKS
An Imprint of HarperCollins*Publishers*
10 East 53rd Street
New York, New York 10022-5299

First Avon Books paperback printing: July 2001

Avon Trademark Reg. U.S. Pat. Off. and in Other Countries, Marca Registrada, Hecho en U.S.A.
HarperCollins® is a trademark of HarperCollins Publishers Inc.

Printed in the U.S.A.

10 9 8 7 6 5 4 3 2

Preface

For years, all of London has known of the legendary Saint of Seven Dials, that shadowy figure who steals from the rich to give to the poor. To the denizens of London's slums and rookeries, he is worshiped as a hero and savior, while the gentlemen of the *ton* curse and scowl whenever his name is mentioned. His infamous calling cards are only proof of his impudence, they say, and an embarrassment to master and servant alike when they appear in place of purloined valuables.

The ladies of London Society are torn, sympathizing with their fathers and husbands even as they sigh over the mysterious, romantic thief. What sort of man must he be, to take such risks for such a noble cause? they wonder. But though his identity is shrouded in secrecy, his fame continues to spread . . .

Chapter 1

London
April 1816

She'll marry you, never fear."

Lady Pearl Moreston froze, her hand suspended over the crystal handle of the parlor door of Oakshire House, the finest mansion on Berkley Square. How dared her stepmother make such a promise—and to whom? Instead of opening the door, which stood slightly ajar, she waited to hear what reply might come.

"But she's refused me twice already, Your Grace." Pearl identified the tremulous tenor as belonging to Lord Bellowsworth. "It seems clear that her wishes—"

Obelia, Duchess of Oakshire, cut him off. "Her wishes have nothing to say to the matter. Do you wish to wed the Lady Pearl or not?"

1

Scarcely waiting for the young marquess's stammering assent, the Duchess went on. "When you get her to Hyde Park, take one of the less frequented paths—the one leading off to the north, about a quarter mile from the entrance. You know the one? Good. No, don't interrupt. She'll be down at any moment. Go all the way to the end, to the little copse you will find there, and renew your addresses, as . . . forcefully as you can."

"Forcefully? I—I'll try. But what if—"

"I told you not to interrupt. I have arranged to have someone discover you, seemingly by chance, who will attest that he found the two of you in a most compromising situation. The Duke will be only too happy to consent to the match, whatever his daughter's wishes might be. Her hand—and her fortune—will be yours."

Pearl waited to hear no more. Breezing into the room, her head held high, she exclaimed, "A delightful plan, to be sure!"

Lord Bellowsworth started violently and began to stammer, but the Duchess merely smiled. "Lady Pearl. What a surprise. We were speaking hypothetically, of course."

"Of course you were," Pearl agreed. "A hypothesis I fear I cannot help you to prove. You'll excuse me, my lord, for feeling indisposed for our drive today."

"Of . . . of course. That is to say . . . I never meant . . . I'll give you good day, my lady, Your Grace." Bowing and blathering, he backed out of the parlor and fled Oakshire House.

Pearl turned to her stepmother, whose petite blond beauty, so similar to her own mother's, even now diluted her anger with long-remembered sorrow. "I know you have been anxious for me to marry, but I confess I had not expected you to resort to such measures as these to ensure it."

The Duchess appeared more vexed than apologetic. "You leave me little choice," she said, flouncing across the room to seat herself in a high-backed chair that rather resembled a throne—her favorite. "Your father is concerned about your future, and I feel bound to make him easy on the subject."

"And, of course, the fact that the Fairbourne estate will fall to me if I am yet unwed on my twenty-first birthday has nothing to do with your solicitude." Pearl spoke dryly, hiding any pain she felt from both herself and her stepmother. Seven years ago, when her father had first remarried, she had wished— She cut off that regret ruthlessly.

Obelia tossed her golden curls. "You'll have a substantial fortune in any event. If you marry well, you'll have no need whatsoever for that property, which by rights should go to Edward with the rest when he inherits. You cannot fault me for looking out for my son's interests."

"Edward will scarcely be paupered by my inheritance of the smallest of the seven Oakshire estates." She adored her five-year-old half-brother, currently in the country while his mother enjoyed the London Season. But even for his sake, Pearl refused to sacrifice Fairbourne, a lovely little estate in the north of Oakshire, where she had spent many happy months as a child. She had definite plans for the land and people there—plans to put some of the theories she had studied into practice.

"That is not the point. It will divide the Oakshire

estate and lessen its consequence, which I cannot imagine you would wish. Besides," the Duchess continued peevishly, "that addendum to the entail was intended to provide for any daughter who might prove unmarriageable. As you've had any number of offers, it clearly does not apply in your case. I believe the lawyers will agree, when I explain how matters stand."

Before Pearl could reply, her father appeared at the parlor door. "I don't hear my two favorite girls arguing, do I?" he asked jovially. "What is it this time? The color of the new draperies?"

Obelia rose to greet the Duke, ushering him to the chair next to hers. "Of course we're not arguing, my love. We both know how that upsets you." She shot an admonitory look at Pearl. "I was merely pointing out to dear Pearl the advantages of matrimony, as I have been so blessed by that state myself. I do so wish to see her comfortably settled. Don't you?"

The Duke frowned, as he always did when this subject arose—which it did all too frequently, in Pearl's opinion. "So long as she's happy, and needn't be too far away," he conceded. "I won't let my 'Pearl beyond price' go to just anyone, you know. But I leave that in your capable hands, Obelia, as I've told you often enough. And Pearl's, of course."

"Of course," echoed the Duchess, clearly less than perfectly pleased by his caveats. "You may always trust me to do what's best for *both* of our children, my love."

He smiled fondly at his wife, and Pearl rose abruptly. "If you'll excuse me, I have some reading I'd like to finish."

Her father waved her away with an indulgent smile—he'd always been proud of her academic turn of mind—but Obelia arched one delicate brow. "Your bluestocking tendencies make my task more challenging, Pearl, but I shall prevail, never fear." Her look, which escaped the Duke's notice, made her words into a threat that Pearl now understood only too clearly.

Since Pearl's sixteenth birthday, Obelia had been throwing her in the way of every eligible male she could find. This Season she had redoubled her efforts, bringing in the most exclusive French modistes and coiffeuses to enhance her stepdaughter's slim figure and honey-colored tresses, and planning lavish entertainments. Now she seemed determined on stronger measures.

Pearl left the parlor, but not before she heard Obelia say to her husband, "I know dear Pearl's future worries you, Clarence, but fear not. By the time you return from Brighton, all will be settled. I have everything well in hand."

"I know you'll do your best for her, my dear," the Duke responded with an indulgent chuckle.

Pearl bit her lip. She had forgotten that her father was to leave within the hour. Without his support, she would have to rely solely on her wits to evade Obelia's determined plotting, and by the time she reached her opulent lilac sitting room she had the beginnings of a plan.

Her abigail, folding the Mechlin lace shawl Pearl had earlier rejected, looked up in surprise at her entrance. "My lady? Did I forget an item in your toilette?" Dark, perky, and petite, Hettie swept her mistress with a critical eye, clearly finding no fault until her gaze reached her face. "Something has happened." It was a statement, not a question.

Despite her anger at Obelia's machinations, Pearl could not suppress a smile. Hettie knew her better than any person living. "I'm afraid so," she replied. "And I need your help." Quickly, she related what had happened downstairs.

The daughter of Pearl's nanny, Hettie had known her mistress since they were both in the nursery, and enjoyed far more intimacy than was customary between a lady of the upper Quality and her abigail. When Pearl concluded, Hettie's indignation equaled Pearl's own. "You, marry that mealy-mouthed young popinjay? What can Her Grace be thinking?"

Pearl shrugged. "She wants me wed, and he is the most malleable of my current crop of suitors." She waved a hand toward the dozen or so bouquets displayed about the room, from the gilt mantelpiece to the exquisite inlaid mahogany tables, in testimony of their numbers. "But her reasons don't matter. Now that I know to what lengths she will go, I must put myself out of her reach—for a few days, at least. Until my father returns."

"Out . . . out of her reach? What do you mean?"

"I'm leaving."

Hettie gaped, her usual cleverness not in evidence at the moment. "For Oakshire, you mean? Without informing His Grace or—"

"No, she'd only fetch me back to Town, or take advantage of my journey to compromise me somehow, if not with Bellowsworth, then with some other young lord whose ambition outstrips his integrity—any one of them, in other words. I mean to disappear entirely, right here in London. Will you help me?"

Hettie's brown eyes recovered a measure of their customary shrewdness. "I'll not do anything to put you in danger, my lady. I'll go tell His Grace the Duke first. This start of yours—"

"It's no start, I assure you." Even as she spoke, Pearl's nebulous plan took on more clarity. "It's an idea I've toyed with for some time. One day I'll have the management of Fairbourne and be responsible for hundreds of people. I've studied agricultural, economic, and social reform, but what is that but theory? I've been coddled and protected my entire life. Even my charitable projects have been strictly chaperoned and supervised, so that I never have any actual contact with those less fortunate."

Hettie still looked doubtful, so Pearl tried another tack. "I've been perched on a lofty, confining pedestal, first by my father and then by every man aspiring to my hand. If I don't escape it, I may begin believing all they say about me and become the most conceited, arrogant, autocratic woman who ever lived."

Hettie chuckled. "With Her Grace putting you in your place ten times a day? Not likely."

"I suppose I do have something for which to be grateful to her after all." Ignoring Hettie's snort, she hurried on. "How would you like it if every man who paid you court was interested only in your money and connections, never in yourself?"

"Don't forget your looks, my lady," Hettie added dryly. "Those violet eyes of yours aren't exactly in the common way."

It was Pearl's turn to snort. "All part of the package of externals. I'm one of the best-educated women in England, but no one cares about that. Never has one of my suitors asked my opinion on any political or economic issue, or on philosophy, science, or anything else. All they can see is a glittering ornament that would add to their own consequence. I'm sick to death of it!"

At this appeal to her romantic nature, Hettie nodded with sympathy, and Pearl began to relax.

"I wish to experience life without the trappings of rank," she continued. "To see how the common folk live. Perhaps even to work with my own hands. I'm certain it will be of benefit to me."

Though she still looked doubtful, Hettie only asked, "What do you want me to do?"

Pearl smiled in relief. "First, help me out of this dress."

Whistling cheerfully, Luke St. Clair strolled along Jermyn Street as the cool of early evening turned the afternoon's haze to tendrils of mist. Casually, he scanned those entering and exiting the gaming houses, looking for an easy mark. His gaze slid over one well-dressed man and then another. No, obviously merchants. Ah! That middle-aged man alighting from a crested carriage. Clearly one of the *ton*. He'd do nicely.

Luke hunched his shoulders and slowed his pace, in keeping with today's disguise as an inebriated old man—down at his heels, but not quite seedy enough to look threatening. He ambled in the direction of his selected target, then stumbled just as he reached the man.

"Sorry, milor'," he mumbled, steadying himself

against the gentleman's arm to break his supposed fall. Even as the nobleman superciliously swept aside Luke's abject apology, his purse was liberated from his pocket.

"Be gone with you, old tippler. Keep your distance from your betters," the haughty lord advised him with a sneer.

Biting back an instinctive retort, Luke managed a servile bow that made his cheap white peruke slip down to partially conceal his face as he backed away from the man. Not until he turned onto Haymarket Street a moment later did the hue and cry begin.

With a chuckle, Luke straightened his wig and quickened his pace, though not enough to draw attention. Then the words, "Stop, thief!" rang out behind him. Ducking around the next corner into an alley scarcely wider than an arm-spread, he broke into a run.

This was always his favorite part. Leaving the alley for Coventry Street, he glanced back to see two dandified bucks of the *ton* hot after him, brandishing sticks and shouting absurd threats. Perfect.

Or not so perfect. The young gentlemen were apparently among the more fit of their species, for another quick glance showed them gaining. Luke put on a burst of speed, leaping over an ash can before sending it clattering behind him. So much for his disguise! No description of the thief would mention an elderly man now.

Still, he knew this part of London better than the alley cats did. With the young sprigs hot on his heels, he led them a merry chase toward Soho Square, taking care to trail them through every puddle of mud or filth he could find along the way. "That's for you, Mum," he muttered at the sound of sudden cursing behind him.

Slipping around a corner, he then nipped into the dark recess of a doorway, pressing his back against the wooden panels. He managed to catch a few much-needed breaths before his pursuers approached. As they came closer, he snaked one hand behind him to test the door handle.

It opened easily, and he nearly fell into a brightly lit room filled with women in various stages of undress—actresses preparing to perform here at one of the minor opera houses. Quickly, he shut the door behind him so that his pursuers wouldn't hear their squeals.

"Lucio, as I live and breathe!" cooed a buxom redhead Luke remembered well from last Season. Indignation turned to delight as others realized who had burst in upon them.

Doffing his peruke, Luke greeted them all with his most charming smile. "My apologies for an unannounced entry, ladies. I won't be staying long." He'd dallied with at least three of them in the past, taking nearly as much pleasure from the knowledge that he was cuckolding their noble protectors as from their more obvious charms.

The outer door opened again, and at once two of the actresses stepped in front of Luke, who quickly ducked down behind them. Between their skirts, he could see the dumbfounded faces of his erstwhile hunters.

Shrilly, the women protested the intrusion, claiming a modesty that should have provoked laughter rather than the embarrassment the two young dandies evinced. Stammering apologies, they quickly backed out to continue their search elsewhere. The moment the door closed, the women again converged on Luke, giggling and pulling at his jacket. Obligingly, he took it off, but only long enough to reverse it and pull a cap from the pocket.

"I am eternally in your debt," he declared to the group as a whole. Despite their chorus of protests, he dropped a quick kiss on the cheek of the redhead, winked at the two blondes he'd known previously, and, with fulsome compliments, took his leave.

Peering from the doorway, he watched his pursuers turn another corner, apparently heading toward Seven Dials. He waited another moment or two before emerging to stroll toward Mayfair, in the opposite direction.

Pulling the purloined purse from his pocket, he counted his takings as he walked. Not as much as he'd hoped, but it would pay his rent for the month and buy a new washtub and iron for Mrs. Breitmann, who eked out a living for herself and her five children by taking in laundry. Of course, there was still Grady O'Malley to spring from debtor's prison in Newgate, as well as a few things he wanted for himself. Luckily, he was headed toward the richest part of London.

Luke paused at the edge of Berkley Square in the gathering dusk, gazing at one of the finest mansions in Town. Yes, that one would do nicely—or perhaps that one there, two houses down. He'd wander through the mews and discover which one might be having guests tonight. That would make his job easier.

He felt not the slightest twinge of guilt for what he was planning. These people had more wealth than they could ever use, and deserved none of it. With the exception of the close circle of friends he'd made at Oxford, in his experience every member of the *ton* was arrogant, self-absorbed, and completely unappreciative of his or her privileged state.

Smiling to himself, he again considered the fine mansions before him. Gilded cages, that's what they were. He far preferred his life of unfettered freedom to one of circumscribed luxury with no thrills, no challenges, no worries whatsoever. . . .

"Are you sure you want to go through with this, my lady?" Hettie asked anxiously as Pearl closed the gate at the back of the kitchen gardens, emerging into the alleyway behind the great houses of Berkley Square.

Her escape accomplished, Pearl let out her breath and faced her abigail. Tucking a stray strand of hair into the tight bun she now wore, she checked the fit of her borrowed clothes—a worn work dress of Hettie's, with the hem let out to cover the much taller Pearl's ankles.

"Of course I'm sure. And it's 'Purdy,' remember? If you call me 'my lady,' we'll be found out at once." Slipping out of the house unseen had been difficult enough, despite the commotion surrounding the Duke's departure. She had never quite realized what an army of servants her family employed.

"Oh, look at that poor cat, trying to pull a fish from that crate there," she said then, her attention diverted. "Do you suppose it has kittens somewhere?"

Hettie chuckled. "It looks sleek and fat enough to me, my—Purdy. Stuffed on mice from Lord Tinsdale's stables, no doubt, not to mention scraps from his kitchens. A cat's not likely to starve in Mayfair."

"Oh. No, I suppose not."

Hettie glanced away, but not before Pearl saw the combination of worry and merriment in her eyes. No doubt she believed that Pearl was merely amusing herself with her playacting. But of course Pearl had a far higher purpose. *Think of Fairbourne!*

"Eh, there!" A rough, masculine voice accosted them. "Be either of you wenches looking for a job t'night?"

Pearl turned indignantly, ready to blast the footman—for that's what he appeared to be—for calling them wenches, but Hettie placed a restraining hand on her arm.

"What sort of job?" she asked the man. "We'll do nothing unsavory, I assure you."

Pearl had to admire Hettie's command, putting the man in his place without betraying them. She herself would have botched it, but Hettie knew this world as Pearl did not—yet.

The footman dipped his head respectfully, rather to Pearl's surprise. "No, nothin' like that, ma'am. Just some extra brass, is all. Lord Mountheath be hiring on extra help for the evening. So if you've the night off and wishing a bit on the side . . ."

"Just a moment," said Hettie, and pulled Pearl aside. "Well, my lady?" she whispered. "It's a chance to put your plan to the test—but it's risky."

Risky indeed! Pearl herself was expected at Lady Mountheath's ridotto tonight, and nearly everyone she knew who was currently in Town was likely to be there.

"Do you think it would be possible for me to work only in the kitchens, or somewhere else out of sight of the guests?" She'd never liked the Mountheaths, and suspected their servants would like them even less. If she really wanted to see first-hand the hardships of the working class, this seemed a heaven-sent chance.

"I'm sure they can find you a dirty job some-where—Purdy." The twinkle in Hettie's eyes told her that her abigail expected her to back down, which only stiffened her resolve.

"I'll do it," Pearl said with a determined nod. "Though I'd very much prefer it not involve cham-ber pots," she added hastily, hoping she would not live to regret this mad, if noble, scheme.

Hettie turned back to the footman. "What posi-tions are they hiring for?"

An hour later, Pearl found herself in the Mountheaths' kitchen, transferring tray after tray of tiny pastries from the enormous oven to glittering crystal platters. This wasn't turning out at all as she'd expected, she decided, as she burned her fin-gers for the third time. Kitchen maids didn't wear gloves, of course—which she now realized was foolish. Surely they needed them far more than did any lady in a drawing room.

In addition to her lofty social goals, Pearl had wished to discover how people might respond to her without the aura of the Duke of Oakshire sur-rounding her. So far, she was simply being ignored.

She burned her fingers yet again, this time more severely. With a yelp, she dropped the hot tray, scattering its dainties over the kitchen floor. Muttering an apology, trying to ignore the mutterings of "clumsy wench," she knelt to sweep up the ruined pastries.

"Here, I'll help you with that."

Glancing up in surprise at the masculine voice, she found herself face-to-face with one of the serving men. Though his brown hair and regular features were not much out of the ordinary, there was something compelling, even magnetic, about the intelligence—and intensity—of his dark, dark eyes.

"Thank you," she murmured. "I'm . . . not normally so fumble-fingered."

He took her bare hand in his much larger one—also ungloved—and turned it over. An alarming tingle shot through her at his touch—perhaps the first time in her life a male hand had touched hers, skin to skin. She nearly snatched her hand away, a stinging rebuke for his impertinence on the tip of her tongue, but remembered just in time that the servant "Purdy" must not react the way Lady Pearl would.

"You should put something cool on that before it blisters." His voice was rich, deep, and surprisingly cultured—not at all what she'd expected of a belowstairs servant. He held her gaze as securely as her hand, and something unfamiliar stirred deep within her.

Vainly, she reminded herself that this man was not of her class at all. "Thank you," she repeated, gently disengaging her hand. "I'll do that."

She rose, but already he had whisked a damp

dish towel from a nearby table. With a smile and a too-familiar twinkle in his eye, he wrapped it around her damaged fingers, reestablishing that disturbing flesh-to-flesh contact.

" 'Ere, now! None o' that!" exclaimed the head cook's assistant. Pearl released the serving man's hand guiltily. "Back to work, both of you, if you're wanting to get your shillin' for the evening." She thrust a filled tray into the man's hands. "Take this out to the buffet tables, then hop it back here for another."

With a ghost of a bow in Pearl's direction, he complied, his eyes still twinkling.

Pearl watched him go, a curious frown pulling her brows together. No, he didn't act like a servant at all. But then, what did she really know of how servants behaved toward each other?

"You there! Purdy! Get the rest of those crab puffs onto trays. We're falling behind in here."

With a start at her assumed name, Pearl quickly turned back to her task, taking more care for her fingers. As she worked, she gained confidence in the task. This wasn't so hard.

"More servers!" the butler called down the kitchen stairs. "We still need more servers out here." He followed his words into the kitchen and glanced haughtily around at the hired drudges—a motley group, to be sure. "You there!"

Cautiously, Pearl glanced over her shoulder at the butler, to find him staring straight at her. "M-me?"

He gave a single, supercilious nod. "You appear the most presentable of this lot. You'll do." With a jerk of his head, he indicated that she should follow him.

Pearl froze. She couldn't go out there! If she was recognized, the scandal would be . . . well, more than she cared to imagine. Wildly, she glanced around the kitchen for Hettie, but she was nowhere to be seen.

"This instant, missie, *if* you please." Pearl had met royalty who exuded less authority than this man. Mechanically, she moved to obey, hoping a solution might magically present itself.

"Clear away the empty trays and bottles from the buffet tables and bring them back here," he said carefully, having apparently decided she was a half-wit. "Mrs. Mann will tell you what to do next. And you won't need this." Before she could stop him, he whipped off the kerchief she'd been wearing to conceal her hair.

Again she stopped, but by now the attention of the entire kitchen was focused on her, so she meekly followed the butler up the stairs. Emerging at the top, she quickly surveyed the glittering ballroom, thronged with people, nearly every one of whom knew her. She should have quit on the spot rather than risk this, she realized belatedly. What was a shilling, after all? A single button on one of her fine gowns was worth more than that.

She kept her head down, avoiding eye contact, as Hettie had taught her. And, amazingly, no one seemed to notice her. The eyes of the noble assemblage slid over her as though she were invisible.

In the midst of her relief, she felt a sudden pang. Did *she* regard servants—not counting Hettie, of course—in this same dismissive way? She'd never thought about it before.

Pearl reached the buffet table without incident

and began stacking trays, trying to cause as little clatter as possible, hoping to avoid notice. So far, so good. As soon as she returned to the kitchen, she would find Hettie and leave.

She placed a final tray atop the stack, added a few empty bottles, and headed back the way she had come.

Head down, she saw no faces, only feet. Even so, she had to pass near one all-too-familiar pair: her stepmother's, in the new gold-laced slippers she had exhibited with pride just last week. How had Obelia explained Pearl's absence tonight? she wondered.

Please, please, she chanted silently to herself as she slipped past. Her incoherent prayer apparently successful, she neared the edge of the room and the safety of the kitchens. She had almost reached the door at the top of the stairs when a feminine voice accosted her.

"Mama wishes to have more champagne sent up." It was Fanny Mountheath, one of the daughters of the house, a girl Pearl had never liked, though they frequently met in company. "Pray tell the wine steward."

Pearl nodded silently and kept moving, afraid her voice would give her away.

"Wait!"

Her insides contracting, Pearl paused, still not making eye contact.

"How extraordinary. You look amazingly like— But no, how absurd. Still, I must show Lucy. Wait here. Lucy! Oh, Lucy!" She bustled over to where her sister stood, some distance away.

Pearl took her chance and hastened to the door. As she struggled to open it while balancing the trays, a bottle rolled off the top and hit the polished marble floor, shattering with a resounding crash. Her heart in her throat, she fled down the stairs.

Chapter 2

❝Hettie! Hettie, where are you?" Pearl called frantically, not caring now what the servants thought of her. "We have to leave—now!"

Dropping the trays onto the closest table, she looked wildly about the kitchen, but still saw no sign of Hettie. She dared not wait, however. At any moment, Fanny might send someone after her, or even venture into the kitchen herself, to show off the novelty of the serving girl who looked like Lady Pearl, and then all would be discovered. She absolutely refused to risk such humiliation.

Snatching up her kerchief and cloak, she darted toward the back door, ignoring the cries and protests around her. She ducked through the door and raced up the stone steps to the kitchen gardens, then paused. The afternoon's haze had become evening fog, and she had no clear idea of where she might go—other than home.

"You look like you could use some assistance again, miss."

Whirling, she saw the same serving man who had bound up her burned fingers earlier.

"As I'm leaving myself just now, I'd be pleased to offer you my escort," he said, extending his arm. "Shall we go?"

Pearl placed her hand on his arm, then snatched it back, alarmed at the jolt that went through her bare fingers on contact with his rough sleeve—and the very solid arm beneath. Whoever this man was, whatever her involuntary response to him, she didn't dare trust him far enough to go off alone with him into the night!

The commotion in the kitchen rose to a clamor. "Where is she?" came Fanny Mountheath's plaintive wail.

Abruptly, Pearl changed her mind, though she didn't touch him again. "I'd be delighted to accept your escort," she said hastily. "Let's go—quickly."

With a grin that was perhaps a shade too understanding, he led her through the gate and into the alleyway at a brisk walk. As they turned the corner, shouts erupted from the house behind them.

"Time to run," the man suggested.

Pearl nodded and hiked up her skirts—slightly—to keep pace with him. The country lass she was pretending to be would be used to plenty of walking, of course. Unfortunately, she was not, constrained as she'd always been by the dignity of her station. Still, she trotted along gamely enough.

Her rescuer sent her one approving glance, then

turned his attention to their course, leading her around one corner and then another. "Quick! In here," he said, as heavy footsteps approached from behind.

Before she could protest, he seized her by the arm and pulled her after him into an empty stall in some nobleman's stables. He touched a finger to her lips to check her indignant exclamation, and the shock of the sensation startled her speechless. Though he withdrew the finger at once, her lips continued to tingle. She had to fight the urge to lick them.

Footsteps—several sets, by the sound of them— passed by outside. Her companion waited a minute, though it seemed far longer in the warm, intimate darkness, then slipped back out of the stall, motioning for her to follow him.

Though he was only an inch or two above average height, the man was powerfully built, Pearl noticed. That made her feel somehow vulnerable—an unfamiliar sensation, and one she didn't particularly care for. For a second or two she held a fierce debate with herself, but then hurried after him. What else could she do, under the circumstances?

Leading her back the way they had come for the length of two houses, he turned up another alleyway, then another. By a circuitous route, he led her farther and farther from the Mountheaths' house and then from Mayfair itself, until they were in a part of London totally unfamiliar to her.

As they progressed, the streets became narrower, darker, and dirtier, and Pearl's misgivings mounted. Smells she had never experienced before assaulted her nostrils unpleasantly. Mounds of garbage and other, nastier refuse lay uncollected in stinking corners, while rats skittered out of the way at their approach.

When it was clear there was no longer any danger of pursuit, they stopped in a squalid alley no more than four feet wide. Her companion did not appear to be out of breath, but Pearl gulped in lungfuls of the fetid air after such unaccustomed exercise. When her mind finally began working again, she turned curiously—and cautiously—to her savior.

"Thank you," she panted. "But . . . why did you help me?"

He grinned across the meager width of the dim alleyway and her breathing accelerated again, though not from exertion.

"I was leaving anyway, and you appeared in rather urgent need of help. Never let it be said that Luke St. Clair would turn his back on a damsel in distress." He regarded her for a long moment, then, in a deeper voice, asked, "Might I have the honor of knowing whom I have rescued?"

Pearl hesitated, wondering whether she'd betrayed herself already. "My name is Purdy," she said at last, making an effort to speak in a less cultured accent. "I'm . . . no one special. I only wished to make some extra money on my night off." She realized as she spoke that the words sounded rehearsed.

He placed a hand on her arm, its warmth comforting even as it flustered her. "Don't discount yourself so easily," he said with gallant sincerity. "You're far more special than you believe." His low, melodious voice was as warm as his touch, his eyes alight with interest, if not suspicion. "What were you taking a night off from? What do you normally do?"

Oops. She and Hettie hadn't worked out that detail of her story yet. "Er, actually, I've just come to London from the country. I—I have no regular position as yet. My friend, Hettie, was going to help me find one."

His raised eyebrow told her he was well aware that she was hiding something, but he merely said, "I see. Then pray allow me to escort you back to wherever you are staying, before Hettie becomes concerned about you. Was she also at the Mountheaths' house tonight?"

Something in the timbre of his voice seemed to set up an answering vibration within her, a response she could no more define than control. Between that and her acute awareness of his touch, she had to force herself to focus on the sense of his question.

"Yes. Yes, she was," she finally responded. "But . . ." She paused to choose her words carefully. "But I was not actually staying with her, yet. I—I fear I do not know where she lives, exactly."

An almost imperceptible change came over his manner, and he dropped his hand from her arm, leaving Pearl feeling oddly bereft. "Then to wherever you wish to go. You must be staying somewhere." He spoke slowly now, as if to a child.

Obviously, he had concluded that she was simple, as the Mountheaths' butler had. Not that she could blame either of them. She suppressed the urge to correct his assumption, realizing that it might afford her a modicum of protection.

"No, I'm . . . I'm not staying anywhere, really. That is . . ." Pearl twisted her apron between her hands, trying without success to recall whether Hettie had ever mentioned any relatives in London. Her mother, Pearl's old nurse, still lived in Oakshire. They hadn't discussed where they would stay after their stint at the Mountheaths'. No doubt Hettie had believed Pearl would be ready to return home after a few hours of honest work.

"Hettie and I were on our way to her . . . her cousin's home when we accepted tonight's employment," she improvised haltingly, feeling like the fool he now took her for. "Until I find Hettie, I have nowhere to go."

Mr. St. Clair regarded her with thoughtful concern. "I cannot leave you here in this alley. I'd offer to take you back to the Mountheaths', but I assume you had good reason for wishing to leave?"

"No! I can't go back there, not just now. But . . . I suppose I must, later. After the ridotto is over. To find Hettie."

"Later, then." Still enunciating his words carefully, he continued, "In the meanwhile, we should get off the streets. This is not one of the safer parts of London."

Pearl blinked. "Oh. Oh, I see. I hadn't thought—" She realized belatedly that it should have been obvious. Certainly they were well outside her accustomed environs. "Where do you suggest we go?"

"My lodgings are just a short walk from here. You are welcome to stay there until I can find your friend for you."

She stared, momentarily aghast. Go with this man, this servant, to his *lodgings*? How dared he insult her so? She opened her mouth to give him a blistering set-down before the reality of her situation intruded. He was attempting to help her, after all, and had no idea who she really was.

Slowly, reluctantly, she nodded. Careful to use short, uncomplicated sentences, she said, "Thank you, Mr. St. Clair. I must accept your kind offer. But only until we can find Hettie."

He offered her his arm with a gallantry that would have done credit to a titled gentleman and she gingerly took it, trying to appear unaccustomed to such courtesy. Leading her out of the alleyway, he turned to the left. Though this street was wider, it was no less squalid. From somewhere in the fog above them came the sound of a man and woman arguing, then a splintering crash. Pearl winced.

"Where are we, exactly?" she asked her escort.

She thought he hesitated for a moment before answering, "This part of London is known as Seven Dials."

Pearl started. "Seven Dials! What . . . what a curious name," she concluded lamely, remembering in time that she had just claimed to be unfamiliar with London. "Why is it called that?"

"Because of the way seven streets converge, like the spokes of a wheel," he explained, but Pearl was not listening.

Seven Dials! This was one of the most notorious rookeries of London, home to thieves, prostitutes, murderers, and other sorts that she was not even supposed to know existed. But though her physical existence had been sheltered, Pearl had read widely enough that little about London—or the rest of the world—was truly unknown to her. Intellectually, at least.

Though initially horrified to discover where she was, now her natural curiosity reasserted itself. Had she not begged her father to allow her to witness such places, when first she had learned of them? The nobility owed it to themselves and to England to learn all they could about the condition of the common man, she had insisted. How else could they hope to alleviate the sufferings of those hit hardest by the economic downturn caused by the end of the wars with France and America?

Her musings were interrupted by Mr. St. Clair's announcement that they had reached his building. "It's three flights up, I'm afraid, but not quite so sordid as its surroundings might suggest."

She regarded the steep, narrow stairs dubiously, her earlier doubts resurfacing. But really, what choice did she have? Trying to regard her predicament in the light of an adventure rather than a disaster, she followed him up the rickety stairway.

When they reached the third story, a small brown and white terrier scurried forward to greet Mr. St. Clair, its tail wagging with delight. Then it turned to sniff at Pearl suspiciously.

"This is Argos," he said, scratching the dog between the ears. "A plausible scoundrel, but my closest friend. Argos, this is Purdy. Make her feel welcome."

At his words, the dog's attitude instantly transformed, and he greeted Pearl almost as enthusiastically as he had his master.

"What a sweet little dog!" she exclaimed, kneeling to fondle him. "Hello, Argos. I hope we will be friends, as well." As a child she had been allowed dogs as pets, but since her father's remarriage, animals had been forbidden from every house. She'd missed having a pet.

She glanced up at Mr. St. Clair, to find him regarding her with an odd half smile that made her feel she'd just climbed far more than three flights of steps. Catching her eye, he quickly turned away and cleared his throat. "It's getting chilly. We'd best get inside," he said gruffly.

Fitting a key into the door, he entered quickly to light a few candles, then reemerged to invite her in. "It's not much," he said apologetically, "but I call it home."

Swallowing hard and bracing herself for she knew not what, Pearl followed him into the apartment—then halted, amazed. Elegance, even luxury, surrounded her. On the floor, a thick carpet that could only be Aubusson covered most of the bare, splintered boards. The peeling plaster of the walls was substantially concealed by rich tapestries and paintings by masters she recognized. The furnishings—sofa, chairs, tables, ornaments—were both tasteful and sumptuous.

"My goodness!" If she didn't look too closely at what lay behind the trappings, she could easily imagine herself in a wealthy gentleman's sitting room.

He smiled at her surprise. "I've done my best to counteract my surroundings. My last employer was exceedingly generous in his will, which made it easier for me to do so."

She nodded, accepting his glib explanation. As she was playing the part of a numbwit, she could not very well ask why he remained in such a neighborhood when he clearly had the resources to leave it. Obviously there was more to Mr. St. Clair than met the eye, as she had suspected from the moment he first spoke to her.

"It's—very nice," she said inadequately. "May I sit down?"

Immediately he was full of concern. "Of course! I'd forgotten how exhausted you must be. Here, this is the most comfortable chair. I'll stir up the coals in the grate, and you'll be warm in no time."

Pearl sat, noticing with some irritation that she was indeed tired and a bit sore from their recent exertion. She must make more of an effort to get regular exercise while in Town, or she would end up running to fat. In the country she at least rode regularly.

"Purdy? Miss?"

Abruptly, she realized she had not heard his question. "I . . . I beg your pardon?"

Again speaking slowly, he repeated, "I was asking whether you would like a glass of wine to fortify you. That and ale are all I have at hand, I'm afraid, though I can go out to bring something else back, if you'd prefer it."

"Wine, thank you," she said hastily, unwilling to be left alone here. Though why she should feel safer with him than without him, she wasn't quite sure.

The little dog, Argos—whose very name implied its master had a classical education—came to lie next to her, its head on her foot, while he went to the sideboard to fill two glasses. She took the one he handed her and sipped. Again she had to restrain herself from exclaiming, though her brows rose.

How had this apparently lowly servant developed such expensive tastes?

"Will . . . won't you be missed at the Mount-heaths'?" she asked, in an indirect attempt to obtain an answer—and to hear his voice again.

"I doubt it," he replied. "I was only hired on for the evening, as you were. I'm . . . between positions at the moment myself, as it happens."

Whether he intended it or not, his words reminded her that she had secrets of her own to keep, and therefore would be advised not to probe into his. "How long should we wait, do you think, before going back to look for Hettie?"

He thought for a moment. "How would this serve? You wait here, and I'll go back there now and take a look about. If you can describe her to me, I'll endeavor to have a quiet word with her and let her know where you are. I'll even bring her here myself, if she can get away."

Haltingly, mindful of her ruse, Pearl described her maid. "This is very kind of you," she concluded. Though she still felt nervous about staying alone in Seven Dials, even in this sumptuous apartment, he had offered her the perfect solution. As far as she knew, no one had seen them leaving together.

Again he gave her that odd half smile, and again she was startled by her visceral response to it. "Kindness isn't so difficult, when the object is worthy. There is bread and cheese in the sideboard, should you feel hungry. I should be back in an hour or so—with Hettie in tow, with any luck." Tossing off the remainder of his wine, he rose.

"Argos, you stay here and take care of the lady," he instructed the dog, who lifted his head and thumped his tail in apparent understanding. With a respectful salute, he left the apartment, closing the door softly behind him.

At the sound of the key turning in the lock, Pearl started to her feet in alarm. He was making her a prisoner here! She took two strides toward the door, then noticed Argos regarding her curiously. She relaxed, feeling suddenly foolish. Of course he had locked the door, in a neighborhood such as this one. Doubtless he'd done it to ensure her safety, not for any nefarious purpose.

Laughing at her misplaced fears, she sat down again. "Some adventurer I'm turning out to be," she said to the dog. "All of my daring plans to institute social reform, and here I am completely unnerved by merely witnessing a poorer section of London. I'm as big a ninny as Mr. St. Clair thinks I am."

Argos agreeably wagged his tail and placed one white paw on her knee.

"Feel free to contradict me," she told him. "It's the polite thing to do, when a lady speaks ill of herself."

The dog declined to respond, so Pearl rose again, to explore her temporary quarters. Her first estimation had been correct. The furnishings and artworks were of the very highest quality. Her curiosity about Mr. St. Clair increased.

Going to the mahogany sideboard, she found the bread and cheese he had mentioned and cut herself a generous slab of each. She had not eaten since luncheon, she suddenly realized. Didn't the Mountheaths feed their hired help? Indignation further bolstered her courage.

Returning to her chair with her simple supper,

she amused herself by sharing the occasional morsel with the dog, who obligingly sat up, extended a paw, or rolled over on command. Pearl was charmed. Thus occupied, the hour of waiting passed relatively painlessly.

Luke had misgivings about leaving Purdy alone in his rooms, but aside from his perfectly plausible plan to find her friend, he needed to get away from her, to firmly remind himself that she was off limits. The truth was, he was finding himself far more attracted to the lovely simpleton than was decent.

He chuckled sourly as he descended the stairs to the foggy alley below. When had considerations of decency ever constrained him? Still, he'd never stooped so low as to take advantage of a child, and for all her beauty, Purdy was little more, due to her limited understanding.

The shock of disappointment he'd felt on realizing this, after the instant connection they had seemed to share, had actually been physical in its intensity.

He refused to dwell on it now, though. This was his opportunity to retrieve the evening's haul from its hiding place outside the Mountheath house. By searching for Purdy's friend at the same time, he could kill two birds with one stone. Three, counting this most necessary separation from his delectable guest.

Alone, it took him half the time to reach Mayfair that it had taken him to lead Purdy to Seven Dials. In less than fifteen minutes, he emerged from the mews behind Berkley Square. The Mountheath house was brightly lit, the entertainment clearly still in full swing, with no sign of any disturbance yet. Good.

Casually, so that it would look as though he were merely taking the air if he was seen, Luke angled into the small garden behind the house. Alert for anyone venturing out of the servants' entrance, he knelt to move aside a pair of bricks near a large rosebush, still in bud. There, in the depression he'd located before beginning his night's work, was the cloth-wrapped parcel, right where he'd left it.

He tucked the bundle inside his shirt and slid it around to the back of his waist, where the bulge would be less noticeable. It would be risky venturing back into the house with the goods on him, but he had no choice if he was to find Purdy's friend.

The kitchens were still bustling, though by this late hour the activity was less frantic than it had been when he'd left. Assuming a slack-jawed expression, he approached the cook's assistant.

"You!" she exclaimed. "And where 'ave you been this hour and more? Tipplin' his lordship's wine, by the look of you."

"Nay, nay, 'twas me own gin, missus," drawled Luke with an injured air. "I'll last for a bit, now."

She glared at him. "Off with you! We want no sots working here."

He blinked fuzzily. "What about my shillin'? And I won't leave without my sister Hettie."

Grumbling, the woman sent a maid in search of Hettie, wherever she might be, and counted out sixpence into Luke's outstretched palm. "I'm giving you but half, and may it be a lesson to you."

"Half?" He argued with her, since it would have looked suspicious otherwise, but only until the maid returned to report she'd found no such person as Hettie.

"Are you sure?" he asked, not having to feign his alarm. If the woman couldn't be found, he'd have no choice but to keep Purdy with him overnight. He wasn't at all sure his self-control was equal to that. "She's about this tall"—he held up his hand—"with dark curly hair. A few years younger'n me."

One of the scullery maids allowed that she'd seen someone of that description earlier, but no one had noticed her for the past hour or more, and no one recalled anyone by that name.

"Likely went looking for her wastrel brother," the cook's assistant told him dampingly. "Ought to be ashamed, you ought, worrying her so. Now that's three hirelings who've took off before their shift was done, counting you. You didn't see that blond wench outside, did you? The one you was flirting with early on?"

This was dangerous ground. "Blond? Flirting?" He furrowed his brow as though trying to remember.

"Ah, you're all alike. Begone with you!"

Shrugging and grumbling, Luke headed back to the mews. Not until he was out of sight of the house did he straighten his shoulders and quicken his steps. When the silver inside his shirt clinked, he pulled it out and shoved the bundle in his pocket. At least he'd made a good haul, and from one of the most undeserving households he'd ever met. He'd love to see that arrogant butler's face when his calling card was discovered where the silver had been. But what the devil was he going to do about the girl?

When he reentered his lodgings a few minutes later, she looked up with a hopeful smile, Argos at her knee. He'd spent most of the walk back convincing himself that she held no attraction to him, that he'd always preferred intelligent women, but his body made a liar of him the moment he saw her again.

Her smile faltered as she looked beyond him, then back at him, questioningly.

He shrugged. "Hettie wasn't at the Mountheaths', though someone matching her description was noticed earlier. It appears she wasn't going by the name of Hettie, however."

Purdy bit her lip, looking both alarmed and charmingly confused. Luke felt an almost overwhelming urge to take her into his arms and comfort her. He suppressed it ruthlessly, but not before his wayward imagination wondered what she would feel like, pressed against him.

The helpless expression in her eyes as she gazed at him helped to cool that inappropriate surge of desire. "I . . . I thought surely you would find her there," she stammered. "Without Hettie, I have no idea where to go."

"Perhaps in the morning we'll have better luck," Luke offered soothingly.

"In . . . in the morning?" She seemed not to understand.

Taking a deep breath, he spoke the words he feared he would live to regret. "Unless you can think of somewhere else to go, I see no alternative to your spending the night here."

Chapter 3

Pearl gasped. "Spend the night?" She had intended a tone of imperious outrage, but what came out was more of a squeak.

"You'll be quite safe, I assure you." Mr. St. Clair's fine dark eyes were as intense as before, but with kindness, she thought, rather than desire.

Still, she shook her head. "No, I really mustn't." In fact, it was unthinkable. Why had he not found Hettie?

The abigail to the daughter of the Duke of Oakshire might be well-known in servant circles, she supposed. Perhaps Hettie had used an alias, just as Pearl had. They hadn't discussed it, and had been separated the moment they entered the Mountheath house.

It suddenly occurred to her that Hettie had most

likely gone back to Oakshire House to hunt for her after she disappeared. Her father's men might even now be combing London for her!

The obvious thing, of course, was to give up her entire scheme and return to Oakshire House before a full-blown scandal erupted. Hettie had been right, much as it galled her to admit it. She grimaced at the thought of what her stepmother would have to say to her. The very idea of humbling herself to Obelia was abhorrent.

Mr. St. Clair was regarding her with sympathy mingled with more than a hint of exasperation as she hesitated. "Please believe me, you'll be in no danger whatsoever. The door is quite stout, and I myself would never take advantage of ... such a situation."

Of a simpleton, he means, she thought with a spurt of amusement. She'd best keep up that fiction for as long as possible—an ironic necessity, considering how proud she'd always been of her intellect. With the lightening of her mood, her thoughts cleared.

Despite her strange attraction to this man, it would surely be safer for her to remain here than to venture back out into the streets of Seven Dials at midnight. Even now, she could hear drunken singing and the occasional shriek from the alleys below. She'd heard tales of young gentlemen venturing here on a bet or a dare, or in fits of drunken bravado. And tales of some never being seen again. She didn't want to think what might happen to a lady in those same streets.

Safety, at least, demanded she remain here in this apartment. However, should the merest breath of a whisper of this night ever get out, her reputation would be irretrievably ruined. And that would be . . . would be . . .

The answer to all of her difficulties, she realized abruptly. If she was ruined, her myriad suitors would scatter like rabbits, thwarting Obelia's plans and safeguarding Fairbourne for good. Why had she not considered that solution before? All she had to do was stay away for a night or two, then return with no good explanation for her absence. It was perfect!

Pearl realized she'd been staring blankly at her handsome host while thinking all of this through, no doubt strengthening further his assessment of her intellect. "I . . . Yes. I suppose I must. Stay here, that is." Amazing how stupid she could sound without really trying!

"Good girl," he said approvingly. "I've an extra set of sheets—clean ones—that we can spread here on the sofa for you. I'd offer you my bed, but—"

"Oh, no! The sofa will be perfectly fine," she said hastily, alarmed at the image that suggestion conjured—and even more alarmed by the way that image set her nerves tingling again. Still, as he went to fetch the sheets, she eyed the hard sofa doubtfully, thinking with longing of her feather mattress at Oakshire House. She was mortally tired. *Remember Fairbourne!*

He returned a moment later, and with a deftness that convinced her he was used to doing such tasks himself, he spread the sheets over the divan. "You will let me know if you need anything else?"

She nodded, resolutely ignoring the effect his voice had on her. "Thank you. You're being far kinder than . . ."

"Than you expected? Are used to? If you've been

about the houses of the so-called upper crust, I don't doubt it. But you're most welcome. Not all Londoners are as callous as the Mountheaths and their ilk."

His evident animosity toward the upper classes startled her. Did all the working class feel this way toward her own? Did Hettie? Surely not. She nearly asked him, but realized how odd such a question would sound from a supposed servant. "I . . . suppose not," she said instead. "Good night, then."

He took his dismissal cheerfully. The little dog at his heels, he disappeared into his bedchamber and closed the door behind him. Pearl stared at the door for a moment, frowning, then sat down to take off her shoes—the only articles of clothing she dared remove—before stretching out on the sofa.

It was almost, but not quite, long enough for her. If she were petite and padded, like Hettie, she'd no doubt be comfortable enough, she chided herself. But it was curiosity about her strange host—and the most inappropriate feelings he aroused—rather than the lumpiness of the horsehair-filled divan that kept her awake for another hour and more.

When she finally fell into a fitful sleep, her dreams were disjointed. Oddly secure in the company of a man with strong hands and a melodious voice, she floated through images of sumptuous ballrooms superimposed on the squalor of Seven Dials. In her dreams, she could not figure out which was more real, though it seemed vitally important that she do so. The morning was well advanced before she finally awoke.

"So, you like her, do you?" Luke asked the dog tucked under his arm, as he climbed down the side of the building half an hour after sunrise. Argos's tail thumped against his back in reply.

Shortly after taking these lodgings, he'd concealed handholds and footholds among the crumbling bricks, and now used this route to his quarters nearly as often as the stairway. Today he was using it to avoid waking his guest, who had still been deep in exhausted slumber when he'd checked on her ten minutes ago.

"We can't keep her, you know," he told the terrier, who cocked his head questioningly. "You'd only get attached to her, and then where would we be?" He feared he might already have passed that point himself. "Off with you, then."

He set Argos down as they reached the pavement, and the dog hurried off to conduct whatever business he spent his days about. Luke turned aside to walk briskly in the direction of the Covent Garden market.

Why had he not come up with some alternative to inviting Purdy to stay with him? A woman—particularly one who needed the level of care this one did—was the last thing Luke needed in his life. His livelihood depended on coming and going unobserved and unrecognized. Her presence would complicate his life on more than one level—which meant he'd best take advantage of the time he had now.

At this early hour, the shops and stalls of Covent Garden were hives of activity. Poorer people from the surrounding neighborhood jostled with expensively dressed servants from Mayfair to buy fresh fruits, vegetables, and flowers. An occasional burst of song or shouting from drunken revelers only now making their way home punctuated the market bustle.

Luke stopped to purchase a bundle of tea leaves and a few fresh-baked rolls from stalls at the outskirts before proceeding to the fruit stands. At least he could provide his impromptu guest with a good breakfast before sending her on her way. As he walked, he watched the colorful, shifting crowds for one particular face.

" 'Ere you are, then," piped a clear voice from behind him.

Luke turned with a grin. "Flute! The very man I was looking for." He gripped the grimy hand of his sole confederate, a scrawny lad with a shock of straw-colored hair peeping out from under his tattered red cap.

"You have something, then?" Though he was probably near fifteen, Flute looked no more than twelve, underfed as he'd been by the flash house master he'd picked pockets for until Luke had taken him under his wing two years since. Now, with better victuals, he was beginning to fill out, though slowly.

"Aye, some plate and baubles for you to take to the fencing ken," said Luke, falling easily into the street cant. "After your cut, you can give enough of the ready to Mrs. O'Malley to spring her feckless husband from Newgate, then bring the rest to me."

He pulled from his pocket the parcel he'd retrieved last night and handed it to the boy. Flute tweaked open the wrapping to catch a glimpse of assorted silver and a diamond necklace, and whistled approvingly before stuffing it into his own pocket.

"Mrs. Breitmann sends thanks to the Saint," he told Luke then. "Her old tub was past fixing, so the new was in the nick o' time."

Luke resisted the urge to tousle the boy's hair, knowing how it irritated him. "Good lad. Off with you, then." With a quick nod, they went their separate ways, careful as always not to spend too much time in each other's company in public.

That task settled, Luke took his time selecting the choicest hothouse oranges. Then, on sudden impulse, he stopped by one of the flower carts and bought two bunches of violets and another of daisies. Perhaps they would make Purdy smile—something he'd like to see again before she left. He wondered fleetingly whether she'd ever received flowers before in her life. Probably not, poor girl.

Finally he headed back. On reaching his crumbling building, he decided to take the stairs rather than risk crushing the flowers. He unlocked the door, then knocked softly, not wanting to startle the girl. When there was no answer, he cautiously pushed the door open.

Purdy was sitting bolt upright on the sofa, blinking dazedly. "Where . . . How? I, er, did not hear you go out."

"I didn't wish to wake you."

She looked absolutely adorable with her honey-blond hair half tumbled from its bun and her expression charmingly confused. Adorable and delectable. It was a crying shame she was . . .

"I brought breakfast," he added, cutting off that line of thought. "And some flowers for the table." He produced them with a flourish.

She brightened at once. "Oh, how very thoughtful!"

The smile he had hoped for flashed out, and again Luke felt that odd warmth surge through him at her eager pleasure at small kindnesses. What a difficult life she must have led. "Come, have a seat while I serve it up."

She complied hesitantly as he pulled tea leaves, rolls, and oranges from his sack. He handed her a knife so that she could peel her orange while he set water to boil, but when she fumbled ineffectually with it he took it back, afraid that she might cut herself.

"Have one of these rolls," he suggested, deftly peeling her orange for her. "They're still warm."

Her cheeks pinkened with embarrassment, but she mutely accepted his help and his suggestion, taking a big bite of the sweet bread. "Oh, this is very good," she exclaimed in evident surprise, making him wonder what she'd had to subsist on before.

"Where did you say you were from?" He spoke casually, not wanting her to suspect how curious he was about her.

Still, her expression became wary. "Near Oaklea," she replied after a hesitation that came either from caution or a spotty memory. "To the north of London."

Two days' ride north, in fact. Oaklea was barely more than a village, but Luke knew his geography well. "Did you travel to London by stage or with friends?"

Again she looked confused for a moment before replying. "Hettie's father is a farmer and let us take his gig. We traveled slowly, so that we would not have to change horses."

All the way to London in a farm gig? More like five days, then. Luke restrained himself from asking about their accommodations along the way, or what kind of father would let two young women—one of them of childlike intellect—come so far alone. "Did you live on the farm, too?"

She nodded, then shook her head. "Near, but not on it. I . . . I lived in a cottage near the village until my mother died. Then I decided to come to London to find work."

"I'm sorry for your loss," he said softly, but she averted her gaze—no doubt to hide tears.

"Thank you," she murmured, before devoting her attention to the now-peeled orange, clearly wishing to drop the subject.

Luke respected her feelings, though there were a dozen more questions he'd have liked to ask. Instead, he watched as she took a bite of the orange, then had to avert his own eyes rather than risk revealing the sudden surge of desire that shot through him. He simply had to get his unruly passions under control before he frightened her.

A moment later, Purdy asked a question of her own. "Have you always lived here? In London, I mean?"

Trying not to notice the way her pink tongue licked the juice of the orange from her perfect lips, he responded, "Near London, anyway. I grew up just outside of Edgeware."

He recalled the tiny hovel he and his mother had shared, and the abuse she had endured—always for his sake—at the hands of the upper classes, whose sewing she took in and whose great houses she helped to clean.

"What brought you into London?"

The question caught him off guard, though he should have expected it. Impossible to tell the truth—that he'd been lured here as a lad to learn thievery after his mother's death. That after escaping that life, he had later returned to revenge himself on those he considered responsible for that death. That only here could he simultaneously embarrass the *ton* and help those who were even more reduced by circumstances than his mother had been.

"There was no living to be had elsewhere," he said at last. "Probably much the same reason you came to London yourself."

She blinked, then apparently decided against further questions for the moment, again applying herself to her breakfast. Luke wasn't sure whether he was relieved or disappointed.

Though her curiosity about her rescuer was by no means sated, Pearl needed to think through her own circumstances before pushing further. How much did she dare tell him? As little as possible would be safest.

Still, this was a far better opportunity than she had expected, aside from the chance to free herself from her stepmother's matchmaking plans. She had wanted to see how the common people lived, and those in Seven Dials were the very commonest— with the exception of Mr. St. Clair, who seemed most uncommon indeed.

She had hoped, upon awakening, that she had

merely imagined the effect the man had on her, but if anything it was stronger than ever today. His voice flowed over her like warm silk, dizzying her senses in a way she could not call unpleasurable. His eyes, far more intelligent than she'd have liked, also stirred up odd longings she couldn't quite decipher. Hastily, she turned her thoughts back to the matter at hand.

While it pained her to think how Hettie must be worrying, wherever she was, she hadn't the faintest idea how she was to find her, or even get a message to her, without giving herself away. By now Hettie was sure to have returned to Oakshire House, and Pearl was by no means ready to go back. Not yet. But was spending the next few days in Seven Dials—in Mr. St. Clair's disturbing company—really a viable option?

Her ingrained sense of propriety—and, yes, her pride—recoiled at the thought, useful as it would be for her purposes. Yet the reformer in her exulted at this chance to educate herself in a way few of her class ever had—and, perhaps, the chance to do some actual good among the wretched poor of London's slums. And the woman in her . . . No, she wouldn't dwell on that.

Finishing both her breakfast and her ruminations, she asked hesitantly, mindful of the role she was playing, "If we are unable to find Hettie today, would you . . . mind too much if I stayed here for a few days?"

Mr. St. Clair, having just taken a sip of tea, sputtered and coughed. Pearl feared that boded ill, but as soon as he recovered he said cheerfully enough, "Of course I don't object. But don't give up so easily.

We'll find your friend, never fear. Why don't you tell me everything you can about her?"

Pearl examined his face for signs of reluctance—or lechery—but found only kindness and curiosity. She really had been exceedingly fortunate that he, and no one worse, had appeared to assist her. His curiosity was the biggest threat. That, and her undeniable attraction to this totally unsuitable man.

"Hettie is very nice," she offered unhelpfully after a moment. "I told you last night what she looks like—shorter and plumper than I, with curly brown hair."

If he felt any exasperation, he hid it admirably, only saying patiently, "Yes, I remember. But what is her last name? Where is her father's farm? Can you remember anything at all that she said about where you would be staying?"

"We were to stay with her cousin," she said, sticking to the story she'd given him last night. "I don't think her last name is the same as Hettie's, though." She couldn't give him Hettie's last name, either, for she could too easily be traced to the Oakshire household.

"And her father?" His wonderful voice was still patient. "He has a farm near Oaklea, you said."

Pearl hoped she wouldn't regret naming a village barely three miles from her father's primary estate in Oakshire, but it was the first thing that had popped into her head. She must not allow Mr. St. Clair to distract her so! "Yes, just a small one. He's a tenant—"

"Of the Duke of Oakshire, I presume."

She glanced up at the change in his tone. "You do not like the Duke of Oakshire?"

He was frowning, but at her question he smoothed his brow with a visible effort. "Actually, I know very little of him. I simply believe that farmers should be allowed to own the land their families have tilled for generations."

"So do I," she agreed eagerly, though she knew what she said would be heresy to most of her class. She opened her mouth to elaborate with her theories on how such a radical shift might benefit the economy, but remembered in time that she was supposed to be simpleminded. So instead she merely said, "I've . . . often thought that."

He smiled at her approvingly, warming her again—dangerously. "Come, let's go back to the vicinity of the Mountheath house to begin our search. You can give me more details as we go."

Rising, he plucked her cloak from the back of a chair and draped it over her shoulders. At home, Pearl received such courtesies as a matter of course, never thinking a thing about them. So why should this instance, by this man, cause her arms to tingle? For a fleeting moment she considered what Society would be bound to believe, once it became known that some nameless commoner had compromised Lady Pearl.

They would think that he and she had . . . The tingling increased, and she felt herself pinkening. No, she didn't dare think along such lines. It was absurd, of course, yet far, far too easy to imagine!

She thanked him haltingly, chiding herself for such foolishness, then tied her kerchief securely over her hair. Wishing vainly for a thorough wash and a change of clothes, she accompanied him out the door and down to the street.

Seven Dials by daylight was far less frightening, but no less squalid. A woman sat in a narrow doorway nursing an infant, while two painfully thin toddlers, dressed only in tattered rags despite the chill wind, played in a rubbish heap nearby. A few steps farther along, a man wearing the remnants of a cavalry uniform sat slumped against a wall, his single leg extending into the alley as he shook his tin cup at them.

Pearl choked back a gasp of pity, momentarily distracted from the man at her side. "Was that man a soldier?" she whispered.

Her companion nodded. "One of thousands reduced to begging, discarded by their country after serving in its cause against the French." His voice was bitter.

Though she had read such accusations in the *Political Register*, until now Pearl had not fully believed her own government, run by men like her father, could be so callous. But here was the evidence before her. She wished she had money with her, that she might ease the poor man's straits, though she knew it would do nothing to solve the larger problem.

"Hey, mister, Mr. Saint, sir, can you help my sister?" A little girl, no more than five years old, her face as dirty as her torn dress, ran up to tug on Mr. St. Clair's sleeve.

He glanced quickly at Pearl, then said, "Not right now, Emmy. I'll be back soon."

"But she's so sick. Mama thinks she might die." The tyke's chin trembled as tears made pale tracks down her smudged cheeks.

When he hesitated, Pearl put a hand on his arm.

"Let's go see what we can do," she suggested. "Please. I don't mind."

He shot her a grateful glance that made her heart tremble, then nodded. "Very well. Lead the way, Emmy."

The child led them into a dark doorway, down a narrow hallway, then through another door into a cluttered room with several straw pallets along one wall. A thin woman knelt over one of the pallets, where a girl perhaps a year younger than Emmy was shaking violently.

Pearl recognized the symptoms at once, and spoke before Mr. St. Clair could. "How long has she been like this?" she asked the woman sharply.

The woman turned, her tearful eyes wide and frightened. She looked first at Mr. St. Clair, with dawning hope, then at Pearl. "Thank ye for comin', Mr. St. . . . Clair. Thank ye from the bottom of me heart. I fear we may be losin' poor Mimi. She started shakin' just a few minutes since, but can't seem to stop."

Both Pearl and Mr. St. Clair moved forward, but she reached the girl first. "Do you keep poison out for rats?" she asked quickly.

"Aye, we can't keep 'em out of the food otherwise. D'ye think poor Mimi . . . ?"

"Yes, I do. Have you any asarabacca about?" The woman regarded her blankly. "Mustard, then?" Already Pearl was reaching for the child, prepared to thrust a finger down her throat if nothing else would serve.

"Mustard? Aye, but—"

"Bring it, please. Quickly." The tiny girl convulsed again, a blue rim appearing around her lips.

Pearl took the mother's place at her side, supporting her. "There, there, sweetheart. You'll be all right. Everything will be fine."

"Do you have it, Mrs. Plank?" Mr. St. Clair asked urgently. Pearl had nearly forgotten his presence. "Good. Hurry, woman!"

He took the bottle and handed it to Pearl, who quickly pried little Mimi's tightly clenched teeth open and poured a liberal amount down her throat. After only a few anxious seconds, the little girl retched, expelling the contents of her stomach, mustard and all. Pearl continued to hold her as her tremors slowly subsided. Finally, with a little sigh, she fell asleep.

"I think she'll be all right now," Pearl whispered to the girls' mother, transferring the tiny bundle into her eager arms. "Give her some water when she wakes, as much as she will drink. You should also have her seen by a physician as soon as possible."

The woman nodded. "I'll . . . I'll try. I don't know how to thank you, Miss . . ."

"Purdy. I'm just glad I was able to get here in time." She turned to Emmy, who had watched in silence the entire time. "You may have saved your sister's life. You should be very proud."

Emmy responded with a gap-toothed smile. "Thank you, Miss Purdy. Thank you, Mr. Saint." She then flung herself at Pearl and hugged her tightly, before turning back to watch her sleeping sister.

Pearl stood, smiling. This was what she had always loved best about living on her father's estates—the personal contact with the tenants, the knowledge that she could render needed assistance. It was good to know the skills she'd accumulated there were useful here in London, as well. This was far more satisfying than playing the part of a glittering ornament in some ballroom.

"Shall we go?" murmured Mr. St. Clair at her side, careful not to wake the sleeping child.

"Oh! Yes, of course." With a last glance at the tiny apartment where she had made a difference, Pearl followed him back out into the sunlit alley. "I'm so glad we were coming by just then," she commented as they continued on their way.

"Yes." At his tone, she glanced up at her companion, to find him regarding her intently. Her heart quickened its pace. "You saved little Mimi's life. I wouldn't have known to do that. Where did you learn such skills?"

She realized abruptly that, in the face of the emergency, she had completely forgotten her role as a simpleton. "Ah, on Hettie's farm, of course. The . . . the dogs there are always getting into the rat poison."

"Of course." His intense, dark gaze did not leave her face, and she felt it coloring under his solemn regard. "I can see that there is more to you than meets the eye, Purdy." His expression told her that he intended to find out what.

Chapter 4

"Would you like to go back to my lodgings for some more tea, to settle yourself?" Luke asked the unusual woman at his side. "Or would you prefer to go on at once?"

Purdy blinked up at him, again giving the impression of a lovely idiot, something he had now begun to doubt. Or was that wishful thinking on his part? In daylight, her eyes were an astonishingly beautiful violet-blue.

"Let's go on," she said. "I should try to find Hettie."

"Very well. This way, then." Luke noticed that she was again speaking with an uncultured accent. During the crisis at the Planks', both her manner of speaking and her vocabulary had improved markedly. He decided not to tell her he'd noticed—not yet, anyway.

He led her through the alleyways of Seven Dials, avoiding the foulest areas. Even so, he heard an occasional indrawn breath of dismay at the poverty and filth around them. Whether dim-witted or a clever liar, Purdy clearly had a compassionate heart.

In ten minutes they had reached more respectable environs, where tradesmen and regularly employed workers lived. In another ten minutes they approached the outskirts of Mayfair. "Not far now," he said encouragingly.

Purdy nodded, but pulled her kerchief lower, so that it concealed part of her face as well as her hair. Again Luke wondered what she'd been running from the night before. He couldn't believe that the girl had committed any sort of crime, but as they neared the Mountheath house, her steps slowed.

"I, ah, what should we do now, do you think?" she asked him, her voice reflecting her uncertainty. "Hettie won't be here today, surely."

He placed an arm around her shoulders, hoping to bolster her courage. Oddly, he still felt protective toward her, even knowing that she was hiding things from him. He'd never felt that way about any woman before. Earlier he'd assumed it was because of her mental deficiency. But now . . .

"We can go around to the mews and ask for news of her," he suggested. "Perhaps you'll see the footman who hired you."

She nodded, swallowing. Luke frowned but said nothing further, and she accompanied him around to the back of the square without further protest, though she hung back when they neared a small knot of stable hands. Before anyone had spotted them, she halted.

"I . . . I don't see him," she whispered, clearly anxious to retreat. Unwilling to add to her distress, Luke refrained from urging her forward.

"Would you like me to make inquiries on your behalf?" he asked gently. It would be risky, of course, if last night's thefts had been discovered, but he realized he was willing to do almost anything to erase the fear from Purdy's sweet face.

"If you wouldn't mind terribly?"

The gratitude in those lovely violet eyes made him feel willing to slay a dragon for her, if necessary. "Just a moment, then," he said, stifling a smile at such an absurd notion. "You can wait here beside the gate, out of sight."

Giving her shoulder a reassuring squeeze, he walked over to the stable hands, hoping the girl wouldn't flee before he returned. Just before he reached the group, a liveried groom emerged from the servants' entrance at the rear of the house and hurried in the same direction.

"Hoy there, lads!" he called out to the workers, who immediately broke apart and grabbed their shovels and brooms, attempting to look busy. "More news from Hodge, who had it direct from his lordship himself."

Luke slowed his pace to a stroll, making it look as though he were merely headed down the alley toward the houses beyond the Mountheaths', so he could listen.

"We're all to keep our eyes peeled for anything out of the ordinary. Her ladyship's suspicions were right, it seems. Not just jewels were stolen last night, but some of the plate, as well."

An excited murmer arose. One of the hands even exclaimed, "Was it the Saint, think you?"

Luke had all he could do to maintain his leisurely pace as he came level with them, only a few yards away, his ears straining. Luckily, he'd seen none of these men last night, so they wouldn't recognize him.

"Aye, it were him, all right. Hodges was in a fair fury when he found his calling card in the plate closet. But there's more." The groom raised his voice to be heard above their mutterings. "The thievery here was bad enough, but the blackguard did even worse two houses down." He nodded in the direction Luke was heading. "Miss Fanny's maid, Maggie, overheard her ladyship saying there was a kidnapping last night, as well."

A stunned silence greeted his words, and Luke nearly stopped to hear the rest. "Who?" one of the men finally asked, as the groom seemed determined to milk the situation for its drama.

"The Lady Pearl, daughter to the mighty Duke of Oakshire," he said at last, just before Luke had to pass out of earshot or become obvious for lingering. "Snatched right out of her very bedchamber, she was! Mark my words, the Saint of Seven Dials will hang for last night's work."

Peering out from her hiding place beside the Mountheaths' back gate, Pearl frowned as she saw Mr. St. Clair veer away from the group of stable hands and continue on down the alley. Too far away to hear anything herself, she could see that the servants were excited about something, waving their hands and chattering to each other. Perhaps Mr. St. Clair had decided it wasn't a good time to be asking questions.

Of course, that was just fine with her. She much preferred to avoid anything that might link her to the Mountheaths'. Or, worse, to the Duke of Oakshire. But now her confederate was walking briskly in the direction of Oakshire House itself! Had he discovered the truth about her after all?

She lingered, debating whether to wait for him to return, or to slip away before he could, just in case. Or she could simply return to Oakshire House and suffer the consequences of her ill-advised flight, as she'd have to do eventually anyway. She grimaced at the thought.

Without her father there, she'd be completely at the mercy of the Duchess, who would doubtless be very creative in meting out what she considered appropriate punishment—especially when she realized that her plans for a quick match had been overthrown. Obelia had never been susceptible to the tears and pleading that worked so well with the Duke.

No, Pearl wouldn't give her stepmother that satisfaction. However, she might try to contact Hettie without being seen. . . . Backing away from the gate, Pearl glanced around. If she could find something to write with, and on, then perhaps—

"You weren't leaving, were you?"

The voice, directly behind her, startled Pearl breathless. Whirling around, she found herself face-to-face with Mr. St. Clair, a knowing gleam in his eye.

"How . . . ? You . . . Leaving?" she stammered, her heart pounding. "Of course not. But where did you come from?"

"I cut through the gardens of the next house over and circled around. I didn't mean to frighten you, however. Were you getting bored waiting?" He still watched her expectantly.

Pearl quickly shook her head. Her shock had faded, but her heart didn't slow its beat noticeably. "No, I was going to come after you. I had an idea for contacting Hettie."

With a flash of inspiration, she realized she could ask him to deliver a note for her. No one at Oakshire House would have reason to connect Mr. St. Clair with her, and a note given to one of the scullery maids, addressed to Hettie, should be passed along without suspicion. At worst, the servants might speculate that Hettie was carrying on a flirtation with the unknown man.

She somehow suspected that Mr. St. Clair would be very good at flirtation.

"You can tell me as we walk," he said, interrupting that thought. "Right now I think we'd best be going. It appears there was some criminal activity here last night. If we linger, we might be noticed— and questioned."

"Criminal—oh, my!" The last thing Pearl wanted was to be questioned by Mountheath servants in her present guise. "Yes, let's leave, please."

As he led her away from Berkley Square, she realized that her eagerness might be incriminating. Did Mr. St. Clair believe *she* had done something criminal? Of course, he had been equally eager to leave the area, just as he had been last night. What might Mr. St. Clair be hiding—and just how safe—physically safe—was she with him?

"I'm sorry," he said after they'd walked a few minutes in silence. "You must be thinking all manner of terrible things. The truth is, I owe money to one of the Mountheath footmen. Money I don't have at this precise moment. It's why I needed to leave last night, and why I'd as soon not draw attention to myself today, but it's not very fair to you. I thought you deserved to know."

Pearl's mounting tension melted away at this entirely reasonable explanation. "Thank you. I admit I was becoming a bit worried."

"Yes, I thought you must be." His eyes held more than a hint of a question, however.

She cast about for an equally plausible reason for her own flight last night. "I have no wish to encounter a particular servant there, either. He made . . . improper advances to me last night, and became rather insistent when I refused."

His brows drew down alarmingly. "What kind of a man would force himself on— Who was it?"

His protectiveness warmed her, even as she had to hide a spurt of amusement. Again he'd almost called her an idiot to her face. "It was the butler," she replied, her resentment of that autocratic man who'd been her undoing overcoming her judgment for the moment. "I don't know his name."

"Hodge," he said through gritted teeth. "I should have known."

Nervously, Pearl wondered what she'd done. She couldn't have Mr. St. Clair risking himself on her behalf—especially for an insult she'd invented. "No harm was done," she said hastily. "I'd simply prefer to avoid him in future, that's all."

With a visible effort, he brought his sudden anger under control. "Yes, of course. I understand. You needn't worry I'll challenge him to a duel—much as I might like to."

They veered south, taking a different route from before, but Pearl barely noticed, startled by his words. She'd assumed dueling, illegal though it was, was restricted to the upper classes, where the law was willing to look the other way. It appeared she was wrong.

That this man, who had only met her last night, would even consider taking such a risk on her behalf stunned her. Certainly she was getting the education of her life!

He led her around another corner, into sudden, bright sunshine. Before them lay a large open square, as large as any of the grand squares of Mayfair, simply crammed with carts, small shops, and wide expanses of bunched flowers of every description, color, and scent. To Pearl's dazzled senses, it was like a wonderland dropped down into the heart of dirty London.

"Covent Garden market," he said when she paused. "I thought to buy a few things for our dinner."

Feeling a bit foolish, she nodded. Odd, that she'd never wondered before where the flowers and fresh produce came from that made their way into Oakshire House every day. Her servants surely knew this place well. She breathed deeply of the mingled scents that rose up to greet them, briefly envying those servants.

"Have you fought duels before?" she asked then, recalling her earlier surprise. She felt an urgent need to know what Mr. St. Clair's life was like, to understand him.

He grinned, making her heart flutter, then offered her his arm and started forward again, threading their way between the market stalls. "Only two or three, in my hotheaded youth. And with swords rather than pistols. Thus the risk was less, as was the chance of discovery by one of the masters."

"Masters? Do you mean at school?"

"Yes, at school," he said with a grimace, as though he'd let information slip that he'd have preferred to keep to himself. "I was . . . able to attend for a few years, before my circumstances were reduced."

That explained his cultured speech, about which Pearl had been curious from the start. Perhaps he was not so far removed from her world after all. "You've had a gentleman's education, then?"

"It was my mother's dearest wish. Much as it galled me to submit myself to the whims of my supposed 'betters,' I felt obligated to see it through."

Again, that animosity toward the upper classes. Curious, but minding her own accent, she asked, "Why do you dislike the nobility so? They've always been, ah, kind to me."

He paused at a cart filled with vegetables and herbs, looking over the selection before answering. "You've been fortunate, then. Or perhaps you simply haven't had much experience with them."

To hide her amusement at his assumption, she buried her nose in a basket of mint and thyme perched on the edge of the cart and inhaled deeply. "Perhaps."

"I have. Or at least my mother did, enduring their insults and ill treatment, even as she did the work they wouldn't deign to do with their own hands—for my sake."

"You mother raised you alone?" Her amusement abruptly gone, Pearl found that she preferred not to dwell on the shortcomings of her class after all.

He nodded. "My father died when I was very young. He was poor, for he left my mother very little. She was forced to work to support us both."

"Until you were old enough to help?" Pearl tried to imagine what it must have been like for the poor woman and her son—now this magnetically enigmatic man beside her.

"I never had the chance, actually. She died before I was twelve, of a fever she contracted while caring for some titled dame's child. The fine lady wouldn't risk contagion in the nursery herself, of course. And she never so much as inquired after my mother while she was ill."

Pearl bit her lip. No wonder Mr. St. Clair despised the upper classes. She wished she had stories of compassion and caring to relate, to counteract his own experiences, but she couldn't think of a single one at the moment. More than ever, she was determined to keep her true identity from him. She didn't think she could bear to see that loathing in his eyes turned upon her.

"Would you like to take that basket of herbs with you?" he asked her then.

Belatedly, she realized she was still touching the basket, half turned from him in her confusion. "Ah, no. But it does remind me . . ." Turning to the man tending the cart, she asked, "Have you any mallow, or angelica root?"

The man, a burly fellow with a shapeless black felt hat that partially obscured his blunt features, frowned. "Mallow I gots, miss, right here." He lifted a few sprigs of the familiar plant. "No roots, though. You might try Mistress Wiggan's patch, across the way." He pointed to another, smaller cart, heaped with carrots, potatoes, and other roots and tubers.

Luke paid for the mallow as well as a sack of peas, then led her across to the other cart without a word, though she knew he was watching her curiously. "Mistress Wiggan," she called out as they approached it, "do you—Ah, there, I see it. May we have some of that angelica root, please?"

The crone, her tattered yellow skirts swirling about her, turned to them with a toothless grin. "Ha'penny a bunch," she replied.

As before, Luke paid for the roots without question, handing them over to Pearl. Not until they were on their way again did he ask, "I presume you have a particular plan for those items?"

She nodded. "I'd like to stop and check on little Mimi, if you don't mind. These may help in her recovery."

A few minutes later, Luke knocked on Mrs. Plank's door. Though there were several questions he'd have liked to ask his companion, he kept them to himself, merely watching to see what this girl of mystery might do.

Certain now that she was anything but simple-minded, he found his original attraction to her reviving with redoubled force. He was determined to unravel her secrets—and perhaps other things, as well. He would have to tread carefully, though. If she suspected that he knew, she might leave before he had the chance.

"Good day, Mrs. Plank," he said when the woman opened to them. "We wished to inquire after Mimi."

The mother smiled, her tired face brightening until he could see the traces of what might once have been prettiness. "She's still sleeping, but her breathing is regular-like. Again I thank you—both of you."

Purdy spoke up then. "We won't come in and risk waking her, Mrs. Plank, but I've brought something that may speed her back to health." She held out the roots and herbs. "If you will boil these together in water, with a teaspoon or two of vinegar, the resulting tea may prove beneficial."

The woman glanced from Purdy to Luke, who gave her a nod and a smile. "Why, thank you, miss. I'll do as you ask, of course. Your mother raised you right, I must say. Was it from her you learned the herb lore?"

Luke thought she hesitated before replying. "She instructed me when I was young, yes, along with the . . . er, another woman. Together, they knew quite a lot about such things."

Again Mrs. Plank thanked her profusely as they bade her farewell. Walking back toward his lodgings, Luke decided to risk probing a bit. "I rather doubt you induced the dogs on the farm to drink medicinal teas. I presume you've treated people before, as well?"

Her fair skin pinkened deliciously. "I . . . my mother did, and I was always with her. I suppose I learned more from her than I realized at the time."

His eyes did not leave her face, even though he knew his gaze was making her uncomfortable. "You said your mother had passed away. How long ago was that?"

"Ten, er . . . two years ago. But she was, er, ill for several years before she died." She didn't meet his eyes, and it was obvious to Luke, long studied in reading people, that she was lying. But why?

"And the other woman you said taught you about herbs and healing?" he prompted.

She swallowed, reddening further. Lying she might be, but she was not nearly as practiced at the art as he was. "Mrs., um, Horrigan. A . . . neighbor, skilled in the healing arts."

They had reached the stairs to his lodgings, so he forbore questioning her further—for the moment. Placing a hand at her elbow, as much for the pleasure of touching her as to assist her, he escorted her up the stairs.

As they approached his door, a scruffy little mound of brown and white fur jumped up and ran toward them, short tail wagging furiously.

"And what have you been up to today, Argos?" Luke asked, scratching the terrier between the ears. The tail wagged faster. "Ah." Kneeling, his back to the girl, he unwound a scrap of paper from around the dog's collar. The note would be from Flute, and could mean only one thing: Someone in the neighborhood was desperately in need of help.

Surreptitiously scanning its contents proved him right. Mme. Billaud's son Christophe had broken his leg—no doubt climbing out of windows again—and the surgeon refused to see him unless she paid in advance. With her husband recently dead, she had no way to come up with the money.

Palming the note, he put it in his pocket as he drew out his key. Normally this would mean that the Saint of Seven Dials would ride again tonight, but with Purdy here, he wasn't sure how he would manage it without both arousing her suspicions and putting her at risk by leaving her alone. He opened the door and bowed her inside, still frowning.

"Is there something I can do to help?" she asked, startling him back to awareness of her presence.

"Help? What do you mean?"

She lifted a hand in a vague gesture, then dropped it. "You seem, ah, upset about something. As you've been very kind to me, I'd like to help with whatever it is, if I can."

Luke stared at her for a moment, thinking hard. Not only had Purdy revealed unexpected skills, she was more perceptive than he'd given her credit for, as well. Was it possible that she *could* help?

Deciding there was little to lose, he asked, "By chance, did you ever watch or help your mother set a broken bone?"

Her eyes widened, but she answered quickly enough. "I've seen it done, yes. Why do you ask?"

"I've just remembered that a boy nearby has broken his leg. I had promised to help, or bring help, but, er, events of the past night and day drove it from my mind."

Her smile sent a jolt of desire straight to his vitals, and this time he did not try so ruthlessly to suppress it.

"As I was that 'event,' it seems fair that I help remedy your lapse," she said. "Let's go at once—the poor boy may be in considerable pain."

"Thank you," he said, thinking of other things she could remedy for him. Later. There would be time for that later.

Pausing only to slice bread and cheese that they could eat along the way, Luke led her back out into the streets, hoping that together they could render aid to poor Christophe—and that it would not take too long.

When they reached her second-story apartment, Mme. Billaud greeted him with delight, chattering in her native French, but paused at the sight of the girl behind him. "Surely this is no surgeon?" she asked, still in French.

Mme. Billaud, he remembered belatedly, spoke almost no English. He would have to translate for Purdy—though that had advantages, as well as drawbacks. "She knows much of healing arts," he replied in French. Then, to Purdy, "I'm merely reassuring her that you'll try to help."

Purdy nodded. "May we see the boy?"

He conveyed the request, and Mme. Billaud led them to a curtain that separated the sleeping area from the rest of the small room. From his cot, Christophe grinned up at Luke with his usual impudence, but the white line around his mouth attested to the pain he was suffering.

As she had at the Planks', Purdy hurried forward, her focus instantly on her patient. Gently, she probed the injured leg, while Luke asked the boy to point out where it hurt most.

After a few moments, she turned to Luke with a relieved smile. "It appears to be a clean break—I can feel no displacement. If we can find something to use as a splint and some bandages, I believe we can do as much for him as a surgeon could."

A tension Luke had been unaware was constricting his chest suddenly loosened as he returned her smile. "Excellent!" Then, again in French, he explained to Mme. Billaud what they would need. Nodding and chattering, the woman hurried out, saying that a neighbor had just the thing.

Purdy spent the few minutes while she was gone soothing the boy with her voice while she made certain his leg was as straight as possible.

"Can I be of assistance?" Luke asked her as she struggled to turn Christophe's knee slightly without causing the boy any more pain than necessary. He'd never known anyone before with her capacity for compassion.

She sent him a quick smile, which again went straight to his nether regions. "Thank you, but I believe that will do it. We're ready for the splint now."

Even as she spoke, Mme. Billaud returned with the required items. Handing them to Purdy, she asked whether she needed anything else.

"No, this will do the job nicely, madame."

"And will he be all right?" asked the anxious mother.

"Yes, I believe so. The break is not bad." Purdy was working as she spoke, binding the two wooden splints on either side of the leg with tightly wrapped bandages.

Watching her deft ministrations, it was several seconds before Luke realized with a shock that Mme. Billaud's questions had been in French—as had Purdy's replies. The girl spoke French with the ease of a native! She seemed unaware of having done anything unusual, however, still intent on her work.

When she finished a few minutes later, she turned to Luke. "Tell Mrs. Billaud that her son must not use this leg at all for the next few days. After that, he should be able to get around a bit, if she can find or fashion him a crutch to keep his weight off of the leg."

Hiding his smile, Luke dutifully relayed her instructions so that she would not realize her earlier slip, then bade Mme. Billaud and her son good-bye. What other abilities or knowledge might Purdy be hiding? he wondered, as they reached the street again. He decided to try a small test.

"The Billauds are but lately come to England," he told her as they walked. "They tired of the tug-of-war over their homeland between the Treaties of '14 and '15, and came here to escape it."

She nodded absently, staring at a pair of ill-clad children arguing over a crust of bread, a touching concern creasing her pretty brow. "Were they Belgian, then, caught between the French and the Dutch?"

Aha! No farm maid would have known that. "Indeed they were. You have kept current with European politics, I see," he said dryly.

With a start, she turned wide, guileless eyes to him, though he detected a flicker of wariness in their depths. "I, er . . . not really. I recall Hettie's father talking about it once."

And remembered treaties, dates, countries? Unlikely, but he did not say so. "Of course. Shall we return to my lodgings, or would you prefer to make another attempt to contact your friend? You said you had an idea?"

Now, knowing that she was as intelligent as she was beautiful, he found himself almost overwhelmingly attracted to this girl of mystery. The feeling was almost frightening in its intensity. Tempted as he was to taste her delights, he realized it would be safest to get her out of his life without further delay.

She glanced at him, a troubled frown between her brows, as though she were wondering how much he had guessed, but she nodded. "Yes, I've remembered that Hettie has a . . . a friend who works at Oakshire House. In the kitchens."

That seemed plausible, if Hettie, like Purdy, was from the Duke of Oakshire's lands. "You believe this friend might know where she is?" Unfortunately, after what he had overheard earlier, Oakshire House was the last place the Saint of Seven Dials could safely go.

"Perhaps. At the very least, she could surely get a note to her from me, so that I can tell her where I am. Then she can come to fetch me." She smiled brightly at her solution, again giving the impression of childlike intellect—intentionally, of course.

"A reasonable plan," he agreed. "However, this may not be the best time to carry it out." At her questioning look, he continued. "In addition to the robbery at the Mountheaths', it would seem that an even more serious crime was committed at Oakshire House last night."

Purdy gasped. "At Oakshire House? What . . . ?"

"I told you that I overheard the Mountheath servants speaking earlier. They were saying that a highborn lady, in fact the very daughter of the Duke of Oakshire, has been kidnapped."

Chapter 5

Pearl stared at him in horror, though her first wild fear that something had happened to her father was allayed. Kidnapped? They believed she had been kidnapped? What hornet's nest had she stirred up?

"A kidnapping—in the middle of Mayfair?" Had Hettie hinted at such a thing, or had the others simply assumed it? What on earth must Hettie be doing right now? Pearl imagined her stepmother grilling the girl mercilessly.

"Hard to believe, I admit. And of course I merely overheard some servants talking, so it's possible it's exaggerated gossip. Still, if I were to appear just now at Oakshire House with a mysterious note—"

"Someone might assume it was a ransom note and have you arrested," she finished. And if the authorities discovered she'd spent the night at his lodgings, he might well hang for a crime that had never been committed!

Horror swept through her again at the thought. This man might not be of noble birth, but he evinced the most noble character she'd ever known, so obviously concerned as he was for the unfortunate around him. No, even for Fairbourne, she could not risk Luke St. Clair's life.

"Very astute," he said then, and she had to think for a moment to recall her last words. Another slip on her part.

"I . . . I've heard of such things as ransom notes," she offered, trying without much hope to salvage her charade. "Hettie and I used to read adventure stories together, you see."

"And did this mythical Hettie teach you French as well? And geography?" Though his eyes—those intense eyes—held more warmth and amusement than condemnation, she knew she was trapped. He *had* caught her lapse into French earlier, though he'd pretended otherwise.

She flinched away from that too-knowing gaze to focus again on the ragged children and their stick-swordfight across the alley, until welcome pride came to her aid. "Hettie is not mythical," she said haughtily, raising her chin to face him again. "She's my . . . my friend."

The gentle question in his eyes was nearly her undoing. Perilously close to admitting all, she had to remind herself how foolish that would be. He could have no idea—yet—of who she really was. Once he did, there would be no more support, no more heated glances.

Somehow, in just one day, he had become a friend—and perhaps a little bit more. But that would end the moment he discovered she was one of the hated noble class.

He put a hand on her arm, and instead of spurning the intimate contact, Pearl found herself leaning into it, taking comfort from it, her quick spurt of pride forgotten. "Come," he said quietly. "Let's go back and sort everything out."

"Back?" Sternly, she tried to subdue the tremble in her voice.

"To my lodgings. Unless there really is somewhere else I can take you?"

If he escorted her back to Oakshire House, there was a chance he'd be arrested before she could explain. Taking his proffered arm, knowing this was almost as dangerous, she accompanied him back the way they had come.

"I've been trying to puzzle you out," he said conversationally as they walked. "Perhaps you can tell me how well I've done." He shot her a grin in response to her questioning frown—a grin that sent tendrils of warmth curling through her body.

"Here's my guess," he continued. "You're actually of gentle birth, and have worked as a governess in some exalted household. That would explain your education. You were forced to leave when some supposed 'gentleman' of the household tried to take liberties." His eyes darkened with anger for a moment, then with something else. "Not that I can blame him completely."

Again she felt herself coloring—something she'd done more in the past day than in the whole year preceding it. "That's . . . a surprisingly good guess," she said, trying to ignore his effect on her. After only a slight hesitation, she elaborated on the story he had begun. "It was the butler, actually—which is why I was so anxious to avoid the attention of Hodge at the Mountheaths'."

"And Hettie? A fellow servant?"

"My pupil's abigail. She, er, helped me to escape. I fear we did not think things through as thoroughly as we should have, however." Mixing some truth into her story made her feel better. It felt somehow wrong to lie to this man, even though she knew he was hiding things as well. Besides, lying was beneath her—though at the moment she had little choice.

They were mounting the steps to his lodging now, and Pearl felt her heartbeat quickening with every step, along with a sense of anticipation for she knew not what.

"Has Hettie returned to the house you left by now?" he asked. "In Oaklea—or perhaps much closer to London?"

Pearl watched his strong brown hands—bare hands—as he unlocked the door. "I don't know," she confessed truthfully, following him into the apartment. "We were separated at the Mountheaths' before we'd decided just what to do. She may have gone back by now—which I cannot do." She ignored the latter part of his question.

A quick upturn of his lips told her he'd noticed. "Very well, mystery lady, that will do for now, I suppose. If you're not willing to go back, we'll have to find you other, more permanent employment. Without references, however, another governess position will be difficult to procure." He closed the door, shutting out the rest of the world.

She couldn't stay, of course. She didn't dare, now that he knew this much about her, now that she suspected he was as drawn to her as she was to him. No, she would have to slip away at her first opportunity and return home—and he mustn't be anywhere near her when she did so.

"You've been very kind," she said, meaning every word. "Even knowing so little about me, knowing that I was hiding things from you. Thank you."

His smile warmed his eyes, warmed her— dangerously and deliciously. "You're very easy to be kind to. At first I may have acted out of simple pity, but now that I know . . . er, know you better, it's more than that. I'd like to help in any way I can—as you've helped me, and the denizens of this place. You are a gallant young woman, Purdy."

His use of her assumed name served as a much-needed reminder that he knew nothing about her— and that she knew even less of him. They were from different worlds, and she would soon be gone from his. There could be no future for their budding friendship. The realization struck her with a sharp sense of loss.

"I simply try to do what's right," she said, as much to herself as to him. "The world doesn't always make that easy."

"Well I know it. Instead, it places barriers in the way of good intentions." He spoke as though to himself, but then caught her eye again. "As you have discovered yourself," he concluded, shaking off his sudden gravity with a smile.

She nodded. "But our good intentions will triumph," she said with complete conviction. "They must."

Something kindled in his deep brown eyes, capturing her. "Such an idealist," he murmured. "I like that."

Pearl became suddenly, acutely aware of how alone they were, here in the close confines of his lodgings, how near he stood. Not another person in the world knew where they were. She continued to drown in his gaze, her heart thudding in slow, heavy strokes.

"Do you?" Her voice sounded breathless to her own ears and she felt herself swaying toward him.

"Very much." The spark in his eyes flamed into something far more intense, though they held a question, as well.

Without stopping to think how inappropriate, how foolhardy, how—anything—this was, conscious only of her own need, Pearl tipped her face up for his kiss.

His lips lowered to hers, first to gently brush, then to explore, and finally to claim. She responded, still without thought, reveling in his strength, his masculine scent, the sense of being cherished. Instinctively, her hands sought his shoulders, while his clasped her waist. His mouth on hers felt like heaven—like something she'd waited for all her life.

The one or two kisses a calf-eyed suitor had stolen in a shadowed alcove when she was seventeen had been nothing like this. This was real, a kiss between adults—and it stirred a sharp longing in her for something more.

As though sensing her longing, he tightened his grip on her waist, deepening his kiss, then slid one hand slowly, sensuously up her back until his bare fingers rested at the sensitive nape of her neck.

Pearl allowed her own hands to wander as well, skimming along his broad shoulders and upper arms, then back up until she threaded her own ungloved fingers through his disordered dark curls. His slight moan elicited a similar one from her own throat, a sound she vaguely identified as a growl of desire.

Spanning the back of her neck with one hand, he slid the other back down to her waist, then lower, pulling the length of her body against his. A bulge in his nether regions pressed against the very heart of her desire, igniting a need she'd never known she had—a hot, burning need to become one with this man.

When he moved the hand at her nape around to cup the swell of her breast, it never occurred to her to protest. Instead, she shifted to give him better access. She tilted her head back and he trailed kisses down her throat, to the high collar of her gown, then back to her lips. He released her breast to unfasten the top button of her bodice.

A passion like none she'd ever imagined roared up, threatening to consume her—consume them both. She wanted this, more than anything she'd ever wanted. This was right. This was real. This was—

"I want you, Purdy," he murmured against her lips.

The alias was like a splash of cold water, tempering her ardor with a sudden chill of reality. What on earth was she doing?

Though her body thrummed an insistent protest, she forced herself to pull away from him. "I . . . I'm sorry," she panted. "I never—"

He released her at once, self-awareness, even guilt, fighting with the desire in his eyes. "Oh, Lord. Purdy, I'm sorry." He raked a hand through his hair, making it stand wildly on end in a way she found oddly endearing. "I've subjected you to the very thing you were escaping."

She couldn't suppress a smile. "You were no more subjecting me than I was subjecting you, so you need not apologize. Believe me, what I escaped was nothing like that." True enough! "Still, I fear this is . . . unwise."

He swallowed visibly, though his eyes seemed to devour her—despairingly, she thought. "Unwise indeed. First thing tomorrow, I'll begin making inquiries about a position for you, and for a respectable place for you to stay while we search. And I do apologize, Purdy. I . . . I knew better."

"So did I," she replied, pulling her gaze away from his smoldering one before it could reignite what she'd so reluctantly broken off. "Let's . . . not speak of it any further."

She felt rather than saw him nod. "What say you to some dinner and an early night? Tomorrow we must accomplish more than we managed today." Moving away from her with obvious reluctance, he went to the sideboard and began pulling out the makings of a simple meal.

Though her eyes followed him hungrily, Pearl

seated herself at the table. "Is there something I can do to help?"

He turned and almost caught her staring. She had to will her color not to rise. "Do you think you can shell these peas?" he asked, clearly remembering her clumsiness with the orange that morning.

She chuckled, finally getting her unruly passions under control—for the moment. "As you've guessed, I've had little experience in the kitchen, but I believe I can manage to shell peas without doing myself an injury."

For a few minutes they worked in companionable silence, she shelling the peas into a pot for boiling while he unwrapped a couple of meat rolls he'd bought while they were in the market. While the peas boiled, he deftly peeled the remaining orange from breakfast.

"The bread isn't as fresh as it was last night, but it should still be edible," he commented, cutting a few thick slices. "Now."

With a flourish, he set out bread, cheese, meat rolls, orange sections, and the bowl of peas, as well as two plates of fine china that again made Pearl wonder about this man of contrasts. Belatedly, she realized that she could at least have set the table while he worked. Two days among the working class had not been enough to cure her habitual assumption of rank, it seemed.

"Thank you," she said graciously, in an attempt to compensate for her uselessness. "It looks delicious."

Though the fare was as simple as she'd had, devoid of French sauces or elegant garnish, Pearl found it delicious. It was said that hunger was the best sauce, she reflected—not that she'd had the chance to put it to the test before. And more than one sort of hunger was at work here.

Even with the table between them, she could feel a physical link to this man humming through her blood. Though she knew it was madness, she wanted nothing more than a repeat of that kiss, that embrace. . . . The sooner she left Luke St. Clair's company, the better, obviously!

Partly to distract herself, she asked, "Last night you mentioned that your last employer had been generous in his will. What sort of work did you do for him?" The question was more blunt than she'd intended, but this might be her last chance to assuage her curiosity about him.

He took his time chewing and swallowing a bite of meat roll before answering. "I, ah, tutored his son briefly, then worked as his personal manservant. He preferred to have few people about him, so I was able to make myself indispensable."

She forced herself to focus on his words rather than his lips. His answer seemed reasonable, but she had the distinct feeling he was telling her less than the truth. Only fair, she supposed, considering how little he knew about her. "And you've lived here since he died?"

"More or less. I can pick up a living here, of sorts. In addition, I can occasionally help people whose lives have been destroyed, directly or indirectly, by the nobility."

"Like your mother's," she said softly. No, she certainly did not want him to know the full truth about her.

Though he frowned in apparent surprise, he nodded slowly. "Yes, I suppose I'm still trying to repay her, to avenge her, in the only way I can."

Avenge. It seemed an odd word choice. "She must have been a remarkable woman."

Now he smiled, with a wistfulness that tugged at her heart. "She was. A true lady in everything but birth."

Pearl caught the implication that her lack of noble birth elevated his mother even higher in his eyes. Luke's clear animosity toward her class pricked her pride, putting her on the defensive. "Perhaps birth—or lack thereof—has little to do with nobility of heart," she suggested.

The wistfulness in his eyes changed to something more cynical. "If anything, noble birth seems to preclude nobility of heart, at least in my experience."

Pearl shifted uncomfortably in her chair, trying to frame an argument, but he spoke again before she could. "You are a perfect example, Purdy. I've never met anyone, except perhaps my mother, who so clearly evinced nobility of spirit. Yet you're as common as I am, are you not?"

She swallowed, trapped. "My . . . my mother was a gentleman's daughter," she offered as a nod to the truth. She couldn't bring herself to say more, dreading the condemnation in his eyes.

To her surprise, his smile forgave her—and caused her pulse to race again. "Mine may have been as well," he admitted. "But the true nobility, the peers of the realm, are in a class apart—and they flaunt it whenever they can, to the detriment of those they consider beneath them."

Though his words were harsh, his eyes were not. They held hers with a gentle seeking that snatched her breath. Though she wanted to deny his words, she responded only with an uncertain nod. He seemed to consider it enough, for he reached across the table to take her hand in his—again, bare flesh touching bare flesh. Her senses pulsed with awareness.

"This may sound trite," he said, still holding her gaze and her hand, "but I believe we are kindred spirits, you and I. Perhaps it was fate that threw us together after all."

Pearl's heart began to hammer so that it seemed impossible he would not hear it. Fate? She didn't believe in fate . . . did she? And how could hers, Lady Pearl's, lie with this man's? Impossible! But the idea appealed to her on a primal level, even while her reason told her it was absurd.

When she did not answer, Luke rose, her hand still in his. Mesmerized, Pearl stood as well, their bodies only inches apart. This time, when he took her in his arms, she would not call a halt, she decided. People would believe the worst anyway— why should she not have this moment of bliss?

Instead, he brought her hand to his lips with the courtliness of royalty.

"You've shown me a side of life I'd nearly forgotten," he told her, then touched her fingers with his kiss—a gentle brush that sent flame licking along every nerve in her body. "Thank you."

She managed to summon a smile, when what she wanted was to feel his lips, his hands, upon her. "And you have shown me a side of the human condition that I sorely needed to learn about. For that, as well as your unselfish help to a stranger in need, I thank you."

For an instant his grip tightened, and she thought he would pull her back into his arms after all. She was ready, more than ready. . . . He released her and bowed.

"A noble spirit indeed. But even so strong a spirit as yours must be tired after a day like today. Rest, and we'll start fresh in the morning." He turned from her to stack their plates and cutlery in the washtub.

She knew she should offer to help, but now that the moment of madness had passed, she fully understood just how dangerous it was for her to get too close to this man. Instead, she went to the divan and unfolded the sheets, spreading them out in preparation for another night on its unyielding surface. When she finished, she turned to find him regarding her with a smile and a steaming pitcher.

"I was remiss last night, but here is hot water and a basin, should you wish to wash before retiring. My apologies for not thinking to offer them before—I am unused to guests."

"Pray don't mention it," she said quickly. "But thank you." A wash sounded heavenly. "I'll . . . see you in the morning." Even as she spoke, however, she knew her words were false. By morning she must be gone, or she would be lost forever.

Luke settled himself in bed, intending to thoroughly examine the bewildering mix of emotions that had assailed him over the past few hours. He needed to analyze his feelings, decide just how important Purdy had become to him in one short day and evening. Instead of a dispassionate analysis, however, he found himself reliving those amazing few moments of passion.

He'd been intimate with a number of women, of course, but this was different somehow. Though Purdy's inexperience had been evident, if anything that only added to her appeal, exciting him far more than the practiced caresses of an opera dancer or a straying wife. He'd felt a connection with Purdy, a need that went beyond mere physical arousal. A rightness.

And it scared him.

For the first time, he allowed himself to toy with the possibility of a permanent attachment, something he'd always assumed was impossible for him. But perhaps, just perhaps, it wasn't.

Purdy fit into his lifestyle, his role here in Seven Dials, with remarkable ease. She possessed skills he lacked, skills which complemented his own. Of course, she still knew nothing of his usual methods, and he knew without asking her that she would disapprove, even be shocked.

He felt sure, though, that he could make her understand. And if he couldn't, then perhaps, with her help, thievery might become less necessary to achieve his ends. With the delectable memory of her body and lips pressed to his, he drifted off, to dream of an improbably rosy future with Purdy at his side, day and night.

The sun was well risen when he awoke, the first time in ages he could remember sleeping past dawn. Luke stretched and smiled, remembering the day—and evening—just past, his pleasant dreams, and his hopes for the future. He would speak to her today, he decided. Discover whether his hope was justified. Quickly he rose, washed, and dressed, before going to listen at his bedroom door for any sound of Purdy stirring.

Silence. No doubt she'd needed sleep even more than he had. After all, she'd not only traipsed over half of London at his side, but had healed two children yesterday.

Again he smiled. Valiant, self-effacing Purdy, so unaware of her own talents and charms. She would bring out the best in him, if any such thing existed.

Cautiously, he cracked open the door, anticipating the sight of her in tousled, innocent sleep.

The divan was empty.

Frowning, he stepped into the room, sweeping it with a glance before striding to the window to draw back the curtain, chasing away the shadows. Her sheets were neatly folded at the end of the divan, and a quick check revealed that the door was unlocked.

She was gone.

Chapter 6

Pearl stretched, reveling in the luxury of her own soft down mattress when she awakened after only a few hours' sleep. No one in the household knew she had returned as yet.

After slipping out of Luke's lodgings shortly after midnight, she had made her way back to Mayfair. The fog, combined with the necessity of hiding every time anyone approached, had made the walk of little over a mile take more than two hours. On reaching Oakshire House, she'd had to be even more cautious to avoid waking the servants who slept in the kitchen.

Eventually she had achieved her own bedchamber, with no one the wiser. At any moment, however, someone was sure to . . .

At a slight sound behind her, Pearl rolled onto

her side to see Hettie emerging from the hidden servant door, a dejected look on her pert face. The motion on the bed drew her eye, however, and for a long moment she stared, stunned, at the figure there. Then she ran forward with a glad cry.

"My lady! Oh, my lady! You're back! I'd near despaired of ever . . . How did you . . . ? When . . . ?" The questions tumbled out of her mouth too quickly for completion.

Pearl sat up to return her abigail's embrace, pleased that her first welcome should be such a happy one. "Yes, Hettie, I'm back, and perfectly safe, I assure you. What a lot I have to tell you! But first, pray, lower your voice and tell me what story has been put about to account for my absence."

Hettie gave her one more fierce hug, then sat back to examine her mistress's face. A small nod evidenced her satisfaction with what she saw there, and then she began. "I couldn't find you at the Mountheaths', then I heard you'd fled the place. I didn't know what to think. I assumed at first someone had recognized you, but no one mentioned the Lady Pearl having been there."

"Fanny Mountheath saw me and remarked on the resemblance," Pearl explained, "so I left before she could assemble a crowd, which would have guaranteed my discovery."

"So I was nearly right, then. Anyway, I stayed for another hour hoping you'd return, then when you didn't I spent most of the night searching the area."

Pearl took her hand. "That was dangerous, Hettie. You might have been set upon by footpads, or worse!"

Hettie shrugged. "I didn't think of that at the

time, and no harm came to me. I didn't dare venture beyond Mayfair, however, and I finally came back here, but you hadn't come home, either." She paused questioningly.

"I'll tell you everything later." Well, perhaps not *everything*. "First, I need to know what has transpired here."

"I tried to get in without being seen, but the house was in an uproar on account of your disappearance, and I was spotted and called to face the Duke and Duchess. His Grace was most upset, I fear, and Her Grace as well—though for fear of scandal, I'd warrant, rather than out of true concern for you." Hettie's dislike of the Duchess was evident.

Pearl sighed. "My father returned home, then? Oh, dear. I never meant to cause him distress—nor you, Hettie. I'm sorry you were subjected to the Duchess's wrath, as well."

"I told them you'd gone to visit a friend, but that I couldn't remember who. I fear I wasn't very convincing, for they didn't believe me. His Grace was certain you'd been kidnapped, while the Duchess seemed to think you'd planned the whole thing to discredit her. I was dismissed before I could discover more."

"Dismissed?" Pearl was startled. "From their presence, you mean?"

"No, from their employ," Hettie replied sadly. "I am to leave for my mother's house today. Her Grace insisted that I had failed in my duties and could no longer be useful here."

Pearl snorted. "Well, *that*, at least, will soon be rectified. What story have they told the world? That I was kidnapped?"

Hettie shook her head. "It's what's being whispered belowstairs, and may even have leaked outside the house, but Their Graces' explanation is the 'absurd' one I offered—that you're visiting a friend."

"And that's the explanation we'll maintain," declared Pearl decisively. Her original idea of claiming to be ruined would only serve to ensure Hettie's dismissal. In addition, it might be dangerous for Luke, should her father insist on investigating.

Luke would have discovered by now that she was gone, she realized. What might he be feeling? No doubt he would believe she had panicked and fled . . . which was not so very far from the truth. She realized Hettie was waiting for her to continue, so reined in her errant thoughts.

"Come, dress me for breakfast while we work out the details of my story so that it will not conflict with what you've already told them."

Half an hour later, again dressed in the height of fashion in a pale blue day dress, Pearl descended to the breakfast room, ignoring the openmouthed stares of the servants she passed along the way. The Duke and Duchess were already at the table when she entered and greeted them as though nothing whatsoever were amiss.

Obelia gasped, and her father leaped to his feet, rushing to encase her in a comprehensive bear hug. "Pearl! My precious! You are safe!" he exclaimed with such feeling that she suffered her first serious twinge of guilt.

Her stepmother remained seated. "Where have you been—for *two* days and nights?" she asked in ominous tones. "We were forced to assume the worst."

Would the worst be that she was dead, or ruined? Pearl wondered. Probably the latter. She directed her explanation to her father. "I'm so terribly sorry to have worried you so. It was wrong of me. I was distraught and did not think things through as I ought."

The Duke led her to her place at the table and signaled for a servant to bring her a plate. "Distraught?"

She nodded. "The Duchess and I had a falling out over my unwed state, and I feared—foolishly, I now realize—that she might somehow compel me to marry whether I wished it or not." She shot a glance at Obelia, but her stepmother looked not the least bit conscious.

Her father patted her hand soothingly—at which Obelia's face darkened with suppressed anger.

"I thought to go to Oakshire to compose myself," Pearl continued, "and perhaps seek Rowena Riverstone's advice." Rowena and Pearl had been friends from girlhood, as Sir Nelson Riverstone's lands adjoined the main Oakshire estate, dwarfed by it though they were. Obelia had done her best to discourage the association, deeming Rowena Pearl's social inferior, but the young ladies still corresponded. It should seem a plausible story, therefore.

The Duchess, however, was having none of it. "You haven't had time to go to Oakshire and back," she pointed out. "Nor did you take a carriage." Her fine blue eyes fairly blazed with suspicion.

Pearl sent her what she hoped was an apologetic

smile, though her anger at her stepmother made it difficult. "I was *escaping*, you see, so my own carriage would scarcely do—it would have been too easily marked. I traveled post."

Obelia's lip curled with distaste, but Pearl continued before she could speak. "As I went along, I had time to more calmly ponder my situation, and realized I was being foolish. So after a single night on the road I decided to return rather than worry you both unnecessarily." She turned the full force of her charm on her more susceptible father.

As she'd hoped, he smiled down at her indulgently. "It was dangerous, my heart, to travel so far alone, but I am happy beyond words that you are back safe now."

The Duchess began sputtering. "My dear, surely you are not going to simply *accept* this glib explanation? Think of the inconvenience she caused you, forcing you to turn back before reaching Brighton to deal with the crisis here. And a night on the road, without even her abigail in attendance? Scandalous! If it were to become known, her reputation would be in shreds!"

Pearl thought wryly that it was a very good thing her stepmother had no inkling of the truth. "I stayed at a respectable inn—the Hound and Hare." She named the place where they always stopped when traveling between London and Oakshire. "Everyone there knows me, and I was assigned a maid for my stay."

She turned back to her father. "I deceived Hettie so that she could not betray where I'd gone. I feared if I brought her with me she would dissuade me from my plan. She tells me she has been dismissed, but she truly did nothing wrong. Pray tell me I may keep her on, as we deal so well together."

It pained her to lie to her father, but she felt the end justified the means. And indeed, her words had the desired effect.

"Of course, if there was nothing she could have done, then we cannot hold her accountable," the Duke said, giving her hand a loving squeeze. Pearl ignored the indignant sounds coming from across the table.

"Thank you, Father. And I truly am sorry for the worry and inconvenience I've caused. I promise it won't happen again." With that promise, the face of Luke St. Clair arose unbidden in her mind—a face she would almost certainly never see again. Feeling suddenly forlorn, she felt her smile waver.

"Happen again? I should say not!" exclaimed Obelia before the Duke could respond. "Our mission now must be to squelch whatever rumors are abroad and repair your reputation. Thank heaven I have not yet sent your regrets for the Chathams' ball Tuesday. You must make an appearance at Princess Charlotte's reception tonight, as well. If we hold our heads high, there's a chance it may all blow over."

Pearl's spirits sank lower, but she dared not protest, much as she'd have preferred her reputation unrepaired. To do so might provoke her stepmother to the point that she would check out the facts of her story, which could be damaging to others besides herself. So she nodded meekly while Obelia chattered on.

"Tomorrow we'll attend services, of course, so that you can be seen again, and Monday we have invitations for both afternoon and evening. The

Chatham ball Tuesday, and then our calendar begins to fill up as the Season progresses. If all goes well, you will still have a chance at a respectable match. A quick betrothal and wedding would be just the thing, in fact."

Pearl bit back her instinctive retort and let the words wash over her, painting a picture she could only regard as bleak. Despite her regrets for causing her father needless worry, she began to regret returning even more. What might Luke be doing now? Was he searching for her, or would he be relieved that she was no longer his problem?

And why should it matter to her so desperately?

"So you have not seen her?" Luke asked, then sighed as Mme. Billaud shook her head a second time. For the past three hours he had scoured all of Seven Dials, and now had reached the last place he might reasonably look in this part of London. No one Purdy had met during her brief stay had seen her today.

He thanked the woman, listened to her effusions about young Christophe's improvement, then bade her good day. What now?

At first he'd hoped Purdy had merely gone out for a breath of air, or perhaps to the market, but now he had to admit that she had left entirely—and that it was doubtless his own fault. He'd frightened her with his advances, even if she'd denied it. Perhaps she had even been frightened by her own eager response, which he had certainly not imagined.

But where would she have gone? Back to the household she'd left? Or might she even now be wandering the streets of London, seeking fruitlessly for a new position? With her looks, the odds of someone taking advantage of her innocence seemed high.

But no. He reminded himself that she was not at all the simple girl she had first pretended to be, but was in fact a very intelligent young woman, presumably with a decent education. And that, of course, must be why she had fled. She had correctly judged that Luke would not force himself on a girl of meager intellect. But what had he done, the moment he knew the truth?

Luke tried to tell himself that it was for the best that she was gone—best for him, best for her. At his side, little Argos whined, and he leaned down to scratch the dog between the ears.

"I miss her, too, lad. But where else can we look?" Sinking down on an overturned whiskey crate, he tried to recall every word of their conversations, seeking for clues. Instead, he found himself remembering the lovely expression of her vivid blue-violet eyes, the way her body had felt against his, the indescribable bond he had sensed when they kissed . . .

No! He had to think. She was from Oaklea, if she'd told the truth, but she wouldn't have attempted traveling all the way back there alone, surely. He recalled other things she'd said, though little of it had been personal. She'd admitted—defensively—that her mother was a gentleman's daughter.

Perhaps her mother—or she herself?—was the byblow of some gentleman, or even a nobleman. That might explain her evasiveness. Perhaps she even felt unworthy of him due to her illegitimate birth. That was laughable, of course, but he couldn't discount the possibility.

With a deep breath, he made a sudden decision. Whatever the truth, wherever she was, he owed it to Purdy—and to himself—to make certain that she was safe. And once he'd done that, well, he'd just let fate take its course—his as well as hers.

If he was to effectively search for Purdy among the houses of the *ton*, he'd have to move among them as one of their own—which meant it was time to resurrect Lucio di Santo. Relieved to be taking action at last, he headed briskly back toward his lodgings, already mentally composing the necessary letter.

Pearl concealed a yawn behind her ecru lace and ivory fan as Lady Minerva Chatham regaled her with yet another version of the gossip surrounding her disappearance five days ago. The dancing would begin at any moment, and Pearl was wondering whether there was any way she could plausibly escape to one of the anterooms instead of being trapped on the dance floor for another interminable evening.

"Of course it all seems silly in retrospect," her companion was saying, "but you must confess that a possible kidnapping, particularly by so romantic and mysterious a figure as the Saint of Seven Dials, made for a captivating tale."

"The Saint of Seven Dials? I thought he was only a legend, Minnie, yet you are the second person to mention that name since my visit to poor Nanny."

The story Obelia had decreed they would tell everyone was that Pearl had gone to visit her sick nurse for a couple of days. The fact that her old nurse—Hettie's mother—was neither sick nor within a day's ride of town had no bearing on the matter.

"Oh, the Saint is very real, I assure you!" Lady Minerva exclaimed. "You must not have been in Town for his last rash of thefts, but the disappearance of the Mountheaths' plate and jewels from under their very noses was quite in keeping with his legendary audacity. Some believe he may actually be a member of the *ton*, stealing from the wealthy to give to the poor, like Robin Hood of old." Her fine complexion pinkened visibly at the notion.

"Very romantic indeed," said Pearl dryly, but her thoughts were already leaping to an incredulous guess. *Saint of Seven Dials*. Luke St. Clair. Mrs. Plank had called him "Mr. Saint." He had been at the Mountheaths' that night, too, and as eager to depart as she herself had been. . . .

The strains of the opening minuet recalled her to her surroundings in the Chathams' opulent ballroom. Glancing up, she saw the Marquess of Ribbleton approaching to claim the promised dance. She'd missed her chance to slip away—not that the Duchess would have allowed her to hide for long anyway.

"I'll tell you everything else I've heard about the Saint later," Minerva promised in a whisper as her own partner advanced from the other direction. "It's just the sort of adventurous tale you like."

Pearl smiled her thanks, then turned to greet Lord Ribbleton. It was quite true that she enjoyed the occasional novel of derring-do to lighten her otherwise serious reading. But fiction was one thing, and a real-life criminal something else entirely.

Still deep in thought, she took her place opposite the Marquess, murmuring something appropriate in response to his fulsome compliments on her appearance.

As the evening progressed, Pearl's thoughts returned again and again to Luke and the puzzle he presented. After her brief taste of another sort of life, her own felt more artificial and hollow than ever, and not nearly as interesting. For two nights and a day, she had been more alive than at any other time in her whole sheltered, pampered life.

"You are unusually pensive tonight, my lady," commented Lord Harrowby as he led her from the floor after a country dance. "Still concerned about your old nurse, are you?"

"What? Oh, yes. Poor Nanny," Pearl responded absently, noticing that Lord Harrowby's hair was almost the exact same shade of brown as Luke St. Clair's, though he was not so tall.

Glancing up at Sir Cyril Weathers, who met her at the edge of the floor to claim the next dance, she decided that he was of approximately the same height as her Luke, though slighter in build. Mentally, she shook herself. What was the matter with her, trying to see bits and pieces of Luke St. Clair in every man present? Sternly she marshaled her thoughts. He was not "her" Luke!

"What think you, Sir Cyril, of the result of the Corn Laws, now that the wars are over?" she asked, to distract herself.

Though clearly surprised that a lady would broach such a subject, Sir Cyril expounded at length on his views, which Pearl quickly realized came exclusively from a particular editorialist in the *Times*. All too soon, her mind was wandering again.

As the dance ended, she noticed yet another man who reminded her strongly of Luke—height, hair color, and general build were all the same. He walked toward the buffet table, and she mused that he even moved in much the same way, though of course she should not be noticing such a thing about any man.

Pearl accepted Sir Cyril's thanks for the dance, then turned back to watch the man she had noted. As soon as he turned, of course, she would realize who it was and laugh at herself for her fancies. But until then, she unwisely allowed herself to imagine Luke St. Clair in her world—what they might speak of, the things they might do together.

No man had ever affected her like this before, she knew. Could one kiss—one very heated kiss!—be enough to send her into such infatuation? Or was it more than that? Luke had spoken of fate. . . .

She and Sir Cyril reached the edge of the floor, and already her next partner was approaching. Summoning up a polite smile for Lord Edgemont, Pearl took one last glance at the gentleman who had reminded her of Luke. At that precise moment he turned, and it was all she could do to suppress a gasp.

Could it be only her imagination, or was he indeed the very image of Luke St. Clair? Scarcely hearing Lord Edgemont's greeting as he bowed over her hand, she finally pulled her gaze away to respond.

"I find myself quite thirsty, my lord." Her voice sounded high and strained to her own ears. "Would

you mind terribly if I took this opportunity to re-
fresh myself with some lemonade and a cake or
two?"

At once Lord Edgemont offered to procure for
her whatever she desired, but that did not suit
Pearl's purpose at all. She needed to get a closer
look at the gentleman near the buffet tables.

"We'll go together," she told her escort. "I wish to
look over the selection myself. I also perceive that
there are a few guests to whom I have not yet been
introduced."

Completely oblivious to whatever reply Lord
Edgemont might make, or even whether he was following her, Pearl headed toward the tables and the
man who looked so disturbingly familiar, an impossible hope beginning to form in her breast.

Chapter 7

"So there are no young ladies here of an age to have a governess?" Luke asked the footman refilling the tray of lobster patties. "I was certain my aunt said that her protégé worked for the Earl of Chatham."

The footman shook his head. "Lady Minerva hasn't had a governess for nigh on two years, since she turned eighteen," he offered. "Could be one of the maids will have heard of this Purdy, though."

"Thank you." This was the third great house where Luke had made inquiries, though without much hope. Purdy had mentioned a connection to Oakshire House, but an invitation there was rather above his touch.

He was about to ask the footman whether he'd heard of a Hettie, when he was accosted by a hand on his shoulder. "There you are, Luke, old boy. Hobnobbing with the servants again? Your aunt's friend will turn up sooner or later, never fear. For now, I've got some people you must meet."

Luke turned to Lord Marcus Northrup with a genuine smile. Among the few members of the *ton* Luke knew personally, Lord Marcus was his closest friend. They had met at Oxford, where they'd discovered a number of common interests, including a delight in playing pranks upon bullying upperclassmen. The youngest son of the Duke of Marland, Marcus had given Luke invaluable advice based on his experience with four older brothers. He was also as adept at gaining entry where they weren't allowed as any professional housebreaker Luke had encountered.

Upon receiving Luke's note saying he'd arrived in Town, Lord Marcus had immediately responded, as always, with an invitation to stay with him in Grosvenor Street, where he shared a house with two of his older brothers when in Town. Luke had accepted at once, as he'd done a few times previously, when he'd needed—or simply wanted—to move in more fashionable circles for a while.

"Of course, Marcus. Sorry if I seem preoccupied by this silly errand. I did promise my Aunt Lavinia, but there's no call to be obsessive about it." Obsessed he certainly was, but he couldn't let Marcus know that. "To whom did you want to introduce me?"

Lord Marcus grinned, making him look far younger than his twenty-five years. "As this is your first visit to Town in a year, quite a few people. In fact, here comes a lady you really must meet—a true original. Diamond of the first water, bluestocking and philanthropist all in one, but quite influential for all that. She could be your entrée into the highest circles, if she finds you tolerable. Let me make you known to her."

Luke barely listened. Already he was considering whether he could visit any other great houses tonight in his search for Purdy. Only a few days without her, and he felt as though a vital part of himself had gone missing. He had to find her, and soon! Still, he pinned on his best social smile and turned to make his compliments to the remarkable lady in question.

"Lady Pearl, may I present an old school chum of mine, the honorable Lucio di Santo, nephew of the Conte di Santo of Italy, though of good English stock on his mother's side. Luke, the Lady Pearl Moreston, daughter of the Duke of Oakshire."

While Marcus nattered on, Luke stood frozen, his gaze locked with that of the young lady in question. The room seemed to spin about him, Marcus's voice coming from a great distance. How could this be? It was impossible—it *must* be impossible!

This divine creature before him, Lady Pearl Moreston, Duke's daughter and influential pillar of Society, was none other than his poor, lost Purdy. Though his reason protested, his body and soul thrummed in instant recognition. What an end to his quest this was!

Lady Pearl's heightened color and arrested expression left no doubt she recognized him as well, and for a moment he thought she might either faint or give him the cut direct. But after a hesitation not quite long enough to be considered rude, she inclined her head.

"I am delighted to make your acquaintance, Mr. di Santo. Have you been in London long?" Her eyes held a subtle accusation that no one but he could have noticed.

"I arrived at Lord Marcus's house only two days since," he said with perfect truthfulness. He doubted the accusation in his own eyes was as subtle. His deception had been nothing to hers!

Lord Marcus stepped in before unwise questions could escape him. "Indeed, we'll have to civilize him all over again, I fear, he's so rarely in Town. He came to us at Oxford after being largely raised abroad, and since then he's been splitting his time between the Continent and the countryside. It's not often you'll find someone so cosmopolitan who is so unfamiliar with London and its ways," he concluded with a chuckle.

Luke politely echoed the chuckle, as did Lady Pearl—and hers sounded as forced as his own.

"I presume the cosmopolitan Mr. di Santo has had opportunities to polish his social skills in other milieux." Though she spoke casually, even flippantly, Luke could see the intensity behind her gaze.

He swept her a bow that would not have been out of place in the courts of Spain or Italy. He'd made a point to learn that Continental flair, though of late he'd had little opportunity to practice it. Dash, he had discovered, could compensate for a variety of social sins.

"I am willing to let you put my skills to the test, my lady," he said, hoping for a chance to discover more about her.

She raised one delicate brow. "Are you indeed? Perhaps I should present you to my father. He is said to be most discerning." A test indeed.

"I would be most honored," he replied with another half bow. He may as well brazen the game through, and this might be the opportunity he needed to speak with her alone.

The curiosity in her eyes now tinged with alarm, Lady Pearl inclined her head. "Let me make my excuses to my current partner, and I will take you to my father and the Duchess."

Marcus shot Luke a questioning glance as she turned away, but he merely shrugged, having no wish to be drawn into explanations. Pearl spoke briefly to a supercilious stick of a man, accepting a glass of lemonade from him before returning to Luke's side.

"Mr. di Santo?"

He extended his arm and she placed her fingers upon it, sending a shaft of pure desire straight to his vitals. Stunned and, yes, betrayed as he felt at discovering his "poor" Purdy's true identity, Luke found his physical attraction to her as powerful as ever.

This vision in satin, lace, and jewels seemed impossibly far removed from the girl he had rescued, far above the touch of a mere mortal like himself. Still, he was determined to breach the wall of reserve their changed circumstances had erected, and get at the truth.

"It appears your straits were not quite so dire as you led me to believe," he murmured as they traversed the edge of the ballroom.

"Nor yours," she returned, just as softly. "Which story—" She broke off as they were accosted by an overblown matron in yellow and green silk.

"Lady Pearl, my darling dear!" the woman gushed. "The Duchess, precious Obelia, tells me the gossips were all put about for nothing. I'm so excessively relieved for you!" The enormous chartreuse feather topping her turban bobbed violently as she nodded her head.

"Thank you, Lady Varens. I assure you it was all a tempest in a teapot—a simple matter of miscommunication. I went to visit my old nurse, who is ill, but my message was garbled. Next time I shall write it out myself, or speak to my father personally."

So that was the cover story for her absence. Luke burned to know what she had really been doing in the Mountheath kitchens that evening, since the story she had given him was clearly moonshine. Spying on a social rival, perhaps?

After a few more inanities, Lady Varens allowed them to progress, but before he could revive their interrupted conversation, Lady Pearl stopped before a handsome older couple that could only be the Duke and Duchess of Oakshire.

"Father, Your Grace, I'd like to make known to you Mr. Lucio di Santo, an old friend of Lord Marcus Northrup."

She stepped aside, and Luke bowed low, as he had before, keenly aware of her watchful eye upon him—no doubt waiting for some monumental gaffe.

"It is above all things an honor to put myself at your service, Your Graces. I apologize if I do wrong to intrude upon you in this way. I find some things are done a bit differently in Italy."

The Duke, an imposing man with sandy hair touched by gray at the temples, smiled affably. "Pleased to make the acquaintance of a friend of one of Marland's lads, of course. My Pearl will see you introduced about, won't you, my dear?"

The Duchess extended her hand then, simpering a bit, as ladies frequently seemed to do upon meeting him. "I'm charmed to make your acquaintance, Mr. di Santo. You have spent much time on the Continent, I presume? It is quite a dream of mine to travel, I confess."

Luke was now forced to lie outright, something he'd hoped to avoid in front of Purdy—er, Lady Pearl—though why, he didn't know, as she'd scarcely been honest with him.

"I spent several years in Italy, under the guardianship of my uncle, the Conte di Santo," he said, giving the story known to all of his Society acquaintances. "My mother's family is English, and insisted I receive a proper English education, but my manners have been largely shaped abroad."

"And charming manners they are," the Duchess assured him with a flirtatious flutter of her lashes. Her eyes, a paler blue than Lady Pearl's, held a calculating gleam he'd never noticed in her daughter's. "Pearl," she continued, "pray be certain to save a dance for Mr. di Santo. It will make him feel more welcome in England."

Luke dared a quick glance at Lady Pearl and caught what looked like the ghost of a grimace, though it was quickly concealed. That evidence of her reluctance struck him like a blow.

"I'm certain Lady Pearl's dances are all engaged by now, but I am honored by the sentiment," he said quickly.

The Duchess's smile held more than a hint of malice, he thought, as she responded, "Oh, I'll warrant her waltzes are yet free—are they not, Lady Pearl?"

The beauty at his side stiffened slightly, but did not allow her social veneer to crack. "They are indeed, Your Grace—and I would be honored, sir." Though her smile did not quite reach her eyes— those remarkable blue-violet eyes he remembered so well—Lady Pearl concealed her feelings better than the Duchess did.

Taking leave of the Duke and Duchess, he led her back toward the buffet tables. "You needn't dance with me, of course," he said stiffly, the moment they were out of earshot. "It's clear you would prefer not to."

Her expression, since the first shock of meeting him, had been almost blank, but now she turned to him with a rueful smile and suddenly she was his Purdy again. His hurt and resentment began to melt away, and he had to fight a sudden, mad urge to take her in his arms.

"It's not that. Obelia knows I never waltz, and this is just one more way she's found to punish me."

"I could see that there was some friction between you and your mother—"

"Stepmother," she corrected quickly.

Ah. "But I have no desire to be an instrument of punishment." Did he? "It has been some time since

I've danced, in any event," he concluded truthfully. Not since his last brief stint as di Santo last Season, in fact. Still, to touch her again . . .

"I do not mind, truly. If I can appear to enjoy myself, it will rob the Duchess of her victory. Besides," she added with an all-too-familiar smile that disordered his thoughts, "a waltz is likely to be our best chance for uninterrupted conversation this evening, and I imagine you have as many questions to ask me as I have to ask you."

Indeed he did. Her smile set his senses stirring, even as he told himself he must forget his feelings for this woman he had thought was his destiny. Everything she had told him before was a lie—but why?

He bowed. "Then I shall look forward to our dance," he said with perfect sincerity. In the meantime, he had a few questions to ask Marcus, who seemed to know quite a lot about the Lady Pearl.

Pearl watched Luke's retreating back with a bemused smile. What was it about this man that could so thoroughly undermine her defenses even when she knew he had been completely dishonest with her? She didn't know, but found herself, for the first time in her life, anticipating a waltz with pleasure.

It wasn't the first time Obelia had trapped her into a waltz, though this instance had to be from pure spite, as the nephew of a minor Italian noble would scarcely meet her exacting standards for a suitable match. Though Obelia had seemed impressed, if only by Luke's appearance and manners. Pearl wished her father were not so blind to his Duchess's flirting.

Still, in this instance she could hardly blame her. Dressed in the height of fashion, Luke was a sight to turn feminine heads young and old. Again she felt a delicious thrill go through her at the thought of dancing in his arms. To think, only half an hour earlier she'd been fantasizing about him being a part of her world! And now—

"My lady?" Lord Hardwyck broke into her thoughts. "I believe this is my dance."

She went with him without protest, though in truth the middle-aged earl always made her uneasy. His manners were polished, but there was a certain ruthless self-assurance about him that chilled her.

Though nearly as rich and powerful as her father, he coveted her fortune and the prestige she could bring him, she knew. He had yet to abandon his suit, even though she had twice refused him. Luckily, he was far from a favorite with her father, as they often found themselves on opposite sides of political issues.

"You appear to be in excellent health tonight, my lady," he commented as they took their places for the cotillion. "It would seem your recent, ah, adventure agreed with you."

Pearl forced a trill of laughter. "Adventure? Hardly that. Simply a visit to my old nurse, and a missent message. But I thank you for the compliment."

His dark eyes slid over her speculatively, possessively. "Health is always attractive in a young lady. It adds a luster to her other charms."

To her relief, the music started then and the movements of the dance precluded further conversation. Lord Hardwyck was a highly regarded member of Society, she knew, but there seemed something almost oily about him at times. This led her thoughts back to Luke, of course. Why did she not distrust him as she did her current partner, even though she knew for a fact he had lied to her on at least one occasion? She honestly couldn't say.

At last the dance ended, and she scanned the crowd, experiencing a moment of panic when she didn't see Luke anywhere. What if his appearance here had merely been part of some scheme, and he had already vanished, as he had from the Mountheaths'?

Lord Hardwyck spotted him before she did. "That fellow there, coming this way. Do you know who he is?" he asked her.

She turned and nearly sagged with relief. "A Mr. di Santo, newly arrived from the Continent, I'm told," she responded evasively, wondering at the intensity in the older man's gaze. "Why?"

He blinked, and seemed to recall himself, turning to her with an ingratiating smile. "For a moment he reminded me of someone, that is all. But the name means nothing to me. Until we meet again, my lady." He lifted her hand and kissed it lingeringly. With one last, frowning glance in Luke's direction, he turned on his heel and disappeared into the throng.

She was just as pleased to see him go. An instant later, Luke was at her side. "My promised waltz, I believe?" he asked with the same cocky smile she remembered from the night he'd helped her to escape from the Mountheaths' ridotto. Her heart turned over.

"So it is. I half feared you would not claim it," she

said as the opening strains of one of the newer waltzes sounded, reminding herself that she still knew very little about this man.

"While I wondered whether you would choose to remember it," he responded, taking her gloved hand in his own to lead her onto the floor.

"As I said, it's likely to be our only opportunity for conversation." She spoke quickly, to distract herself from his touch, but when he quite properly placed a hand at her waist an instant later, the feelings that surged through her were anything but proper.

At once, Pearl was transported back to those delicious few moments in his lodgings when she had thrown propriety to the winds. She could almost feel his lips upon her throat, his hands upon her—

"I was concerned that you might leave before I could satisfy my curiosity," she said breathlessly, trying to subdue her wayward emotions, trying to remember that this man was a virtual stranger.

"And leave my own unsatisfied as well?" The intensity in his eyes gave his words a dual meaning, making her heart pound. She hoped he could not hear it over the music.

Refusing to blush, she smiled up at him daringly. "Then shall we begin?"

"Certainly," he replied, tightening his grip on her in preparation for swinging her into the dance. Her senses responded instantly, without her volition. "I have hopes we might both find complete satisfaction."

She could not prevent the color rushing to her face as she realized that there was nothing she would like more than to find complete satisfaction with Luke. Not until the waltz was well under way did she find her voice again.

"Will you go first, or shall I?" Pearl asked then. "We . . . don't want to waste this chance, after all."

His hand at her waist shifted, no more than half an inch, but it sent flames licking up her back. "We certainly don't. What do you wish to know?" His voice seemed husky with some suppressed emotion.

Pearl looked up and became trapped in his hot, dark eyes for a long moment. Swallowing, she pulled her gaze away and was able to breathe again. "My most burning question," she said, licking her lips, "is who you really are—Luke St. Clair, or Lucio di Santo? Or neither?"

He twirled her, remarkably well for someone who hadn't danced regularly, before replying. "I'd have to say both. I was raised Luke St. Clair, but everyone in *your* world knows me only as di Santo."

Her world. The distinction made her bristle, tempering her errant desires and allowing her to think again—to remember what he might be. "So 'my world' is not worthy of your honesty?"

"*My* honesty?" He tightened his grip again, and instantly her rebellious body responded. "Perhaps Luke St. Clair is not worthy of your world—or *its* honesty," he suggested, his expression now unreadable.

Pearl knew it was a reference to her own deception, but was determined to puzzle him out before offering any explanations herself. "Just who *is* Lucio di Santo?"

He flashed her an enigmatic smile that didn't quite reach his eyes, still watching her intently. "You may recall my telling you that I contrived to attend school—Oxford, in fact."

She'd had no idea at the time that he'd gone to such a prestigious university, but she nodded. "Because your mother wished it, you said."

"Yes." She felt his slight withdrawal, his hand pressing less firmly at her waist now. "But money alone would not have guaranteed my acceptance there. Background—and blood—is at least as important."

Watching his brows draw together in distaste, she leaped to a guess. "So you were forced to rely on this uncle, this Conte di Santo. Someone to whom you'd have preferred to have no obligation. Someone who cast off your mother? Did he force you to take his name as a condition for sponsoring your education?"

Now he frowned down at her in apparent surprise. "Something like that, yes."

"And you resent him for it. So as soon as you left Oxford, you repudiated everything he stands for, to include his name." Pearl felt rather pleased with herself for having unraveled the mystery on her own. Most of it, anyway. "But . . . why have you now taken that name again, venturing back into this world you so obviously despise?"

His expression softened, stealing her breath. "To find you, of course."

Pearl missed a step in her surprise, and he had to support her until she caught the rhythm of the dance again. "Me?" To her disgust, the word came out as a squeak.

"Poor little Purdy, alone in the world—how could I rest until I knew what had become of her?"

His hand at her waist seemed to burn through the thin silk of her gown. "I had no way of knowing that she was really the great Lady Pearl, in disguise for purposes of her own.

She flushed at the mockery in his tone, knowing she deserved it. "Yes, I deceived you, too, and I'm sorry. At first I was afraid, and then I feared I might put you at risk by telling you my true identity." She did not add that she had also feared losing his respect.

"Then will you tell me why you were at the Mountheaths' in the guise of a servant in the first place?" His voice was gentle now, that very gentleness sweeping away the last vestiges of her resistance.

She gazed up at him, no longer caring what showed in her eyes, ready to pour out the truth to him. Before she could speak, however, the dance came to an end. Already the young viscount who had reserved the next one was coming forward to claim her.

"We'll talk again later," she promised Luke quickly, even as he released her waist, leaving a lingering heat where his hand had been. "Call on me tomorrow and we'll contrive something—a drive, perhaps."

He nodded, then gallantly took his leave, brushing his lips across her inner wrist just above her glove in a caress that left her tingling to the tips of her breasts. "Until tomorrow," he murmured, and then he was gone.

The lively country dance that followed required no conversation, for which Pearl was grateful, as her thoughts and emotions were chaotic. She managed to catch one more glimpse of Luke, only to see him and Lord Marcus taking their leave of Lord and Lady Chatham. Though all prospect of enjoyment for the balance of the evening went with him, Pearl could not help exulting.

Luke was at least marginally of her world, whether he wished it to be so or not. At the very least, they could continue their friendship. Beyond that, she did not dare to think—yet.

The next day, Pearl received her usual retinue of callers, the gentlemen bearing flowers and compliments, the ladies bearing gossip. She listened with only half an ear, responding automatically, until Clorinda Stuckton introduced a topic of particular interest.

"I saw that you danced with Mr. di Santo last night, Lady Pearl. Did he say anything . . . scandalous? I had *such* tales about him from Fanny Mountheath!"

"Tales?" Pearl carefully schooled her voice and expression into the same indifference with which she'd greeted all previous gossip.

Clorinda nodded eagerly, and the other ladies—and one or two of the gentlemen—leaned forward to hear what she had to say. "For one, it is *rumored* that he was, ah, instrumental in Lord and Lady Simcox's divorce!" Her voice sank to a whisper on the last, shocking word.

All Society knew, of course, that Lord Simcox had obtained the rare decree last year on grounds of his wife's infidelity.

"One can scarcely blame Lady Simcox," said Miss Chalmers with a giggle, though her mother

frowned her disapproval. "He was easily the hand-
somest man at the Chatham ball last night."

One or two of the gentlemen protested, and the
ladies set about soothing and teasing them, turning
the conversation. Pearl wasn't sure whether she was
disappointed or relieved.

Though she had not known the particulars of
the scandalous Simcox divorce at the time, Pearl
had mentally congratulated Lady Simcox on her
escape from a drink-sodden, ill-tempered husband,
nearly thirty years her senior. The idea of Luke's in-
volvement, however, put things in a different—and
disturbing—light. She was more eager than ever to
continue her conversation with him.

Clorinda Stuckton took her leave, and a moment
later a new caller was announced. Pearl felt a thrill
of anticipation, only to have it quashed—again.

"Lord Bellowsworth!" trilled Obelia to the newcomer. "I vow, I was beginning to fear we should
never see you again. I was quite cast in the dismals
when you were not at the Chathams' ball last
night." She waved him to the seat next to Pearl, just
vacated by Sir Cyril, who was taking his leave.

"My apologies, Your Grace. My mother was feeling poorly, and I did not feel easy leaving her. She is
much recovered today, however, so I was eager to
pay my respects." He turned his wistful, worshipful
gaze on Pearl, who managed to suppress her sigh of
impatience.

"Such a doting son," the Duchess declared approvingly. "I always say a young lady can tell much
about how a man will treat a wife from observing
how he behaves toward his mother, do I not,
Pearl?"

"Frequently," Pearl responded with an automatic smile. She was rather surprised Lord Bellowsworth had the courage to call, considering the embarrassment attending his last visit.

His next words explained the seeming anomaly. "Your Grace was more than kind to invite me to call today, after my neglect of you this past week. Dare I hope this means I am forgiven?"

"Tut-tut, my lord," the Duchess responded. "You've done nothing requiring forgiveness. In fact, I was hoping you might be prevailed upon to escort Lady Pearl to the theater tonight. The Duke and I had planned to accompany her, but it appears he may have to attend some dreary diplomatic function instead."

Pearl had hoped that after what she'd told her father, Obelia might suspend her matchmaking efforts, but such was clearly not the case. If anything, she seemed to have intensified her efforts. She nearly gasped in her outrage that Obelia would treat her like a charity case in front of half a dozen visitors.

"I regret that you did not consult with me, Your Grace, before inconveniencing Lord Bellowsworth," she said icily. "As it happens, I have already agreed to allow another gentleman to escort me tonight."

"Indeed?" The Duchess arched one eyebrow, plainly disbelieving. "Who might that gentleman be, and when did you have opportunity to make such an arrangement?"

At that perfectly propitious moment, Luke was announced. Pearl gave her stepmother her sweetest smile, trying to ignore the fluttering which suddenly gripped her stomach.

"I'll be attending with Mr. di Santo. We discussed it during our waltz last night—the one you yourself suggested, Your Grace."

Chapter 8

L uke paused in the doorway of the opulently elegant Oakshire drawing room upon hearing
his Society name on Lady Pearl's lips. She was stun-
ning today in a simple pink day dress, her honey-
colored hair falling in artless ringlets past her
shoulders. Warily, he moved into the room, then
swept his hostesses an elaborate bow.

"Your Grace, my lady. I am flattered to find myself a topic of discussion between you."

"Why, Mr. di Santo," exclaimed Lady Pearl, as
though she had but that moment become aware of
his presence, though a twinkle in her eyes told him
otherwise. "I was just informing the Duchess of our
plans to attend the theater tonight. Did you not say
that *Othello* is one of your favorite plays?"

Luke did not hesitate for an instant. "Indeed I

did, my lady. As I said last night, I am delighted to have the opportunity to gratify two passions at once—for the theater, and for more time in your company."

He thought she colored slightly at the word "passions," and he hid a smile. Woman of the world she might be, but her fundamental innocence was intact. Though her deception still stung, he was pleased to discover that had not been a part of it.

He turned to the Duchess. "Your Grace, I wish to thank you again for your suggestion last night that I dance with the Lady Pearl. Your endorsement was most gratifying."

Now the Duchess pinkened, her smile a shade less gracious than it had been. She glanced quickly at the tall blond man seated by Lady Pearl, and he responded with a concerned frown. A match she was promoting, perhaps? Luke kept his expression carefully bland.

"I was merely being hospitable to a newcomer to Town, Mr. di Santo," the Duchess replied after an awkward pause. "The Lady Pearl is—"

"Uniformly charming," Luke concluded for her. "I know it is extremely unlikely that she is not already engaged, but I came today in hopes of persuading her to drive out with me this afternoon."

He turned his smile upon Pearl. "Lord Marcus suggested that you might acquaint me with any particularly English customs that may differ from those abroad." Marcus had done no such thing, of course, but Luke didn't think he'd mind having his name invoked for such a cause.

Before the Duchess could speak—to forbid the drive, judging by her expression—Lady Pearl spoke. "I had merely planned to shop for a new bonnet, but that can easily be put off until tomorrow. I should be delighted to assist in educating you about Society's expectations." And her own expectations as well, said the look accompanying her words.

"You are all generosity, my lady," he declared, enjoying both the Duchess's sudden frown and Lady Pearl's wariness. In fact, he was enjoying everything about this situation far too much. "Might I be presented to your other guests?" He turned to face the man he instinctively regarded as a rival, foolish as his own aspirations toward Lady Pearl must be.

"This is the Marquess of Bellowsworth, a longtime friend of the family." The Duchess's voice held a hint of severity that was no doubt supposed to put Luke in his place. Clearly, she had deemed him unworthy of her stepdaughter.

She was right, of course, but he was not about to let her know that. "Bellowsworth," he said with only the slightest inclination of his head, mimicking the supercilious, bored attitude of the most self-important of his Oxford classmates—which was to say, the ones he'd liked least.

The young man reddened and cleared his throat. "Servant, di Santo," he said with an attempt at equal unconcern, which would have been more impressive had his voice not broken on the final syllable.

Luke turned from him, not quite quickly enough for rudeness, to face the two ladies who had sat watching this entire byplay with obvious interest. "And these must be sisters," he exclaimed, "so similar in coloring and charm."

"Lady Wittington and her daughter, Miss Chalmers," the Duchess corrected him, while the elder of the two ladies tittered with delight. Luke swept them a bow only a shade less elaborate than the one with which he'd greeted his hostesses.

"I am honored to make your acquaintance," he told them, making eye contact with first the mother and then the daughter, until each blushed and lowered her eyes in flattered confusion. He was pleased that his lack of recent practice had not robbed him of the social skills he'd once worked so hard to attain.

He took a seat then, though the gangly marquess prevented him sitting as near to Lady Pearl as he'd have preferred. His plan was to take Bellowsworth's chair the moment it was vacated, but he soon learned that the marquess would be staying for luncheon. As he could not very well invite himself to a meal, he shortly thereafter took his leave.

"I'll see you at five o'clock, for our drive," he said to Lady Pearl, bowing over her hand in parting.

This time she kept her expression and color strictly under control, though a flicker in her eyes told him she had felt the same jolt he had when their fingers touched. "I shall look forward to it. Until then, sir."

Back outside, Luke walked in the direction of Grosvenor Street, and the town house Lord Marcus shared with Lord Peter and Lord Anthony Northrup. He hoped he could persuade Marcus to trust him with his phaeton for this afternoon's drive. Stealing one might conceivably mar the impression he'd been at such pains to make on Society.

Luncheon was an interminable meal for Pearl, what with the inane conversation between Lord Bellowsworth and her stepmother, and her own impatience to have another private conversation with Luke. What, exactly, would she ask him—and how? She must not allow the pleasure of bantering with him to dissuade her from her object.

"Why are you smiling, my lady?" asked Lord Bellowsworth, interrupting her thoughts. "Surely you do not find the theft of Lady Mountheath's diamonds amusing?"

Recalling what Lady Minerva had told her last night, Pearl's interest was caught. "No, of course not. I was thinking of something else. Has the thief not yet been taken?"

Lord Bellowsworth shook his head. "It is only a matter of time, however, for I've heard the authorities are pursuing a promising lead."

"Indeed? Then they have hopes of finally catching this legendary Saint of Seven Dials?" Her suspicions last night now seemed absurd, but still Pearl could not suppress a shiver of something that might have been apprehension.

The Marquess snorted. "Legendary thief he may be, but his days are numbered now. Lady Mountheath's necklace has been recovered—or, rather, a portion of it. It appears the villain broke it up to sell it, to divert suspicion."

The Duchess gasped. "Broke up that lovely necklace? Oh, poor Madeleine!"

Somehow, Pearl couldn't seem to muster much sympathy for Lady Mountheath over the loss of a few expensive baubles, remembering some of the wretched souls she had encountered in Seven Dials who never knew when another meal might be forthcoming.

"So the magistrates were able to discover who sold the necklace?" she prompted.

Bellowsworth gave the Duchess's hand one last sympathetic pat and turned back to Pearl. "Yes, it seems the diamonds came to the shop by way of a known purveyor of stolen goods. Under questioning, the man was induced to give a description of the fellow who sold him the stones."

"A description?" Pearl was pleased that her voice did not squeak on the question, as her breathing seemed to have stopped. "Did you hear what it was?"

Lord Bellowsworth favored her with a rather sour smile. "Smitten by the rogue like all of the other young ladies? I'd thought you too sensible for that, Lady Pearl. In any event, it is doubtful that the lad who sold the diamonds was the Saint himself. More likely one of his henchmen."

"Do you mean it was a boy, my lord?" asked the Duchess. "Did not everyone believe the Saint of Seven Dials to work alone? How abominable if he is recruiting children to his dirty trade!"

"My sentiments precisely, Your Grace," agreed the Marquess. "As I heard it, the lad was a mere ten or twelve years of age. Some have suggested he might be the blackguard's son. Once he is apprehended, I've no doubt we will quickly come at the truth of the matter—as well as the Saint himself."

Pearl swallowed hard. His son? Could Luke possibly . . . ? But no. She'd already worked out his past, and his reasons for keeping it a secret. Besides, if he'd had a son, surely she'd have seen the boy while at his lodgings. Nor was he old enough, surely, to have a child of that age.

Relieved by this reflection, she managed a smile. "However do you come by such timely information, my lord?"

"My cousin Randolph—Lord Grimsby, you know—is a magistrate in Town," he explained. "While not directly involved in this investigation, he has been kept apprised, and has passed his information on to me. Or, rather, to my mother. She was afraid to sleep in her bed until he was able to assure her that the scoundrel was as good as caught."

"How commendable," she responded absently, her thoughts already returning to Luke St. Clair—or di Santo? She intended to have *all* of his secrets, whatever they might be, uncovered by the end of the day.

Luke pulled Lord Marcus's phaeton to a halt outside Oakshire House. "Remember, Flute, not a word from you. We still have a deal of work to do on your accent."

His all-purpose manservant, valet, and groom nodded with a cocky grin, putting a finger to his lips. "Mum it is, guv."

He shot Flute a quelling glare, which appeared to dampen the lad's spirits not a bit. Dressed in fine livery, and with a false mustache, he looked older—though still more like a page than a manservant. Still, he was all Luke had. "Good lad. I'll be back in a few moments, with the young lady I told you about."

Flute hopped down to hold the horses while Luke strode to the imposing entrance of Oakshire House, exuding a confidence he could not quite feel.

Coming here today, inviting the Lady Pearl for this drive, had been unwise, despite his promise to her last night. Once he'd assured himself that "Purdy" was in no danger, he should have discreetly disappeared from the social scene, with a suitable excuse to Marcus. But he'd found himself unable to stay away.

He reminded himself yet again that pursuing any sort of relationship with Lady Pearl was out of the question. Her world was not his world—nor did he wish it to be. At some point over the course of the afternoon and evening, he would have to tell her so, and say his inevitable farewells. First, however, he was determined to discover the truth about her foray into the London slums and into his life—a life he knew would never be the same.

He was shown into the same opulent drawing room as before. The Duchess, to his relief, was not in evidence, and he had not even seated himself before Lady Pearl appeared, now clad in a round dress of jonquil dimity.

"I see I may number promptness among your other virtues," he said with a bow, trying to ignore the immediate effect she had on him. "It is one not many ladies share—or so I have heard."

"I have never seen the point in leaving a gentleman to cool his heels once I have agreed to receive him. If I do not desire his company—which is the case more often than not—I simply tell him so," she said with an arch smile. At the moment, she seemed impossibly far removed from the simple servant girl he had rescued last week.

"Then I am doubly honored. Shall we go?" He extended his arm and after only the slightest hesitation she placed her gloved hand upon it.

"My abigail will be down in a moment. I had thought to leave her behind, but the Duchess would not hear of it. However, we may speak freely in her presence." Even as she spoke, a dark-haired woman in a stylish maid's frock appeared.

Luke grinned. "Hettie, I presume?"

The maid flushed scarlet, glancing at her mistress in confusion before bobbing a curtsy. "Yes, milord."

He sobered at once. "I'm no lord, Hettie, just a plain mister. Please remember that."

He spoke as much to Lady Pearl as to her abigail, and she responded for both of them. "I daresay you won't let us forget it, *Mr.* di Santo. Shall we go?" Though her voice was light, it held a hint of a rebuke.

Remembering some of the things he'd told her last week about his feelings toward the nobility, it was no wonder she was displeased. No matter, he told himself firmly. If the great Lady Pearl wished to take his attitude personally, there was little he could do about it—nor should he wish to, of course.

A moment later, he was helping both ladies into the phaeton. Pearl sat beside him as he took up the reins, while Hettie sat up behind, with Flute. He prayed his little protégé would remember his instructions and play the mute.

"I hadn't realized you would have a chaperone of your own along," Lady Pearl commented as he whipped up the horses. Her tone was playful, whatever irritation she had felt in abeyance for the moment.

Luke restrained himself from glancing back. "He's still in training, which is one reason I suggested he come along. This should be a good learning experience for him."

Her quizzical glance reminded him that people of her class didn't make "suggestions" to their servants, but it was too late to recall his words. Not that he would. "Our, ah, conversation last night was cut short," he said, deliberately diverting her attention from Flute. "You implied you wished to continue it today?"

To his surprise, she colored slightly. "Yes, I realize it was rather improper of me to invite *you* for a drive, but it was all I could think of. May I assume that your manservant is as discreet as my Hettie?"

"He scarcely speaks at all." Luke spoke loudly enough for Flute to hear him. "As I recall, you were going to tell me what you were doing in such unusual guise last week." Though she had said he might speak freely, his caution was instinctive.

She slanted a glance at him that made his blood quicken. "I don't believe I've heard your full tale yet, have I?"

"You've heard most of what's fit to tell."

"I don't mind hearing the unfit parts," she retorted.

"Ladies first," he said with a grin. Not that he intended to tell her the entire truth in any event. It would be far too risky for both of them. Nor was he quite ready to lose whatever remained of her good opinion. Far better he simply disappear and leave her with whatever illusions she still possessed.

For a long moment she did not reply, but

watched the park gates draw near as they clattered along Mount Street. "Oh, very well," she said at last, as he slowed the horses.

The traffic was thick at the Grosvenor Gate, requiring all his attention to navigate the pair of chestnuts through the queue of carriages and riders entering the park for the fashionable hour. Once they were able to progress again along the carriage path, he turned to her expectantly. "Well?"

She gave a little laugh, which seemed directed more at herself than at him. "It seems rather silly, now I try to put it into words. I . . . I was hiding from my stepmother, so that she could not force me into marriage."

He was startled by the fury that gripped him. "Force you? By what means could she possibly do such a thing?"

"That's just it," she replied with a self-deprecating smile that reminded him sharply of Purdy. "In retrospect, I realize she couldn't. She had, however, tried to maneuver me into a compromising situation. It was only by chance that I discovered her plan in time."

"But once forewarned . . ." He felt his anger fading, though his opinion of the Duchess was lower than ever.

"Precisely. Simple caution would suffice. In fact, that is my current strategy to avoid her machinations. It is easier, however, with my father's support. I left because he was going out of Town."

Luke's skepticism must have shown, for after only the slightest pause, she continued earnestly. "I did have another motive—one you may find just as silly, but which was important to me. I wished to discover for myself what it was like to live as a commoner, without the advantages of rank and wealth. And indeed, thanks largely to you, it proved a more educational experience than I'd hoped."

"I don't think that's silly at all," he said truthfully. Though it was in keeping with what Marcus had told him about her, he doubted one girl in ten thousand would have attempted such a thing—or even considered it. "If more of . . . your class were to do what you did, I imagine we would see real reform in short order."

"My thoughts exactly." She leaned toward him in her intensity, placing a hand on his sleeve. Her nearness and the sweetness of her scent nearly distracted him so that he had to force himself to focus on her words.

"I believe that those who hold the fates of others in their hands owe it to themselves as well as their dependents—and their country—to fully understand every viewpoint," she said. "What better way than by experiencing it firsthand?"

He smiled, and she suddenly seemed to recall herself. Flushing, she drew away from him.

"I apologize. I tend to become strident on this topic, as anyone who knows me will tell you. You must think me quite the zealot."

"No, I think you remarkably clear-eyed," he told her, though he had to pull his gaze away from those passionate violet eyes. They reminded him far too vividly of what he could never have—something he had never realized he wanted before last week. "In my experience, most of the nobility goes through life with blinders on, willfully oblivious to anything they don't wish to see."

She fell silent again, and he feared for a moment that he had insulted her. Everyone she knew—family, friends—were of that class, after all. When she finally spoke, however, it was slowly and thoughtfully.

"You can't imagine how refreshing it is to hear someone else espouse these views. I've read them, of course, in the *Political Register* and other such places, but that isn't the same. And those who hold such leanings tend, for obvious reasons, not to move in the same social circles as the Duke of Oakshire."

She met his eyes candidly. "I love and respect my father, of course, and he has even listened to my views, but I can tell that he considers them the idealistic dreamings of a female who knows little of the world. And perhaps he is right. Soon, however, I shall have the opportunity to put my ideas into practice and demonstrate that they are sound."

Her breast rose and fell, her beautiful eyes gleaming with fervor. Luke had never desired her more. Almost, he missed the purport of what she was saying, so entranced was he by the way she conveyed it. Almost. "What opportunity is that?" he asked.

Now she smiled, with a conspiratorial air that stirred his senses. "If I can keep my stepmother and her string of eligible suitors at bay until the end of June, I will become mistress of Fairbourne, a small estate in Warwickshire. Once I have it secure, I may manage it as I see fit. A test, if you will, of my theories."

His eyes widened with admiration—and surprise. It was nearly unheard of for a woman to hold property, he knew, even a woman of her rank and independence. "And you feel able to do this on your own?" he asked before considering his words.

Lifting her chin defiantly, she replied, "I see you are not so completely different from the others after all. You consider a mere woman unfit for such a responsibility?"

"No! That is—" He was interrupted by a duck taking sudden flight from a pond by the path, startling the horses so that they nearly shied into an oncoming carriage. For a moment, he had all he could do to bring them back under control, unused as he was to driving. By the time he was able to turn back to her, he had his answer ready.

"I wouldn't feel up to such a task myself, you see. But I forget—you are Lady Pearl, daughter of a Duke, raised to the task. Still, it seems an ambitious goal for just one person—of either sex—to attempt."

She regarded him suspiciously for a long moment. "I'll have stewards, of course, who will carry out the bulk of the changes I am planning. And they will have men under them. I'll hardly be working alone."

He couldn't resist a grin. "What, no women in supervisory capacities? Do you consider them unfit for such responsibility?"

After a moment's startled pause, she laughed— the first full laugh he'd heard from her. It was a lovely sound, and oddly erotic to his heightened senses. "Why, Mr. St. Clair, I do believe you're more radical a reformer than I am!"

"Mr. di Santo, if you please," he reminded her. "And I was merely pointing out the inconsistency in your position, not necessarily espousing it myself."

"Your point is taken." She was still smiling, apparently considering him an ally now. Was that good or bad? He wasn't sure, but he liked it. "I'd be very interested in hearing your opinion on my specific plans, actually. Your perspective might open my eyes to other, ah, inconsistencies."

He bowed as best he could, considering that he was seated and holding a pair of reins. "Having seen the efficacy of your social crusading at firsthand, I would be delighted to be of assistance, my lady. But oughtn't I be getting you back soon? It grows late."

She sighed with a regret that lifted his spirits, foolish though that was. "Yes, you're right. But we will have more opportunity for conversation this evening at the theater, I hope, though the Duke and Duchess will be accompanying me after all."

"We may talk during the performance, then?" They had reached a cross path, so he was able to turn the horses. "I've never sat in one of the boxes, you see. I'm afraid it wasn't just for the Duchess's benefit that I claimed to be unfamiliar with London customs."

"You may safely follow my lead, Mr. di Santo." Her smile was both mischievous and indulgent. "I'll be certain to nudge you when silence is expected."

The thought of her nudging him in a darkened theater sent a shaft of anticipation—and overwhelming desire—through him. He strove to subdue it, remembering what he needed to tell her. "Thank you. If a simple nudge doesn't silence me, feel free to knock me to the floor."

She laughed again, but then he added, "Even if

you do, I'll treasure the experience. It's likely to be the only such opportunity I will ever have."

That sobered her at once. "Why do you say so?"

He guided the horses out of the park gates to return her to Berkley Square. Though he hated what he had to say, he forced himself to speak matter-of-factly the words that would sound the death knell to the hopes and dreams that taunted him.

"Because I am but a visitor in your world, Lady Pearl. Now that I've reassured myself as to your safety and your future, I must leave it—and the sooner, the better."

Chapter 9

Pearl stared at Luke in dismay. Since meeting him, life had taken on a luster it had lacked for some time. Indeed, the idea of unraveling the mystery he presented had promised to make the Season bearable.

"Why must you leave Society? You seem to fit in remarkably well. I cannot believe you are as alien to my world as you claim to be. What of the time you spent with your uncle? And at Oxford?" *And last Season, with Lady Simcox*, she thought but did not say.

They turned onto Berkley Square and he pulled the phaeton to a halt before her house, his manservant leaping down to place the steps for her descent. She did not move, but held his gaze with her own, compelling him to answer.

"I've become rather good at playing whatever role is expected of me," he finally replied. "But that does not make the role *me*. Can you understand that at all?"

Recalling everything he had told her, she nodded. "I understand that you hold the upper classes to blame for your mother's misfortunes—and your own. And I can see why you choose not to affiliate yourself with them . . . us. But do you not see?"

Fired by a sudden idea, she spoke eagerly. "You can do more to change my world from within than without. That is what I am striving to do, after all. You can help me." A vision of him by her side, working for the same causes, thrilled her in more ways than she cared to examine.

He shook his head with a wistful smile, and she tried to take what little hope she could from that wistfulness, even as her spirits plummeted again. Climbing down from the phaeton, he walked around it to help her to the pavement.

She placed her hand in his and descended, but instead of releasing her once she was on the ground, he covered her gloved hand with both of his. The sense of connection was so strong she had to force herself not to lean into him, though she gazed up into his dark eyes.

"I admire what you are trying to do, my lady, and I am grateful that I've had this chance to speak with you again. Let's make the most of this last evening we will have together, and not allow our differences to mar it."

She read intense emotion in his gaze—an emotion she needed to understand. Before she could try again to convince him, the front door opened, and she had perforce to allow him to escort her up the wide stone steps and make his farewells.

"I shall look for you at the Drury Lane Theatre in two hours' time, sir," she said. "We can continue this discussion then."

He bowed over her hand, his fingers warm against hers. "Until tonight, then." With a nod to the butler, he released her hand, leaving it suddenly chilled, then turned away.

Head held high, Pearl entered the house without a backward look. She could not have the servants gossiping that Lady Pearl had formed an attachment for this newcomer. But as she mounted the stairs to her chambers, she knew that she was in danger of doing precisely that.

Of course she was fascinated by the man, by his contradictions and unconventional history. He was unlike anyone she had ever met before. She must convince him to join her cause, where he could surely do much good. *That* was the reason that she must somehow convince Luke to stay in her world.

For a moment she remembered again the feel of his lips upon hers. Every time she was with him, he made her feel things she had never before imagined. . . . But no, she mustn't dwell on that, or it would drive her mad.

She refused to consider what losing him forever might do to her.

"The theater? With the Lady Pearl?" Lord Marcus was visibly impressed. "Dancing last night, driving this afternoon, and now this? I've never heard of her showing this sort of preference toward any man before. And you met her only last night?"

Luke nodded, earning him a growl from Marcus's valet, who was striving to repair the damage done to Luke's cravat by the inexperienced Flute. "We seem to have a few interests in common. 'Preference' is perhaps a strong word, particularly since I doubt I'll be in London long enough for anything to come of it. She's rather above my touch anyway, wouldn't you say?"

Marcus snorted. "Yours and everyone else's! Any number of fellows have attempted to run the gauntlet of gaining both the Duke's and the Duchess's approval, courting Lady Pearl in the approved style, only to be refused in no uncertain terms. I confess, I'm rather surprised her parents are allowing your suit."

"They haven't had an opportunity to intervene— yet," Luke told him with a grin. Then, to the valet, "Thank you, Clarence. A vast improvement indeed. Were you watching, Flute?"

The lad nodded, and Luke turned back to Lord Marcus. "And as I said, there's no suit for them to allow. I expect I'll be gone in a day or two, after which it's unlikely I'll ever see her again." In vain, he tried to ignore the hollow feeling that assailed him every time he reminded himself of that—which he tried to do frequently.

"So soon? I thought you were fixed here for the Season. You'd take to London if you'd just give it a fair shot, you know. We could have some grand times." He grinned, reminding Luke of the trouble the two of them had courted, standing up to older and more influential students in defense of those who were younger and poorer.

"And the Lady Pearl may not be as out of reach

as all that," Marcus continued. "Stranger things . . . well, not stranger, perhaps, but no one thought Lady Haughton would have Jack Ashecroft—Foxhaven, now—a Season or two back. Have my brother Peter tell you about it sometime. Of course, Jack had a title in his favor, but his reputation was even worse than—" He caught himself. "That is to say . . ."

Luke was touched by his friend's eagerness for him to stay. "That's not the point, I'm afraid." And indeed it wasn't. Already his funds were running out. "I'm expected by my aunt in the country. She quite depends on me."

For a brief moment, he allowed himself to imagine what it would be like to have someone—anyone—truly dependent on him. Unlucky for them, assuredly, and more responsibility than he ever wished to shoulder. Just as well it was unlikely ever to happen.

"Well, you're welcome here for as long as you wish to stay—if not this time, then on a future visit," Marcus assured him with every appearance of sincerity—a sincerity Luke knew he didn't deserve.

He stifled a twinge of guilt, wishing he could take his friend into his confidence but knowing how foolhardy that would be. "I'll keep that in mind, Marcus. Thank you."

"Pearl, it simply will not do for you to encourage Mr. di Santo," Obelia insisted as the carriage neared the Drury Lane Theatre. "A single dance mattered little, but this will be your third time in his company in a single day. Pray remember that your reputation may be in question already, due to your foolishness last week."

Pearl shrugged, enjoying the scandalized rise of her stepmother's brows. "I find his conversation both entertaining and informative," she said. "He has experiences outside the purview of other gentlemen of my acquaintance."

The Duke chuckled. "That's my Pearl, always learning. Surely books would be safer, however, my dear." As always, he sought to appease both Pearl and his Duchess.

Pearl was in no mood to be appeased, however, still irritated by Obelia's insistence that they accompany her to the theater after all. If she could not manage a few moments of private conversation with Luke, this was likely to be the last time she would ever see him—something she refused to accept.

The moment they were inside the theater, she walked ahead of the Duke and Duchess, eagerly scanning the crowd for Luke. Her eagerness received a slight setback when she spotted him. Two ladies, clearly from the lower fringes of Society, were claiming his attention, tittering and simpering behind their fans as he spoke to them. At least he did not appear to be *encouraging* their flirtations, Pearl reassured herself.

"There you are, Mr. di Santo," she greeted him with forced cheerfulness. "I feared we should never find you in this crowd."

Luke bit back an oath and turned with a smile. He'd known it was a mistake to come here tonight, where he would be known by far too many unsuitable people—unsuitable to introduce to Lady Pearl and her parents, at any rate.

To his relief, the two women who had been flirting with him—acquaintances from last Season—discreetly melted into the throng as he bowed over Lady Pearl's hand. He kept it no longer than propriety demanded, keenly conscious of the Duke's watchful eye.

"Then I would have found you, my lady," he assured her. "You outshine everyone else to such a degree that you would draw me like a beacon."

"Very prettily said, Mr. di Santo," the Duchess commented, rather sourly, he thought. "So nice to see you again so soon."

The Duke's greeting was more affable, but his slight frown as Luke extended his arm to Pearl bespoke his concern—not that Luke could blame him. As the four of them progressed toward the ducal box, Luke was acutely aware of Pearl's gloved fingers upon his arm.

"I hear that Edmund Kean is very good," he said as they walked, mostly for the benefit of the Duke and Duchess. "I'm pleased I'll have a chance to see him before I leave London."

"I've seen him perform several times," she replied almost absently. "His Iago is said to be particularly brilliant. I'm certain you will enjoy his portrayal."

They chatted about the play and Shakespeare in general until they reached the elegant, curtained box with its excellent view of the stage. Four plush chairs awaited them, and Luke noticed how deftly

Pearl placed herself between himself and her father, with the Duchess on the Duke's other side.

Just before releasing his arm to seat herself, she pressed it to get his attention, then followed that with a significant look. Luke held her gaze and nodded slightly, to convey that he understood. She wished to speak with him alone, if possible.

She sent him the very slightest of smiles, drawing his attention to her full lips in a way she likely didn't intend. For a moment, he could think of nothing but what those lips had tasted like beneath his own. So soft, so yielding . . . Guiltily, he jerked his glance away and took his seat—which was closer to hers than he'd realized.

Conscious of the Duke and Duchess just beyond, he focused on the audience below, willing his body to behave. At the moment, his reaction to Pearl was rather too visible, if anyone were to—

"Look at those two ladies wearing identical gowns," he said, pointing to divert attention from the bulge in his breeches. "They appear to have just noticed each other."

Pearl looked at the two women he indicated, then laughed. "Ladies?"

"I admit I used the term rather loosely." Indeed, it was obvious even from this distance that both were women of easy virtue, on the prowl for protectors. To his relief, he knew neither of them—not that Pearl would ask, of course.

As they watched, the two advanced on each other, their mouths moving with what were doubtless insults as vulgar as the tight-fitting red dresses they wore. There was a time when Luke would have been attracted to women like those. He wondered whether he ever would be again, now that—

"Oh! It's as good as a play," Pearl exclaimed, as the women began snatching at each other. One yanked a scarlet feather from the other's hair, only to have the shoulder strap of her dress torn away.

At that point, two men appeared from opposite directions, to pull the women apart before they could inflict more damage on each other. A smattering of applause from the surrounding boxes showed that they were not the only ones to witness the spectacle.

"Never a dull moment at the theater, eh?" asked the Duke with a chuckle. "I often think the audience is more amusing than the play, myself. I've often said so. Don't you agree, Mr. di Santo?"

Luke swallowed. The Duke of Oakshire was an almost legendary figure, overshadowed only by the Royal Dukes and the Regent himself on the political as well as the social scene. That the man should be making small talk with him seemed somehow unbelievable.

"I've never before had opportunity to observe the audience from such a vantage point," he confessed. "I understand now why the boxes are so coveted."

The Duke chuckled again, though his eyes were disturbingly perceptive. Luke realized how easy it would be to underestimate this man—no doubt a mistake others had made in the political arena, and lived to regret. Did Lady Pearl realize what a dangerous man her father could be? He rather doubted it. For the moment, though, he appeared to be in the Duke's good graces, so he tried to relax.

When the curtain rose a few minutes later, Luke

tried to concentrate on the performance, but Pearl's proximity made it difficult. His every sense was keenly attuned to each tiny movement of her hand, each change in the angle of her head. Her scent, delicate and feminine, made its way to his nostrils with erotic effect. Sliding a glance her way, he fixed on a single curl of her honey hair kissing her throat. How he envied that curl!

His surreptitious gaze wandered to her face, only to find her watching him as slyly as he was watching her. They exchanged a slow, tiny smile that had him instantly hard with desire again. In vain, he tried to remember other women he had known intimately, to overshadow this subtle flirtation with the memory of more overt physical pleasures.

It did no good. In Pearl's presence, such memories had no power whatsoever. The realization was profoundly disturbing.

Distracted by his thoughts, he was caught off guard when Pearl leaned toward him, her curls brushing his shoulder as she whispered, "That is Mary Sedgehill, playing Desdemona. She is held to be almost as good as Kean. What do you think of her?"

Luke swallowed, striving yet again to rein in his unruly body and focus on the stage. Did Lady Pearl have any idea of what she was doing to him? Almost certainly not.

"She seems very good," he whispered back, barely knowing what he said. Unable to resist the temptation, he allowed his hand to brush hers where it lay on the arm of the chair.

Her eyes widened slightly, and though he could not tell in the dimness, he imagined that her color rose. They both turned back to the stage, but he suspected—hoped?—that she was now as aware of him as he was of her.

What was it about this man, Pearl wondered, that affected her so profoundly? A simple brush of his hand on hers, and she felt her insides turn to warm liquid, her every nerve focused on that point of contact. She stole a quick glance at his hand where it lay just grazing her own. Large, much larger than hers, and undeniably masculine, even sheathed by buff-colored kidskin.

Unbidden came the thought of that hand—both of his hands, ungloved—touching her body as they kissed. She imagined those hands touching her in other places, even more improper places. . . . Her face heated, reflecting the burning between her thighs.

Preoccupied as she was, the intermission seemed to come in no time at all. It was as well she knew *Othello* by heart, for she hadn't heard more than a dozen lines in the first act. The Duke and Duchess would be receiving a continuous stream of visitors during the intermission, as they always did. She stood.

"Father, I'll take this opportunity to show more of the upper gallery to Mr. di Santo, if you don't mind." She usually contrived to escape the parade of obsequious toadeaters, having no patience with that sort of hypocrisy, and her father well knew it.

"As you wish, my dear," he responded with a wave of his hand, though Obelia's brows arched with disapproval. "We'll look for your return in fifteen minutes."

Luke was already standing at her side, so she took his arm and escaped from the box with him, her senses thrumming with the close contact after her thoughts during the performance. "What would you like to see?" she asked him, realizing belatedly that her words could have more than one meaning.

He smiled down into her eyes, his own dark ones kindling in a way that set her very blood afire. "Everything," he replied huskily. "What would you like to show me?"

With an effort, she pulled her gaze away, her breathing suddenly shallow. "The, ah, view from the topmost balcony is said to be quite impressive." Her voice sounded high and unnatural to her own ears.

"Lead on, then." She didn't dare look, but suspected from his tone that he was grinning at her. Tilting up her chin, she ordered herself not to blush.

"We only have a few minutes, and we may be interrupted at any moment, but I wished to have a private word with you." She spoke softly but quickly, before she could change her mind, using the words she had rehearsed earlier today. "Do you still intend to leave London—my part of London— shortly?"

"I must," he murmured, his head close to hers. "I don't belong here."

She fought the distraction of his nearness. "I have a favor to ask of you, but it would entail delaying your departure. You know that my stepmother intends me to marry before my twenty-first birthday at the end of June. I'd like your help in thwarting her plans."

"How?" As they talked, they moved slowly in the

direction of the balcony, avoiding the more thickly crowded areas of the mezzanine.

Pearl swallowed, then plunged ahead. "If it were assumed that I had ... formed an attachment, it would deflect other suitors, and force my stepmother to expend her energies elsewhere."

He halted to face her, his expression inscrutable. "Are you asking me to court you openly?"

"No, not truly." *Not unless you want to.* "Just pretend that you are doing so, as I will pretend to welcome your advances. Once my birthday is past, I could seem to change my mind. You would be free to go back to whatever life you prefer. And I'll be able to live my life as I wish."

She rather hoped that by then she would have convinced him that he could do more good from within Society than from without. And perhaps she could convince him of other things, as well. . . .

"I see." He walked on in silence for a few moments. Whether he was relieved or disappointed at her caveat, she could not tell. Then, "Will your parents not send me to the right-about? It is clear already that the Duchess, at least, does not approve of me dancing attendance on you."

Now she smiled, relieved beyond measure that he had not rejected her idea out of hand. If he had, she'd have had to summon her courage to propose a second, far more scandalous scheme to achieve her ends. "Father will permit it if I ask him. He rarely denies me anything that I truly want, and the Duchess will not gainsay him."

They had reached the fourth balcony now and paused, as though admiring the view. Luke appeared to be deep in thought. Finally he stirred and looked at her again, searching her face with serious eyes. Pearl returned his gaze earnestly, her heart in her throat, hoping she had not gone too far and alienated him beyond recall.

Suddenly his expression softened, and he smiled. "I begin to see why the Duke can deny you nothing. If you really think it will help, I'll pose as your most earnest suitor for as long as you consider it expedient."

Pearl was startled by the elation that surged triumphantly through her at his words. It was only to be a sham, she reminded herself sternly. "Thank you . . . Luke. I'll do everything in my power to make certain you do not regret this."

She took his arm again and they headed back toward the Duke's box in silence. What Luke was thinking, she had no idea—nor was she entirely sure she wanted to know. It was enough that he would stay.

Luke untied his cravat and tossed it over the back of a chair in the sumptuous guest room of Marcus's town house, careful not to awaken Flute, asleep in the dressing room. He needed solitude to think.

He was a fool.

Never, never should he have given in to temptation and agreed to Lady Pearl's scheme. She was an idealist, a dreamer, and he should have told her so. Instead, he'd stared into her beautiful blue-violet eyes and said exactly what she wanted him to say. Even now, the memory of her beseeching gaze had the power to stir him powerfully.

Hell, just thinking about her had him rock-hard with desire. And he was supposed to *pretend* to be courting her for two entire months? To look but not to touch? It would be sheer torture. But that wasn't even the worst of it.

Only a few things worth selling remained in his lodgings in Seven Dials—assuming that by now the place hadn't been stripped bare. To maintain his charade as a man about Town for another two months, more money—much more—would be necessary.

Marcus was kindly providing him with a place to stay and regular meals, but he could scarcely keep wearing the same two sets of evening clothes indefinitely—nor the single pair of daytime breeches he owned. Marcus hadn't commented on it yet, but he must think it as odd as Luke's preference for dining at home rather than at one of the clubs.

Then there was the matter of flowers and other trinkets for Pearl, to keep up appearances. He'd love to give her something that would bring a smile to those luscious lips. But he knew only one way to obtain the necessary money.

He'd have to turn to theft again.

Why the thought should bother him, he wasn't sure—it never had before. The *ton* had far more than they could ever use or need, and it had always seemed only fair that he, and others like him, benefit from their plenty. Stealing from them was a form of justice—to himself, to his late mother, and to the downtrodden denizens of the London slums. But would Pearl see it that way?

No, almost certainly not. And therein lay the rub.

Luke removed his coat and waistcoat, then his shirt, and shrugged. He'd simply have to make certain she never found out, that was all. What other choice did he have, situated as he was? None. His conscience still niggled at him, but he refused to acknowledge it. He'd do what needed to be done, just as he always did, and leave any moralizing for another day.

Climbing under the sheets, he closed his eyes to dream of Pearl and the future they would pretend awaited them. A future that could never be.

Two days later, Luke was the subject of considerable speculation. The news that Lady Pearl finally had a favorite had made its way through the active gossip chain of Society, and all of fashionable London was abuzz with the news.

Marcus was the first to congratulate him. "You're a sly dog, you are, Luke," he exclaimed when they met at his house for luncheon. "All that talk of going back to your aunt, but I knew that the proper inducement could keep you here in Town. Do you think Oakshire will actually give his consent?"

"I sincerely doubt it," Luke confessed truthfully. "But so long as he doesn't forbid me to my face to see his daughter, I intend to continue doing so."

"And the Duchess? Has she had nothing to say on the matter? No offense, Luke," Marcus added quickly. "You're the best of good fellows, but—"

"But basically a nobody," Luke concluded for him. "No offense taken, as you're quite right. The Duchess has asked a few pointed questions—it's clear she considers me a fortune hunter—but her main interest seems to be whether or not I'll come up to scratch."

"Women do love to plan weddings," Lord Marcus agreed with a grin. "So will you?"

Luke shrugged. "I've known the lady for less than a week. And, as you so diplomatically pointed out, my chances of gaining her father's consent are small in any event."

A betrothal was out of the question, of course. Such a step would require the drawing up of settlements and an inevitable inquiry into Luke's background and finances—dubious in the one case and nonexistent in the other. He reminded himself of that fact frequently, whenever his hopes and desires threatened to overset his reason.

That evening he was to be Pearl's escort at a musicale at Oakshire House itself, where all of polite Society from the Prince Regent on down would be in attendance. When he arrived, one glance told him that he was the most inexpensively dressed man there. While his evening clothes were fashionable, he hadn't had the time or the funding to have them made by one of the premier tailors. Unfortunately, it showed.

"I'll do my best not to embarrass you," he murmured to Lady Pearl as they moved from the receiving line into the main hall. "This is all a bit over my head, you know."

She squeezed his arm encouragingly. "You're doing splendidly. Your manners are better than many a titled gentleman's, I assure you, and that's what really matters."

He couldn't help being touched by her faith in him, though he feared it was misplaced. When he'd ventured into great homes in the past, he'd relied on remaining inconspicuous to get by. As Lady Pearl's rumored favorite, that would scarcely be an option tonight.

Rather than a single musical performance at a set time and place, the Duchess had decreed five different venues throughout the mansion. At least one performance, therefore, was going on at all times, and the guests were free to wander as they chose from one to another. For several minutes, Luke and Pearl stood listening to a particularly brilliant pianist in one of the smaller parlors.

"Remarkable, is he not?" Pearl commented in an undertone. She had not released his arm all evening, but Luke did not mind in the least.

"Mmm," he responded noncommittally, as music was something he knew very little of. He was simply enjoying Pearl's nearness, occasionally allowing himself—unwisely—to fantasize that things were other than they were, that he had a chance of spending his life with her, his nights with her. . . .

"Let's go see if that flutist is still performing in the atrium," she suggested when the pianist ended his piece with a flourish. "There's supposed to be a soprano here, as well, who they say was the toast of Italy. Perhaps you'll have heard of her through your uncle?"

That was impossible, of course, but Luke merely said, "Perhaps. Did you catch her name?"

"Signora Donatelli or something like that— Oh! There is Lady Minerva beckoning to me. She'll want to meet you, I know."

Luke obediently accompanied her to the young lady in question, relieved that the topic of his Italian uncle had been dropped. Lying to Pearl was becoming increasingly difficult.

"Pearl! I vow I'm simply perishing to meet your Mr. di Santo. I hear such *interesting* things about him," exclaimed Lady Minerva the moment they were within earshot. The petite blonde's beauty was only slightly marred by the avid curiosity in her bright blue eyes.

Pearl merely smiled, answering her implied question with an introduction. "Lady Minerva Chatham, meet Lucio di Santo. Luke, Minnie is one of my closest friends."

"Hmph. Not close enough to have anticipated this development, if development it is," said Lady Minerva with a toss of her golden curls. "Mr. di Santo, pray fetch us something to drink, so that Pearl and I may have a proper coze."

At Pearl's slight nod, he bowed. "It is my great honor to be of service to two such exquisite ladies. Will ratafia do, or would you prefer champagne?"

Lady Minerva tittered at the compliment and waved her furled fan at him. "Oh, champagne! Pearl choosing a favorite is a festive occasion, after all. But pray take your time about it."

Luke left them to their chatter, taking a roundabout route to the buffet tables, where champagne was in abundance. Having no particular desire to carry the glasses longer than necessary, he moved slowly, nodding and speaking briefly to various new acquaintances along the way. He peered into the atrium to discover that the flutist was indeed still playing, storing that information to share with Pearl later.

As he finally approached the tables, his attention was caught by an elderly dowager a few steps in front of him. Dressed all in black silk, the woman positively dripped with jewels, from the emerald-encrusted comb in her hair to her diamond-studded slippers.

Speaking with an equally antiquated gentleman, she gestured with her left hand, and a heavy ruby and diamond bracelet nearly slipped from her wrist. She bobbed her head emphatically at something the old gent said, then gestured again. This time the bracelet did come free, its clasp either broken or undone, to slide along the folds of her voluminous skirts to the floor, where it formed a glittering puddle.

The two octogenarians moved on, oblivious, leaving Luke to stare at the sparkling bit of temptation in his path. Only for an instant, however. With the nonchalance of long practice, he moved forward without breaking his stride, seeming to focus on the table ahead while surreptitiously ascertaining that no one else had noticed the old lady's accident.

Drawing level with the bracelet, he paused, facing away from it, and pulled out his handkerchief. He touched it to his nose, then moved it back to his pocket, dropping it at the last moment so that it landed nearly atop the fallen bracelet. Swiftly he knelt, scooping up the jewels along with his handkerchief.

This bauble would pay for a new wardrobe from Weston himself, unless he missed his guess, perhaps with enough left over to buy a pretty trinket for Pearl. He was just tucking the handkerchief-wrapped bracelet into his pocket when a strong hand gripped his wrist.

"And what might you have there, sir?" The Oakshire House head butler, radiating outraged sensibility, peered at him down a hooklike nose.

Luke froze, groping for a glib explanation. The last thing he could afford was a scene! He cleared his throat, his mind working frantically.

"Oh, darling, you found it!" Like a vision in shimmering lilac, Pearl swept between Luke and the butler, deftly taking the bracelet from him before the butler could. "I was certain I'd dropped it in the atrium. How clever of you to retrace my steps and find it here!"

The butler's demeanor changed at once, and he backed away with a respectful bow. "My apologies, sir! My lady, if I can be of any service?"

"Thank you, Upwood. I'll certainly let you know," said Lady Pearl, pointedly dismissing the man.

The butler retreated, still mouthing apologies, and she turned to face Luke. "Now, perhaps you would care to tell me how you happened to be in possession of the Dowager Lady Glinnon's bracelet?"

Chapter 10

Pearl strove valiantly to keep her expression neutral, betraying neither the shock nor the disappointment she felt. It appeared her first suspicions had been correct after all: Luke was clearly the notorious Saint of Seven Dials. But that he would resort to thievery here, under her father's roof . . . !

"Why, Luke?" she asked softly.

She saw several expressions chase each other across his face as he too-obviously toyed with various explanations. Finally, guilt won out and he dropped his gaze. "I'm sorry, Pearl. I've lied to you."

"I'd rather figured that out." Still, she tried to keep accusation from her voice, tried to understand. "Come, let's go into the library. We should be able to talk there.

Though she half feared he would protest, he accompanied her without a word. The library, a smaller replica of the one the Duke maintained at his main Oakshire estate, was deserted, as Pearl had hoped. She took a chair facing the door, so that they could not be surprised, and motioned Luke to one close by. Silently he took it, still avoiding her eye.

"And now, if you please, the truth—all of it."

He frowned. "You won't like it, you know."

"Probably not," she agreed. "But I'd rather hear it than not. I told you everything you asked about my unconventional behavior last week. Now it is your turn."

He took a deep breath, then looked directly at her, his expression now candid. "Very well. The story I told you last week was far nearer the truth than the fantasy I have woven for Society. I really am plain Luke St. Clair, and no one else."

Pearl blinked, unable—or unwilling—to understand. "But your time at Oxford? Your friends there?"

"Lucio di Santo was the identity I assumed to attend school, using references I forged myself—documents, correspondence, everything. Background—and blood—is at least as important for entry as tuition. And those I fear I had to manufacture."

"So your uncle in Italy . . . ?"

"Is completely fictitious."

"But the tuition? Someone must have—"

He shook his head. "I paid it myself. I merely made it look as though it came from another source."

"And the money, then and now?" she asked even

more quietly. "I presume it cannot actually be credited to a generous employer?"

For a moment, he closed his eyes, as though waging an inner battle with himself. Then he met her gaze again, his own still frank. "No, it is as you've guessed. All stolen. I'm nothing but a common thief, Pearl—it's all I've ever been. I had no right to let you believe otherwise, to let you—"

She held up a hand to stem his apologies, ignoring the pain in her heart. "No, you did not. Still, I would hardly call the renowned Saint of Seven Dials common."

His eyes widened, then narrowed. "Who told you that?"

She gave a mirthless little laugh. "What, do you still have so little faith in my abilities? I admit I was slow on the uptake, or tried to be, though all of the evidence was before me. Did I not see you helping the denizens of Seven Dials myself?"

He shook his head and started to speak, but she hurried on.

"I heard little Emmy Plank call you 'Mr. Saint' with my own ears. Then, of course, there was the theft at the Mountheath house, combined with your eagerness to leave it on the very night it occurred."

Whatever he had been about to say in protest, he abandoned with a sigh. "I admit, once I discovered that rumors of my existence had spread to your social circle, I feared you might make the deduction on your own. I only wish I had told you the truth beforehand. Before you ever had a chance to consider me a fit companion, to introduce me to your parents—"

"Or to talk you into a counterfeit courtship," she

concluded, tears suddenly beginning to prick behind her eyes. "Did you agree only to afford yourself better means to steal? Shall I find one of your calling cards about the house?"

His shock appeared sincere—or perhaps she only wanted to believe that.

"Of course not! I agreed only for . . . for the reasons you laid out—though against my better judgment, I confess. I knew I hadn't the resources to extend my stay. That was why I had already told you I must leave. That's the truth, on my honor."

She understood, or hoped she did, though knowing he was right gave her little comfort. "A rogue's honor," she murmured, but then saw the pain in his eyes. "I'm sorry. Had I known what I was forcing you to, I would never—that is—"

"No!" He spoke urgently now, the intensity that drew her like a moth to a flame very much in evidence. Even knowing what she did, her wayward body ached for him. "You are in no way at fault. I'll make it clear to the authorities that you were completely blameless throughout."

"The authorities?"

"Do you not mean to call them? The Saint of Seven Dials is a wanted man, you know."

It was her turn to be appalled. "Of course not! How can you even suggest such a thing?"

"Why not?" He seemed honestly curious.

She stared at him, even in this extremity noticing the sweep of his dark hair, the masculine line of his jaw, his noble—yes, noble—forehead.

"You need to ask? You did me a great service last week, thinking me nothing but a simple serving maid. If you think I would repay that kindness with betrayal, then you must truly consider me no better than the worst of my class after all."

His expression became tinged with something like awe. "But I have betrayed you, lied to you. I can't imagine any woman, of any class, overlooking such a thing."

"Perhaps I'm not just any woman," she replied with a shaky smile, trying to salvage what remained of her pride.

"No, that you certainly are not." His eyes were admiring, but held a shadow of pain, as well.

Uncomfortable at being credited with more virtue than she felt she possessed, Pearl forced a light tone. "In any event, it would be far too ironic to have you arrested for stealing Lady Glinnon's bracelet, as it is undoubtedly paste."

He blinked. "Paste?"

"Quality paste," she allowed, amusement at his expression distracting her for a moment from her own despair. "She loses things constantly, so her family has had all of her jewels replaced with exact replicas. It's well known that she never wears the real ones in public. In the morning I'll return the bracelet, saying I found it after the guests left, and no one will think a thing of it."

Shaking his head, he chuckled. "It appears I have lost my touch already." But then, sobering, "You understand, though, why I must leave?"

Reluctantly, she nodded. "I do. But ..." she paused, suddenly remembering her alternate plan. It was madness, of course—worse than madness. Her heart pounded at the very thought. Quickly, before she could dissuade herself, she continued. "But I have a favor to ask of you first."

"Another favor?" He looked wary, and she couldn't blame him. Nor was her request likely to reassure him.

Scarcely daring to breathe, she hurried on. "Several times it has occurred to me that the one foolproof way to evade the Duchess's machinations would be to render myself unmarriageable." She couldn't quite meet his eye as she continued, "I'd like you to ruin my reputation—irretrievably—before you go."

He stared. "I beg your pardon, my lady? Surely you're not asking me to—"

"To deflower me, yes." Ignoring the quivering in her belly at what she was suggesting, she kept her voice and expression cool, as though discussing one of her social reforms. "Without my virtue intact, Obelia will be unable to prevail upon anyone to marry me. My estates will be secure, and I will be able to proceed with my plans for them."

Luke still looked as though he could not believe he had heard her aright. "You cannot have thought this through. You would be shunned by Society. You may wish to marry at some time in the future, to have a family—"

"Indeed, I have thought it through." So thoroughly, in fact, that even now she felt her color rising, a heat growing at the heart of her femininity. She had to admit to herself that she wanted him for reasons that had nothing to do with terms of inheritance—with Fairbourne.

"I care nothing for Society," she continued determinedly after a moment. "I plan to spend all of my time at Fairbourne once it is mine. I am far too strong-willed to marry, and I don't foresee that changing. A husband would only attempt to impose his will over mine. I would resist, and we should both be miserable. I'll deal much better alone."

And lonely . . . but she would not think of that. Not now. Not yet. Not while she still might have one night of passion with Luke. "Will you do it?"

Slowly, he shook his head. "I'm sorry, my lady. I simply can't—"

She could have cried with frustration, but instead she stood, holding out a hand to him. "Wait. Before you refuse, I wish to show you something."

As though in a daze, he took her proffered hand and rose. Without another word, she led him to the corner of the library to the right of the fireplace. There, she turned an almost invisible catch to open a narrow door, disguised as part of the mahogany paneling. She peered into the dimly lit servants' corridor, listening intently for a moment, before leading Luke through the door and closing it carefully behind them.

"A secret passage?" he asked in surprise.

"Not particularly secret, but hidden, yes. Many of the larger houses have them, so that the servants can perform their various duties without intruding upon the public rooms. I am surprised you have not found them of use yourself in your, ah, career. Come."

Though she still spoke lightly, her heart pounded at what she was intending. He mustn't suspect, though. Not yet.

Still seemingly bemused, he followed her as she led him quickly up a narrow flight of stairs, around a corner, and down another passage. To her relief, they passed no servants along the way—doubtless they were all busy serving the guests. At the end of the corridor, she cautiously opened another door, the one into her own sitting room.

"Wait here a moment," she whispered to Luke. Then, stepping into the room, "Hettie?"

Her maid, employed in winding up some ribbons at Pearl's dressing table, started violently. "My lady! Whatever are you doing in—"

"Escaping," Pearl responded, cutting her off. She closed the door behind her, Luke still in the passageway. "I've done it before, you know. Pray go downstairs for me and tell the Duchess that I have the headache. Mr. di Santo has gone, as he felt uncomfortable facing the company without me, so pray make his apologies as well."

Hettie sent her one piercing stare, but then nodded. "Of course, my lady. Then I'll return to help you out of your things."

"No need," Pearl assured her. "If you'll just undo these hooks at my back before you go, I'll put myself to bed. I really am quite tired. I shall see you in the morning."

Obediently, Hettie unfastened the back of Pearl's gown and then left, using the regular door, as she was going in search of the Duchess in the public rooms. Pearl locked it behind her.

At once she returned to the hidden door, half afraid Luke would have guessed her intention and disappeared. He was still waiting, however, and she ushered him into her rooms. "We can be private now," she told him, ignoring her growing nervousness.

He appeared to detect it, however, for he gave her a long, searching look before saying, "You had something you wished to show me?"

"Yes. That is . . ." Mindful of her unhooked dress, she awkwardly backed her way to her desk, to pick up a periodical. "The *Political Register*," she said inanely. "Have you read it?"

His expression told her how odd her behavior seemed, though he followed her to the desk. "Not recently. Is there a particular article you want me to see?"

How on earth did one launch a seduction, anyway? she wondered frantically. In a moment, if she didn't do something, he would be gone, and her last chance with him. He reached for the magazine, but she tweaked it away before he could touch it, holding it behind her.

"Luke, I . . ." Boldly, she met his eyes, hoping he might read there what she couldn't seem to put into words.

That he read something there was clear. In his own eyes she saw a sudden longing, which became naked desire for an instant, before he as quickly concealed it. That one brief glimpse gave her badly needed courage, however. Dropping the magazine behind her, she laid one hand on his arm.

He covered her gloved hand with his own, still gazing into her eyes. "Pearl, you are playing with fire that you don't understand. You are such an innocent."

Fire indeed. The flame behind his dark eyes singed her to her toes, but now she did not hesitate.

With her other hand, she touched his cheek. "I know I am, but I want you to change that," she said softly. "Please, Luke."

He closed his eyes, and she could sense the struggle within him. The knowledge that he was tempted emboldened her further. She slid her hand from his cheek to the nape of his neck, swaying infinitesimally closer to him. A quick glance downward showed that he was most definitely affected.

His eyes opened, smoky with desire, though he held himself rigid beneath her touch. "Do you have any idea of what you're doing to me?"

"Yes, for you do the same to me," she said. "Please don't deny me, Luke."

With a groan, he crushed her to him, covering her mouth with his own. She returned the kiss with all her being, fire licking along her extremities. This was what she had dreamed of ever since leaving his lodgings a week ago. This and more. Wanting to feel again his skin against hers, she stripped off her gloves one by one, without breaking the kiss. As she'd done once before, she threaded her bare fingers through his hair.

At her touch, however, he seemed to regain his senses. Pulling back, he regarded her from only a few inches away. "We can't, you know," he told her. "*I* can't. I would never forgive myself."

"I'll never forgive you if you don't," she replied with a smile, intoxicated by his nearness and the sense of her power over him. "It is my life, Luke, and I've made my decision—for independence. Help me to achieve it."

For another long moment he gazed at her, conflict warring within his eyes. She saw his surrender the moment he made it. With a glad little cry of triumph, she welcomed his kiss, his touch. He stripped off his own gloves, then clasped her free hand, flesh to flesh, while his other hand went to the nape of her neck, drawing her closer.

She pressed her length against his, reveling in his masculine hardness. Tall herself, it seemed right that he was several inches taller. Skimming her hands up the firm planes of his chest, she untied his cravat, then began working on his waistcoat buttons. She half expected another protest, but it did not come.

Instead, he shrugged out of his coat, then reached behind her. He paused, on discovering her dress was already unfastened, then chuckled deep in his throat. "Decisive indeed," he murmured against her lips.

"I'm accustomed to getting what I want," she whispered teasingly. "And I've wanted you almost from the moment we met." His waistcoat undone, she started on his shirt.

"It appears that rank has its advantages after all," he said with another chuckle. "Who am I to deny a grand lady like yourself?"

Who indeed? Pearl wondered. But only for an instant. Her whole being was focused on getting closer to him, on having the desire singing through her veins fulfilled. She had his waistcoat off him now, and his shirt. Luke had somehow worked her gown down to her waist and was nearly done unlacing her light corset. A moment later, nothing but her thin chemise separated her breasts from his bare chest.

"I presume you have a bed nearby?" Luke asked

as she stepped free of the shimmering lilac folds of her gown. Pearl nodded toward her bedchamber door, which stood ajar. To her amazement, he swept her into his arms and actually carried her to the next room. If any other man had done something so high-handed, she'd have been outraged or even frightened. But with Luke, it only increased her desire.

Before she was done considering her amazing attitude toward this man, he deposited her on the sumptuously quilted feather bed. Sitting on the edge, he removed his shoes—and then his breeches. Following his lead, Pearl whisked her shift off over her head while his back was turned. Then he faced her, his eyes aflame.

For an instant, at her very first sight of an aroused male body, Pearl quailed. Surely . . . surely this would be impossible? How . . . ?

Luke smiled tenderly and kissed her. "I'll be gentle, I promise. I don't want this to be something you'll remember with regret—ever."

She relaxed. "I trust you." And she meant it. Amazingly, she had never trusted anyone as wholeheartedly as she trusted this man who had lied to her almost from the moment she'd met him. "Show me what to do."

"Ever my little academic," he said with a grin. But then, pulling her against him, he sobered. "I want you, Pearl. And I want you to want me. But you must be absolutely sure."

In answer, she lay back, pulling his face down to hers for a kiss, running her hands up and down his bare back, enjoying the warm, firm smoothness of his skin. Shifting slightly, he did the same. His fingers seemed to leave a trail of fire everywhere they touched. She wanted more—much more.

He gave it to her.

Slipping one hand between them, he ran his palm down her belly, making her quiver. Then, before she could even realize what it was she needed, he buried his fingers in the cluster of curls between her thighs. She gasped with pure pleasure, a pleasure so sharp it was almost pain. But still he was not done.

Slowly, agonizingly slowly, he massaged the spot that was the focus of her desire, then slipped one strong finger inside her. Instinctively, she tightened around him and he drew in a quick breath. Then, still slowly, he moved his finger out, then back in, setting up a rhythm that her body echoed, demanded.

Though she wanted these wonderful sensations to go on forever, she still wanted more. Cupping his muscular buttocks in her hands, she pulled him closer, until the hard shaft that had shocked her with its size brushed against her, right next to his questing fingers.

When he broke the rhythm within her, she nearly cried out in protest, but at once he replaced his finger with the very tip of his shaft. Slowly he reestablished the rhythm, sliding ever so slightly inside her, then withdrawing. Without thought, she moved her hips to greet him, urging him deeper with each thrust.

They rocked together, first gently, then more and more forcefully, until finally he drove into her with his entire length. Pearl gasped, her body seeming to explode into a shower of colorful sparks. Never had she imagined such sensation, such ecstasy, was possible. She tightened around him convulsively as he thrust again and again. Then, with a shuddering sigh, he thrust one last time, even more deeply, and remained there, his arms wrapped tightly around her as he expended himself into her depths.

For several long minutes they lay entwined. Pearl felt her heartbeat gradually returning to normal as a sweet lassitude came over her. Refusing to think beyond the moment yet, she gloried in the contentment pervading her mind and body.

All too soon, Luke stirred, but only to touch her cheek gently, and to kiss her lightly on the lips. The warmth had not left his eyes. "No regrets?" he asked softly.

She smiled at him—at her lover. "None at all. I never imagined . . ."

"Nor did I." Now his expression was one of wonder. "Pearl, I . . . I . . ." He seemed on the verge of disclosing something vitally important, his eyes burning into her with their intensity. Then, suddenly, his expression changed. Swallowing visibly, he pulled away from her—first emotionally, then physically.

She started to protest, but restrained herself. He was right, of course. She had known—they both had known—that he must leave, most likely never to see her again. Better that whatever feelings they shared remained unspoken. But while the logical portion of her mind explained all this to her, her heart wailed in silent sorrow for what could never be.

In silence, he resumed his clothing and she her shift and then a nightrail, he apparently as deep in thought as she. Was it possible that he also wished . . . ? But no, she could not ask him. It would not be fair to either of them.

Luke finished dressing and faced this woman who had become so inexpressibly dear to him. He had to leave, of course, for her sake even more than his own. But saying good-bye, most likely forever, was going to be the hardest thing he'd ever done.

"You won't return to . . . to thievery, will you?" she asked hesitantly, her concern evident.

He blinked in surprise, realizing he hadn't even thought that far ahead. "It's what I do best," he reminded her—and himself. "And it's not as though I have another trade to return to. Besides . . ."

"Besides, the poor people of Seven Dials depend upon you." Her smile was tender, sending a shaft of sweet agony through him, but he shook his head.

"No, I can't let you believe that I steal only for altruistic reasons. When I see a need, I try to help, yes, but my primary motive has always been—"

"Revenge." She finished his sentence again, this time correctly.

He nodded. "I told you how my mother was treated, how she died. For most of my life I have seen the Quality as the enemy, people to be taken advantage of whenever possible, as some small recompense to her, and to me."

But did he feel that way now, knowing that Pearl was of that previously hated class? He wasn't sure. Of course, his revenge had gone far beyond mere thievery. He'd nearly lost count of the number of titled gentlemen he'd cuckolded, seducing their paid mistresses and, once or twice, even their wives. And now he'd gone even further, snatching the virtue of a Duke's only daughter.

Luke turned away from Pearl's earnest gaze to stare blankly out of the window, hating himself.

"The fact remains that you have benefited many people, perhaps even saved their lives, through your generosity." Her simple faith in him made him feel even worse. "I understand why you might feel you can't just abandon them."

Warily, he met her eyes again, willing himself not to flinch away from the warmth and understanding—so undeserved!—he saw there. "I know you won't set the authorities on my tail, and I'm grateful for that."

She dismissed that with a quick wave of her hand. "That was never in question. But the authorities are already on your tail, or very nearly. That is why it's far too risky for you to resume your activities as the Saint of Seven Dials."

This was news to him. "What do you mean?"

"According to Lord Bellowsworth, a boy has been recognized, disposing of some of the items, er, missing from the Mountheaths'. No doubt he is being followed, in hopes of leading the law officers to you." Now she looked doubtful. "Do you truly have children in your employ?"

How to respond without blackening himself further in her eyes? "Not children, precisely, no. But I have Flute."

"Flute?" Her puzzlement was obvious.

"You met him once, actually, on our drive. He has been useful to me in both of my guises."

Her brow cleared, then drew down in a frown.

"You have put that boy at risk, taking in stolen goods? Even helping you to steal?"

He opened his mouth to defend himself, to tell her that he had rescued the orphaned Flute from a far worse fate at the hands of a vicious master, but then closed it again. Better that she believe the worst of him. She would forget him more quickly that way.

Instead of condemning him, however, she only said, "By returning to thievery, you will put him at even greater risk—and yourself as well. I have a proposition instead."

"Another proposition?"

She chuckled, but there was no real mirth in the sound. "I don't wonder you are concerned, but this one is solely for the benefit of the wretched denizens of Seven Dials. I have money enough to spare, and will soon have even more. I can supply you with whatever is necessary to meet their needs—and yours."

Until the addition of those last two words, he had almost been tempted. It would be so simple. But the idea of Pearl supporting *him* was intolerable. He would not become one of her social projects. "Thank you, but I'll manage," he said, perhaps more stiffly than he intended. "I always have."

For a moment she looked as though she meant to argue, but then, apparently realizing she had offended him, she let the matter drop. Instead, she said, "As we're unlikely to see each other again, will you tell me more about yourself, and your past, before you go?"

He suspected he had not heard the last of her

plan to help him, but he welcomed the change of subject. He led her back into her sitting room, to stand before the hidden servants' panel.

"Are you certain you wouldn't prefer that I simply disappear without a trace?"

She smiled briefly, acknowledging his teasing and her own curiosity, but then became serious. "It is possible that my father may already be making inquiries into your background, which could well prove disastrous for you. If—"

"He'll find nothing," he assured her, grateful again for her concern. "At worst, your father will conclude that I am an imposter, a fortune hunter. He'll discover nothing whatsoever about my real background, simply because it doesn't exist."

Clearly confused, she frowned. "Don't be absurd. Of course you have a real background, however unsavory it might be. What of your mother? She was a real, flesh-and-blood woman, was she not?"

"She was," he conceded. "But I can tell you little more about her, save her heroic character. Her name was Dorothea St. Clair—though even whether that was her true name, I can't say for certain. Even as a child, I knew she was afraid of something or someone. We moved frequently until I was eight or nine years old, sometimes at a moment's notice."

He paused, remembering. "I never knew my father," he continued after a moment, "nor did she tell me anything about him, except that he was a good man, and that he was dead. I did ask her once, shortly before she died, whether I was illegitimate, but she denied it." He had never dared to believe her, much as he'd wanted to.

"You told me she died when you were still

young—eleven or twelve?" Pearl prompted him. "What did you do then?"

Again he hesitated. "I stayed with my old nurse-maid briefly, but she did not have the wherewithal to care for me, nor did I feel she should have to. I went out to find employment and fell in with . . . an unsavory crowd." It was an understatement, but he saw no point in arousing her pity.

"Is that when you turned to thievery?" she asked gently, apparently guessing some of what he'd left unsaid.

"Yes. I joined a ring of pickpockets, whose leader offered to teach me the trade. I was reluctant at first, of course, but I soon discovered that it paid far better than anything else a twelve-year-old boy could do. Well enough that I was able to lay enough money by to break away from them eventually."

"And go to school." Her gaze seemed almost admiring, which shamed him.

"Yes, to school. You'd think once I had a university education to my credit, I'd have turned to a respectable trade, wouldn't you?" he asked wryly.

"Why didn't you?" No condemnation, just simple curiosity.

Luke shrugged, then sighed. "I did try, actually. I held two or three different positions—first as a clerk, then apprenticing with a barrister. I don't take orders well, however, nor do I do well in situations where I have to acknowledge others as my betters."

"Perhaps because they really are no better," she said with a smile. "I have little patience with fools myself."

He had to restrain the urge to laugh wildly—for

surely there could be no greater fool in England than Luke St. Clair! It was high time he took his leave.

But what he would do then, he honestly didn't know.

Chapter 11

The distant, forlorn look in Luke's eyes as he told his story made Pearl want to fold him against her breast and comfort him, but she did not dare—not now, knowing what his touch did to her. Knowing he must leave.

Watching him as he spoke, the light of the fire playing about the firm line of his lips, his expressive brows, Pearl felt again, more poignantly, the crushing disappointment that had assailed her the moment she saw Lady Glinnon's bracelet in his hand. But now an idea occurred to her.

"Since you know so little about your parents, it is possible your birth is perfectly respectable," she said when he did not reply. "Have you considered that?"

"As a lad I thought of little else." His chuckle

seemed a bit forced, she thought. "I spent long hours fantasizing about my royal heritage—how one day, out of the blue, someone would appear to tell me I was actually a prince, or heir to a dukedom." He shook his head. "At best, I suppose I might be the byblow of someone important."

"Don't you want to find out? Have you tried?" She tried to bank the sudden, wild hope flaring to life from the ashes of her despair.

But his expression hardened, closing her off. "No. What would be the point? As things stand now, I am beholden to no one, free to live my life as I choose. Besides, I have no place to start looking, even if I wanted to—which I don't."

Despite the pain his words caused her, Pearl's quick mind was already formulating the beginnings of a plan. She would say nothing to him about it yet, as he was so resistant—not until she knew what fruit it might bear.

Instead, she asked, "So what now, Luke? Do you mean to vanish at once, or will you go back to Lord Marcus's house?" She needed to know how to find him, just in case.

He regarded her warily. "That depends upon you. On what you mean to do now that I've given you . . . what you wanted." The words were harsh, and he seemed to realize it, for he softened them with a smile.

The thought of never again experiencing the wonder they had shared tore at her, but she had known beforehand that was the way it must be. "I won't put you at risk, of course," she told him. "Not until you are safely away will I make use of my, er, changed circumstances. I trust that you can disappear without a trace, as you have done before? Back to Seven Dials?"

He nodded, though his eyes searched her face. She was careful to allow no trace of hope to show there.

"Tomorrow, then? Once I know you have gone, I can confess what has happened. I'll . . . say that you seduced me, then fled. That you were not what you seemed to be."

"Yes, you can claim to have been deceived, along with the rest of the *ton*." Now a smile lurked behind his eyes, though she read pain there, too.

She fought down a sudden surge of panic at the idea of facing the censure of her peers alone. "I think you enjoy deceiving the *ton* rather too much," she said with mock severity, to distract herself.

"I have in the past," he confessed, suddenly sober again. "But now—" He pulled a small stack of calling cards from his pocket, fingering them for a moment before suddenly flinging them into the fire. "There. That is the end of the Saint of Seven Dials."

He faced her again. "I hope you'll believe me when I say that never for a moment did I enjoy deceiving you, Pearl."

She reached up and touched his cheek with a smile, enjoying for one last time the rough feel of the light stubble on his jaw against her bare fingers. "You had no choice—and I forgive you."

He took her hand from his face and kissed the very tips of her fingers. "Yours is the truest heart I've ever known, my Lady Pearl," he said, sincerity shining from his eyes. "Farewell."

Releasing her hand, he moved as softly as a

shadow to the hidden servants' door. Then, with one last bittersweet smile, he was gone.

Pearl stood rigid before the cold fireplace, the fingers he had kissed at her own lips. Despite what she had told him, despite her need to secure Fairbourne, she doubted she would ever tell another soul what had happened here tonight.

Luke slipped soundlessly along the narrow passage, pausing when he heard voices, waiting until they moved on before proceeding. Hurrying down two flights of steps, he cracked open a door that led to the kitchens. He watched and waited until he had a clear path to the outer door, then whisked out while the servants weren't looking.

Quickly he moved through the kitchen gardens, then out to the alleyway behind the great houses. There he paused for a moment, breathing in the cool night air. Looking up, he identified the window that would be Pearl's. What was she doing now? Thinking now? He prayed she wasn't already regretting what they'd done . . . what *he'd* done.

He had difficulty regretting it himself. Never had he bonded so completely with a woman, been so willing to sacrifice everything for her. He turned away and began walking quickly in the direction of Lord Marcus's house, self-loathing again effacing his euphoria.

Sacrifice? Instead, he'd sullied the only thing he cared about. He should have stood firm, knowing the world as he did. Knowing the risks.

Unbidden, a vision rose before him, of Pearl at her most alluring, pleading with eyes and body, using her considerable intelligence, equally attractive to him, to formulate persuasive arguments. In her, Luke had finally met his match.

But what of that? By her own admission, they must never meet again, nor would he be fool enough to attempt it. If he thought he could protect her from scandal by standing at her side, he wouldn't hesitate, but his presence would only make things worse. Especially if he were arrested for thievery. A fat lot of good he could do her swinging from a gibbet.

Pushing his conflicting feelings down deep, into an obscure corner of his heart, he quickened his pace until he was nearly trotting. Letting himself into Marcus's house, he hurried up to his temporary chamber without encountering any of the servants. Good.

"Flute?" he called softly. "Are you here?"

The lad emerged from the dressing room, rubbing sleep from his eyes. "I were just takin' a bit of a catnap, sir. You're back early, ain't you?"

"Yes. Wake yourself up, Flute, and pack up my things. I wish to be gone within the hour—before Lord Marcus returns."

Instead of evincing surprise, Flute nodded sagely. "Got wind of the Runners, did you? I meant to tell you as soon as you got back."

Luke paused in the act of pulling out pen and paper for the note he meant to write to Marcus. "The Runners?" Did everyone know of this investigation except him? "Tell me."

Flute frowned, tugging at his straw-colored forelock. "You didn't hear, then? Seems I was recognized by someone hereabouts as the one what fenced them baubles last week. Old Fenster described me to the

Runners, the snitch. After all the business I brung him. Then today, Missy from the kitchens tells me one of 'em was here, talking to the stable lads."

"Bow Street Runners? Here?" It appeared they'd be leaving just in time—if they *were* in time. "Have you noticed anyone watching the house?"

"Not sure I would have, since I dursn't show my face outdoors after what Missy said. She's a lively lass, she is."

Luke shot him a grin. "You'll meet more lively lasses, you young rapscallion. Now stop your mooning and finish packing while I write my excuses."

Ten minutes later, the note to Marcus written and Luke's single trunk packed, the two headed cautiously down the back stairs. Leaving Flute with the trunk just inside the servants' entrance, Luke stole back to prop the note against the library mantelpiece. Marcus likely wouldn't believe his explanation of an urgent summons from his aunt, but it was the best he could think of under the circumstances.

Returning to Flute, he told him to remain where he was while Luke went out to reconnoiter. Sure enough, a man was leaning against a lamppost across the street, watching the house. They'd need a distraction.

Still dressed in his finery, Luke was less likely to excite suspicion than his confederate, particularly if the Runners had Flute's description. Pinning an expression of grave concern on his face, Luke walked right up to the man.

"Sir," he exclaimed, "one of the stable lads says you are an officer of the law. I hope you can help my friend—he was set upon by footpads not a block from here!"

The man straightened at once to regard Luke warily. "I heard nothing," he said. "Are you sure?"

"Sure!" Luke waxed indignant. "I was with him at the time, man! I helped to frighten them off, but my friend sustained a blow, so I was obliged to go for help. My good friend Lord Marcus is away from home, or I'd have enlisted his aid."

At the invocation of Lord Marcus's name, the man snapped to attention. "Of course, sir! Which way did you say, sir?"

Luke pointed in the opposite direction from the one he and Flute would take. "In the alley behind those houses there. If someone else has rendered him aid by now, perhaps you can catch the men who did this—there were three of them."

"Three. Very good, sir." Without further hesitation, the man hurried off in the indicated direction.

Quickly, Luke returned to Flute and together they disappeared into the shadows to make their way back to Seven Dials. As the streets got narrower and dirtier, Luke felt his spirits, briefly elevated by the encounter with the Runner, sinking into his shoes. In vain he tried to tell himself that he was happier here, free of the restraints trammeling the upper classes. At the moment, all he could see was the squalor.

Abruptly, he realized that he was seeing Seven Dials the way Pearl must have seen it, that first night he met her. Not for a moment had she quailed, though the filth and poverty had to be a shock to her. Instead, she had looked for ways to help those in such need.

"Shall we separate here?" Flute recalled him from his thoughts when he nearly walked past the building where he had his lodgings.

"I think you'd better stay with me for the time being," Luke replied. "It's entirely possible your crib is being watched, if the authorities know who you are."

"Are you sure, sir?" Flute had only visited Luke's lodgings once or twice before, and always surreptitiously, so that they couldn't be tied to each other by witnesses.

"Have you anywhere else to go?"

Flute shrugged. "I can always find a corner somewhere. I've done it often enough."

But Luke had had enough this night of abandoning those who trusted him. "This will be warmer. Come on."

As he had feared, the place had been ransacked in his absence. For a moment anger assailed him. After all the help he had given these people, he'd have thought— But no. For the residents of Seven Dials, gratitude could scarcely compete with hunger, or even the need for spirits to dull their pain.

Prying up a corner floorboard, Luke was relieved to find that the thieves hadn't found his "safe"—the place he kept a few small but valuable items. From the little recess he pulled a pair of diamond earrings, a dozen gold coins, and an emerald watch fob. His retirement fund.

Flute gave a low whistle. "Good to see they didn't get everything—not by a long shot! You want I should fence those for you?"

Luke shook his head. "Too risky, especially now

you're being sought. The jewels were recognizable enough that I stashed them away for a rainy day some months since. Luckily I've also saved the gold, and it should see us through." He pocketed two of the coins, then rewrapped the rest and replaced the bundle.

Only as he spoke did it occur to him what a momentous decision he'd made. Though he wouldn't accept Pearl's charity, he didn't intend to steal anymore. Not for himself, and not for anyone else. No matter how he justified it, doing so injured him more than it did his victims, destroying a tiny piece of his soul with every theft.

No, the Saint of Seven Dials would never ride again.

Pearl slept surprisingly well, considering the dramatic turn her life had just taken. Awakening to bright sunshine that chased away all fantasy and pretense, she found she still could not regret what she and Luke had done the night before. The experience had completed her somehow, even though she'd never known before that anything was missing from her life.

With her usual impeccable timing, Hettie entered as Pearl stretched, carrying a steaming basin for her morning wash. "I see you're feeling much recovered this morning, my lady," she said with a smile.

"Indeed I am," Pearl declared, hugging her secret knowledge to herself. It seemed remarkable that Hettie could not perceive a change in her, so profound was her shift in perspective today.

Standing, she turned her face to the sunshine streaming in the window. Even the slight soreness between her legs could not dampen her spirits. She felt like dancing. As she remembered her plan, her smile broadened even further.

"I have a new project in mind, Hettie, and again I'll need your help."

Not surprisingly, her abigail regarded her with alarm. "Not another disguise, surely, my lady?"

Pearl laughed, a bit too gaily, for Hettie's alarm did not abate. Forcing herself to something more resembling her usual mien, she reassured the maid. "No, a mere fact-gathering mission. Who on our staff would you trust to make inquiries, perhaps unusual inquiries, and keep anything he found to himself?"

Hettie thought for a moment. "William, the head coachman, has been with the family the longest, but I doubt he'd do anything behind the Duke's back. There's Jimmy, who works in the kitchens, who'd do anything for a price—but he's a bit too fond of talking. Wait!" She snapped her fingers. "John Marley. He's worked his way up from stable lad to footman, and I'd trust him with my life."

"But will he not feel obliged to report to my father?"

With a slight blush, Hettie shook her head. "Not if I ask him to report only to you. He . . . seems to have a fondness for me."

Pearl grinned, where two weeks ago she would have frowned at such an admission. Though servants were generally discouraged from forming attachments for each other, just now she could not bring herself to condemn romance in any form. "He sounds perfect. Once I have breakfasted, ask him to attend me in my sitting room."

An hour later, seated in her favorite chair, Pearl regarded the young footman, who stood glancing nervously from her to Hettie and back. Though not particularly handsome, he had an honest, pleasant face. And Hettie trusted him. He would do.

"John, have you ever been to Edgeware?" she asked without preamble.

Too well trained to show surprise, he merely nodded. "Yes, milady, twice."

"Good. I have a task for you." Quickly, mindful that morning callers might be arriving downstairs at any moment, she outlined what she wished him to do. Recalling every snippet of information Luke had given her about his childhood, she shared everything that might be helpful to the investigation.

"Report directly to me—through Hettie, if you prefer—with any information you find. Of course, you'll be well compensated, as this goes beyond your usual duties. I will see Upwood does not question your absence."

The footman accepted his dismissal with a bow. "Thank you, milady. You can count on me. If the information you seek exists, I will find it." His speech, a shade better than the average footman's, made it clear he was still striving to better himself. Pearl thoroughly approved such an effort.

"Thank you, John. I'm sure you will."

"Very well, Mr. di Santo. You may check back in a week to see if we've found anything for you." The bespectacled clerk at the tiny employment office closed his book, pointedly dismissing him.

Luke gave the man a terse nod and took his leave,

fighting an urge to tell the officious clerk to go to hell. This was the fourth office he'd visited, giving his Oxford name at two of them, for those positions where a formal education would be required, and his real name at the others, for more humble prospects. Using either name was risky, of course, but he was reluctant to invent yet a third one.

This whole process was even more degrading than he had expected—a massive step down from pseudo-gentleman or even legendary thief. He wondered whether he'd be able to hold to his resolve after all.

It had been nearly a week now since he'd left Mayfair behind him, and he'd made a point of reading the scandal sheets every day. So far there'd been no mention whatsoever of any furor to do with the Lady Pearl. That could only mean that she hadn't told anyone after all. It made his position here safer, but he couldn't help wondering at her reasons.

Whether she was too ashamed to admit their liaison, or whether she remained silent out of concern for him, it made no difference, he reminded himself. They were of different worlds and it was best for both of them if they remained in those separate spheres.

He was in no very pleasant frame of mind when Flute greeted him at the door of his lodgings.

"I saw me old master," he said, his expression as sullen as Luke himself felt. "Had to nip 'round a corner so's he wouldn't spot me. I won't be able to work that crossing as sweeper no more. If he don't finger me for the reward, one of me old chums will."

Luke nodded heavily. "No, you mustn't risk it.

We'll find you something less visible to do, until the Runners have given over looking for you."

Flute's "master" was the head of a flash house, a den of thieves, from whom Luke had rescued the boy two years since. The scoundrel had never forgiven Flute for leaving, of course, and would snatch at a chance to make an example of him to the other boys.

"I could always go back to work for him again," Flute ventured, though without much enthusiasm. "He weren't as bad as some—didn't beat us unless we went two days in a row without bringing him brass, except when he was in his cups."

Luke supposed that, in comparison to his earlier life as a climbing boy, picking pockets had seemed a soft job to Flute. His master there was far more lenient than the old chimney sweep who'd forced him through the narrow, soot-filled pipes of London until Flute got too big for the task. But he wasn't about to let the boy go back—it would be an admission that he had failed him completely.

"Nonsense," he said with a heartiness he was far from feeling. "You've got some education now. Didn't I teach you to read and write? We'll find you something far better, though it may not pay as well at first."

"Aye, sir, we will." Flute grinned, his spirits reviving. The total confidence he showed in Luke's abilities was rather unnerving, outstripping Luke's own confidence substantially.

He tousled the lad's hair, laughing at his protests. "I've got some fair prospects now," he lied. "If I get the position I'm hoping for, I'll be able to hire you myself, as my manservant."

"Really, sir?"

Luke steeled himself against the eagerness in the boy's eyes. Somehow he had to make good on his words—and he would. "Really. So why don't you practice right now, by polishing these boots for me while we eat? I have a few more stops to make before nightfall."

Flute took to the task with enthusiasm, and Luke watched him for a moment before turning away to cut up bread and cheese for their simple midday meal. Despite his resolve to reform, he couldn't help thinking that one spectacular theft might be enough to set him—and Flute—up in relative comfort for a year or more.

Without Pearl his life had no meaning anyway. What was the point of integrity, after all, without her there to applaud it? And then there were all of the people who still desperately needed whatever help he could offer. Perhaps one last burglary would be worth the risk after all.

Handing Flute his plate, Luke sat down to plan while he ate.

Pausing to let Hettie slide one last pin into the cluster of curls on top of her head, Pearl listlessly thanked her and descended to the main parlor. Her spirits had gradually fallen over the past week as life returned to the same dull routine it had followed before her adventure and all that happened afterward. Rise, dress, eat, freshen up, receive callers . . .

No news had come about Luke's antecedents— not that she had really expected any yet. Entering the parlor, she was both pleased to see that she had only two callers, and irritated that those callers were two of her least favorite people.

"I give you good morning, Lord Bellowsworth, Lord Hardwyck," she greeted those most persistent suitors with what she hoped was enough cordiality to conceal her feelings about them. "Such a pleasure to see you here again."

"Lord Bellowsworth was just about to tell us some news from his cousin, about that investigation we discussed last week," Obelia informed her, her eyes rebuking Pearl for her tardiness.

About the tardiness she could not care in the least. But about the investigation . . . "Have they caught the Saint of Seven Dials, then, Lord Bellowsworth?" She was careful not to display undue interest, though her insides contracted in sudden fear.

Both gentlemen had risen at her entrance, but now they reseated themselves, one on either side of her.

"No, but they expect to have him within the week," Bellowsworth replied. "His henchman—the lad—was traced to Mayfair itself, if you will believe it. He was seen by several servants in Grosvenor Street, but their stories apparently conflict. Just yesterday, however, he was spotted working as a crossing sweeper near Covent Garden. One of the Runners is shadowing him even as we speak. As soon as he returns to his master, we'll have him!"

Lord Bellowsworth preened as though he himself were responsible for the all-but-certain capture. Pearl could only smile fixedly and pray that Luke—and Flute—were too clever to be caught so easily.

"I don't know why they bother, myself," drawled Lord Hardwyck, flicking an imaginary speck of dust from his pearl-gray glove. "Where's the real harm in the fellow, after all? He merely redistributes a few trifling bits of money or jewelry before Parliament can do so. And he gives the ladies an object of interest to swoon over."

He sent Pearl an indulgent smile, which she forced herself to return. Lord Hardwyck had always been insufferably condescending, toward her and other women. Just now, though, she preferred his viewpoint to that of Lord Bellowsworth.

"Besides," he continued, "if the man is caught, he'll become a martyr, I doubt not. How would ordinary fellows like ourselves glean any attention at all from the fair sex if he were being paraded about the city in irons?"

"You do yourselves a disservice, my lord, I am sure," exclaimed the Duchess. "Does he not, my dear?"

Thus appealed to, Pearl was obliged to agree. "Indeed. How could any woman of sense prefer a common thief—or even a legendary one—over men of rectitude and substance?"

Both men bowed, acknowledging the ladies' compliments, but Pearl scarcely noticed. Where might her thief be now? She yearned for him with every fiber of her being.

Just then, a cough at her elbow alerted her to the butler's presence. His expression implied a private matter, so she stood and followed him to the door of the parlor.

"Yes, Upwood, what is it?"

"I would not normally interrupt you, of course, my lady, but I was told you had given very explicit instructions. Young John Marley has completed the commission you gave him." As were most of the Oakshire servants, the butler was far too well trained to betray the curiosity he undoubtedly felt.

"Thank you, Upwood. Tell him to attend me in my private sitting room at once."

The butler bowed and left without another word.

Returning to the others, Pearl said, "I fear my abigail has had a small mishap with the gown I intended to wear to tonight's rout. I must choose another one at once, so that she will have time to purchase matching accessories. I know you will excuse me."

It rankled to give such a frivolous excuse, but in her excitement to hear what John Marley might have to say, she could think of nothing better. At once the gentlemen stood to take their leave, protesting that they had outstayed the customary quarter hour already. Obelia frowned, but made no objection, so Pearl was free to hurry up to her rooms.

There she found not only John Marley, but an elderly woman she had never seen before. Hettie was hovering nervously in the background.

"And who might this be?" Pearl asked, then immediately regretted her imperious tone. The old woman looked harmless enough—even kindly.

"Milady, I—I hope you'll forgive me," stammered the footman, "but I thought you would want to hear Mrs. Steadman's tale from her own lips. It's a rather remarkable one."

Pearl turned to the woman with interest. "Indeed? Pray, have a seat, Mrs. Steadman. I presume you have some connection to Luke St. Clair?"

The old woman walked with halting steps to the

nearest chair and eased her narrow frame into it with a sigh. "Aye, my lady, that I do. I were his nurse when he were a lad, and his mother's nurse before him, God rest her."

Eagerly, Pearl moved to the chair opposite her and leaned forward. "Then Mrs. Steadman, you are precisely the person I most wished to see! Surely you must know the truth about Mr. St. Clair's background."

Again the woman nodded. "Aye, that I do—more than he ever knowed himself, for his mother wished it that way. Now that he's a man grown, though, it's time he knew. It's that grateful I am that your man here came calling, for I hadn't the faintest idea how to go about finding the lad. You'll bring me to him, won't you, or tell him the news yourself?"

"Tell him what? What news?" Pearl could not quite conceal her impatience at the woman's meandering way of coming to the subject.

"Why, that his name weren't never St. Clair at all, though his mamma was born Sinclair. Master Luke's real last name is Knox, and he's the rightful Earl o' Hardwyck!"

Chapter 12

P earl stared at the old woman for several long heartbeats, certain she had misunderstood. "But . . . but the Earl of Hardwyck was just here. He was downstairs not five minutes ago. How can Luke possibly . . . ?"

"That would be his uncle," Mrs. Steadman said with a grimace. "Mr. Wallis Knox. He may think he's an earl now, but he's not. Lady Dorothea meant Luke to take his rightful place once he was grown, and I'll do all I can to help him do it."

"*Lady* Dorothea?"

The old nurse nodded. "Daughter to Earl Sinclair, she was, a lady from birth. It was enough to make a body weep to see her living like she did after she run away and all, but she had Master Luke to think of."

"I'm afraid I still don't understand." Indeed, Pearl felt the woman's rambling explanations were adding to the mystery rather than unraveling it. "Perhaps it would be best if you started at the beginning. Your mistress—Luke's mother—married the Earl of Hardwyck, and Luke was their son? This can be verified?"

"Oh, aye. It's all in the parish registry at Knox Abbey, the marriage and Master Luke's baptism, too."

And there must be copies of those records right here in London, Pearl realized. She could have those facts checked this very day.

"I remember both days like they was yesterday," Mrs. Steadman continued, her eyes growing misty with reminiscence. "So happy, my lady was! Just as well she didn't know then what was to come."

Again, Pearl had to fight her growing impatience to know everything at once. "And what *did* come? Her husband died, I presume?"

"Died!" The woman turned her head as if to spit, then recollected where she was and merely snorted. "Murdered, I'd say. And my lady believed the same, though she couldn't prove it. She had her proof a year later, though, when the blackguard tried to kill both her and Master Luke. What kind of a monster tries to do in a three-year-old child, I ask you?"

Though still not convinced of the old woman's sanity, Pearl could not help but be horrified. "Monstrous indeed! Who would do such a thing—and why? And how?"

The old nurse took each question in turn. "Who? Why, Mr. Wallis Knox, o' course, him what styles himself Earl of Hardwyck now. The why is plain to see. With his brother and Master Luke out of the way, it all come to him—the title, the money, and the land and all."

Pearl couldn't deny that Lord Hardwyck was generally considered one of the richest men in England, his fortune rivaling, perhaps even exceeding, her father's. A strong motivation indeed! Still, it seemed so unlikely. . . .

"And the how?" she prompted, as her informant had paused, apparently to commune with her memories.

Now a tear trickled down the lined, careworn face. "Fire. My lady couldn't bear to live in the grand mansion after her poor husband was murdered. Even then, she was afraid of Mr. Knox, I reckon. So she moved into the Dower House at Knox Abbey, seeing as how it was standing empty. She said it was plenty big for her and Master Luke, and only brought along me and one other servant."

Fearing the woman meant to go off on another tangent, Pearl gently brought her back to the matter that most concerned her. "The Dower House burned, then? How can you be certain it wasn't an accident?"

"I saw Cranley, Mr. Knox's henchman, skulking about the grounds only an hour before the fire started. I meant to tell my lady about it, but I forgot." Her wrinkled face crumpled into tears. "Maybe if I had . . ."

Pearl laid a gentle hand on her shoulder. "But Lady Hardwyck escaped, did she not, along with her son? Had you prevented the fire, perhaps another attempt would have been made—a successful one." As she spoke, she realized that she had nearly accepted the woman's story as truth.

Drying her eyes with the corner of her apron, the old nurse nodded. "Aye, you be right, milady. And Lady Dorothea seized her chance with both hands, as they say, once she realized what had happened. She bundled us all out of the house in the nick o' time. Mary, the housemaid, was up at the big house—helping with the brasses, I think she was. So it was just the three of us in the Dower House. We hid in the wood a quarter mile away and watched it burn to the ground."

Now Pearl began to understand. "So Lord . . . er, Mr. Knox never knew you all escaped?"

"Nay, she wanted him to think we was all dead, so's he wouldn't ever try to harm Master Luke again. She took us to a cottager whose baby she'd helped birth when the midwife couldn't come. They was willing enough to help us—giving us spare clothes and baby things, and promisin' to hold their tongues."

Pearl listened, rapt, as the old nurse related the rest of the story, of how Lady Dorothea had gone into hiding, masquerading as a commoner to protect her son. Finally, she brought it up to the point where Luke went off on his own after his mother's death and Mrs. Steadman lost track of him. By the time she was finished, more than an hour had passed.

Turning to Hettie and John, who had been listening as attentively as she to the astonishing story, Pearl said, "John, I have one more task for you. I will write a letter for you to take to Somerset House."

She would request documentation of the transfer of title and property to the present Lord Hardwyck, as well as all pertinent dates attending previous title holders. As he was known to be a suitor of hers, her request would not look particularly odd.

"And Hettie, ask the coachman to ready the small, closed carriage—the one without the crest. I have a visit to pay."

Luke returned from yet another discouraging day of seeking employment to see a sumptuous dark blue carriage standing in the narrow street directly in front of his building. It looked absurdly out of place, and his first thought was that some fool gentleman had lost his way. This might be the very opportunity for gain he had both hoped for and dreaded.

It might also be a trap. Suppose the Runners were trying to flush him out with this strange ruse? In that case the carriage was being watched, and the last thing he should do was approach it.

He glanced up and down the street, but saw no one other than a pair of drunkards slumbering in a doorway. Moving from shadow to shadow, he maneuvered himself into position to glimpse the interior of the carriage without attracting the attention of the coachman atop it. A lone figure sat within, apparently female. His heart beginning to hammer with a hope he could not quite admit, he crept closer.

Yes, the occupant was definitely female—but

short. Dropping back into the shadows, Luke circled around the side of his building until he could see his own door. There she stood—his own Pearl, the one who had haunted his dreams and daydreams since the moment he left her.

As he watched, her shoulders slumped in apparent dejection and she turned away from the door, her pale pink skirts brushing the filthy balustrade as she started back down the stairs. Now Luke stepped forward, his sudden eagerness sweeping caution away.

He met her at the first turning, and was able to observe her expression an instant before she saw him. He read there wariness, frustration, and suppressed excitement, which gave way to shock, then pleasure.

"Luke! Oh, Luke, you are here after all!"

Her obvious delight sent a shaft of exultation through him. Then, as quickly, he realized how he looked, dressed as he was to apply for more menial labor. And how inappropriate her presence here was.

"What are you doing here?" he demanded, more harshly than he had intended in his concern and embarrassment. "This is madness, my lady. The risk—"

"Was worth it," she assured him, though the joy in her eyes dimmed a fraction at his tone. "I have something to tell you—something extremely important. Will you join me in the carriage?"

He realized that she could hardly go alone with him into his lodgings, with two servants watching—much as they both might have preferred it. His body was already responding to her nearness, interfering with his ability to reason.

"Very well," he said, caution belatedly returning. This all seemed deucedly odd, but he could not believe Pearl would betray him. Not knowingly, anyway.

As they descended to the carriage, he again peered up and down the street. Was the shadow at that alley entrance a mere trick of the light, or was someone there? Suppose Pearl had been duped, so that she would lead the authorities to him?

Still, he did not have the strength of will to leave her, after being so depressingly certain he would never see her again. Whatever followed, he would have a few moments with her. Silently he accompanied her to the carriage, handed her into it, reveling in her touch, then climbed in himself. The moment the door was closed, she turned to him eagerly.

"Oh, Luke, I have the *best* news! I've discovered who you really are, and it is far better than I ever dared to hope!"

Distracted by her loveliness, her lips, her scent, despite Hettie's presence in the carriage, it took a moment for the meaning of her words to penetrate. "What do you mean?" he asked in sudden alarm, when they did. "How could you possibly—"

"I had inquiries made, in the vicinity of Edgeware. Something you no doubt could have done yourself, had you wished to." Though her words held a rebuke, her expression was still one of suppressed joy. "When you hear, you will wish you had done so years ago, I assure you!"

Luke doubted that, but her excitement was contagious. "Then tell me, do," he said with a smile. Sweet, valiant Pearl, so much more concerned for his welfare than her own. "And then," he added more severely, "we'll speak about the danger you courted in coming here."

Sweeping his scolding aside with an imperious wave of one dainty gloved hand, she placed the other on his sleeve. "I was able to find your old nurse, Mrs. Steadman," she explained.

Now she had his full attention, the very name bringing back a flood of memories he had suppressed for years. He listened while she related to him the story of his early years, events that predated those memories. Though she spoke with compelling conviction, he could not seem to make the story his own. Surely it must belong to someone else. Someone more . . . worthy.

"So you see," she concluded, "you are no more a commoner than I am. Indeed, your family is even older than mine, and nigh as wealthy. You are an Earl, Luke. A peer of the realm!"

Slowly, he shook his head. "It all sounds like something out of a novel—and Nanna was always fond of the novels my mother read to us. I fear you have been deluded by an equally deluded old woman."

She frowned, clearly disappointed that his enthusiasm did not equal hers. "I am having the verifiable facts checked, of course—the marriage and birth records, the fire. I couldn't believe it at first, either."

"Even if the circumstances turn out to be true, it doesn't follow that they relate to me. There can be no proof that I am who you say I am. Certainly I possess none."

"Mrs. Steadman was your nurse, was she not?" Pearl asked impatiently. "To whom else could they possibly relate?"

But Luke was not convinced. The very idea that he himself might be one of the class he had hated all his life was repugnant, and far too much to swallow at one bitter gulp.

"She might have read of it in the papers," he pointed out, quite reasonably, he thought. "She is old—her mind may not be what it was. She may have woven this pretty fiction from that story to comfort herself with the idea that she was once someone important."

"From what you've told me, it doesn't seem so terribly unlikely that your mother was a lady born. Are you unwilling to believe that of her?"

Pearl knew him far too well, he realized, her shrewd question having just the effect she'd hoped. No, he couldn't deny that his mother had always seemed out of place in her situation, nor that Nanna had called her "lady" from time to time, in private. If he had thought about it at all, he had assumed it was merely a gesture of respect.

"Of her, no. I am another matter, however. And even if all of this were true, there is still the matter of proof. Without that, my lot is unlikely to be affected by this revelation."

She stared at him. "You sound as though you don't *wish* to believe it is true. Are you so bent on despising the nobility that you feel compelled to reject the very possibility that you may be one of them?"

Again, her perception was disturbing in its acuity. "I've never despised *you*, Pearl," he said, ignoring the real purport of her question. "You know that."

"That's not what I meant, and you know it." The eager excitement in her eyes had turned to frustration and dismay, but he refused to share her hope. "Assuming the facts check out, as I am convinced they will, do you mean that you will make no attempt to reclaim your rightful place?"

"Rightful? If you knew the sort of life I have led . . ."

She placed her gloved hand over his bare one, distracting him again. The bond between them was as strong as ever. "I do know, Luke. You have told me, remember?"

But he shook his head. "Only the generalities, not the specifics." Even now, he writhed inwardly to remember some of the things he had done. "I'm no hero, Pearl, believe me—nor even a fit object for your pity."

"Pity?" She released his hand as though it burned her. "Do you think that is what I feel for you? Pity? That I'm doing this out of some sort of charitable concern for the poor, misunderstood Saint—"

She broke off, apparently remembering Hettie's presence, though the maid made no indication that she heard the slip. Eyes downcast, she seemed to be doing her best to appear invisible and uninterested, but Luke was sure she was absorbing every word. How much had Pearl told the girl? He had Flute's safety as well as his own to consider.

"I think you are grateful that I was able to assist you when you made your ill-advised foray into the backstreets of London," he said dampingly. If her abigail did not already know of their liaison, she

would not discover it from him. "You thought this
would be a fitting way to repay me, and I thank
you. But it is up to me what I do with the knowledge."

Pearl swallowed visibly. Unshed tears glittered in
her eyes, tearing at his heart. He wanted to kiss
them away, to fold her in his arms and assure her
that she was the most precious thing in the world to
him. Instead, he steeled himself with the reminder
that he was in no way worthy of her, even if her unlikely tale turned out to be true. The choices he had
made put her forever out of his reach.

"Surely you cannot wish to continue in a life
of . . . of the sort you have been leading?" Her voice
quavered, but did not break. "What of poor Flute?
And what of your uncle, enjoying his ill-gotten
gains at the expense of your father's death and your
mother's suffering? If anyone merits your
vengeance, surely he does."

He felt his resolve beginning to waver. But was it
because of the strength of her reasoning or the
strength of his feelings for her? "I'm sorry, Pearl,"
he forced himself to say. "I must go—and so must
you. You are not safe here."

Not safe from the inhabitants of Seven Dials . . .
or from him. Before he could change his mind, he
stepped out of the carriage.

Pearl extended a pleading hand. "Luke, please—"

"Farewell, my lady." He took her outstretched
hand and lifted it briefly to his lips, then turned
quickly and walked away, not even caring what direction he took.

For a moment he feared that she might follow

him, but he heard no sound of pursuit, neither footsteps nor carriage wheels. Still, he quickened his pace. He needed time to think, to decide, perhaps to plan a course of action, away from Pearl's intoxicating presence.

Pearl sat for several long moments in stunned disbelief. She had been so certain Luke would forget his prejudices upon learning he was himself a peer. His difficulties—their difficulties—would be solved. He could return to her world. . . .

Yes, she now had to admit what she had managed to conceal from herself before. Her motives had never been entirely selfless. She wanted Luke to come back to her, to become a part of her life. To experience again—

But he had rejected that life. Rejected *her*. Suddenly overwhelmed by the enormity of her failure, she covered her face with her hands and wept.

"Oh, my lady, pray do not cry," Hettie exclaimed, putting a gentle hand on her shaking shoulder. "He's not worth it—no man is. An ungrateful wretch, that's what he is, after all you tried to do for him."

Pearl's head snapped up. "You do not know him. Don't pass judgment on him."

Hettie blinked, and at once Pearl apologized. "I do appreciate your concern, Hettie, but I shall be fine." That quick burst of anger had not been without effect, however, for it had supplanted her despair. Now she could think again—and plan.

Opening the panel on top of the carriage, she directed the coachman to drive back to Oakshire House. Luke St. Clair was much mistaken if he believed Lady Pearl Moreston would admit defeat so easily. She could be every bit as stubborn as he.

Luke walked the streets for hours, but when he returned to his lodgings to find Pearl's carriage gone, he was no closer to a decision than he had been when he left—except one. If what she claimed was true, and the man styling himself as Lord Hardwyck was really responsible for Luke's father's death and his mother's poverty, then that would have to be repaid somehow.

But how? After sending Pearl away so brusquely, would he ever know the truth? She had admitted she had no proof beyond Nanna's word as yet, and it was entirely possible no such proof existed. Even if it did, and Pearl obtained it, she would see no point in telling him now.

Flute opened the door before he could fit the key into the lock. "I'm glad you're back, sir. Something havey-cavey is going on. Not ten minutes ago, this was slipped under the door." He handed Luke an envelope. "I reckon the Runners must know we're here."

Turning the envelope over, Luke read the one-word inscription and smiled ruefully. "No, not the Runners, but someone every bit as persistent." He broke the seal, as recognizable as the hand that had written his name, and read through the letter twice.

Pearl had already obtained the proof she sought, corroborating Mrs. Steadman's story. Wealth and influence could always speed the wheels of bureaucracy, he thought cynically. Had he requested the same information, it doubtless would have taken months, had it been granted at all.

Pearl now had in her possession documents attesting to the marriage of James Knox, Earl of Hardwyck, and Lady Dorothea Sinclair, daughter of Earl Sinclair. Also records of the birth and baptism of one Luke Hartwood Knox, their son, and heir to the earldom.

Luke closed his eyes. As though it were yesterday, he could hear the dreaded middle name on his mother's lips, letting him know yet another childhood escapade had been discovered. The birth date listed was his own.

It was true, then. He really was a member of the very class he had despised all his life. If he could find a way to prove his identity, he would have wealth, influence, even a seat in the House of Lords. He *could* become as vain, pompous, proud, and shallow as any of them. Or he could throw this letter away and pretend nothing had changed at all.

But then he thought about his mother, and the father he had never known. What kind of life might he have led, if both had lived? His mother—and Pearl—were proof that blue blood did not preclude strength of character. Would he have been able to rise above a privileged state and become a worthwhile human being? He would never know. The chance had been denied him—by one man.

"Should we escape out the window?" asked Flute worriedly. "Or do you think they'll be watching for that? Are we done for, sir?"

Brought back to the present, Luke smiled grimly. "Not yet, Flute. Not quite. But if I have anything to say to it, someone else may be. What do you know about the Earl of Hardwyck?"

Flute blinked in confusion. "Not much, sir. Only

that he's one of the richest swells in England. Wouldn't know him to look at, though. Why?"

"Then he no doubt lives in one of the biggest houses in London. Let's find out which one. It would seem I have a score to settle with him."

Chapter 13

Pearl had not the slightest desire to attend the Countess Lieven's rout, but knew Obelia would never believe the excuse of another headache. Besides, if she stayed home she would only give herself a real one, stewing over Luke's shortsightedness that afternoon and her own thwarted desires. Better to get out and distract herself as far as was possible.

"My lady, you are a vision. That color particularly becomes you," Hettie informed her as she handed Pearl a pale green fan that perfectly matched her gown. "See for yourself." She positioned the pier glass so that Pearl could observe her entire ensemble at once.

She barely glanced at her reflection. What did it matter, after all? "Thank you, Hettie," she said ab-

sently. "You've done a wonderful job, as always."
She headed for the door, forcing her abigail to trot
after her to toss a silver lace shawl over her shoulders before she left the room.

The Duke and Duchess awaited her below, where
they were to have a family dinner before departing
for the rout. Both echoed Hettie's opinion that she
looked particularly lovely tonight, and she thanked
them automatically. Odd, that her exterior should
be so unaffected by the wretchedness within, she reflected, picking at the lobster bisque before her.

By the time they reached the Russian Embassy,
Pearl had roused herself somewhat. She had no desire to appear so preoccupied that people would
question her about it. Therefore, she greeted the
Ambassador and his wife with the graciousness
trained into her almost from the cradle.

"You have outdone yourself, Countess Lieven,"
she exclaimed as she passed through the receiving
line at the top of the grand staircase. "I had no idea
so many hothouse flowers could be had in all of
London so early in the Season."

"One merely needs to know whom to ask,"
replied the Countess in her beautifully accented
English. "Flowers are a passion of mine, so I have
made it my business to know where the best are to
be found, at any time of year."

Unfortunately, that brought to Pearl's mind a vision of Covent Garden market, with its masses of
flowers. She managed to refrain from asking if those
she saw here had come from that source—so close
to Luke.

Moving into the main ballroom, she could not
help scanning the assemblage for the one face she

knew would not be present. Instead, she spotted the man responsible for his absence—Lord Hardwyck, who was in truth no lord at all. Seized by a fit of perversity, she moved in his direction.

He saw her before she could speak, and bowed deeply. "If this was your second choice of attire for the evening, my lady, I must express my appreciation to your abigail for her clumsiness," he said by way of greeting.

For a moment she was confused, then recalled the excuse she had used to escape him and Lord Bellowsworth that morning. "The mishap was less than I feared. Merely a torn flounce, easily repaired," she replied easily. "Would that all injuries were so easily put right."

As he could have no suspicion that she knew the truth, her veiled barb had no effect.

"Indeed. And would that an unblemished gown could make all women beauties. Though your ensemble is lovely, you would outshine every woman here were you clad in homespun, my lady. You are perfection itself." His dark eyes were disturbingly similar to Luke's, but with none of the same warmth. Before she could stop him, he seized her hand and brought it to his lips.

Vividly reminded of Luke doing the same that very afternoon, Pearl had all she could do not to snatch her hand away.

"Perfection surely entails more than fine clothes or a pretty face, my lord." Her tongue nearly stumbled over the undeserved title. "I would far rather be admired for character—a rarer commodity."

He smiled. "Character can only be appreciated upon closer acquaintance. I would deem it an honor to be granted the opportunity to understand yours, Lady Pearl."

"In some cases, greater knowledge of a person reveals rather a lack of character," she informed him. "Or even a lack of integrity."

"Certainly it is lamentable when such is the case," he agreed, "but I have no fear it might prove so in yours."

The man's complacency nettled her further. Did he feel no shame whatsoever for what he had done years before?

"You would be equally willing, then, to open your own character to examination?" she could not resist asking, watching for some chink in his polished veneer.

"A dull study, no doubt, but I would never deny you anything you deemed a pleasure, my lady. Shall we retire into one of the anterooms to commence this closer acquaintanceship you suggest?" He extended an arm to her expectantly.

Appalled, Pearl realized belatedly that he had interpreted her digs as flirtation. The last thing she wished was to be alone with this man.

"I think not," she replied icily. "I merely spoke hypothetically. Excuse me—I believe my father wants me."

As the Duke had his back to them, it was clearly a fabricated excuse, and therefore an insult. Lord Hardwyck's eyes narrowed with an unpleasant glitter, but he only said, "Later, then, my lady."

Inclining her head slightly when she would have preferred to cut him entirely, Pearl moved away, silently resolving to be more careful in the future. She should have known that a man who could cold-bloodedly plan the murder of his brother, sister-in-law, and infant nephew would be impervious to any verbal slings she could cast his way. After more than twenty years, he must feel so secure in his position that he feared no retribution.

Surely, now that he had her letter detailing the proof, Luke could not allow those crimes—crimes against him, against his parents—to go unpunished?

She would give Luke a few days to do the right thing, she decided, difficult as it might be to refrain from taking a hand in things herself. But she was determined that the false Lord Hardwyck should not profit from his crimes for longer than that. If Luke would not act, she would—whatever the personal cost.

Luke stood outside the glow cast by the numerous lamps leading up to the entrance of his uncle's mansion and gazed at the impressive edifice. On the very edge of Mayfair, with a view of Green Park, Hardwyck Hall dominated an area replete with grand houses.

For a moment, Luke could not help thinking that this magnificent place might well be legally his. He tried to imagine what it would be like to be master of such a place, and country estates besides—and failed utterly.

The very idea of such wealth, combined with the overwhelming responsibility that accompanied it, oppressed him. No, he wanted to make the owner of all of this pay for what he had done, but he had no wish to take his place.

"Stay here and watch the street," he instructed

Flute. "I'll go around to the back and find a way in. Give the usual signal if you have any reason to believe I've been detected." Flute could do an admirable impression of a screech owl.

Just now, though, the lad clearly had reservations. "I thought we weren't going to be stealin' no more, sir. And we ain't never tried breakin' into a place as grand as this. There'll be guards and such, surely?"

"I'm touched by your concern, but don't worry. I'm not planning to steal anything this time—just do a bit of exploring." Before Flute could ask the obvious question, Luke left him, to slip around the corner of the walled sweep of lawn fronting the street.

The back of the house held the usual gardens, mews, and stables, if on a rather larger scale than most town houses. At this hour, no one was about but a stableboy, whistling noisily as he scoured an oat bucket. The master of the house was likely out for the evening and probably wouldn't be back for several hours, from what Luke knew of *ton* habits. With any luck, the servants would be taking it easy.

He flitted around the far side of the stables, then along the edge of the back gardens until he reached the house itself. Pausing in the deep, fragrant shadow cast by an apple tree in blossom, he examined the lowest windows on that side of the house— the ones leading to areas only servants would inhabit. The late April evening was warm, and more than one ground-floor window stood open, as did most of the upper ones.

He chose the window nearest the corner. It was open, dark, and its iron-fenced well was amply screened by shrubbery. Moving silently, he hopped over the low iron railing and crouched in the window well to peer inside. All he could see was a slit of faint light from a doorway on the far side of whatever room this was. Good enough. The window was just large enough to admit him with a squeeze.

Dropping into the dark room, he identified bags and crates by feel. A storeroom, then, probably close to the kitchens. Peering through the slightly opened door, he saw a dimly lit hallway, deserted for the moment. Quickly he slipped out of the storeroom and crept to the stairway at one end. A smaller set of stairs led off to one side, and he took those, hoping they might lead to a secret panel in one of the upper rooms, as the servants' stairs in Oakshire House had done.

They did. The first panel door he found led into an ostentatious dining room with a brilliantly polished table that would easily seat twenty people. Nothing here interested him, however, so he closed the panel and moved on. Next he came to the library. A quick check of the desk revealed only writing paper and pens—nothing of a personal or business nature. Glancing around at the hard leather chairs and undisturbed bookshelves, he concluded that Hardwyck rarely used the room.

Going up another flight of stairs, Luke tried another panel. This one led into an elegant parlor, revealed only by exterior lamplight filtering in through the tall windows. Tired of this hit-or-miss exploring, he crossed the room and cautiously cracked open the door there, to discover a large passageway, well lit by sconces set at intervals along the walls, stretching in either direction.

Still moving softly, wary of servants, he traversed the corridor, peeking into rooms along the way. These were the public rooms, and included among other things a music room, a ballroom even larger than that at Oakshire House, and a gallery hung with at least two dozen portraits. He couldn't resist a quick exploration of the latter.

The first few portraits were very old, their subjects wearing costumes from fifty, one hundred, or even two hundred years earlier. Luke gave them only a cursory look. Even knowing that these people might well be his own ancestors, he felt no particular connection to them. He moved on to more recent paintings.

And stopped, stunned.

There, staring out of a canvas halfway along the gallery, was his mother, just as he remembered her—except for the elaborate gown she wore. If Pearl's letter had not been proof enough that Nanna's tale was true, this portrait convinced him beyond doubt. Below the painting was a brass plaque which read, "Lady Dorothea Hardwyck, 1791." One year after he himself had been born.

He then glanced at the next portrait and received an even greater shock. Except for the clothing and hair, longer and lighter than his own, he might have been looking at his own reflection! Yes, according to the plaque, this was his father, the fourth Earl of Hardwyck, painted the same year as his mother's portrait.

Here, then, was all the proof he would need, should he do as Pearl wished and press his claim to the title. And perhaps the means to his revenge, as well.

For a moment he struggled with himself, assailed by all of the advantages Pearl had put forth to him that afternoon. But then sanity prevailed, and he again considered the obligations that went with such a position: lands, tenants, even a seat in Parliament. Simple Luke St. Clair, responsible pillar of Society? Preposterous!

Even as he renewed his original decision, he heard footsteps in the passage outside the gallery. Quick as thought, he pressed himself into an alcove behind a piece of marble statuary. The footsteps neared, then receded. Whoever it was had not come into the gallery.

He waited until he heard a door open and close, then stole back down the corridor to the parlor he had first entered. Retracing his steps, in five minutes he was climbing back through the storeroom window into the cooler evening air. Flute was waiting where he had left him, across the street from the grand front of Hardwyck Hall.

"Did you find what you were looking for, sir?" Clearly, he still found Luke's behavior odd.

"I did indeed, even though I had no idea when I went in what it was I sought." A slow smile spread over his face as the idea that had first occurred to him while standing before his father's portrait took clearer shape. "How would you like to help me become a ghost?"

Flute stared at him in dismay. "Are you asking me to turn you in for the reward money? I won't do it, sir, and that's flat. I'd rather starve first."

Luke gave a shout of laughter, then realized it wouldn't do to draw attention to himself. "No, no, nothing like that, lad, I promise you. I don't mean to become a *real* ghost. Let's head back to my lodgings, and I'll explain as we go."

Quickly, he outlined his plan, which involved obtaining an ensemble similar to the one in the portrait. His hair was too short and dark for the part, so he'd need a wig as well, several shades lighter.

"If I play my part well," he concluded, "Lord Hardwyck will either believe his house is haunted or that he's gone mad. Either way, I daresay I can convince him to do whatever I wish inside of a week."

"But . . . but why, sir? Why this particular nob? And why would he have a picture in his house what looks so much like you? Is he some kind of kin to you?"

"I always knew you were a sharp lad, Flute. Yes, I believe this fellow to be my uncle. Further, I believe he may have killed my father, years and years ago." Luke debated whether or not to tell him the rest, but Flute was already ahead of him.

"If your uncle's a lord, then what does that make you, sir? You're one o' *them*, ain't you?"

For a moment Luke wished he hadn't been quite so vocal about his hatred of the nobility. Clearly Flute had picked up more of his attitude than he had realized over the past two years.

"It looks like I may be, yes. But that's neither here nor there," he added quickly, before Flute could speak. "This earl is one of the worst of the lot, and I want to make him pay for what he's done. Will you help me?"

Flute considered for a moment, then nodded, his thin face breaking into an impish grin. "Aye, I'll help. Thinking how much you done for me and others as a nobody—so to speak—I'll trust you to do what's right and more, once you've got brass and some clout."

Luke frowned. That was too similar to what Pearl had said, for his comfort. Was he going to be pressured by Flute as well? "I don't want to be one of them," he said dampingly. "I just want to give this one what he deserves. That's all. Still willing?"

"Oh, aye." Flute sobered a bit, but his eyes lost none of their twinkle. "Whatever you say, sir. What do we do first?"

By the end of the next day, Luke had everything he needed and once again stood watching Hardwyck House.

"If I didn't know better, I'd think you were a ghost myself, sir," Flute whispered. "Look! Here comes the carriage. It'll only be a moment now."

Luke nodded, the curls of the powdered light brown wig brushing the ruffles of his antique shirt where they billowed out of the equally archaic coat. He felt as though he were about to step onstage. "There he goes. Come."

They both followed the same route Luke had used the night before. Though a light drizzle was falling, the storeroom window was still ajar. From a dark corner of the gardens, Luke pointed. "That's the window, there. You know what to do, if anyone is about later?"

Flute nodded. "I'll make sure their attention is on the other side of the house, not to worry. Two in the morning, you said?"

"That should be enough for the first night, yes. I'll see you then." Slipping from the shadows, Luke

crept to the house, hopped over the railing, and
again let himself in through the window, taking care
to leave it just as he found it.

Perhaps he should have left Flute out of this entirely, he thought as he continued the explorations
he'd begun the night before. Certainly he could
have handled this himself. But acting as lookout
made the lad feel useful, and kept him out of more
substantial trouble, as well. He'd have to give some
serious thought as to what Flute could do once this
caper was over. He was bright enough to get bored
easily, and that was dangerous, as Luke knew from
long experience.

Deep in thought, making no sound in his soft-
soled slippers, he drifted around a corner and came
face-to-face with a young housemaid dusting a set
of Grecian urns. Her mouth formed a perfect O and
her eyes went wide and wild. For several long
heartbeats, they stood still, staring at each other,
then she took a quick step backward.

Instinctively, Luke reached out with one hand to
reassure the terrified girl, but before he could speak,
she let out a shriek, whirled, and ran. Belatedly, he
realized that speaking or touching her would have
ruined the effect. Before she could bring any witnesses, he ducked back around the corner and
through the nearest door, into what appeared to be a
bedchamber.

He checked the wall near the fireplace, hoping to
find another hidden door to the servants' passages,
but without success. Turning, he examined the
room by the dim light filtering in through the partially curtained windows, searching for a suitable
hiding place. Only as he secreted himself behind the

voluminous bedcurtains did he notice the ornate initials carved on the mahogany headboard: *JLK*. Had this been his father's room at one time, then? Perfect.

Before he could consider how to put that interesting tidbit to use, he heard heavy footsteps in the corridor, coming closer.

". . . too many sweetmeats last night," came a male voice. "Mrs. Duggin warned you about that. Dreaming, you were."

"No! I truly saw it! From another age, he was, floating inches off the floor, with eyes like dark fire. Looked right through me, they did—then he reached for me, never making a sound."

Luke smiled silently at the housemaid's description, far better than anything he could have devised. Imagination was a wonderful thing. The door to the chamber opened then, and he held perfectly still, barely daring to breathe. The faint glow of a candle penetrated the heavy draperies surrounding him.

"See? Nothing here, either," said the male voice. "If any room was going to be haunted, it would be this one."

Luke's ears pricked at this, and he was glad when the maid asked, "Why?"

Unfortunately, the male servant did not explain, but merely said, "If no one's told you the story, it's not my place to do so. Come, let's go back to the kitchens. I'll have Mrs. Duggin fix you a cup of something to calm your nerves, and you can work downstairs for the rest of the evening."

The door closed, leaving Luke in darkness and little wiser than he'd been before. Now he was sure, though, that this had been his father's room. And it appeared that at least some of the Hardwyck servants knew his death had been untimely, if not unnatural. He smiled grimly.

This first encounter had been accidental, but had turned out exactly as he might have wished. No doubt the housemaid would tell the story of what she'd seen to every other servant in the house. They'd be on the lookout now, but they would also be predisposed to terror—just the atmosphere he needed to carry off his plan.

A more thorough search revealed a hidden door on the wall opposite the fireplace, leading into the servants corridor. Deciding he'd done enough for one evening, Luke waited half an hour, then made his way back to the storeroom and out of the house. Flute was surprised to see him so soon, but he quickly explained that they'd be back the next night—and the next.

"For how long, sir? You're sure to be caught eventually if you keep breaking into the same house."

"For as long as it takes," he replied. "But less than a week, I hope. I'll simply play it by ear. Meanwhile, I have a different task for you. I need to find out what the servants are saying about their ghost, and how far and how fast the rumors spread."

"Can do, sir!" Flute exclaimed eagerly. Ferreting out information had always been a specialty of his, and he took pride in it.

"Good man. Now let's rest up. We've got several interesting nights ahead of us."

After her last encounter with Lord Hardwyck, Pearl would have preferred never to see the man again. But chance, or fate, seemed to have other ideas. Two days since, she had nearly bumped into him while shopping on Bond Street. Last night he had attended the same two functions at the same times she had, though she had avoided any interaction beyond a nod of greeting.

And now, tonight, Obelia had joined with perverse fate by actually inviting Hardwyck to accompany them to the theater. Conversation with him would be virtually impossible to avoid. Pearl whetted her tongue, determined to say and imply only what she intended this time, as they approached Covent Garden.

The environs reminded her vividly of Luke, though this was a different theater. His lodgings, however, were only a few streets away. Four days had passed since she had spoken with him, sent her letter. What had he been doing all this time?

"I give you good evening, my lady," Lord Hardwyck greeted her as she stepped from the ducal carriage. Was it her imagination, or did the man appear on edge—even nervous?

"Lord Hardwyck." The very name on her lips seemed a betrayal of Luke. She stepped back while he exchanged greetings with the Duke and Duchess, then reluctantly placed her fingertips on his outstretched arm to follow them into the theater.

"I apologize if I somehow offended you a few nights since, my lady," he said quietly as they walked. "It was unintentional, I assure you."

She slid a sideways glance at him. "Your offense to me was but trifling," she said. "Far worse things are done by man to fellow man every day, or so I hear."

Now there was no mistaking his nervousness. "You hear? What do you hear, my lady?"

"Rumors. Only rumors," she replied lightly, though she watched him closely now. He appeared to realize he was staring at her intently, for he shifted his gaze away.

"Rumors can be oddly distorted, especially at a distance of years," he murmured, so low she barely caught the words. "I try not to put stock in them, myself."

Something had brought his old crimes to mind, that was clear. Might that something have been Luke? "A wise policy for one's peace of mind, no doubt," she responded noncommittally.

He shot a sharp glance her way, but said nothing more, instead quickening his pace to close the gap with the Duke and Duchess, who were now some way ahead.

With what Pearl could only consider true poetic justice, the play they had come to see was *Hamlet*. Though Hardwyck made only the idlest of conversation, seeming to prefer now to speak with Obelia rather than herself, Pearl could not help watching him closely as the play progressed.

As the spirit told Hamlet of "murder most foul," Lord Hardwyck shifted uncomfortably in his seat. And when Hamlet exclaimed to his father's ghost, "O my prophetic soul! mine uncle!" he flinched visibly.

Pearl smiled inwardly. Whether or not something had occurred previously to remind him of the events of the past, this production was bringing it home to him forcefully, it was clear. The moment the curtain fell for the first intermission, he rose.

"I cannot thank you enough, Your Graces, for the invitation," he said, though he spoke so absently that it seemed he scarcely knew what he was saying. "Pray forgive me, but it seems something I ate at dinner has disagreed with me. I fear I must take my leave early tonight."

Obelia was all concern, recommending a particular potion she had found effective against dyspepsia. "An unsettled stomach is such a misery, my lord. We will hope you feel better directly, once you reach home, will we not?" She appealed to Pearl and her husband.

"I'm certain that will be the case," Pearl said with a smile. "The source of the irritation will likely be removed the moment you leave the theater."

With a frown of comprehension, barely even waiting to acknowledge the Duke's halfhearted echoing of his wife's wish for his recovery, Hardwyck fairly fled the box.

At once, Obelia rounded on Pearl. "It's clear you said or did something to offend him. What was it?"

Pearl stared her innocence. "I did nothing, I assure you, Your Grace. I thought he seemed . . . disturbed by the play, but no doubt it was merely the indigestion."

"Leave the girl alone, my love," the Duke advised his Duchess. "Hardwyck always was an odd duck—never trusted him above half, myself."

Obelia seemed about to protest this characterization, but at that point a group of acquaintances descended upon the box to pay their respects, effectively distracting her. Pearl nodded and smiled as was proper, but her thoughts were on Lord Hardwyck's strange behavior. If it wasn't absurd, she would almost have thought he seemed frightened. What *had* Luke been doing?

Wallis Knox, Lord Hardwyck, fit a key into his front door with shaking fingers. The bottle of wine he had consumed at his club after leaving the theater had not calmed his nerves as much as he'd hoped. His phlegmatic butler, along with most of the other servants, had given notice that morning, forcing him to the unaccustomed task of opening the door himself.

Going to see *Hamlet* tonight had been a mistake. He realized that now. He'd always detested the play, and had anyone but the Duchess of Oakshire issued the invitation he would certainly have refused. Especially with so many old memories recently stirred up by these ridiculous "sightings."

As yet, he himself had seen no sign of the alleged ghost. Still, he found it hard to convince himself that four different servants had independently conjured the same apparition. The focus had been James's old bedroom, and the descriptions had matched the portrait in the gallery—the one that had been painted only a month before his brother's death.

He paused in the library for a brandy, downing it quickly before heading for his bed. Though he had never been a superstitious man, Hardwyck now climbed the main staircase with dread prickling along the back of his neck.

At the top of the stairs, he turned to go to his own rooms. Cranley, his personal manservant, would still be here, at least. But then he paused, glancing down the hallway in the other direction. Had he heard something there? For a moment, he half fancied the door to his brother's old room had just snicked shut.

Taking a deep breath, he forced himself to walk to the door of James's room. It was closed. For a long moment he stood there, debating. He was no silly housemaid, he reminded himself, but one of the most influential men in all of England. He turned the handle and pushed open the door.

There it stood, in the very center of the room, just as the servants had described it—an apparition dressed in the style of the end of the last century. As he stared, his brain refusing to accept the evidence of his eyes, its mouth opened and it actually spoke to him, in sepulchral tones.

"Hello . . . Brother."

Chapter 14

T he look on Hardwyck's face alone was worth the last few nights of skulking, Luke decided. For a moment, he thought the man might faint dead away or expire from shock, but then he seemed to rally slightly. He opened and closed his mouth several times before any sound emerged.

"Wh-what do you want?" The question, when it finally came, was barely more than a whisper.

"Justice," Luke replied in the voice he'd been practicing all morning. Flute had assured him it sounded sufficiently ghostly. He watched the emotions playing across his opponent's face in the dim light—fear, disbelief, cunning. This man was almost certainly his nearest living relative, yet Luke felt nothing but a rather dispassionate disgust toward him.

Hardwyck swallowed a few times, then asked, "But how? You are already dead."

Luke had his answer ready. "Truth. The whole truth." He didn't dare anything longer, for fear Hardwyck might penetrate his disguise.

"Truth? About . . . what I did?" Hardwyck glanced over his shoulder, as though considering fleeing.

Luke waited until he had the man's full attention again, then slowly, emphatically nodded. "Truth," he repeated.

"I . . . I only have to tell you? And then you'll leave me alone? Leave this house?"

Again Luke nodded. He had a few ideas for how he might use whatever information he gained, but they didn't involve playing ghost again.

"Very well," said Hardwyck. "It *would* be almost a relief—" He cleared his throat, declining to finish that thought. "Your death wasn't the accident everyone believed. I had debts—gaming debts. I knew—" Again he broke off. "I cut the cinch on your saddle, the morning of your last hunt. Whether you were killed or only injured, I knew I'd have access to the books, at least for long enough to pay off my debts. I . . . never gambled again, for whatever it's worth."

But Luke wanted more than that. "Dorothea," he said.

Hardwyck flinched as though he'd been struck. "How could you . . . ? Did she . . . ?" He glanced around the room, as though expecting yet another spirit to materialize.

Through valiant effort, Luke kept his lips from twitching. He merely waited, impassive.

"Very well," said Hardwyck in a rush. "Yes. I'm

guilty there, as well. Once you were dead, I decided if I was in for a penny, I might as well be in for a pound. I had Cranley burn down the Dower House, with your wife and son inside. He's made me pay dearly for his silence all these years, too, I can tell you."

Luke slowly raised one arm to point at Hardwyck where he stood, trembling and pasty-faced. "Guilty," he pronounced.

Hardwyck's eyes widened. "What . . . what . . . ?"

"Guilty!" Luke repeated, more loudly, taking a step toward his uncle.

"I . . . but . . ." Luke took another step, and Hardwyck abruptly lost his nerve. Letting out an absurdly high-pitched shriek, he turned and fled. A moment later, Luke heard Hardwyck's voice from down the hall. "Cranley! Get up. Pack my things. We're leaving London at once. Never mind why— just do it."

Luke stood where he was for a moment, chuckling quietly to himself. Then he whisked through the hidden door, to take the servants' passage back to his exit through the storeroom. His work here was finished—for now.

"Left Town?" Pearl asked Hettie in surprise. "What do you mean? Why?"

Her abigail shrugged. "Word is, he lit out for the country in the middle of the night, night before last. I thought you'd want to know, but I don't know anything else, beyond the rumors."

"Rumors? What sort of rumors?"

Hettie looked uncomfortable. "I don't usually listen to such foolishness, mind you. But it's certain that the day before he left, most of his servants quit his employ. Belowstairs gossip was that Hardwyck Hall is haunted."

This was so unexpected, Pearl nearly laughed. "Haunted? You're saying *ghosts* drove Lord Hardwyck out of London?"

"*I'm* not saying," Hettie corrected her hastily. "I'm just telling you what the rumors are saying."

Pearl sobered. "I can well believe his guilt might have induced him to imagine vengeful apparitions . . . but not that others would have seen them as well. Perhaps he went suddenly mad, and that frightened the servants."

Hettie shrugged again, unhelpfully. "It seems as good an explanation as any," she conceded.

For a long moment, Pearl considered. She had still had no word whatsoever from Luke. It appeared that he intended to do nothing with the information she had given him. Even now he might be falling back into a life of crime, out of habit or necessity. But with Hardwyck out of London, she should be able to help Luke with minimal risk of retribution from his uncle—the main thing that had held her back before.

"Send John Marley to fetch Mrs. Steadman," she told Hettie with sudden decision. "And check to see whether my father will be free at any time this afternoon. It is time justice was done."

Two hours later, having heard all of the old nurse's story, the Duke shook his head. "It's a damning tale, I grant you. I've never cared for the fellow personally, but the law will want more than one person's twenty-year-old recollections to bring a charge of murder, particularly against someone of Lord Hardwyck's stature."

"I have already checked the available records, Father." Pearl pushed the letters she'd received from Somerset House across the top of the massive desk. "Marriage dates, birth and death dates—they dovetail with Mrs. Steadman's story in every particular."

The Duke looked over the documents and nodded. "That is something, at least. But why are you doing this, Pearl? Where is Mr. St. Clair, or di Santo, or whatever he calls himself? Why does he not press his own case?"

"He seems . . . reluctant to put himself forward," she replied. "To be honest, I suspect he may be intimidated by the responsibility such a position would entail. He was not raised to it, you see, not knowing the truth until very recently."

"What of this Italian uncle of his? Some relation of his mother's?"

"I believe so," Pearl agreed cautiously. Her father, of course, knew nothing of Luke's recent life. The old nurse's story ended shortly after his mother's death. "He put Luke, er, Mr. St. Clair through Oxford, on condition he take his name."

Mrs. Steadman regarded her confusedly, but did not contradict her, to her relief.

"Hmph. Dashed queer business, if you ask me," said the Duke, knitting his bushy brows. "How will your Mr. St. Clair prove his identity? Is there any physical evidence to back up these accusations? The College of Heralds will insist on more than hearsay, my dear, I assure you."

Pearl bit her lip. Luke had offered these same objections, but she had swept them away, assuming he was merely reluctant to take his place among the class he so despised. Before she could confess she had no answer, Mrs. Steadman spoke.

"What sort of proof might you need, Yer Grace? I have Lady Dorothea's diaries, as well as a trinket or two she left to me."

The Duke's brows rose. "Do you have the items here, madam?"

Mrs. Steadman nodded. While Pearl stared at her in surprise, she fumbled through the pockets of her cloak and finally drew out two small leather volumes. Then she unpinned a brooch from her own homespun gown and laid it on the table beside the diaries. "Will these help?" she asked.

Though she itched to have a look herself, Pearl forced herself to sit patiently while her father leafed through the diaries in silence, then picked up and examined the brooch. "This is the Hardwyck crest," he commented.

"Aye, Lady Dorothea's husband gave it to her when they was wed. She never took it off, except to sleep."

He returned to his perusal of the diaries. "These corroborate the story you have told. But I assume you knew that. You didn't, by chance, get your story from these writings?"

The old woman pinkened under the Duke's shrewd gaze. For a moment, Pearl's confidence wavered. Could it all be a sham?

But, "Nay, Yer Grace," Mrs. Steadman replied. "I'm not much of one for readin', though Lady Dorothea did try to teach me. Just never took to it, except to learn to sign my name and such."

"I see." The Duke's expression softened into a smile. "I'd say you were a good and faithful servant to your mistress, Mrs. Steadman."

Then, turning to Pearl, "My dear, if Mr. Knox, or di Santo, or whatever, can substantiate that he is the boy named in these diaries, I believe we'll have a case to put before the House of Lords for transference of the title. Send for the lad at once, so I may talk to him."

"Of course." Pearl's spirits were soaring now.

The Duke continued, "A murder conviction is still extremely doubtful, you realize. Lord Hardwyck's influence—"

"I understand." She refused to worry about that just now. The important thing was that Luke assume his rightful position. "Perhaps we can leave it to Mr., er, Knox himself whether he wishes to pursue those charges. Thank you, Father."

The Duke stood and bowed as she and Mrs. Steadman took their leave. Once outside the library, Pearl turned to the old woman. "Would you like to see your Master Luke, Mrs. Steadman?"

"Oh, aye, milady! Can you bring me to him?"

"I'll bring him to you, instead. Hettie?" She turned to her maid, who had been hovering in the corridor. "Take Mrs. Steadman to the servants' wing and see that she is made comfortable, then call for the carriage. We have another visit to pay."

When he rounded the corner and again saw a dark blue carriage waiting in front of his building, Luke experienced a disorienting sense of having lived this moment before. After only the briefest pause, however, he hurried forward.

He was in a far better mood today than the last time the carriage had appeared. Many times over the past few days he'd regretted his curt dismissal of Pearl after the good she had tried to do him. Now he had a chance to make things right—and to share his story, which she was sure to find as amusing as he did.

Pearl sat drumming her gloved fingers on the edge of the open carriage window as she stared up at his building, an impatient, thoughtful expression on her face. He watched her for a moment, then tapped on the door right next to her. She started violently, then smiled—and it was like the sun bursting forth on a dreary day, chasing away the doldrums.

"Luke! I had nearly given up. No one answered my knock, nearly an hour since, and—"

"And you've waited here that long? I told you last time you are not safe here, as you should know well after your own experiences." Though he tried to be severe, he could not hide his delight at seeing her again.

Her answering grin told him she noticed—and shared that delight, which sent a thrill of something even stronger than desire through him. "Come, we must speak again," she said, opening the carriage door for him. "I have further news."

As before, he entered to sit beside her. "I have news as well," he told her. "Shall I go first, or would you rather?"

"Tell me your news first," she said, gazing up at him with a rapt expression in her lovely blue-violet eyes.

Luke was assailed by a vivid memory of their one

night together—her touch, her sighs. . . . He had to tear his own gaze away to focus his thoughts. "Very well," he said after what he hoped was not too obvious a pause. "I have spoken with my uncle."

"Spoken with him!" Clearly this was not what she had expected. "You mean you confronted him? With the truth?"

"You could say that. Though the truth actually came from him. I persuaded him to a full confession." He grinned, enjoying her astonishment.

"He confessed? To you? How . . . ? When . . . ? But he has left Town, has he not?"

"Night before last, I would imagine. Pity, really— I had high hopes of extorting money from him, but that will be difficult with him somewhere in the country. And one might say that he did not precisely confess to *me*," he clarified, still grinning. "It was my father's ghost who induced him to come clean."

Hettie, seated across from them, let out a small squeak, but comprehension began to dawn in Pearl's eyes. "It was *you* who haunted Hardwyck Hall!" she exclaimed. "I should have guessed it."

"My God, you're quick! Yes, it was I. Once I discovered that I bear an uncanny resemblance to my late father, it seemed the obvious thing to do."

Pearl began to chuckle. "I wish I had been there to see it! Oh! The night before last, you say? Is that when you confronted him?"

He nodded, and to his amazement she went off into peals of laughter. His own lips twitched in response, though he was not sure what the joke was. "What?" he asked, when she finally sobered slightly.

Twinkling, her eyes met his. "He accompanied us

to the theater earlier that evening—to see *Hamlet*. He seemed uncomfortable in the extreme, especially after a few, ah, comments I had made, and left after the first act . . ."

"Only to come home to the ghost of his murdered brother," Luke finished. "No wonder he caved in so quickly! Lord, that's rich!"

When she began laughing again, he joined her, until they were leaning against each other for support. Even Hettie began tittering, if only at the spectacle they presented.

"What a team we have made," he said, as soon as he could speak again. "And now what was your news?"

Pearl sobered, though she had to wipe the tears of laughter from her eyes. "More proof," she said. "Luke, you must come with me—that's why I came today." He started to shake his head, but she laid her hand on his sleeve beseechingly. "Please, Luke. You must!"

"No, my lady, I'm sorry. I—"

With an impatient exclamation, she rapped on the roof of the carriage. At once the coachman whipped up the horses—clearly a prearranged signal. Luke was startled, but not particularly worried, traces of his earlier amusement still lingering.

"Lady Pearl, are you *kidnapping* me?" he demanded, only half serious.

The look she gave him was enigmatic, making him suddenly uneasy. "I suppose you could say that," she replied. "It is for your own good, however, I promise."

Unease turned into alarm. "What do you mean?

Where are you taking me?" He reached for the door. "I can't just—"

"Of course you can." She still clung to his sleeve. "Luke, you must realize by now that you can't allow a man like your uncle to retain a position of power. His retreat to the countryside is only temporary. Eventually, he's likely to discover who you are, what you did to him. Before that happens, you need to be stronger than he is."

Luke stared at her. "I knew that you were ambitious, but I thought you understood that I am not. Do what you wish with your own life, but don't seek to order mine. I'm not one of your social improvement projects."

Pain lanced through her eyes, but she did not release him from her grasp or her gaze. "But you are. I don't mean only to improve you, Luke. My goal is the betterment of society. You are merely one means to that end."

"So I am but a tool," he said, his voice as cold as her words made him feel inside. "I fear I must decline to be put to such noble use, my lady."

Her expression became shuttered, distant, as she directed her gaze out the window. "It is too late for that now. We're here."

Even as she spoke, the carriage halted. A liveried footman opened the door and lowered the steps. The imposing facade of Oakshire House loomed over them. For one mad moment, Luke considered bolting, then realized how foolish that would be. He was not under arrest, or in any real danger, even if Pearl—his Pearl—had suddenly become a stranger to him.

He sent her a long, searching look. She met it defiantly, with uplifted chin. Without a word, he turned and stepped out of the carriage, then followed the footman inside, where he was greeted by the Oakshire butler—the same one who had caught him with Lady Glinnon's counterfeit jewels.

"His Grace will see you in the library," the butler informed him, evincing not the slightest flicker of recognition.

Luke resisted the urge to glance over his shoulder at Pearl before proceeding to the indicated room—the one where he had confessed to her the truth about his past. The butler swung the door wide, and he found himself facing the Duke of Oakshire across a polished mahogany desk.

"My daughter informs me we have an injustice to remedy," the Duke said to him without preamble, waving him to the chair opposite. "To do so, I'll need your cooperation, Mr., ah . . . hm. I suppose 'Knox' will do for the moment, though I understand it's a name you've never used."

Warily, Luke took the seat indicated. No, he was not under arrest, but he might as well be. Instead of a cage of stone and iron bars, it appeared he was headed for a gilded one—and he could see no way of escape.

Pearl sent Hettie to fetch Mrs. Steadman from the servants' wing, then followed Luke into the library. He had not looked at her since leaving the carriage—not that she could blame him. For the first time, she felt a twinge of guilt for what she had forced him to.

"Don't hover there, girl," her father said with a

frown, as she stood uncertainly by the double doors. "Take a seat or leave us alone. We have a lot to discuss."

Still Luke did not turn. Though she suspected he'd have preferred her gone, she could not bear to miss this. She moved forward and took a seat off to the side, out of the way—and out of Luke's line of sight. The Duke quirked an eyebrow at her, clearly surprised that she did not join them at the desk, but then turned his attention back to the man facing him.

"How long have you been aware that you are the son of James Knox, fourth Earl of Hardwyck, lad?"

"Less than a week, Your Grace," Luke answered in an emotionless voice.

"You never sought the truth of your parentage before this?" The Duke was clearly skeptical.

"I had no reason to," Luke replied in the same flat tone. "I was happy with my life as it was." This, Pearl knew, was directed at her. She was glad he could not see her flinch.

"An enviable state," the Duke agreed. "And I presume you had no reason to doubt whatever explanation your mother gave you?"

Before Luke could answer, the library door opened, admitting Mrs. Steadman. "Master Luke?" Her voice quavered uncertainly.

Now he turned, and a fond smile spread across his face, in marked contrast to the coldness Pearl had last seen there. "Nanna!" he exclaimed, rising to greet her.

The old woman hobbled forward as quickly as her aged legs would carry her, to be enfolded in the tall man's arms. "I never thought I was like to see you again," she exclaimed on a sob. "Look how big you've growed! Your lady mother would be so pleased. . . ."

"So you knew?" Luke looked down at the small, wizened figure.

"All those years, you knew, Nanna?"

"Aye. Your mother swore me to secrecy out of fear of your uncle, but I knew. She meant to tell you once you were growed, but she never had the chance—nor did I."

The affection with which he regarded the old nurse tugged at Pearl's heart. She sat perfectly still, unwilling to remind Luke of her presence, waiting to see how the reunion would play out.

"Until now," Luke said. Despite her stillness, he flicked a quick glance at Pearl—a glance that chilled her.

Mrs. Steadman nodded, still gazing up at him worshipfully. "Now you can do as your mother would have wished."

"And what might that be?" Though Pearl caught the ominous note in his voice, the old nurse seemed oblivious.

"Why, to take your rightful place, and pay back all the evil Mr. Wallis Knox has done. To set things to rights. You always was a good, honest boy, Master Luke, if a bit of a rapscallion at times." She patted his arm affectionately. "You deserve the good life you was born to, where Mr. Wallis never did."

His jaw tightened with a spasm of some strong emotion, and for a moment Pearl thought he would refuse. But then his expression softened again, and he smiled down at his old nurse. "Very well, Nanna, I'll do as you ask. For my mother—and for you."

But not for her. Pearl realized she had alienated him irrevocably with her high-handed management of his life. He would do the right thing, because that was the sort of man he was, but he would never forgive her for forcing him to this.

Taking Mrs. Steadman by the hand, Luke led her to the chair next to his and faced the Duke again. "Very well, Your Grace. Tell me what I need to do."

The enormity of what she had lost swept over Pearl. Before her anguish could betray itself in the tears she felt pricking behind her eyes, she rose and hurried from the room. Once outside the library, she leaned against the carved doorframe and gave herself over to her grief, heedless of the footmen passing by.

She had achieved her goal. She had dragged Luke into her world, as she had intended from the first. But a wider gulf stretched between them than ever—a gulf of her own making.

Chapter 15

Luke was finding his gilded cage every bit as confining as he had feared, and even more tedious. No sooner had he completed one thick stack of paperwork or one hearing at the College of Heralds than another had to be dealt with. As May progressed, the fogs disappeared, to be replaced by lovely sunshine, but Luke could enjoy none of it, sequestered as he was at Ibbetson's Hotel, dealing with the interminable business of claiming his title.

A low whine distracted him from the papers spread before him. Glancing up, he saw Argos scrabbling at the door to go out, and sent him a smile of sympathy.

"Can I walk him about a bit, sir—er, me lord?" asked Flute diffidently. Luke had made a detour into Seven Dials to fetch them both before installing himself here for the duration, though now he wondered whether that had been a kindness.

"No reason you two have to stay holed up here," he replied. "Go enjoy the day—but be discreet. We don't know that the Runners have called off the search yet. And 'sir' is fine—nothing is settled yet."

Flute grinned at him uncertainly, clearly still at a loss how to relate to Luke as his fortunes shifted. "We'll be back in an hour or two," he said, heading into the other room. "I'll just get my cap and Argos's lead—if I can get him to hold still for it."

Luke sighed wistfully, wishing with all his heart that he could go with them. He'd far rather be roaming the streets of London, taking each day as it came, living by his wits and luck. The apparently permanent loss of that carefree lifestyle was a constant ache.

And then, of course, there was Pearl.

For the first day or two, he'd been furious at what she'd done, plucking him from his world for her own supposedly noble purposes, giving him no choice in the matter. As the days stretched into weeks, however, he realized that she had only done what he'd most admired about her—acted on her own conscience and principles, regardless of the cost.

And the cost had not been trifling, for her or for him. He'd caught a glimpse of her face as she'd left her father's library—the last time he'd seen her. The loss of his respect, his friendship, had cut her to the quick, that was clear. He looked forward to the time when he could tell her she had not lost those things at all. But when that time might be, he had no idea.

For his life was no longer his own. The transfer of an illustrious title like Hardwyck could scarcely be kept quiet. The Regent himself had summoned Luke for an interview once the Duke of Oakshire apprised him of the news. An impressive figure, for all the cartoonists lampooned him. Luke had been hard-pressed to keep his awe at bay so that he could answer the questions put to him.

The press had sniffed it out within days, plastering it on the front pages of every paper. Now all of Society was doubtless abuzz with the news.

Not that Luke knew firsthand what Society was saying. Though he'd never had any hesitation in pretending to be one of them for his own purposes, he found he couldn't bring himself to join them now. Pretending was one thing. *Being* was another, and he knew he would feel like a fraud. The distinction seemed vague when he tried to pin it down in his mind, but it constrained him nonetheless.

A tap at the door broke into his all-too-brief moment of reflection. As Flute was still in the other room striving to convince Argos to allow him to attach the lead to his new collar, Luke rose to answer it himself.

"Good afternoon, my lord," the now-familiar clerk from the College of Heralds greeted him. Luke frowned at the use of the title, which had yet to be officially bestowed upon him.

"Hello, Mr. Tibbetson. More papers to sign? Or am I summoned to answer yet more questions?" he asked resignedly.

Some of the questions about his activities over the past few years had stretched his inventiveness to the utmost. Thus far, however, he had managed to avoid contradicting himself.

"Not yet, my lord, not at the moment," replied the clerk, adjusting his spectacles on the bridge of his long nose. "First I have news—word from your uncle, at last."

"Indeed?" Luke's interest revived. The one bit of this business he had actually looked forward to—a confrontation with his uncle—had not yet materialized. "Is he coming to Town to contest my claims?"

"No, my lord." Mr. Tibbetson handed him a lengthy document. "In response to the Prince Regent's suggestion, he has relinquished all claim to the title and attendant properties."

Luke perused the paper handed him. Not only was the title his, pending final approval by the College of Heralds and the House of Lords, but all of the Hardwyck wealth and lands as well. The only thing his uncle reserved to himself was the house in Lincolnshire willed to him at his father's death, to which he had already removed.

In return, no investigation would be made into the circumstances of his brother's death or the fire leading to Luke's own disappearance—matters that had not yet found their way to the papers, as the many hearings had dealt primarily with verifying Luke's identity.

"I see," he said inadequately, fighting a distinct sense of anticlimax. "Then it's over?"

"All but the formalities, my lord—though I warn you that those may drag on for some weeks yet."

Luke couldn't help feeling that it had all been far too easy, despite the tedium of the past two weeks.

One very pressing matter still needed to be addressed, however. "When am I likely to have access to my . . . er, money?"

The clerk seemed not at all surprised by the question. "A solicitor will be calling within the hour to arrange the transfer of certain accounts, and you may remove to Hardwyck Hall at your convenience. The rest will follow as everything is finalized."

Just like that. "Thank you, Mr. Tibbetson. You've been extremely helpful through all of this."

"I'm happy to have been of service, my lord." With a deep bow, the clerk took his leave.

For a long moment, Luke stood blinking at the closed door, trying to grasp what had just happened. All along, he had held a deep inner conviction that this was all an elaborate mistake, that it was only a matter of time before the world would right itself and he would be thrown back into the streets. But that, it seemed, was not to be. He was well and truly the Earl of Hardwyck, with everything that entailed.

"My lord?" Flute, standing at the door between the adjoining rooms, jarred him from his thoughts. "Guess I can call you that now, eh? Sounds like it's been worth the work and the wait."

Luke turned, a frown knitting his brows. "So it would seem. I suppose we should prepare to move to my new home." Forcing a lighter tone, he asked, "What think you of taking on a permanent position as my valet?"

Flute gaped. "Me? But you'll have the blunt to hire someone trained to the job—any job. You'll be wanting a whole houseful of servants, I don't doubt."

His spirits rising at Flute's reaction, Luke grinned. "No doubt, eventually. But I'll want someone I can trust closest to me. We'll find someone to train you to the job properly, never fear . . . if you want it?"

"Valet to the Earl o' Hardwyck? I'm not daft enough to refuse, if you think I won't disgrace you. I was afraid—I mean, I was only hoping—" He broke off awkwardly and ducked his head.

But Luke understood, and was touched. "I'd feel as adrift as you would, if we went our separate ways. You've been a great help to me when my fortunes were down. It's only fair that I reciprocate, now that I've the means to do so."

Another whine from Argos prevented any further discussion, which might have embarrassed them both. "Go on, you two, and have your walk. We'll have work to do when you return."

With a tug of his cap, Flute complied, incredulous joy still fighting with disbelief on his thin face. Luke smiled with satisfaction once they were gone. At least he would be able to discharge his responsibility to the one who had depended on him longest. But then he sobered again.

His responsibility to Pearl was far more complicated. If he thought it would make her happy or smooth her path, he'd offer for her tomorrow, of course—but that might only play into her stepmother's hands. And after the way he had treated her on their last meeting, it was entirely possible she never wished to see him again.

Nor, after the life he had led, was he remotely worthy of her, no matter how lofty a title they bestowed upon him. Inside, he was still Luke St. Clair, common street thief—and Pearl would know that, though no one else might.

He knew it was cowardly, but he preferred to wait until everything was settled to approach her again—to discover whether the one thing that mattered far more than money or influence, or even freedom, could ever be his.

"Thank you, Hettie. That is excellent news, indeed," said Pearl, forcing a smile of gratitude for her abigail's help. "Pray convey my thanks to John for his diligence in sharing what he has been able to learn thus far."

"Of course, my lady." Hettie returned Pearl's smile, but worry was evident in her eyes. She took her leave without saying anything more, however.

The moment she was alone, Pearl sighed heavily. She would not cry again. She would not! John Marley had merely confirmed what she had already read in the papers—that all had gone just as she'd hoped it would. Luke had taken up residence in Hardwyck Hall and would shortly be confirmed as Earl of Hardwyck. He would take his rightful place in Society, able to do all manner of good with his vast fortune.

Stupid to repine simply because he had not sent word himself.

More than two weeks had passed since that fateful day in her father's library, and she had heard not a word from Luke since. Now she doubted that she would, until they encountered each other by chance at some Society function, with him in his new role. How awkward that would be! She shuddered at the thought.

Perhaps she should leave London—return to Oakshire now, rather than waiting for the Duke and Duchess to remove there at the end of the Season, now only a few weeks distant. Or better, to Fairbourne, which was as good as hers now. She would have plenty to occupy her there, enough to distract her from what she could never have here. Yes, that would be best.

Her decision made, she went in search of her father to inform him of it. The library was empty, so she glanced into the parlor, where the Duke occasionally relaxed before changing for the evening. He was not there, either, but her stepmother was. Though lately Pearl avoided speaking with her unless compelled, she wanted to commit herself to her plan of action without delay.

"Good afternoon, Your Grace," she said. "Do you know where I might find my father?"

Obelia smiled—that broad, false smile that always presaged something unpleasant for Pearl—and shook her head. "He is out at the moment, but I am very glad to see you just now. Pray come in and close the door. We must talk."

Warily, Pearl advanced into the room as requested and took a seat opposite the Duchess. "Talk? About what?"

"Why, your marriage, of course. Delay would be unwise in a situation such as this, as I am sure you will agree."

Pearl sighed. She had hoped that by now Obelia had given up her hopes of having her married by late June, but apparently that was not the case. "There is no marriage to discuss, Your Grace. I have made it clear that I have no plans to wed, now or ever."

The Duchess's smile did not waver—if anything, it broadened further. "Oh, but you will have such plans before you leave this room. Even you, I am certain, would consider marriage far preferable to ruin."

"Ruin? Whatever can you mean?" Pearl spoke carelessly, but felt the tiniest prickle of apprehension along her spine.

"There is very little that goes on in this house that I do not learn of in one way or another, Pearl."

"Such as?"

Obelia's blue eyes now glittered with malicious triumph, and Pearl's unease increased. "I'm well aware of a certain visitor you, ah, entertained in your chambers a few weeks since, on the night of my musicale."

Though her breathing nearly stopped, Pearl tried to brazen it through. "I have no idea what you mean, Your Grace. I went to bed early with the headache that evening. My abigail can attest to it."

"It was not the headache you went to bed with, missy. *My* abigail can attest that yours was below for much of the evening, with no way to know what you were doing. As well as to the fact that a certain young man left much later, through the kitchens, having apparently used the servants' passageway from abovestairs."

Pearl shrugged with a nonchalance she did not feel. "I am not answerable for the comings and goings of every guest in this house. What young man do you mean, and what has he to do with me?"

"Oh, come, now, my dear. The young man with whom you spent the early part of that evening, of course. Whom you were at such pains to cultivate, in fact, though at the time I don't believe you knew any more about his antecedents than did the rest of Society."

"So he remained at the musicale after I went upstairs. What is wrong with that?" Pearl asked, though she did not meet her stepmother's eye. She felt as though a trap were closing about her—a trap of Obelia's crafting.

"Nothing of course," said the Duchess affably. "But in case you had forgotten, you had your abigail make his excuses to me when you retired—nor did anyone see him in any of the public rooms after that. Lady Minerva commented upon it to me, in fact."

Pearl remained silent, afraid that anything she said might damn her further.

"It was that very evening, as I recall, that your young man disappeared entirely from the Social scene . . . until his recent, miraculous reappearance."

When Pearl still did not respond, Obelia's eyes narrowed, their malice more pronounced, though they lost none of their triumph. "Should you still care to protest your innocence, I can produce the laundry maid, who was obliging enough to disclose to me the condition of your bedclothes the next day."

Though she was careful not to betray anything by

her expression, Pearl cursed inwardly in a way a lady of her breeding would never do aloud. She had not even considered that particular detail. How could she have been so stupid?

"I'd say I have evidence enough to insist upon your marriage," the Duchess concluded. "I have no doubt your father will agree when I share my discoveries with him."

At that, Pearl's head snapped up. "No! Please, you must not!" The very idea of her father confronting Luke, demanding that he marry her—! No, it could not even be considered.

Obelia watched her expectantly, waiting for her inevitable capitulation. But Pearl would not give in without a fight.

"May I ask why, when you have clearly known about this for weeks, you choose to use it against me now?"

For a moment the Duchess appeared disconcerted, but she recovered at once. "When I first learned of your disgraceful conduct, I immediately assumed you had done it merely to thwart me, deliberately choosing to sully yourself with a man of no social standing—one you would not be expected to marry—in order to render yourself unmarriageable at any cost."

Pearl had to force herself not to flinch at this all-too-accurate description of her motives. As stated by Obelia, it sounded sordid, dirty. Not at all the rapturous experience she remembered.

"The fact that your so-called Mr. di Santo disappeared that very night confirmed my suspicion," her stepmother continued. "But when you did not yourself reveal your ruined state, I saw no reason to do so. Not while some eligible suitor might still be induced to marry you, ignorant of the damaged state of his bride."

"I do not consider myself damaged," Pearl informed her coldly.

"Most *men* would," Obelia assured her. "The only one I thought might possibly overlook it for the sake of gain was Lord Hardwyck. He is of a refreshingly practical turn of mind."

"A mercenary turn of mind, you mean."

The Duchess merely smiled. "Just as well nothing ever came of it, considering recent events. Your father tells me everything is now all but settled. What an amazing bit of irony that the true Lord Hardwyck must now marry you, whether he will or no."

Pearl's thoughts flitted this way and that, hammering against her skull like a bird frantic to escape its cage. She could not, *would* not allow Luke to be forced into marriage with her—with the one person he must now despise above every other person alive. He would no doubt believe she had confessed their liaison for that very purpose!

"Your Grace, you must not do this," she said with every bit of earnestness she could command. "I will relinquish Fairbourne to you instead, if that is what you wish."

"And how would you have a legal basis to do such a thing, or I to accept it?" asked Obelia scornfully. "I credited you with more sense than that, Pearl—and more ambition, as well. Why do you not agree, then simply attempt to postpone the wedding date until after your inheritance is secure? It is what I would do in your place."

"Were my motives as mercenary as your own, no

doubt I would do the same." Pearl made no attempt to hide her bitterness. "I might even be willing to marry a man twenty years my senior for the prestige of his position. I fear my ambitions are beyond your ability to understand, however."

"It appears you understand my motives as poorly as I understand yours," snapped the Duchess. "While I believe that estate should go to my son, that goal pales in comparison to my desire to have you wed and out of this house."

This was plain speaking indeed. A month ago, Pearl would have been wounded by her stepmother's words. Now, however, she was concerned only with preventing her from forcing Luke's hand.

"Suppose I agree to wed—but where I will?" She tried to keep the desperation from her voice. "I would still be out of your way. I will even agree to marry before my birthday, if possible."

Obelia regarded her suspiciously. "What do you mean, where you will? Whom can you intend to wed, if not Lord Hardwyck?"

Pearl smiled grimly. There was one man she felt sure she could convince to abet her in her social aims. A man who had offered for her several times already, and whom she believed she could bend to her will, as he had already shown himself exceedingly malleable. A man she could manage, if not one she could love.

Though feeling as if a part of her soul was dying within her, she spoke quickly, before she could change her mind. "I will marry Lord Bellowsworth. Pray send for him, so that I may let him know that I have had a change of heart."

* * *

"That was unusually quick work for Parliament, I must say," Lord Marcus said by way of congratulation. Luke had invited his friend to join him for breakfast, that he might ask his advice on various matters. "Usually they have to debate anything to death before coming to any sort of decision."

Only one week after Luke's removal to Hardwyck Hall, the Committee of Privileges of the House of Lords had acted upon the recommendation of the College of Heralds and confirmed him as Earl of Hardwyck.

"The lords seemed only too eager to have the matter settled," Luke agreed. "It appears my uncle was less popular than I realized, for all the influence he wielded."

"Power breeds enemies," Marcus offered.

Luke took a sip of coffee—excellent stuff, prepared by the French chef he had hired yesterday—and pointed to the morning papers. The news of his confirmation was on the front page of both the *Morning Post* and the *Times*. "So does fame, I imagine. If I am to live up to a fraction of what seems to be expected of me, I will need your assistance, Marcus."

"I'm here to serve, of course," responded his friend with a grin. "Who'd have thought, back at Oxford, that scrawny Luke di Santo would turn out so well?"

"Not I, I assure you," said Luke with perfect truth. Turning to the scandal sheets, he chuckled at the wild surmises about his past and predictions for his future. How could these pundits know what his future held, when he had no clue himself?

Marcus leaned across the table to see what he was

chuckling at. "Everyone is agog to know when you will appear in Society in your new role," he commented.

"So it would seem. Since yesterday, when word first appeared in the afternoon papers, invitations have been arriving."

"And? Whose have you chosen to grace with your grand entrance? I insist upon being present to see the faces of those matrons who warned their daughters away from you last Season."

"I haven't decided yet," Luke replied.

"There's a grand reception at Carlton House tomorrow night," Marcus suggested. "The absolute cream of the *ton* will be there, of course."

"Hmm. Perhaps. I'd have to make certain my new clothes from Weston are ready in time."

"Yes, you'll want to wait until you're properly outfitted," Marcus agreed. "Don't want to give those tabbies any opening to criticize, after all. Begin as you mean to go on."

"My thoughts exactly."

In truth, Luke preferred that his first meeting with Pearl not be in the midst of a crowd, but he still felt uncertain of how he should approach her. Perhaps a casual morning call, and an invitation to go driving, to gauge her feelings toward him? That might serve. He was reluctant to ask Marcus's advice on so delicate a matter.

Idly, he turned over the page, where a noted gossip's speculations about him continued. There, in the next column, another item caught his eye. He stared for a long moment, unwilling to believe what he read there.

"Luke? Something wrong?" Marcus asked in sudden concern.

With an effort, Luke shook his head. "Not a thing. That reception at Carlton House does sound like a good choice for my first public appearance. Will you come with me to Weston's as soon as we finish eating? I'd like to do this thing right."

He swept the paper aside before Marcus could see what had stunned him—an announcement of the betrothal of Lady Pearl Moreston, daughter of the Duke of Oakshire, to the Marquess of Bellowsworth.

Chapter 16

〜〜✕〜〜

Pearl's cheeks were beginning to ache with the effort to maintain a smile when she felt more like screaming with frustration. When she had agreed to this betrothal she had managed to forget, in her desperation to salvage her pride, how irksomely boring Lord Bellowsworth's conversation could be.

". . . So I had to convince Mother that just because a stable cat found its way into the main house, it did not necessarily follow that there were mice in the house," he was saying, as they slowly traversed the main ballroom of Carlton House. "She cannot abide animals of any sort, you know."

"Mmm," Pearl responded, idly scanning the room, though she did not admit to herself who it was she was looking for.

"She insisted that I remain, therefore. I suggested a rat catcher, to ease her mind, but she pointed out that he would have ferrets or terriers with him, which she detests nearly as much as rodents."

Lord Bellowsworth had been obligingly incurious about the reasons for Pearl's *volte-face* after her repeated refusals of his suit. She had cited the claims of filial obedience and he had accepted that without question, as it was an overriding force in his own life. Thus, she was not obliged to pretend an affection she could not feel, much to her relief. Still, that could scarcely console her for the years of tedium she saw stretching ahead.

One of the Prince Regent's numerous footmen passed just then, and Pearl plucked a glass of champagne from the tray he carried—her second of the evening. She hoped it might mellow her sufficiently to allow her to remain civil to her fiancé—and everyone else.

"In the morning, nothing would do but that an army of housemaids go through every corner and cupboard, until she was assured nothing could be hiding anywhere in the house," Bellowsworth continued. "She has such a delicate constitution that I always feel obliged to humor her in these things."

After a discreet—but rather large—sip of champagne, Pearl smiled and nodded. "Of course you do."

Lord Bellowsworth smiled down at her possessively. "Your compassion is one of the many things I have always admired about you, Lady Pearl."

She nearly blurted out, *As well as my fortune?* but limited herself to another smile. The champagne must be affecting her already, she thought with a spurt of amusement—the first she had felt in a week. Since agreeing to this betrothal, in fact.

It had been a mad thing to do, she realized now. At the very least, she should have attempted speaking with her father first. But no, she had been so determined that no one else know the depths of her folly, giving herself to a man who now detested her. Her abominable pride had gotten her into this, and that same pride would simply have to see her through it.

"My mother, of course, is quite anxious to have you call upon her as soon as she feels well enough to receive you," Bellowsworth was saying now. "Her health is unpredictable, so it would be best if you could be ready at a moment's notice, should she have an unexpectedly good morning."

"I'll try to avoid any firm commitments, then," said Pearl, wondering if he realized how absurd such a request was. "At least, to anyone who would be offended by a last-minute cancellation." She drained her glass, to find it immediately replaced with a full one by a hovering footman.

The Marquess frowned slightly, but whether at her words or her imbibing, she didn't know—nor particularly care. Her sense of the ridiculous had reasserted itself with that second glass of champagne, and the evening did not now seem quite so insupportable. She refused to think of all the evenings to come.

"I would attempt to give you as much notice as possible, of course," he said, having apparently caught her note of sarcasm—rather to her surprise. Perceptiveness was not one of Bellowsworth's more prominent qualities. His nose, on the other hand . . .

"Oh, you were teasing. I'm happy to see I have not irritated you with my suggestion," he said then, making her belatedly realize that she was grinning.

"Of course not," she said quickly, taking another sip of champagne, desirous of maintaining the carefree glow it had produced. She wondered whether marriage to Bellowsworth might not make a drunkard of her.

To her relief, their conversation was interrupted at that point by a few well-wishers. This was their first public appearance since the betrothal announcement in yesterday's papers, so few people had yet had a chance to offer their congratulations. Pearl hoped she was saying everything that was proper. That third glass of champagne seemed to have left her a bit fuzzy.

Lord and Lady Mountheath, the Wittingtons, Lady Varens—their exclamations of delight rolled over her, along with various words of advice and a jest or two from the gentlemen. She smiled blandly at it all, wishing, despite the champagne, that she were anywhere but at Lord Bellowsworth's side. A touch on her arm provided a welcome distraction.

Turning, she found Lady Minerva at her side. "I want to add my good wishes to everyone else's," she said, the tiniest frown marring her smile. "The news quite caught me by surprise, I confess."

It was clear she hoped for a private word, so Pearl excused herself from the others to step a few feet away for some quick conversation with her closest friend in London. Well, except for—

Hastily, she closed off that thought.

"I was never more astonished than when I read the notice in yesterday's paper," Minerva whispered, the moment they were out of earshot of the others. "I felt certain that you had a *tendre* for the new Earl of Hardwyck—your Mr. di Santo—and he for you."

Her words cut through the pleasant champagne-induced haze, and Pearl discovered she was not yet quite so numb as she had hoped. "I thought so, too, briefly, but you know how such things are," she replied, waving a hand airily.

"Then this is what you truly want, Pearl? And he is not distressed by this news?" Minerva seemed sincerely concerned.

Though touched, Pearl only shrugged. "I have no idea whether he is distressed," she confessed, ignoring her friend's first question. "I rather doubt it, however. I have not seen or spoken with him in weeks, despite his presence in Town. He has been quite the recluse."

To her dismay, she felt an ominous prickle behind her eyelids. She blinked rapidly, hoping Minerva would not notice. But her friend was staring over her shoulder at something across the room.

"His days as a hermit are over, it appears," she said. "The butterfly has emerged from his cocoon with a vengeance."

Turning, her heart in her throat, Pearl saw him. Luke had just entered the ballroom, sweeping an outrageously elegant bow to the Regent, his daughter, Princess Charlotte, and her new husband, Prince Leopold.

Luke was dressed in the absolute pinnacle of fashion, his deep blue coat fitting him like a glove, setting off his broad shoulders to perfection. The snowy cravat at his throat fell in a mathematical cascade, punctuated by the glitter of a sapphire large enough to be visible from across the room.

"If you don't mind, Pearl, I believe I will renew my acquantance with Lord Hardwyck," Minerva murmured admiringly. "Besides, I'd like to be at hand for your, ah, reunion." With a wink, she drifted in Luke's direction—along with half of the young ladies in the room, Pearl noticed.

With an effort, she dragged her gaze away from his sartorial splendor—to find Lord Bellowsworth at her elbow. "Have you and Lady Minerva finished your coze?" he asked indulgently. "I presume she approves?"

Despite the champagne she had drunk, Pearl found it an effort to smile. "Yes, of course," she said mechanically. What would she say to Luke when they inevitably met? What would he say to her?

Belatedly becoming aware of the stir by the door, Bellowsworth frowned. "I see that the upstart Hardwyck has finally decided to grace Society with his presence. He'd have done better to wait until the press moved on to other news, in my opinion. His appearance here smacks of a taste for sensationalism."

Despite herself, Pearl could not resist another glance in his direction. He was just bowing over Lady Minerva's hand, responding with a smile to whatever pleasantry she had offered. Then, before Pearl could look away, he raised his head and locked his gaze with hers. Though the width of the room separated them, she felt almost faint with shock at the intensity of that gaze.

With a lazy smile that struck her as dangerous, Luke sauntered across the ballroom toward her.

Though he spoke and nodded in response to various greetings as he passed, he never took his eyes from Pearl's. She felt Bellowsworth stiffen at her side, but found herself helpless to do anything but watch Luke's approach.

Before she could begin to marshal her thoughts, he was lifting her hand to his lips. "I understand that felicitations are in order," he said smoothly, though his dark eyes still held an ominous glint.

"Indeed they are," Lord Bellowsworth responded, a shade too loudly. "Lady Pearl has consented to make me the happiest of men."

Luke flicked a glance at him before returning his gaze to Pearl. "I trust you will be able to make her equally happy. In fact, I insist upon it."

Pearl caught her breath at a flash of pain behind his eyes, quickly concealed. Could it be that . . . ?

But Bellowsworth was already blustering. "Your concern is touching, Hardwyck, but unnecessary. Our marital bliss is assured, not that it is any business of yours." Impatiently, he reached for Pearl's hand, which Luke still held.

Again, Luke glanced at Lord Bellowsworth, releasing Pearl's hand an instant before her fiancé could snatch it away from him. His smile held more of challenge than compliance, however. "Then you would be advised not to make it my business. I wish you *every* happiness, Lady Pearl."

Abruptly, Pearl's pride reasserted itself. She would not be quarreled over like a bone between two dogs!

"I thank you," she said haughtily, "but I quite prefer to be the keeper of my own happiness rather than delegate it to anyone." She pinned them each in turn with her glare. "And now, if you will *both* excuse me, I wish to speak with Lady Minerva."

Her friend was hovering just within earshot, too clearly enjoying the exchange. At Pearl's words, she belatedly attempted to look disinterested, but without success. She waited until Pearl reached her to whisper, "I knew he still cared for you! What will you do now?"

Pearl signaled to a passing footman. "Have another glass of champagne, and wish all men to perdition."

Luke watched Pearl stalk away from him with mingled pain and pleasure. She was even lovelier than he remembered, swathed in violet satin that perfectly complemented her eyes, her honey-gold hair upswept to reveal the flawless column of her throat. He wanted her more than ever.

And he would have her yet, he decided. Unworthy though he might be, he could make her far happier than stodgy, prosing Bellowsworth ever could. How she had become betrothed to him, he had no idea, but he would take his oath she had not done so willingly.

He turned back to Bellowsworth, who was also watching Pearl with a slightly puzzled frown. "The lady has quite a mind of her own," he commented. "Are you certain that is what you want in a wife?"

The Marquess glared at him. "I cannot think why you are concerning yourself, Hardwyck. Lady Pearl has been given more freedom than was perhaps wise, but she will make me an exemplary Marchioness. Surely you cannot doubt that?"

Luke shrugged and turned away. "I've no doubt

she will set a new standard—one that most would never dare aspire to." Leaving Bellowsworth to contemplate the meaning of his remark, he strolled back the way he had come.

Lord Marcus greeted him with raised eyebrows. "What have you been saying to Bellowsworth to make him look so peevish? I thought the point tonight was to take Society by storm, not to antagonize its more prominent members."

"Bellowsworth was born peevish," Luke replied. "I was merely offering my felicitations on his recent betrothal."

"Ah, the beauteous Lady Pearl," Marcus exclaimed in sudden understanding. "I just heard about that this afternoon. Bad luck, old chap, but you can have your pick now."

He gestured to the bevy of young ladies surrounding them, most of them regarding Luke with distinct interest—as were their mamas. "May as well, in fact," he continued with a teasing grin, "as you'll have the succession to think of. Being a younger son does have its benefits."

Though Marcus clearly expected him to be nettled, Luke merely replied, "The succession is in no danger, I assure you. In fact, I've already made my choice."

Marcus stared at him in astonishment. "After a mere ten minutes in Society? Who . . . ?" He followed Luke's gaze to where Pearl still stood talking with Lady Minerva. "Not her best friend?"

Luke continued to smile blandly, and Marcus's surprise turned to alarm. "Oh, no. No, it won't do at all, Luke. Surely you can see that? You're in a position to have anything you want. Don't wreck all by

creating a scandal right out of the gate. Bellowsworth may be a stick-in-the-mud, but he's well respected."

"Anything I want?" Luke echoed. "We'll see,
won't we? I may as well put my new position and
influence to the test." Ignoring his friend's worried
frown, he turned to greet Miss Chalmers and her
mother, as well as a cousin they wished to present
to him.

Though he bowed and spoke with his carefully
cultivated Continental flair, his mind was busily engaged in planning his next move. He fully intended
to guarantee Pearl's happiness, whether she wanted
his help or not.

Pearl drained her fourth—or was it her fifth?—
glass of champagne and nodded to Minerva. "Exactly," she said. "I gave him his chance, but he
didn't take it. So now Bebblesworth has his chance.
I don't 'spect much, but I can't very well cry off two
days after it was announced. Can I?"

"I, um, suppose not." Minerva's lips seemed to
be twitching, though it might have been Pearl's eyes
that were twitching instead. Certainly they didn't
seem to be focusing properly. And why should Minerva think her situation funny? "Pearl, why do we
not sit down, in this alcove here?"

"Sit down?" Pearl frowned at her friend. "Why? I
don't want to crease my skirts. Isn't this a pretty
color?" She held out the violet folds for Minerva's
inspection.

"Breathtaking," Minerva agreed. Another footman approached with a tray of filled glasses, but
she waved him away before Pearl could reach for

one. "I think some lemonade—or perhaps tea or coffee—might do you more good."

Pearl blinked at her, then suddenly understood. "Oh, do you think I'm bosky?" She considered for a moment. "You may be right. It's rather an interesting sensation. Quite pleasant, in fact. You should try it."

"Some other time, perhaps." Now Minerva's amusement was unmistakable, but Pearl couldn't seem to feel offended by it. "Wait here by this pillar and I'll see about getting you something more appropriate to drink, before you do something you will regret in the morning."

She went in search of another footman and Pearl waited obediently where she was, though her attention strayed at once to the colorful, shifting throng before her. Was Luke still here? There was her gangly fiancé, surrounded by other pompous-looking men, probably discussing politics or something equally dull. She used to be interested in such things, she remembered, but tonight such topics held no appeal. She was more interested in—

"Hiding, my lady?" As though she had conjured him, Luke stepped around the pillar to join her in the shadowy alcove.

"Of course not. I'm just waiting for Lady Minerva to return," she replied, remembering that she was out of charity with Luke, though she couldn't quite recall why.

"Not waiting for your dashing husband-to-be?" His voice was mocking, and she knew on some level that she should be angry. Instead, she found herself giggling.

"Dashing. I should like to see him do 'dashing,' "

she confided to Luke. "He does 'crashing' quite well—as in 'crashing bore.' "

He stared at her for an instant, then gave a shout of laughter, quickly muted. Glancing hastily around, he asked in a low voice, "Then why did you agree to marry him, my lady?"

Pearl frowned, trying to clear the fog from her brain but failing. "It was him or you, and I thought you were still angry with me," she explained.

"What do you mean?" he asked, staring. "Wait. Let's move back a bit, where we'll be less likely to be interrupted." He led her, now unresisting, to the marble bench at the back of the alcove, partially concealed from the ballroom by a large potted palm.

"Now. What did you mean, it was him or me?"

The delay had given Pearl time to remember why she was displeased with Luke, however. "You've been avoiding me," she said accusingly. "You never called or sent word or . . . or anything. All this time you've been in London—my London—and you've ignored me. It was most ungallant of you."

One of his dark eyebrows quirked upward. "Lady Pearl, have you been drinking?"

"What has that to do with anything? A glass or two of champagne, perhaps." She refused to be dissuaded from her question. "If you do not still hate me, why did you stay away?"

"Hate you?" he asked in amazement. "I may have been angry, but never for a moment did I hate you! You're more precious than . . . that is . . ."

"Yes?" she prompted, her irritation vanishing at what he had almost said.

But he shook his head. "Never mind. I thought it

would be better—for you—if I stayed away, but perhaps I was wrong."

Her spirits plummeted again, as she recalled her entire situation. "Yes. Now I'm betrothed to Lord Beb—Bellowsworth."

"And just why is that?" he probed. "I thought you were determined to remain unmarried."

"I was," she agreed. "But Obelia was going to make me . . . make you . . ."

"Make us what?"

She stared at the marble floor for a long moment, then looked up at him sorrowfully. He might as well know all—he was the only person in the world she could tell. "She found out about your—our—that night we . . ."

Sudden understanding lit his dark eyes. "That I compromised you," he stated quietly.

She nodded. "She was going to tell my father, so that you would *have* to marry me, once you had your title. She'd actually known about us for weeks, but—"

"But had no desire for you to wed a nobody." His voice was bitter, and Pearl wasn't sure whether he was angry only at the Duchess or at her as well.

"I couldn't let her. . . . I thought the last thing you would want was to be forced to marry me," she said in a small voice, staring again at the floor.

His gloved fingers touched her cheek, then lifted her chin so that she had to meet his gaze. What she saw there penetrated the champagne-colored fog and warmed her to her core. "So you agreed to marry Bellowsworth, her first choice, a man you despise, rather than allow my hand to be forced. That may be the bravest thing I've ever known anyone to do, Pearl."

She shook her head slightly. "I . . . 'Despise' is perhaps too strong a word."

"But you don't love him." His eyes still held hers, compelling her honesty.

"No," she whispered. It was Luke she loved. Only Luke. Tipsy as she was, however, she retained enough sense to keep those words to herself.

His fingers glided along her jawline to the nape of her neck, drawing her gently closer. It did not even occur to her to resist. When their lips met, for a long delicious moment she felt as though she had come home after far too long an absence. This was right. This was—

"Pearl! My lord!" Lady Minerva's urgent hiss cut through the euphoric mist. "Are you both mad?"

Startled, they sprang apart. At once, Luke rose and bowed. "My apologies, my lady," he said, though his eyes told her he was not sorry at all. "I had no right to take such a liberty."

"I . . . I suppose not." Pearl tried to gather her scattered wits about her, to act appropriately, mindful of Minerva's watchful eye. Had anyone else seen them?

"Pray forgive me," he said then, his expression making it a question.

She nodded. "Of course. I was at fault as well."

Whatever he read in her own eyes, it apparently satisfied him. With a tender smile, he said, "I'll take my leave of you, then—for the present." Before she could reply, he was gone.

Pearl turned to watch his retreat, a small smile

playing about her lips, but Minerva stepped in front of her, blocking her view of his well-proportioned back. "Here. Have some coffee," she suggested, or rather ordered, thrusting a steaming cup at her.

Taking it, Pearl looked up sheepishly at her friend's disapproving face. "You were right about the champagne, it seems," she said. "I have behaved rather . . . unwisely."

Minerva seated herself on the bench Luke had just vacated. "I should say so! What if Bellowsworth had seen you? Or your parents? Or any of the dozens of gossips present? Pearl, you might have been ruined!"

Wincing at the bitterness of the coffee as she sipped, Pearl nodded. "I'll be more careful in future, I promise." Careful not to be caught, in any event. She knew, though there had been no time for plans, that she would see Luke again.

Minerva apparently detected something of prevarication in her expression, for her concerned frown did not lessen. "Do you not recall what it is said your Lord Hardwyck did last Season, as mere Mr. di Santo? Pray be careful, Pearl. You do not wish to be used and discarded by him as poor Lady Simcox was."

Pearl choked on a sip of coffee. She'd all but forgotten that bit of gossip—nor had she ever questioned Luke about it. "No. No, of course not," she said as soon as she stopped coughing. That couldn't be what Luke had in mind . . . could it?

"Good." Minerva patted her hand. "Now finish up that coffee, and we'll return to the gathering. Tomorrow you may wake with a nasty headache, from what I've seen of my brothers, but you'll be able to view things rationally again."

Draining her cup, Pearl stood. "Thank you, Minerva. I don't doubt you are right." In fact, the headache was already beginning, her temples starting to throb uncomfortably.

"You'll realize then that, handsome and charming as he may be, Lord Hardwyck is safer avoided," Minerva continued. "He may be a lord now, but at heart he is still a rogue without honor, it would seem."

But her own heart was already given to that rogue, Pearl realized. The sober light of another day would not change that. What she would do about that inconvenient fact, she had no idea. She would wait for the promised return of rationality to consider her options. For now, she had to get through the rest of the evening, worsening headache notwithstanding.

"I appreciate your advice," she said to her friend as they headed toward Lord Bellowsworth, still deep in discussion with the other gentlemen. "I shall certainly keep it in mind."

She carefully made no promises to act upon it, however.

Chapter 17

A s Minerva had predicted, Pearl awoke the next morning feeling as though a troop of soldiers had been marching on her head—and across her tongue—all night. "I am never touching champagne again," she mumbled into her pillow.

That was a mistake, for it brought Hettie bouncing through the servants' door. "Good morning, my lady!" she exclaimed, using at least twice her normal volume. "The Duchess wanted you below an hour since, but I convinced her that you needed your rest."

She set down the tray she carried long enough to twitch open the draperies, letting in a blinding amount of light, then carried the tray to her mistress. "I've brought your chocolate and some toast, but can bring up more breakfast if you'd prefer to take it here."

"Why—" Pearl began, then grabbed at her head for fear it might explode, before trying again in a whisper. "Why are you shouting?"

"Shouting?" Hettie bellowed, looking confused, then concerned. "My lady, are you not well?" she asked then, moderating her tone to merely strident.

Still clutching her head, Pearl shook it, very slowly and carefully. To her relief, it remained intact. The smell of the chocolate, normally a favorite beverage, made her stomach lurch.

"No food. No chocolate," she whispered. "Tea, please." She wouldn't have dared request even that except that her mouth was so parched and foul-tasting.

"Of course, my lady. And I will have Her Grace send for the physician at once." Hettie's concern would have been more endearing had it not made her so shrill.

Again, Pearl cautiously shook her head. "No need," she said, her own voice louder than she'd intended. "Merely the aftereffects of too much champagne last night."

Instantly, Hettie's worried frown eased, to be replaced by an almost motherly smile. "Then I know just the thing, my lady." Now she seemed to be making more of an effort to keep her voice low, which Pearl appreciated greatly. "I'll be back in a moment."

"Thank you. And please don't—"

"Not a word, my lady, I promise!" she said with a wink and a grin before disappearing back through the panel, taking the malodorous chocolate with her.

Pearl sighed with relief, then rolled onto her back to stare up at the medallioned ceiling. What had she been thinking, to drink *five* glasses of champagne? Why, she could have . . . Bits and pieces of the previous evening returned, gaining clarity as they accumulated.

Lord Bellowsworth, stuffier than ever. Luke's appearance, in splendid style . . . Luke and Bellowsworth arguing, arguing about *her*! Insufferable men. Then, later, talking to Minerva, then Luke, then . . .

She pressed her hands to her face. Dear heaven, she had told him everything! And then . . . and then he had kissed her. Even now, horrified as she was by what she'd told him and the impropriety of allowing such an intimacy in such a setting, the memory of that kiss had the power to send warmth rushing through her, temporarily easing her bodily anguish.

But not her mental anguish.

She had agreed to marry Lord Bellowsworth with her eyes wide open. He had met with her father, the announcement had been printed in all of the papers, settlements were being drawn up, she had even exacted a promise from him that she would be allowed to manage Fairbourne as she wished.

Everything, in fact, had been arranged precisely as she had requested. And *now*, now she discovered that Luke did not despise her after all. Worse, he now knew that she was betrothed to a man she did not love, and in all likelihood understood the true nature of her feelings toward Luke himself. Pearl writhed inwardly with embarrassment. She had all but thrown herself at the man, while engaged to marry another!

When next she saw him, she would have to behave distantly, even coldly toward him, making it clear that the champagne had been talking last night and not her reason. Otherwise, he might well precipitate a scandal for the pure pleasure of discomfiting Bellowsworth. As new to Society as he was, that would do his standing no good at all.

A little voice told her that she wouldn't care, as long as they could be together. But no. Luke had said nothing last night about wishing to marry her—she was certain she would remember if he had. She would not be made into a laughingstock for the sake of his male pride—or Bellowsworth's. It was up to her to make certain there were no further confrontations between the two.

If she ever felt equal to leaving her bed again. . . .

"Excellently done, Flute!" Luke examined the fall of his cravat in the glass. "We'll make a valet of you yet. You've been practicing, have you?"

"Aye, around that urn on the landing." Flute fairly beamed with pride. "Clarence says I'm getting it right three times out of four now." Lord Marcus had been sending his own valet to Hardwyck Hall for an hour or two each day to assist in Flute's training.

"I always knew you were a clever lad. Now, if you'll just hand me the blue coat— Yes, Woodruff? What is it?" He turned to face his new butler, who stood clearing his throat at the door of his chamber.

"Lord Marcus Northrup is below, my lord," replied the young man, who had served as a footman to the Mountheaths until they turned him off last week without a reference.

It seemed that Miss Fanny had thrown away her favorite fan in a fit of pique, then, regretting her action, had told Woodruff to retrieve it from the dustbin. He had succeeded, but the condition of the fan had been sufficient to throw the young lady into a fury—and Woodruff into the streets.

Luke nodded. "I was just going down. Thank you, Woodruff."

Lord Marcus greeted him in the library a moment later with a relieved smile. "I'm glad I caught you before you went out, Luke. I've been thinking about last night and wanted to talk with you."

"About what?" asked Luke warily, moving to one of the new overstuffed chairs near the windows. Already the library was a far more comfortable room than it had been during his uncle's possession.

Marcus took the matching chair. "Your apparent determination to pursue the Lady Pearl, of course. I don't know how well you know Bellowsworth—"

"As well as ever I want to, I assure you," Luke interjected.

"—but he's rather a favorite, even a coddled son of Society," Marcus continued as though Luke hadn't spoken. "He's an ineffectual fellow, I grant you, but those in positions of influence—particularly the matrons—are rather . . . well, protective of him."

"So you feel it would be a mistake for me to humiliate him?" Luke concluded. "Pity." For that was precisely what he intended to do.

His determination must have been obvious, for Marcus leaned forward earnestly. "I know you care for the lady, and I'm the first to admit that Bellowsworth isn't worthy of her, but can you really afford a scandal so soon?"

Luke had to laugh. "You're a fine one to talk!"

"Yes, but I've never had much at stake. You do."
Marcus frowned worriedly. "Already tongues are
wagging about your exchange last night, and it
won't be long before someone dredges up that old
story about Lady Simcox from last Season."

Now it was Luke's turn to frown. "What story is
that?"

"Hm. Well. I only know what the gossips have
said," replied Marcus, clearly wishing he hadn't
brought it up.

"As I have not been in a position to hear Society's
gossip until quite recently, perhaps you can en-
lighten me," Luke suggested.

Marcus ran a finger between his neck and collar,
glancing out the window, then around the library,
before answering. "The story last year—after you
went back to the country—was that you seduced
her right under her husband's nose. That she
flaunted her infidelity so that Simcox would divorce
her—so she could marry you—but that you left her
in the lurch. I never believed any of it, of course,
but—"

"Like most persistent tales, it's a mix of fact and
fiction," said Luke with a chuckle. "The lady approached me. She was desperate to free herself from
her brutish husband, and I agreed to, er, assist her.
She never had the slightest desire to attach herself to
me—or to any man, I imagine, after what she'd seen
of marriage. She intended to return to her ancestral
home in Cumberland, I believe."

"Then it's true that you and she . . . ?"

"A gentleman never tells," Luke reminded him
dryly. "Now that you've done your duty by sharing

your concerns, perhaps you'll excuse me, Marcus. I have a mind to go riding in the park."

"Would you care for company?"

He shook his head. "I'm trying out a new mount, actually. My horsemanship still leaves much to be desired, I fear."

Visibly relieved, Marcus grinned. "What, does your Aunt Lavinia not keep a stable?"

Luke felt a twinge of remorse for continuing to deceive his friend about his past, but he shook his head. "No, she never travels, so saw no need. I've scarcely ridden at all since Oxford, in fact."

The riding instruction he'd received there had seemed pointless at the time, but he was glad of it now. He saw no need whatsoever to inform Marcus that he had reason to believe Pearl and Bellowsworth would be driving in the park this afternoon. He only hoped he wouldn't make too poor a showing, should he encounter them—as he fully intended to do.

"I'll take my leave, then," said Marcus, standing. Luke accompanied him to the front door. "You'll keep in mind what I said?" he asked, by way of parting.

"Of course," Luke agreed. "I do appreciate your keeping me apprised of everything Society is doing and saying." It would make his campaign easier if he knew precisely what he was up against.

With a cheerful nod, Marcus departed. At once, Luke called for his horse. With any luck, the next hour would be most amusing.

"You seem uncommonly thirsty this afternoon," Obelia commented from her thronelike chair in the parlor as Pearl poured herself another cup of tea.

"I suppose I am," she agreed absently. Hettie's concoction had helped enormously, but she still felt far from her best. Tea was all she cared to put into her stomach thus far.

The Duchess eyed her critically. "I am pleased to see you are feeling recovered. It was beyond all things rude for you to refuse to call upon Lady Bellowsworth this morning, illness or no illness. She rarely invites visitors to her home, you know."

"I'm certain Lord Bellowsworth—and you, Your Grace—would prefer my first impression upon her to be a positive one." Pearl took a large sip of tea. It did seem to fortify her somewhat. "I assure you that such would not have been the case had I gone this morning. I had the most dreadful headache, and was dizzy besides."

"You're not increasing, are you?" Obelia demanded. "That could ruin all."

Pearl nearly spewed out the mouthful of tea she had just taken. "Of course not! And pray lower your voice, Your Grace. That would be a fine thing for one of the servants to hear."

Obelia merely sniffed, taking a delicate bite of the cucumber sandwich she held.

"If you must know, I drank a bit too much of the Prince Regent's excellent champagne last night, and it disagreed with me," said Pearl, deciding honesty was preferable to Obelia's surmises. "And my monthly courses ended just days ago, so you needn't worry about . . . what you suggested."

It appeared that this was plainer speaking than Obelia cared for. "No more details, if you please. I only hope Lord Bellowsworth did not notice your imbibing last night. A man in his position will not want a sot for a wife."

Pearl did not reply, refusing to be drawn into a discussion of her own shortcomings—not that she had any defense for her foolishness, in any event. The silence had become awkward, as so often happened between them, when Upwood appeared to announce Lord Bellowsworth.

On entering the parlor, he offered only a cursory bow to the Duchess before hurrying over to Pearl. "I am so happy to see you sitting up, my lady! Dare I hope you are feeling recovered? Mother was so disappointed that you were unable to attend her this morning."

His solicitousness would have been a pleasant change from Obelia's criticism had Pearl not detected a hint of censure in his manner. "I hope you conveyed my apologies to her," she replied. "I had the most abominable headache, but I am feeling much more the thing now."

"That is excellent news," he exclaimed. "And I have even better news to share. My mother is outside at this moment, in the barouche-landau, and wishes you to come driving in the park with us!" He beamed as though offering her the greatest treat imaginable.

The Duchess spoke before Pearl could summon up the enthusiasm he clearly expected for her response. "Sitting outside in a carriage, my lord? Pray invite the dear lady inside!"

But Lord Bellowsworth shook his head. "She preferred to wait, Your Grace. Climbing in and out of carriages is difficult for her. That is why I was so delighted when she asked me to take her for a drive today. I'm certain the fresh air—warm, with no hint of chill—will do her an enormous amount of good."

"I'll ring for my parasol at once." Pearl realized she might as well get the inevitable meeting over with, though she'd have preferred another day to recover her constitution.

Stepping outside a few minutes later, Pearl saw at once why Lady Bellowsworth might find dismounting from her barouche an effort, for she was an extremely large woman. Blinking in the sunlight, which seemed far too bright for so late in the day, Pearl curtsied to the turbaned, silk-swathed figure reposing under the hood of the carriage.

"I am pleased to make your acquaintance, my lady," she said, when the woman did not speak at once.

Instead of replying, Lady Bellowsworth turned to her son. "Burford, hand her into the barouche-landau, so that I can get a look at her." He hurried at once to comply. "My eyes are prone to inflammation, you know," she continued. "Spectacles do me little good."

Pearl murmured something sympathetic as Bellowsworth seated himself next to her in the rear-facing seat, but the grand dame before her waved a beringed hand to silence her.

"So this is the lady you have finally chosen, is it, Burford? The papers have been uncommonly flattering about her, but I'll form my own opinions. A bit long in the tooth, isn't she?"

"Of course not, Mother!" With an embarrassed

glance at Pearl, he signaled the coachman to start. "I've already told you that she is not yet one-and-twenty."

Lady Bellowsworth continued to regard Pearl, who was torn between laughter and outrage, with a critical eye. "A younger girl would be easier to train," she pronounced. "This one has a very decided expression and her forehead denotes a strong will. I suspect she has been much indulged."

"If Your Ladyship would prefer to select a more suitable bride for your son—" Pearl began hopefully.

"No, no, of course she does not mean that, my dear," Bellowsworth interrupted. "Mother is merely nervous at this, her first drive in some months."

"Driving is not at all good for me," Lady Bellowsworth agreed, diverted for the moment from her critique of Pearl by this reference to her own health. "I find I benefit from a more sheltered atmosphere. Early summer is the only season I can abide being out-of-doors for any time at all, I take a chill so easily."

At once Bellowsworth was all concern. "Is that rug warm enough for you, Mother?" he asked, reaching across to adjust the heavy blanket covering her legs.

"Too warm," she responded, shoving the rug to the floor of the carriage. "And the sun is too bright." In that, Pearl had to agree with her. "It makes my poor eyes water."

"Lady Pearl will be happy to lend you her parasol to shield your face. Will you not, my lady?" Without even waiting for her answer, Bellowsworth reached for the named item.

Pearl relinquished it readily enough, though now she was forced to squint into the sun, as the carriage turned north upon entering the park. Riding backward was beginning to make her stomach lurch, as well.

Lady Bellowsworth continued to complain about one thing after another, keeping her son occupied with trying to alleviate each symptom and freeing Pearl to gaze around her at the fashionable crowds strolling, riding, and driving along the paths. This drive could not last forever, she consoled herself, trying not to think of the years stretching ahead. Perhaps Lady Minerva would be here, or someone else she knew. . . .

"Good afternoon, my lady," came a familiar voice from behind her. Turning, she saw Luke, atop a tall black gelding, looking particularly fine in a dark blue riding coat and buff breeches.

Her heart increased its pace as the events of last night—those she remembered, anyway—came rushing back. She could also feel the color rising to her cheeks. "Good afternoon, my lord," she responded formally.

Across from her, Lady Bellowsworth said something to her son, who shook his head. She then poked at him with Pearl's parasol, and he turned with a pinched frown. "Hardwyck, allow me to present my mother, Lady Bellowsworth. Mother, the new Earl of Hardwyck."

"Charmed, my lady," said Luke, bowing from the saddle.

Lady Bellowsworth squinted up at him. "I cannot see you properly without twisting my neck, Lord Hardwyck. Pray get down."

"I'm certain he has only stopped for a moment, Mother," Lord Bellowsworth protested, but Luke was already swinging down from his horse.

"My apologies for discommoding you, my lady," he said with a charming smile that Pearl was just as glad was not directed at her. "Is this better?"

"Much better. Thank you, dear boy. So you are the new Hardwyck, eh? I met your father once, you know. You're remarkably like him." Lady Bellowsworth was simpering just like every other lady who got within speaking distance of Luke, Pearl noted with amusement.

Luke lightly held his reins in one hand and leaned against the carriage, to Lord Bellowsworth's obvious irritation. "Several people have told me so, my lady. I regret I was never able to know him myself, though a painting at Hardwyck Hall bears out the resemblance."

"A good man, by all accounts," she said, then abruptly recalled her own numerous concerns. "There, Burford, look. My feet are starting to swell, just as they always do. I knew I should not attempt a drive today."

Bellowsworth at once busied himself with trying to alleviate his mother's distress, offering to loosen her shoes or to take her back home at once.

"No, I must elevate my feet, as I do at home. If Lady Pearl could be induced to vacate her seat, I could prop them there."

Lord Bellowsworth was clearly torn between concern for his mother and his duty to Pearl, so she made the choice for him. "Of course, my lady. I would be happy of a chance to walk a bit." Without waiting for any response from Bellowsworth, she stepped from the carriage, Luke moving forward quickly to assist her.

"Now, Burford."

Though it was clear he would have preferred to step down with Pearl, Bellowsworth had no choice but to assist his mother in propping up her feet—a surprisingly involved process.

"So we meet again," Luke murmured to Pearl while the others were thus engaged.

Another carriage was bearing down on them from the opposite direction, so she quickly stepped to the verge of the path, several feet away. Luke accompanied her, his horse in tow.

"He seems a well-mannered beast," she commented, preferring to stick to a safe topic, acutely aware of Luke's nearness and Lord Bellowsworth's darkling gaze.

"He is indeed, which is why I bought him. As you can imagine, I've had little chance during my checkered life to become a proficient rider. Still, he *looks* dashing enough, does he not?"

Examining the tall black gelding with the white star on his forehead gave Pearl an excuse to avert her flushed face. "He certainly does. Has he a name?"

"Star, I was told, but it seems supremely unimaginative. Perhaps you would care to give him a new one?"

Pearl looked up at him in surprise, then quickly lowered her eyes, disturbed by what she saw in his. "That would be . . . inappropriate, I think, under the circumstances." Just that brief glance had her senses humming.

"I considered calling upon you this morning—

which I'm sure would also have been inappropriate." He kept his voice low, so there was no possibility of it being overheard by Bellowsworth.

She nodded. "Yes, I fear it would—"

"That's not why I didn't come," he interrupted her. "I suspected you might not be feeling your best, so preferred to wait to see you again when you would be in full possession of your faculties."

Startled into looking at him again, Pearl exclaimed, "How could you know that?"

He grinned down at her. "Think you I don't know the symptoms—and aftereffects—of too much wine? Permit me to say, however, that you make a most charming drunk."

She felt herself blushing scarlet and glanced nervously over her shoulder at the carriage. Bellowsworth was still fussing with his mother, folding the carriage rug to place it just so beneath her feet.

"Then you know that I was not . . . not entirely responsible for . . ."

"Of course," he said gently. "Nor should I have taken advantage of your impaired state as I did. If I caused you to do anything you now regret, I apologize."

His eyes captured hers, and she read his sincerity there, along with a question—one she dared not answer. Still, she felt compelled to honesty. "I don't so much regret what I did as what I said. I never meant to burden you with . . . with—"

"With the truth?" He raised one eyebrow quizzically. "And why should you bear that burden alone, when the responsibility is as much mine as yours?"

Again she glanced back at the carriage, this time to find Bellowsworth glowering in their direction. She spoke quickly, unsure how much more time they might have for private speech. "No, the fault was mine—you only did what I asked. Therefore you have no responsibility in the matter."

"Do you really think I had no choice?" he asked sharply. "That because you are Lady Pearl, you had merely to command and I to obey, lowly street thief that I was?"

She blinked. "No! I merely—"

"Was I more than a tool to you, Pearl?" His voice was low and urgent now. "I must know. If you wish to have nothing further to do with me, if you really wish to spend the rest of your life competing with Bellowsworth's mother for his attention, let me know now."

She swallowed, knowing what her answer must be, but unable to utter the words. He would know them for the lie they were, however necessary that lie might be. He knew her, she realized, better than she knew herself.

"I . . ." she began, but her voice stuck in her throat. She tried again. "You were never a tool, Luke. You must know that. But you are now free to live your life as you choose. My future is not your responsibility."

"Unless I choose to make it my responsibility," he said with a slow smile that made her tingle right down to her toes.

For an instant, she felt herself swaying toward him, then abruptly caught herself, remembering where they were and who was watching. But the twinkle in Luke's eyes told her he had seen her moment of weakness.

He took her gloved hand in his own and raised it, unresisting, to his lips. "I have just begun a regimen of early morning riding in the south end of the park," he told her. "It is excellent exercise, and a chance to improve my horsemanship. The morning air, I have found, promotes clarity of thought. You should try it."

Bellowsworth joined them then, and Luke released her hand, though not her eyes.

"Come, my lady, it grows late," Bellowsworth said, his voice rigid with disapproval. "Mother believes we can both now fit onto the seat while her feet are yet elevated. In any event, she wishes to return home. We must go at once."

Pearl obediently placed her hand on his arm so that he could escort her back to the carriage. Before disengaging her gaze from Luke's, however, she said, in answer to the suggestion he had left hanging in the air, "Thank you, my lord. I believe I will."

Bellowsworth glanced down at her curiously, clearly thinking she had spoken to him, but Luke sent her a small, secret smile, showing he understood. Doffing his hat to her, he remounted his horse and trotted off without a backward glance as she allowed Bellowsworth to help her back into the carriage.

Despite Lady Bellowsworth's plaintive commentary on her feet, her neck, her eyes, and sundry other body parts all the way back to Oakshire House, Pearl's spirits were sufficiently revived that she was able to smile and nod without the least effort. Lord Bellowsworth watched her approvingly now, but she cared no more for his approval than for his mother's complaints. Her thoughts were focused on one thing alone.

Tomorrow morning, early, she would see Luke again.

Chapter 18

L uke arrived at the gates of Hyde Park before six o'clock the next morning, along with the milkmaids who grazed their tiny herds of cows there. Pearl was not likely to appear for hours, if at all, but he would take not the slightest risk of missing her if she was able to get away. He was certain he had not misinterpreted her response, but it was entirely possible she might have reconsidered. No matter. He was here.

Determined to put his time waiting to good use, he set Star into a canter along a deserted bridle path, then returned at a trot. The horse responded well, though he knew his own seat could be better. He wondered idly how good a rider Bellowsworth was—not that he believed for a moment that Pearl actually cared for the weak-chested fellow.

Turning again, he kicked the horse back into a canter, just as a covey of quail burst from cover in a small copse, right before the gelding's nose. He shied violently, and Luke was nearly unseated. Tightening his knees, he kept a firm hold on the reins and pulled the startled horse to a halt, then patted his neck as they both regained their equanimity.

"Well done!" came Pearl's voice from off to the side. Turning, he saw her trotting toward him from the north on a dainty bay mare. "Either you are making excellent progress, or you are not so inexperienced as you claim," she said, pulling level with him.

She looked divine this morning in a wine-colored riding habit with gold epaulets, her honey-colored hair in intricate loops beneath the matching tall hat. A groom on another bay paced a respectful distance behind her.

Following Luke's gaze, she shrugged slightly. "Hettie wouldn't let me come alone, but John is completely trustworthy—and discreet."

Luke hoped to put that discretion to the test—though perhaps not this first morning. "I'm delighted you could come at all," he said. "I rather feared you would think better of it."

"I did." Her expression was frank—but charming. "I nearly talked myself out of coming, but . . . I needed the exercise," she concluded with a toss of her head, clearly backing away from whatever else she'd been about to say.

Thoroughly bewitched, Luke drank in the sight of her. "Then let's get that exercise," he suggested. "Shall we canter?"

In answer, she flicked her reins and at once her mare sprang forward into an easy lope. He hung back for a moment, admiring her from the rear, before kicking his own mount into motion. At the first turning she brought her mare about, just as he caught up with her.

"Where to now?" she asked.

Glancing back, he saw that the groom had not followed, though he was still within sight at the head of the path. "A trot down and back, perhaps?" he suggested. "You may give me pointers on my form, if you would care to."

One side of her mouth quirked up, but she only nodded. "Very well. You begin and I will follow."

Luke set his horse into a trot, acutely aware of her eyes upon him. He'd never felt less skillful, cringing at every slight mistake he made. When he'd nearly reached the groom, he turned and trotted back, Pearl dutifully following. Back at the turning, he halted. "Well?"

"Your, ah, seat is well enough, though a bit stiff," she said, pinkening slightly. "And you need to lighten up on the reins. Otherwise, it's merely a matter of practice, I should say." She swallowed visibly, not quite meeting his eye.

"I thank you for your advice," he said lightly. Then, in a deeper voice, "Pearl."

She faced him questioningly, almost fearfully.

"Tell me you do not mean to go through with this absurd marriage to Bellowsworth."

For an instant she closed her eyes, as though his words pained her, then opened them with a frown. "It is not as simple as that, I'm afraid. The marriage settlements have been drawn up, the expectations of Society aroused. If I were to cry off now, it would create a scandal, and my stepmother—"

"Hang your stepmother. I thought scandal was what you wanted—so that you could thwart her plans for your future."

For a long moment she hesitated, then dropped her gaze to her hands, encased in their kidskin riding gloves. "I—I thought I did. But the idea of Society talking behind my back, looking down their noses at me, not to mention losing my father's good opinion . . . At the moment, I'm not certain *what* I want."

"As your presence here this morning attests." He kept his voice light, teasing, but watched closely for her reaction. His own course of action—nay, his very future—hinged upon it.

"Yes," she said softly, still not meeting his eye. "I begin to realize that perhaps no price would be too great to avoid a lifetime with Bellowsworth . . . and his mother." She smiled then, dispelling her sudden seriousness. "I'd thought, if nothing else, he would be an easy man to direct, but wresting his reins from her grasp may be more than I can accomplish."

"And scarcely worth the effort," Luke assured her with an answering smile. His way was clear now. "Cheer up, my sweet. You will make no such sacrifice. His mother should be delighted, as she seems a woman unwilling to share."

"But—"

"Meet me here again tomorrow and I will explain," he said with a wink. "One more canter?" Without waiting for her reply, he urged his mount forward. She hesitated only an instant, then, side by side, they rode the length of the path to her waiting groom.

"Tomorrow, then," she said. Luke thought she looked happier than he had seen her in some time, reassuring him that he was doing the right thing.

"Oh, I'll see you before then, my lady, never fear."

Her eyes flew wide in surprise, but instead of explaining, he merely touched his hat and cantered back up the lane, then rounded the curve, continuing on until he was certain she was gone. Another ten minutes or so, and he would return home. He had a campaign to plan.

Pearl returned to Oakshire House in excellent spirits, which for the moment she preferred not to analyze.

"Your ride appears to have done you good, my lady," Hettie commented when she reached her apartments.

"Yes, I believe it has," she replied cheerfully. "I have missed regular exercise. Has the Duchess asked for me?"

Hettie shook her head. "She won't have left her chambers yet, nor His Grace, either. Come, let me brush out your hair."

Pearl allowed her maid to help her out of her habit, then seated herself at the dressing table, clad in her shift. As Hettie plied the silver brush in long, smooth strokes, Pearl allowed her mind to wander back over the past, pleasant hour.

Luke had all but promised to save her from the bleak future that had stretched before her only yesterday. Soon, she knew, her natural curiosity—and desire to control her own destiny—would reassert themselves, but for now she was content to simply trust him and be happy.

"I do hope you plan to ride often, my lady," Hettie commented, laying down the brush and catching up the gown she'd laid out for Pearl's morning wear. "It's put the sparkle back in your eyes."

Pearl smiled at her reflection in the glass. "Yes, I plan to make it a daily habit, weather allowing." She wouldn't miss tomorrow's ride—or Luke's promised explanation—for the world.

Her cheerfulness carried her through breakfast, even though her stepmother spoke of nothing but wedding plans. The Duke excused himself rather quickly, pleading urgent Parliament business, leaving Pearl to smile and nod noncommittally at Obelia's various pronouncements about trousseaux and guest lists.

As had become his habit over the past few days, Lord Bellowsworth appeared almost the moment they repaired to the parlor, the first of their morning callers. "Mother's feet are much better today," he told Pearl by way of greeting. "I knew you would wish to know."

"Of course," she replied, still trying to cling to the remnants of her earlier good mood. "I trust the drive was not too much for her, apart from that?"

He shook his head dolefully. "It's too soon to tell, she says. Though she didn't specifically tell me so, I . . . *believe* she enjoyed meeting you, however."

"And I, her, of course," responded Pearl automatically, her thoughts already straying again to the park this morning—and tomorrow morning.

"How nice that you two get along so well," Obelia exclaimed. "Don't you think so, my lord?"

"Yes, I do—particularly as I have promised Mother that she may reside with us after our marriage. She was prepared to move into the Dower House, but its main prospect is east, and I know the morning sun often gives her the headache, so I would not hear of it. I knew Lady Pearl would not mind, so well known as she is for compassion toward those less fortunate."

This news brought Pearl back to earth with a thud. Share her future home with Lady Bellowsworth? Being talked about as though she were not there every day of her life? Surely no scandal could be too great to avoid such a fate. She hoped Luke's plan, whatever it was, would be successful—and swift.

Meanwhile, she felt obliged to make some small effort to assert herself, against that plan's failure. "Certainly I would not expect her to vacate the home she has been used to at once, my lord," she said. "But I have often heard that two women attempting to run one household is less than an ideal situation."

She did not look at the Duchess as she spoke, but Obelia's faint snort only served to reinforce her words, though that was doubtless not her intention.

Bellowsworth frowned, but before he could voice his concern, a footman entered with an enormous arrangement of spring flowers—the largest Pearl had ever seen. "For the Lady Pearl," he said, looking to the Duchess for direction on where to place them.

"How thoughtful, my lord," Obelia exclaimed to

Lord Bellowsworth. "Here on this table will be fine, James."

Pearl, noting that the frown had not left Bellowsworth's face, rose to pick up the card that accompanied the flowers.

"Read it aloud, my dear, do," her stepmother invited, with a conspiratorial smile at their guest.

"For Lady Pearl, with my undying admiration," he read, "from Luke, Lord Hardwyck."

Obelia's smile vanished. "Well, that is inappropriate, I must say. Even as new to the Social scene as he is, he must realize that."

"From what I have seen of the fellow," Bellowsworth commented sourly, "I rather doubt he cares."

Pearl said nothing, keeping her back to them both as she carefully replaced the card, to hide the smile playing about her lips. She had no doubt Luke had timed the arrival of the flowers to coincide with Lord Bellowsworth's visit. But then she sobered. Gallantries alone wouldn't be enough to get her out of this wretched betrothal.

"Lord Hardwyck," Upwood announced, even as he turned back to the others.

Luke himself strode into the room, pausing to sweep an elaborate bow that encompassed both Pearl and the Duchess. "I give you good morning, Your Grace, my lady, my lord. Ah! I see my small offering has arrived."

With not the slightest trace of apology, he moved to Pearl's side, raising her hand to his lips. "Lovely as always, my lady," he declared, pressing a lingering kiss to the back of her hand.

The heat of his lips burned through the thin lace

of her fingerless mitten, flustering her enough to keep her from grinning back at him. Just as well, as both Obelia and Bellowsworth were watching them in near outrage.

"Will you not have a seat, my lord?" Pearl said, as primly as she could manage.

Without hesitation, he moved to the chair Pearl had vacated, next to Lord Bellowsworth, leaving the chair on Luke's other side for Pearl. Bellowsworth made a motion as though to protest, but then contented himself with a scowl. Pearl, pretending to be oblivious to the interchange, seated herself by Luke, carefully arranging her sprigged muslin skirts about her.

Luke turned to Bellowsworth. "I trust your mother has recovered from her outing, my lord?" he asked affably, ignoring the other man's frown.

"I, er, yes," the marquess responded, clearly caught off guard by the innocent question. "She will be fine after a day or two of rest."

"How are you finding Hardwyck Hall, my lord?" the Duchess asked then, disapproval clear in her voice. "Will you be making many changes there?"

Luke's smile did not waver for an instant. "I've already made a few small ones, Your Grace. Needless to say, it's a far grander house than I've been used to, but I hope to make it livable in time. I mean to ask Lady Pearl for her advice on some of my plans for it, in fact."

"Indeed?" Obelia infused the word with ice. "That scarcely seems appropriate, as she and Lord Bellowsworth are soon to be married."

"Is it not?" he asked innocently. "Her taste is impeccable by all accounts." He shot a glance at Bellowsworth, one raised eyebrow implying that she'd perhaps had *one* lapse in judgment. "I feel I can trust her implicitly in such matters."

"Now, see here, Hardwyck," Bellowsworth began, his face reddening.

Quickly, Pearl broke in. "I am honored by your faith, Lord Hardwyck, and would be happy to assist . . . by giving you the names of the best professional decorators."

"I suppose I must content myself with that—for the present," Luke replied with a comically wistful sigh. "Should I have specific questions, however, would you be so gracious as to answer them?"

"Of course," she said, her lips twitching again. Really, he was behaving most outrageously, and she was enjoying it far too much. "I am flattered that you value my opinion so highly."

The Duchess tried again to turn the conversation to less personal channels. "Lord Bellowsworth, think you that the weather will hold fair for tonight's excursion to Vauxhall?"

"I believe so, Your Grace," he responded, though rather sulkily, Pearl thought. "Rain is less of a danger now that June approaches. If it should threaten this evening, we can always modify our plans."

"Vauxhall Gardens! The very place I'd planned to spend the evening myself," Luke exclaimed, beaming first at the Marquess, then at Pearl and her stepmother. "I've never had occasion to visit it before."

"Our carriage comfortably holds but four," the Duchess snapped, having apparently given up all pretense of civility.

He blinked at her in surprise. "I did not mean to impose myself upon your, ah, family group, Your Grace! But perhaps I will be fortunate enough to encounter you there." He sent Pearl an almost imperceptible wink, which she did not dare to acknowledge under two sets of censorious eyes, though it stole her breath.

A moment later, Luke rose to take his leave, apparently deciding he had stirred things up sufficiently for the present. The Duchess thawed slightly when he bowed over her hand, thanking her profusely for her hospitality. "I have so few friends in Town thus far that I fear I have a tendency to impose upon those few," he concluded.

"No imposition, of course," she replied coolly. "I trust your acquaintanceships will multiply rapidly."

"You are too kind, Your Grace. Well, Bellowsworth? You were here before me, so I presume you'll be going as well. Perhaps you can advise me on a pair of carriage horses I'm considering purchasing."

Lord Bellowsworth rose with obvious reluctance, taking leave first of the Duchess, and then of Pearl. As he took her hand, Pearl thought for a moment that he would say something either of warning or blame, but he merely nodded curtly, then joined Luke in the foyer. As they headed for the front door, she could hear Luke already discussing horseflesh with animation.

The moment the front door closed behind them, Obelia rounded on her. "I will not have you encouraging Lord Hardwyck, Pearl. He may be unfamiliar with the proprieties, but you have no such excuse."

"What have I done to encourage him?" Pearl asked reasonably.

But her stepmother would not be sidetracked. "You had your chance to marry him, and chose Bellowsworth instead. Now you will have the grace to live with that decision. Lord Hardwyck may be wealthier, but he has not a fraction of the influence Lord Bellowsworth has, nor so high a rank."

Pearl could not suppress a laugh. "Do you honestly believe any of that matters to me?"

The Duchess's glare held pure venom. "I will not be made a laughingstock. Society will have no cause to assume I have not raised you properly. You will honor your obligations."

"Yet you seemed willing enough to expose me a week since," Pearl pointed out. "Would that not have achieved the same effect?"

Obelia's lips tightened ominously. "I knew it would not come to that. Had you been willing to wed Hardwyck, all would have been handled quietly. No breath of scandal would have escaped these walls."

"So you were bluffing." Now it was Pearl's turn to become angry. "One might even say you deceived me—tricked me—into agreeing to this match."

"Bellowsworth was your own choice," Obelia reminded her. "I suggested Hardwyck from the first, if you recall."

"You suggested *forcing* him to wed me. A fine foundation for a happy marriage that would have been," Pearl shot back bitterly.

The Duchess merely shrugged. "Men always need a nudge of some sort. What matter whether it is subtle or overt? In any event, you are committed now. I daresay you can contrive to be as happy with

Bellowsworth as with anyone, if you put your mind to it. It's a course I recommend, for you will not be permitted to cry off, I assure you."

Pearl took several deep breaths, striving to bring her temper under control. Much of her anger, she knew, was directed at herself. It was clear now that had she only spoken with Luke before taking this step, all might have been avoided. Still, that did not excuse Obelia's hand in this.

"Very well, I shall not cry off. However," she continued sweetly, "should Bellowsworth wish to end our betrothal, for whatever reason, I will make no effort to dissuade him."

That her stepmother understood her was clear from the sudden alarm in her blue eyes. "You know he would only do such a thing in the face of gross impropriety on your part. I cannot think you care so little for scandal as that. Do you wish to be shunned by the world?"

"I begin to perceive that my definition of the world and yours are somewhat at odds," Pearl began, but Obelia cut her off.

"Promise me that you will do nothing to disgrace your father."

That was a clever stroke, hitting Pearl where she was most vulnerable. After a long pause, she finally said, "I will promise to take his feelings and position into consideration in my efforts to secure a supportable future for myself."

The Duchess relaxed marginally. "So you will not seek to create a scandal?"

"I will not *seek* to do so, no." But if scandal was her only path to happiness, she would not shun it, either, she thought grimly.

Obelia was still regarding her suspiciously, but finally she nodded. "See that you do not. Your father's health may seem robust, but he is not as young as he once was. There is no knowing what a serious shock might do to him."

It was a blatant attempt at manipulation, but it affected Pearl nonetheless. "My father is at least as dear to me as he is to you. You need not fear that I will knowingly cause him distress."

With that half promise, she rose and left the room before Obelia could force further concessions from her—concessions she might not be able to honor. For whether it involved setting the Town on its ear or cloistering herself away in a convent, she would not allow her future to be decided by anyone but herself, she was determined.

Luke had given in to a slight falsehood when he had told the Duchess of Oakshire that he had never before visited Vauxhall Gardens. Though it was true that he had not yet seen it with the eyes of an adult, in his youth he had more than once found its more remote and poorly lit walkways a profitable venue for an enterprising pickpocket.

Arriving just as the sun began to set, Luke paid his admission and entered by the front gate, instead of scrambling over the rear wall as he had on his last visit some twelve years ago. He could not help marveling anew at how far he had come from those hopeless days when he had lived moment to moment, never knowing if the next would see him dead or in prison.

The gardens themselves did not appear to have changed much, though he had never seen the grove and its surrounding colonnades, or the orchestra rotunda, except from a distance. Even as a jaded man of the world, some of the fairyland spell that had charmed him as a lad of fourteen remained.

Dusk deepened, the hanging lamps glowing more brightly as the crowd thickened. Finally, Luke spotted the Oakshire party, walking from the entrance toward one of the supper boxes. Moving forward, quickly but not too quickly, he intercepted them as though by chance.

"Your Graces, Lady Pearl, Lord Bellowsworth." He swept them all his most elegant bow. "What a delight to encounter you here after all. I am particularly pleased at this opportunity to extend my thanks, Your Grace, for your assistance of some weeks since."

"The pleasure is mine, lad," responded the Duke affably. "Will you not join us? We are on our way to our supper box, from whence we can enjoy the fireworks and music that will be starting shortly."

Luke bowed again. "You are all kindness, Your Grace. I thank you." He moved to Pearl's left, ignoring Bellowsworth's darkling glare from her right. From the corner of his eye, he saw the Duchess whispering urgently to her husband.

"You are enchanting as always, my lady," he said gallantly to Pearl, keeping his amusement at the situation from his voice.

She smiled in return, favoring him with a knowing glance that stirred his blood. "You are *too* kind, my lord."

"Have you no party of your own to join, Hardwyck?" Lord Bellowsworth asked peevishly from her other side. "I know you will not wish to crowd us."

"Do not be rude, my lord," Pearl admonished him before Luke could reply. "You know Lord Hardwyck has few friends in London as of yet."

Bellowsworth merely snorted, not even attempting to hide his ill temper. The man appeared to have no inkling of how to court a lady, Luke thought smugly, with a sidelong glance at his petulant frown.

Apparently he was not the only one to make that observation, for he heard the Duke, just behind him, saying in an undertone to his wife, "He's done nothing improper as yet, my dear. Mayhap it will do Bellowsworth good—keep him from becoming complacent, as it were. We don't want him taking our Pearl for granted, after all."

"But Your Grace . . ." the Duchess began, then broke off, apparently realizing that they might be overheard.

Luke grinned. That the Duchess did not approve of him was no revelation, but discovering that the Duke had reservations about Bellowsworth was welcome indeed. Still, he would have to tread warily around Pearl while in her father's company. If he had any reason to suspect that Luke meant to dishonor his daughter, the Duke would no doubt react swiftly and decisively.

They reached the Duke's supper box, which was not crowded in the least, as it was built to accommodate twice their number. The Duchess, in an apparent effort to mollify Lord Bellowsworth, made an inquiry about his mother.

Luke took advantage of his distraction to seat himself next to Pearl at the table. As her father was on her other side, Bellowsworth had no choice but to sit next to Luke, or on the Duchess's far side. He chose the latter, his face reddening ominously.

"I understand Vauxhall is fabled for its sliced ham," Luke commented, as though oblivious to Bellowsworth's discomfiture.

"For the thinness of the slices, yes," Pearl replied. "But its real fame lies in the entertainments. Listen! Already the orchestra is beginning, and as soon as it is full dark we shall have fireworks."

Luke responded in kind, taking no liberties, tempting as Bellowsworth's glower from across the table made it. They chatted lightly of the evening ahead, as well as the other amusements London had to offer, with an occasional interjection by the Duke, or even the Duchess.

Bellowsworth was all but ignored, simply because he never spoke a word. Luke had hoped to goad him into a display of temper, but he began to wonder if the man was capable of anything more explosive than a pout. A challenge, which had been his ultimate goal, began to seem unlikely in the extreme.

Still, seated next to Pearl, who positively shimmered tonight in silver-blue, he found the evening most agreeable. He promised himself far greater pleasures ahead, for both of them.

Wallis Knox, until recently the Earl of Hardwyck, watched the Duke of Oakshire's party from the shadow of a clump of trees at the edge of the grove. He had followed the new earl at a distance since his arrival in London late that afternoon, but this was his first clear view of the man. It confirmed his suspicions.

This nephew, this son of his dead brother James, whom he had assumed dead these twenty years and more, who now sat before him, laughing and chatting, was the very image of James, save that his hair was dark. Yes, there was no doubt of it—this was the "ghost" who had driven him from Hardwyck Hall, who had wrung from him a confession.

Who had humiliated him.

His resources might be limited now, but somehow that deception, that humiliation, would be repaid. Every man had his weakness, and he would discover what his nephew's was.

It was only a matter of time, and time was the one thing he now had in abundance.

Chapter 19

The next morning, despite only a few hours' sleep, Pearl trotted her mare through the park gates, every nerve vibrating with anticipation.

Last night at Vauxhall had been an exhilarating mixture of pleasure and frustration. Pleasure at having Luke so close by her side, guilty amusement at Bellowsworth's discomfiture, but frustration at her inability to have so much as a word in private with Luke. Now, however . . .

"Good morning, my lady!" Luke came around a turn in the path just then, a short distance ahead of her. If anything, he looked even more handsome than he had yesterday, dressed this time in a coat of deep hunter green. "I hoped you would not be able to stay away."

"With your story half told? No chance of that, I assure you," she responded lightly, though her heart hammered in her breast at the mere sight of him. She was not certain she liked having anyone, even Luke, wield this much power over her emotions.

She reached him then, and he turned his horse to accompany her to the same path they had ridden yesterday. Luke glanced back the way she had come.

"Where is your shadow today, my lady?"

"John? I persuaded him to run an errand for me once we left the house. I had to promise not to tell Hettie, however. He seems most reluctant to incur her wrath." She found the budding romance between her abigail and the footman charming, though she knew the Duchess would not.

"Then he is to find you here in the park once his errand is completed?"

Pearl shook her head, willing her color not to rise. "No, I said I would meet him at the corner of Mount Street on my way back to Oakshire House. I . . . did not know whether we would stay on the same paths as yesterday." Was she being too bold? Whenever she was near him, she could not help remembering their one night of intimacy—and wishing for another such experience.

He looked at her then, his dark eyes warm—more than warm. "We need not, you know."

"Where would you like to ride?" she asked breathlessly, meaning something else entirely.

For a long moment, he watched her in silence, the merest hint of a smile playing about his lips. "Perhaps in the direction of Hyde Park Corner?"

"Very well. Those paths are broader, should we wish to, ah, canter." She felt as though they were holding two separate conversations, one spoken and one unspoken. Or perhaps her naughty imagination was oversetting her reason.

They turned toward the south, first trotting, then cantering in the cool early morning air. Pearl was content for a while to simply let the breeze lift her hair, leaving all of her worries behind her. As they neared the southeastern corner of Hyde Park, however, they slowed and reality intruded again.

"You were going to explain your plan to me today," she reminded him, when they had passed several minutes in silence.

Reining his horse to a walk, he drew closer. "I was," he agreed, then fell silent again, watching her, for so long an interval that she wondered whether his thoughts were traveling the same improper channels as her own.

"And?" she prompted.

"I asked you yesterday whether you cared greatly about scandal. I had hoped . . . that is, I thought perhaps I could—"

Transferring both reins to one hand, she reached out with the other, to touch his arm. Even through layers of fabric, the contact had the power to stir her senses. "Luke, I don't care about scandal, truly. At least . . . not much," she admitted. "If you believe the only way to—"

He pulled to a halt, gazing earnestly into her eyes. "I don't want to do anything to hurt you, Pearl, not ever. I'd hoped I could provoke Bellowsworth into challenging me, simply by persisting in my attentions to you. Then I could free you of him quite handily."

"But . . . dueling is illegal," Pearl reminded him, alarmed. "If you shot him, you would be transported—possibly even hanged. I'd rather marry him than risk that, I assure you." Worry became anger. "How could you even consider such a thing?"

He grinned and shook his head. "I didn't intend to kill the fellow. He's such a coward, I had high hopes of persuading him to relinquish his claim upon you in exchange for his safety. I fear I may have underestimated the extent of his cowardice, however. I am not now certain I can provoke him to a challenge at all."

"Unless he has reason to believe you have compromised me," said Pearl, believing she now understood. "Which is why you asked about my tolerance for scandal."

"Yes. But there *is* another way." He was watching her again, gauging her. "One that need not involve you so directly. I can challenge him over some imagined slight."

Though touched by his concern, she shook her head. "No, if he is as great a coward as you believe, he might refuse it, or even bring the law to bear against you, which could be terribly risky given your recent, ah, lifestyle. Any challenge must come from him. Besides," she said with a sidelong glance, "I'd prefer to be . . . directly involved."

The heat in his eyes was unmistakable now. "I was rather hoping you would say that. Pearl, since that night—our one night together—"

"I have dreamed of it, too." Even now, in the full light of morning, in the open air of the park, the memory had the power to arouse her to the point of almost unbearable longing.

"Will you come with me now, Pearl?" he asked with sudden urgency. "It is early yet—no one who is likely to recognize us is about. And Hardwyck Hall is but a short distance away."

"Now I understand your choice of this path," she responded playfully, savoring his obvious desire for her. "But what matter if we are seen? Is that not the point?"

Again he smiled, his eyes all but devouring her where she sat, atop her mare. "Not the entire point, no."

She felt as though his gaze were a physical thing, caressing her body with fire. "Lead on, then," she said, forcing her voice to lightness. "I'll watch your seat, to see if it is still as stiff as it was yesterday."

"Stiffer, I assure you. As you will discover soon enough." Urging his horse to a quick trot, he exited the park and turned to the left along Picadilly. Pearl followed close behind, thoroughly enjoying her view of him, anticipating seeing more, much more, very soon.

They reached Hardwyck Hall in moments. A few early tradesmen were about, but none of the *ton*. Still, Luke led her around to the mews before swinging down from his horse and then helping her to dismount. "If we can somehow contrive to let only Bellowsworth know of this, the rest of Society need not discover it," he said.

"I told you I don't care," she reminded him, and at this moment she meant it. All she cared about was being with Luke again, sating her desire for him, a desire which threatened to rage out of control at any moment.

He dropped a quick kiss on her nose. "I know you did. But I care. I want to spare you any unpleasantness, if possible."

"I'm not finding this unpleasant in the least," she retorted, brazenly tilting her face up to him.

He lowered his lips to hers for a lingering kiss. She had missed this. Yes, a mere moment of heaven with Luke was worth any scandal. "Shall we go inside?" she asked breathlessly when at last he released her lips.

Without a word, he tucked her arm into his and led her to the back door. A single servant bustled about the kitchens, but at a flick of Luke's head, he magically disappeared. They encountered no one else on their way through the house. Up the great stairway, past the public rooms, up again. Pearl scarcely noticed her surroundings, however, anticipating what lay ahead.

Opening one of the many doors on the passage, he drew her into a room and then closed the door behind them. She had a hazy impression of a masculine bedchamber, a large four-poster bed with a deep burgundy counterpane, but her focus was on Luke alone. She reached up to pull his mouth down to hers for another kiss, more passionate than the last. It was like slaking a long thirst, while awakening an even deeper one.

Luke growled, deep in his throat, a sound of animal desire that only inflamed her further. She slid her arms up his back, threading her fingers through his hair, drawing him closer.

"Wait," he murmured against her lips. His arms were around her, and she felt him doing something behind her back. Then he pulled her hands down, his own moving from her shoulders down to her wrists—to strip off her gloves with his own now-bare hands.

She murmured her approval, reveling in once again feeling his skin against her own. Along with their gloves, they seemed to have stripped off the last of their inhibitions, as well. They fumbled with each other's clothing, clumsy in their haste.

When Pearl would have torn the stubborn fastenings from her habit, Luke stopped her, forcing her to wait while he undid every hook rather than damage the gown. She understood the necessity, but chafed at the delay. The moment the last hook came free, she shrugged out of the dress, stepping over the rich wine-colored fabric now pooled on the floor—the same color as the bed.

The bed. Luke seated himself on its edge to finish divesting himself of his boots and breeches. She slipped out of her undergarments while he did so, ready and more than ready to move to the next stage. Before he could rise, she was as naked as he, and moved quickly to join him. He looked up at her questioningly, and with a grin she pushed him back upon the bed.

"So the lady is in an authoritative mood today, is she?" he asked with an answering smile.

"She is." To demonstrate, she clambered atop him, pinning him to the down mattress, her hands on his shoulders.

His eyebrows arched with surprise, though there

was no dimming of the desire in his eyes. "I place my fate in your hands, my lady."

"Mmm. And not only your fate." With all of his masculine length before her, she set about exploring it in detail. First the firm planes of his chest, the muscles well defined under a sprinkling of curly down. His sides, smooth but hard, tapering down from the width of his shoulders to the narrowness of his hips. His flat, firm belly. Lower . . .

He gasped as her fingers encircled his shaft, still startling in its size. But now she felt no fear—only desire to have him within her once again, fulfilling the need she felt for him. She shifted above him until she straddled his hips with her thighs, then leaned down to kiss him, the length of his shaft trapped between them.

"You've become quite the seductress after only one lesson," he commented when she raised her head again.

"Ah, but it was such an excellent lesson." Still playful, she nuzzled his throat, then his chest, skimming her palms across his flat male nipples, hard with his arousal.

Without warning, he pulled her back down against him. "Time for another lesson, then, in just how effective your wiles are." Moving his hips slightly, he brought his shaft into direct contact with her most sensitive spot, causing her to gasp in her turn. Now he moved her slowly atop him, so that she slid along its length, every inch a new ecstasy.

She continued the rhythm on her own, freeing his hands for other pursuits. Reaching behind her, between her spread legs, he found her cleft and explored it, first with one finger, then two. She tightened convulsively around him, sensing that she was nearing her peak.

He must have sensed it, too, for he lifted her again, to impale her with his maleness. No tentative gentleness this time, but a thrust into her depths, joining them in a rhythm as old as humanity itself.

Pearl felt herself disintegrating around him, melting into fragments of pure sensation. Still he thrust, and still she climbed, until she cried out in an incoherent expression of ultimate pleasure. While she still throbbed about him, he thrust again and again, until his moans mingled with hers as he reached his own fulfillment.

Together they slowly descended from the dizzying heights, nerves tingling with the aftermath of the climax they had achieved. Pearl lifted her head to gaze on his face, not caring what he might read in her eyes. With a slow smile, he drew her mouth down for a kiss, long and languorous.

"You are the most amazing woman I have ever known," he murmured at length. "I love you, Pearl."

The longed-for words reverberated through her being, bringing a pleasure nearly as intense as the physical one they had just shared. By way of reply, she kissed him again, trying to communicate all she felt through her lips and her body, still joined with his. To her surprise, she felt his shaft swell within her in response.

"To hell with Bellowsworth and Society," Luke growled when she lifted her head again to regard him questioningly. "What would you say to an elopement? With a fast carriage and good horses along the way, we could reach Scotland in three days' time."

It was the first time he had mentioned marriage directly, and she blinked in surprise. "Now? Today?" The fog of euphoria cleared slightly, allowing traces of reason in. "What if we were overtaken?"

"That doesn't sound like a refusal, at least." His eyes twinkled warmly.

She smiled. "Not a refusal at all. But—"

"But we should plan, to maximize our chances of success. You're right. And we will ... in a few moments." As he spoke, he began to move within her again, rolling her onto her side.

Pearl would no more refuse him in this than in an elopement. She kept rolling until he was atop her, and let him direct the renewal of their passion, even sweeter than before, now that she knew he wanted a lifetime with her.

"I must get back," Pearl said regretfully, some time later, when they both lay sated again. "Everyone will be awake and about by now, and my absence will be noticed. I don't wish to put Hettie in an untenable situation again."

Luke could not protest, much though he'd have liked to. "Very well, my sweet." With a last, quick kiss, he rose, then helped her out of bed for a longer kiss that promised the future.

As at Oakshire House, they dressed in silence, but this time punctuated by smiles and touches. They were linked now, and would remain so, whatever came. Luke had never felt more content.

Once they were both dressed, he led her back through the house and out the kitchen door. No servants were in evidence, and he congratulated himself on having the foresight to warn them away before leaving the house this morning.

Pearl apparently noticed as well. As he put his hands to her waist, preparing to toss her into her sidesaddle, she commented, "It seems you took the precaution of sending most of your servants away for this occasion. Were you so certain of me?"

She was smiling, clearly not upset by the thought, but he felt obliged to defend himself anyway. "I merely wished to be prepared for all eventualities, of course."

Chuckling, Pearl opened her mouth for a retort. Before she could speak, however, another voice cut through the morning quiet of the mews.

"So it's true. Lady Pearl, I would not have believed it of you!"

As one, they both spun to face Lord Bellowsworth where he stood at the entrance to the mews, his eyes wide with horror.

"Back to Plan A," Luke muttered under his breath. Releasing Pearl's waist, he strode toward Bellowsworth. "You are abroad early, my lord." Though he spoke softly, his voice held a warning— one his unexpected visitor did not heed.

"Not as early as the two of you, it seems." Bellowsworth's eyes flicked from Pearl to Luke and back, his expression still disbelieving. "I am shocked, my lady. Beyond shocked. Whatever am I to tell my mother?"

Luke had to swallow a laugh at this unexpected conclusion, but managed to keep any hint of amusement from his voice. "You won't be telling anyone,

Bellowsworth. To do so would be to besmirch the Lady Pearl's honor."

Tearing his eyes away from Pearl, Bellowsworth finally focused on Luke, now directly before him. "I'd say you've done that already, Hardwyck."

"And?" Luke asked ominously.

"And . . . and you'll both be sorry for it, when word gets out. The Duchess will be most displeased, my lady."

Luke sighed inwardly. The man was a complete milksop—he simply could not be provoked. Deliberately, he removed his gloves. Out of the corner of his eye he saw Pearl watching, her eyes wide—but not as wide as Bellowsworth's.

"What . . . what are you doing?" he stammered.

Instead of replying, Luke struck him across the face with his gloves—not violently, but smartly enough to sting. The soft *thwap* of kidskin against flesh was amplified by the silence around them. Behind him, Pearl gasped—as did Bellowsworth.

"I knew you were not worthy of her," Luke said, almost conversationally. "As you will not defend the lady's honor, I see I must. Name your seconds."

For a moment, he thought Bellowsworth would refuse—or faint dead away. But the man apparently had some vestigial backbone after all. "Very well, Hardwyck," said in a strangled whisper. "I'll . . . I'll send his name to you shortly."

"Have him call on Lord Marcus Northrup." Luke coolly reminded him of the proper procedure. "He will act for me." Marcus's face, when informed of this fact, would be most amusing. Luke rather looked forward to seeing it.

"Very . . . very well." Bellowsworth seemed completely at a loss, shaken almost to the point of tears. "May I escort you home, Lady Pearl?"

Luke tensed. How dared he . . . ?

"Thank you, no." Pearl's voice held not the slightest quaver. "It seems more appropriate that my *protector* do so."

Luke had to bite his lip to stifle his amusement at the double entendre. Whether Bellowsworth caught it, he could not tell, for the man merely flushed scarlet and bowed stiffly before disappearing around the corner as quickly as he had appeared.

The moment he was gone, Pearl ran to Luke and surprised him with a fierce hug. "You were marvelous!" she exclaimed. "But now we must manage our elopement before this meeting can take place."

Luke set her away from him, both hands on her shoulders, with a frown. "What do you mean? I'm quite looking forward to meeting Bellowsworth on the field of honor—not that the man seems to have any."

"Exactly. I don't think he'll go through with it. More likely, he'll report the whole thing to the authorities and attempt to have you arrested. We dare not risk it." Her violet eyes were wide with concern for him. Luke was deeply touched, but he shook his head.

"I'm sorry, my love. Whatever the risk, I cannot fail to appear, particularly as I was the one to offer the challenge. Even a thief such as I has more honor than that."

She opened her mouth to protest, but he silenced her with a quick kiss. "Besides," he continued, "Bellowsworth may surprise us and come prepared to duel. For all we know, he's a crack shot."

"This is supposed to comfort me?" she demanded, her fine eyes now snapping with anger. "Men can be so absurd, with their high-flown ideas of honor. History is littered with *honorable* corpses. I would not have you become another one."

"Never fear, my sweet," he said, reaching for her again. "I promise to be careful. Now let me see you home."

She spun away from him. "I'll see myself home. It appears I am the only one I can truly rely upon after all."

Her grand exit was somewhat marred when she had to wait for Luke to help her into her saddle. It gave him one more chance to reason with her.

"Pearl, it will all turn out right, you'll see. No one will be killed, and Bellowsworth will relinquish his claim on you. We won't have to elope after all."

She stared down at him from atop her mare, her expression unreadable. "Then I suppose it is worth the risk—for you. Good day, my lord." With that, she turned her mount, flicked the reins, and was gone.

Luke stared after her with a frown. Now, what the devil had she meant by that? He would call upon her later and find out. Right now, he'd best alert Marcus to expect a call from Bellowsworth's second, whoever it might be. Grinning in anticipation, he vaulted into the saddle.

"I should never have gone there. You were right, damn you. I was so certain you must be mistaken."

Wallis Knox sat at his ease in the small tavern where he had told Bellowsworth to meet him, dispassionately watching his confederate as he threatened to dissolve into a puddle of nerves.

"Then it is as well that you went, is it not?" he asked dryly. "You would not have wished to marry the girl while she was carrying on an intrigue with my nephew."

Bellowsworth propped his elbows on the table and dropped his head into his hands. "No, I suppose not. But now I must fight a duel with the blackguard, and I've no doubt he means to kill me."

"You challenged him? Good for you! I didn't think you had it in you." It was just what Knox had hoped for, in fact, though from what he knew of Bellowsworth, he'd rather feared—

"No, he challenged me. I could hardly refuse, could I?"

Knox stared. "*He* challenged *you*? And how did that come about, may I ask?"

Haltingly, Bellowsworth related the entire conversation between himself and the upstart Lord Hardwyck. At the conclusion, Knox's mouth twisted unpleasantly.

"He was right, you know. You're *not* worthy of her." The marquess's head came up in protest, but Knox waved him to silence. "Fear not, however. You'll be in no danger. I'll see to that."

"But . . . how?" Resentment battled with hope in Bellowsworth's pale brown eyes.

"I've been making inquiries, and have even put to use certain information you have given me, of which you apparently missed the significance. All things considered, it is entirely possible that we can have young Hardwyck taken up by the authorities before your dreaded meeting takes place."

"Taken up . . . ? On what charge?"

Smiling, Knox took a long draught of ale before answering, enjoying the other man's impatience. "My dear Lord Bellowsworth," he answered at length, "I have every reason to believe that Luke di Santo, now styling himself Earl of Hardwyck, is none other than the notorious Saint of Seven Dials."

Chapter 20

Pearl was still seething when she rounded the corner of Mount Street. How dared Luke risk their future this way? Couldn't he see that Bellowsworth was not worth any such sacrifice? She focused on her anger, refusing for the moment to consider the significance of his final remark.

Looking up, she saw John Marley waiting for her atop the bay gelding. His relief when he spotted her was obvious. "I'd begun to worry you'd gone home by a different way, my lady," he commented, falling into position behind her.

"My apologies, John. I found riding particularly exhilarating today, so continued longer than I had intended." Much of her earlier exhilaration and contentment had been swamped by anger and worry, however.

The Duchess emerged from the breakfast room as Pearl entered the front hall. "So you return at last," she said by way of greeting. "Do not tell me you were riding until now, as your abigail informed me."

"I was indeed, Your Grace. The morning is exceedingly fine. I brought a groom, for propriety's sake." Pearl kept her voice pleasant, though it cost her an effort.

"Get upstairs and change out of your habit at once," her stepmother said then, abandoning the argument before it could begin. "Morning callers may arrive at any moment, and you will wish to look your best—particularly for Lord Bellowsworth, who I daresay is still somewhat offended by the attention Lord Hardwyck paid you last night."

"I daresay," Pearl echoed, a spurt of amusement lightening her mood briefly as she remembered the look on Bellowsworth's face twenty minutes since. "If he does not call, we will know just how offended, I presume."

Before Obelia could do more than gasp in outrage, Pearl headed up the wide staircase, anxious for a few moments alone with her thoughts. Hettie was waiting in her chambers, however, so her musings had to be put off while her maid scurried to divest her of her habit and help her into a primrose-yellow morning gown. Brushing out Pearl's hair, Hettie regarded her mistress knowingly in the glass.

"You've had quite a morning, I take it, my lady," she commented.

Pearl frowned at her abigail's reflection. "Why do you say that? Simply because I am so late returning?" In truth, it had been the most momentous morning of her life, but she could not tell

Hettie that—not yet. Not until she had puzzled things through.

"That and . . . other things. You have a different look about you, somehow. I hope everything is all right?"

"I hope so, too," said Pearl with a sigh.

Hettie did not probe further but completed Pearl's toilette in silence, then left her in much-needed solitude. Pearl knew that the Duchess would be sending for her the moment their first caller arrived, but she was determined not to go down beforehand. Instead, she went to the window near the fireplace and gazed sightlessly down at the gardens below.

We won't have to elope after all.

The words she had avoided contemplating returned the moment she dropped her guard. Surely . . . surely he had meant that if Bellowsworth released her from their betrothal, they could marry more conventionally? But he had not said so. He had only suggested an elopement when no other way out of her predicament presented itself.

Now it seemed he was eager to grasp at any alternative, even at grave risk to himself. He would sooner risk death or arrest than sacrifice himself on the altar of matrimony.

Pearl tried to tell herself she should be pleased. A quick elopement would have meant giving up Fairbourne, as her birthday was still more than three weeks distant. Now it would be secure. Somehow, though, that reflection brought her no satisfaction. The thought of living on and managing the estate— alone—seemed unutterably dreary. With whom would she share her successes? To whom would she turn for advice and reassurance?

It seemed she was not quite so independent as she had believed. Vainly, she tried to summon pride to her aid, but even pride failed her. Without Luke, her sense of purpose seemed to have evaporated. Listlessly, she turned from the window just as a tap came at the door.

"Her Grace bids you join her below, my lady," came a maid's voice through the panels. "Callers are arriving."

With a spurt of hope that one of the callers might be Luke, here to dispel her worries, Pearl checked her appearance one last time in the glass and left her chamber.

Luke was not below, however. Old Mrs. Haverstock, widow of their former vicar, was the only caller, joined shortly by Lady Wittington and Miss Chalmers, who apparently spent every morning of their existence calling upon others. Over the next two hours, a fair number of ladies and one or two gentlemen came to pay their respects and exchange gossip, but there was no sign of Luke—nor of Lord Bellowsworth.

At length everyone had gone and Pearl followed the Duchess to the dining room for luncheon. She was famished, as she had completely neglected to eat breakfast. Her stepmother's first words took the edge from her appetite, however.

"I knew it. You have offended Lord Bellowsworth more severely than I feared, else he would have called this morning."

This time the memory of this morning's encounter brought no amusement with it. "So it would seem. Or perhaps his mother required him."

But what kept Luke away?

As the afternoon drew on, Pearl again allowed herself to hope that he might appear to invite her for a drive—but he did not. Nor did he make an appearance at Lady Wittington's ridotto that evening. Bellowsworth was absent as well, though he had originally planned to meet Pearl there.

Though the Duchess clearly considered this a most ominous sign, Pearl was quite grateful for *his* absence, as any meeting right now would be awkward in the extreme, and perhaps even disastrous should he find himself unable to hold his tongue about what he had seen this morning. But it did not make up for Luke's failure to appear.

The next morning, she arrived at their accustomed path in Hyde Park even earlier than before. John had insisted on remaining with her this time, after Hettie had impressed upon him the importance of doing so, but Pearl did not care. Just a few private moments with Luke would be sufficient to allay her fears . . . she hoped.

But though she waited for well over an hour, cantering up and down the lane, he never joined her.

As she rode slowly back to Berkley Square, Pearl's imagination ran riot with wild fears. Had the duel already taken place? Had Luke killed Bellowsworth after all, and been forced to flee the country? Or perhaps Bellowsworth had ordered his arrest for challenging him, coward that he was. Could a peer be arrested for such a cause? She did not know. But what if that peer was also accused of thievery? Just how much did Bellowsworth know?

These and even more horrifying suppositions occupied her throughout breakfast and another tedious bout of morning callers, rendering her quite unsociable. The last caller was leaving, and already Obelia was frowning in preparation for another tirade, when a late visitor was announced.

"Lord Hardwyck," the butler intoned.

Hope, relief, disbelieving joy, all sent Pearl's spirits soaring—until she saw Luke's face. "My lord?" she asked uncertainly as he bowed over her hand, mindful of the Duchess's proximity. "Is anything wrong?"

He met her eyes then, his own tired and bleak. "Merely a matter of a missing servant, my lady," he responded. She could hear the effort it took to keep his voice steady. "I confess I am concerned, however."

"La!" exclaimed the Duchess. "You will find, Lord Hardwyck, that servants can be most unreliable. If someone offers them better wages, they are gone in an instant, with no thought of the loyalty they owe you."

"Of course, Your Grace," he said stiffly, moving to take a seat. Pearl had never seen him so dejected.

He did not remain long, as it was already past the fashionable hour for calls, but Pearl was determined to have a private word with him before he left. Under the pretext of asking his opinion on a bit of needlework she'd done, she managed to lean close enough to whisper without her stepmother overhearing.

"Is it Flute who is missing?"

He nodded. "Since yesterday morning. I fear— Yes, the combination of blue and green is most pleasing," he concluded in a louder voice, as the Duchess turned a suspicious eye upon them.

A moment later he rose, preparatory to leaving. "Perhaps if you are not otherwise engaged, you might care for a drive this afternoon, my lady?"

"Must I remind you, Lord Hardwyck, that Lady Pearl is betrothed?" The Duchess was clearly outraged—again.

"Am I not to be allowed to take the air until Lord Bellowsworth sees fit to grace me with his company?" asked Pearl, just as haughtily. "I am not yet his wife, that he may order my comings and goings. I should be pleased to drive out with you, my lord."

"You are all kindness, my lady." Turning to the Duchess with a deep bow, he added, "I promise to behave with all propriety, Your Grace. A drive, nothing more."

Obelia sniffed, but offered no further objection until he was gone. Then she turned to Pearl, her fine eyes narrowed. "May I have a similar promise from you?"

Wide-eyed, Pearl responded, "Of course, Your Grace. What do you take me for?"

"Perhaps the less said on that subject, the better." With that stinging retort, she swept from the room.

Pearl, after a moment's consideration, decided to take her meal in her chambers. Not only would that spare her further barbs, but she wished to plan for her outing. She must be ready for any eventuality, even a sudden elopement, though she knew in her heart that was less likely than ever.

She remained in her chambers until Luke arrived. There still had been no word whatsoever from Lord Bellowsworth, which she knew must look exceedingly odd to Obelia. She wondered whether she had mentioned it to her father.

The moment she heard Luke's voice below, she hurried downstairs, unwilling to leave him to tête-à-tête with her stepmother for even a few moments.

"I'm so pleased the weather has held fine," she said brightly, intercepting him before he could enter the parlor. "Here is my maid now. Shall we go?"

Luke still appeared somber and unwilling to tarry, so with only a formal bow to the Duchess, he motioned for Pearl to precede him down the front steps to his waiting curricle. The groom holding the horses was unfamiliar to her, which she presumed meant that Flute had not yet returned.

Luke took up the reins, the groom sitting up behind with Hettie, as Flute had done on their previous drive. Though she was fair to bursting with curiosity, Pearl waited until they were well away from Oakshire House to speak.

"Any news?"

"I'm afraid so," he replied quietly, but whether because of lowered spirits or because he did not wish to speak freely before the groom, she couldn't tell. "He was arrested in Seven Dials yesterday. I just discovered it an hour ago."

"Arrested?" Pearl whispered, a hand at her throat. "What did . . . He didn't . . . ?"

"No. He was simply visiting a friend there. I was finally able to find someone who saw what happened. I feared it might be the case, when Argos was found dragging his lead, not far from where I . . . from where Flute's friend lives."

Pearl believed she understood. "Then it was because of, ah, prior events that he was apprehended?"

"So it would seem."

They drove in silence until reaching the park gates, at which point Luke pulled to a halt and turned to the groom. "Sam, take Lady Pearl's abigail for a turn about the loop here. The lady and I wish to walk for a bit."

Luke helped Pearl out of the curricle and the groom obeyed without question, though Hettie frowned and craned her neck to watch her mistress as they drove on. "Sam is new," Luke explained the moment they were out of earshot. "One or two of my other servants have vouched for him, but I don't know him well myself yet. No point in running unnecessary risks."

"How much *do* your servants know about you?" Pearl asked curiously.

He shrugged. "Flute knows the most, of course, and a fair number are lads I knew from before—lads who deserved a chance at a better life."

"Boys who also helped you to steal?" she asked dubiously. She'd nearly managed to forget that distasteful aspect of Luke's former "career."

"No, no. Flute is the only one who ever worked directly with me, and never in any actual robberies. He merely helped me convert my, er, takings into coin. I had opportunity to get to know several of his street mates, however, and did what I could to better their lot—which wasn't much, until recently."

Pearl's heart swelled with admiration for the man he was, then and now, but she returned to the matter at hand, knowing they didn't have much time. "But now Flute has been arrested as your former accomplice?"

"Yes. I had the news of Mrs. Plank—she's the one who found Argos. It seems Flute walked him down to Seven Dials to visit a few old cronies of his, while he was making himself scarce yesterday morning."

Pearl flushed at the memory of why Luke would have given him such instructions, but he continued without seeming to notice.

"Apparently word was all over the streets today that Flute was apprehended not far from there—at my old lodgings, in fact. It seems the place was still being watched. I'd have thought Bow Street would have moved on to other matters by now. The Mountheaths must be paying them well." He shook his head.

"Do you know where he is being held? Perhaps we need merely pay a fine, or—"

"Yes, that's odd, as well. He's already been locked up in Newgate, though there's been no time for a hearing as yet. An unusual precaution, considering the trifling nature of his crime, I must say. As unusual as the publicity surrounding his capture."

Pearl thought for a moment as they slowly strolled along. "Perhaps they are concerned—or hoping?—that the Saint might try to rescue him."

Luke sent her a grim smile. "My thought exactly—which leaves me with a bit of a dilemma, as you might imagine. I can hardly leave him there to rot in my stead, after all."

"But if they are expecting you . . . Wait, I may have an idea. But first, tell me of your meeting with Bellowsworth. Has it not yet taken place?"

He shook his head. "His second—Ribbleton—did not even call upon mine until late last evening, Marcus tells me. They've set the meeting for Friday morning, two days hence."

She snorted. "I'd have thought he'd have wanted to get it over quickly, but perhaps he is hoping the

delay will allow him a chance to avoid it alto-
gether." A sudden thought struck her. "Could he
have been involved in Flute's arrest, think you?"

"I doubt it, as it must have happened before I issued the challenge. Merely a lucky coincidence for
him, I imagine, should my rescue attempt prove un-
successful."

"But it won't! Here's my idea." Quickly she outlined her simple plan, but he was shaking his head
even before she could finish.

"I can't let you involve yourself in this, Pearl. It's
too risky."

"Far less risky than if you go alone—as yourself.
Surely you must see that? Even if we are unsuccess-
ful, no blame will attach to me. But what about your
part in this scheme? Can you do it?"

"I'm sure I can, but—"

"Then it's settled." Her tone brooked no argument. She knew she was being high-handed again,
but she didn't care. Luke's safety was too important
to her.

He walked beside her in silence for a long while,
frowning, clearly weighing various options. Finally,
just as the curricle approached them again, he said,
"Very well. But I reserve the right to call the whole
thing off if I believe for a moment that you could be
in any danger."

"Agreed," she said cheerfully, her spirits higher
than they'd been since they parted yesterday.

They hadn't had any opportunity to discuss their
own future, but she was willing to leave that for another time. It was enough to know he still cared,
and that she could be of use to him.

"It has been some time since I went on a charitable crusade," Pearl said as Luke handed her back into the curricle. "I'm sure I will feel the better for the one I plan tomorrow."

"An admirable undertaking, my lady—one I mean to emulate someday." Luke took his place on her right and flicked the reins, putting the pair into a trot.

As the Duchess had never shown any interest in charity, Pearl was confident she could convince her stepmother to let her go alone, with only a servant or two. As they drove back to Oakshire House, she was already eagerly anticipating tomorrow's adventure.

Luke had to admire Pearl's command as he followed her into the courtyard of Newgate Prison the next morning, along with John Marley, her erstwhile groom, and her abigail, Hettie. Dressed in nondescript, unidentifiable livery, Luke was masquerading as a manservant, while she was every inch the grand lady out to do good among the poor and downtrodden.

"You there! Guard!" she called to a uniformed man standing near the outer door. "I have brought clothing for the prisoners, and wish to dispense advice to some of the women as well. Summon the chaplain, if you please."

At her nod, Luke and the others pulled bundles of old clothing, discards of the Oakshire servants, from the carriage.

"Of . . . of course, my lady," the guard stammered, then disappeared inside.

Pearl turned to Luke the moment the guard was

gone. "Where is he being held?" she whispered. "Were you able to find out?"

"On the second story, near the back right corner, in an individual cell." Two of his footmen, formerly fellow climbing boys with Flute, had been only too eager to undertake a reconnaissance mission last night to discover the specifics.

"I'll make certain we go near that area, then will keep everyone's attention diverted and trust you to do the rest. If we should—" She broke off as the guard returned, followed not by Reverend Cotton, whom Pearl had encountered twice before when performing similar charity work, but by an officious gaoler who identified himself as a Mr. Werner.

"My lady, we are most honored," he exclaimed, "and the prisoners will be most grateful, I assure you. Your generosity will earn you an exalted place in heaven."

Pearl inclined her head regally. "No doubt, Mr. Werner. At present, however, I am merely concerned with giving some relief to these poor unfortunates here below. Pray take me to them."

"Your . . . your ladyship wishes to enter the prison itself? But the conditions are most unsanitary and unsafe. If you will just leave the—"

"No, Mr. Werner, to witness those conditions is a part of my mission, that I may report upon them to my father, the Duke." Luke had to hide a grin at her imperiousness. "If you fear for my safety, I suggest you summon every possible man to accompany me as a guard. Perhaps they may be edified by what I shall have to say as we proceed."

The turnkey scurried to do her bidding, returning a few minutes later with half a dozen men, most of them looking as brutish as any of the criminals in their care. "Shall we go, then, my lady?"

Pearl motioned for the rest of the clothing to be brought from the carriage, and had it distributed among her increased entourage. Luke passed into the dark confines of Newgate along with the rest of them.

"The very air here is depressing," exclaimed Pearl, sniffing disdainfully. "This atmosphere cannot be conducive to a spirit of rehabilitation, Mr. Werner. Pray make a note of it." She thrust a small notebook and a pencil at the gaoler.

The man muttered something, nodding and scribbling, as Pearl continued her pronouncements on the lack of light and the narrowness of the passages. When they reached the first block of cells, she stopped in evident horror.

"Such crowded conditions, Mr. Werner! Unsanitary indeed, and most prone to the spread of contagion, I should imagine. Are all prisoners crammed into bunches like this?"

"Ah, no, my lady, not all," he stammered. "The more dangerous criminals, and the condemned, are often put into private cells, separating their vicious influence from the others." He pointed down a dim passage to their left.

Pearl turned to look, then caught Luke's eye with a questioning glance. He nodded, almost imperceptibly. Based on his information, somewhere along that corridor was where Flute was imprisoned.

"I feel the need of a few more of your men about me," Pearl declared with an elaborate shudder that made Luke smile in spite of the seriousness of the situation. "Then I wish you to take me to the women's cells. Here, let these items be distributed here."

As Mr. Werner called for more guards, Pearl had most of the men's clothing separated into a pile, which she indicated the largest of the guards should distribute to the prisoners. In the confusion, it was an easy matter for Luke to slip down the corridor leading to the private cells, pressing himself into the first doorway he reached until the augmented group had moved on.

As he had hoped, and as Pearl had no doubt intended, whatever guard had been posted outside Flute's tiny cell had now been pressed into service for her protection. Trying not to think about what risk she might be running or the sights assailing her sensibilities, Luke hurried to the last door on the right, to whisper through the keyhole.

"Flute? Are you in there?"

"Aye, sir!" came the immediate reply. "Squint said you'd be comin' for me today."

"Just a moment, then." A quick glance up the passage showed it still empty. Pulling a set of lock picks from his pocket, Luke fit one into the keyhole with a deftness borne of long practice. In a few seconds he had the door open.

Flute greeted him with a grin. "I'm right glad to see you ain't lost your touch, sir!"

"As am I," Luke responded, "but we haven't much time. Come—no, this way." He led the way, in the opposite direction Pearl and the others had gone.

Just as they reached the corner, however, a burly guard appeared right in front of them. "Hoy, there! Who are you and where d'ye think ye're goin'?"

Rather than attempt a reply, Luke smiled at the man, grabbed Flute by the wrist, and turned to run the other way. After a startled moment, the guard followed in hot pursuit, but Luke hoped they had all the lead they would need.

Rounding another corner, he saw Pearl and her entourage just entering the women's wing. She glanced his way and at once halted and raised her hands to distract the attention of the others. Luke slowed his pace to a quick walk.

"My good men, upholders of the laws of England!" Pearl cried as he approached. "As we observe the plight of these pitiable women, I want to be certain you see everything with eyes full open, as I shall. For you will be held accountable at the final judgment for how you treat these poor misguided wretches."

Luke and Flute approached the group, then turned down another passage leading back toward the main entrance, before the guard in pusuit came around the corner behind them.

"Where . . . where did they go?" he heard the guard say as he reached the group, interrupting Pearl's impromptu sermon. Luke and Flute kept walking, making as little noise as possible.

"I beg your pardon!" came her indignant response. "Why are you not with your fellows? Mr. Werner, did you not promise me every available man for my protection?"

"I did indeed, my lady," responded the gaoler. "Mr. Fithers, why were you not at your post earlier?"

Luke did not wait to hear the man's explanation. Still holding Flute by the wrist, he rounded the next corner, then released him. "Here, put this on." He

handed Flute the suit of clothes he'd brought along
for the purpose.

"Aye, sir!" Donning the cleaner, more respectable
garb, Flute grinned. "She's a plucky one, and no
mistake."

"She is indeed," Luke replied. He hoped she
would not bring any suspicion on herself for
thwarting his capture just now.

Then Flute startled him by asking, "D'ye mean to
marry her, sir?"

Luke led him to the prison entrance, still merci-
fully unlocked and unguarded, before answering.
"Time enough to worry about that later. Right now
my concern is to get you safely home."

Warned by his tone not to pursue the matter,
Flute accompanied him out into the street and
around the corner in silence, leaving Luke to his
thoughts.

The past half hour had reminded him vividly of
who he'd been until just a few weeks ago. He also
knew now beyond all doubt that the authorities had
not given up their hunt for the Saint of Seven Dials.
Though a lifetime with Pearl would be heaven on
earth, had he any right to risk her happiness, even
her safety, should the truth about him become public knowledge?

He honestly didn't know.

Chapter 21

The hour Pearl spent at Newgate was one of the longest of her life. The suffering and squalor she saw there only reinforced her determination to institute social reforms, but it was Luke who primarily occupied her mind. She had deflected the pursuing guard, but had he escaped Newgate without being recognized? Where would he hide Flute so that he could not be found? And what of that dreaded duel tomorrow?

These and other questions hammered so persistently at her brain that it was all she could do to keep up her role as Lady Bountiful among the prisoners. The masses of clothing she had brought were distributed, she gave what she hoped were appropriately rallying speeches to two groups of women prisoners, and finally felt she could reasonably leave.

"I have your word, Mr. Werner, that the quality of the food will be investigated?" she asked the gaoler as they made their way back into the noon sunshine.

"Of course, my lady. And the overcrowding, as well. If you could prevail upon your esteemed father to influence Parliament to set aside funds for a larger facility . . ."

"Yes, I certainly will," she agreed. "And now I have other work to do." Glancing up and down Ludgate Hill as she climbed into her carriage, she saw no sign of any disturbance, and hoped that meant Luke had escaped cleanly with Flute. Bidding a dignified good day to the turnkey and the rest of her temporary entourage, she signaled the coachman to whip up the horses.

Pearl's apprehensions lasted until midafternoon, when she received a scrap of paper, brought to the house, so the footman said, by a filthy street urchin. On it was scrawled but one word and an initial, but it was enough to relieve her mind:

Success.—L

She tucked the paper into her bodice just before her stepmother returned to the parlor, her afternoon conference with the housekeeper concluded.

Pearl still had countless questions she wanted to ask Luke, about today, tomorrow, and the future—Flute's and theirs—but for now she tried to be content. Still, needlework had never seemed so dreary. She was about to excuse herself, intending to retire to her books in hopes of more effective distraction, when a visitor was announced.

"Why, Lord Bellowsworth!" the Duchess exclaimed as he entered. "I vow, we had nearly despaired of seeing you again, it's been so long. I assume it was some urgent business which has kept you away from us?"

"My apologies, Your Grace," he replied with a bow. "I have been extremely busy, yes." He sat in the chair she indicated and answered a few more questions rather absently, then turned to Pearl.

"I was hoping that you might consent to step out with me, my lady—perhaps into the gardens? We could . . . talk."

Obelia answered for Pearl. "Yes, you two young people run along. I'm certain you have much to say to each other after several days apart."

Pearl rose obediently. "Certainly, my lord." Though not particularly eager for a private conference with Lord Bellowsworth, it would be preferable to stilted, empty chatter—or worse—in her stepmother's presence.

They passed through the house in silence, out to the formal rose gardens behind. The blooms, nearing their peak, filled the air with fragrance as they traversed the graveled path. When they reached the wooden bench beneath the arbor, Lord Bellowsworth finally spoke.

"I had hoped to receive word from you before this, my lady, putting an end to our betrothal. Under the circumstances, I cannot imagine why you have not done so."

Though he spoke stiffly, Pearl understood that he was hurt by her faithlessness and felt a pang of guilt. Pompous and boring he might be, but none of this was his fault. While she was quite certain he had never truly loved her, discovering that she preferred another must have been a blow to his pride, no small thing for a man to absorb.

"My lord, I owe you the deepest of apologies," she said sincerely. "It was never my intent to deceive or dishonor you, but the Duchess—"

"Would not allow you to cry off?" he asked, his frown lightening with sympathy.

She shook her head, trying to frame the words that must be spoken. "I realize, however, that her feelings are of no consequence—nor even my father's. I had no right to leave you dangling in this way."

To her surprise, he took her hand in his. "Lady Pearl, if your esteemed parents insist, I am yet willing to marry you, if you can but assure me that you are virtuous. Lord Hardwyck is not the sort—that is, I have reason to believe—"

"I love him, my lord," she said simply, stopping him midsentence.

His eyes widened. "But you scarcely know the fellow! You can't possibly know—"

"I know enough." Pearl sat down on the bench, and reluctantly he sat beside her.

She continued, "I confess I had a *tendre* for him before I knew anything about his title, but I did not believe my feelings were returned." That was close enough to the truth to cause her only the slightest of qualms.

"I understood from the start that you accepted my suit out of obedience to your parents, but if you cared for another . . ." He still seemed unconvinced.

"My stepmother—the Duchess—can be most persuasive." There was no need for him to know what weapon she had used for that persuasion.

Now he nodded in understanding. "Yes, I have noticed that myself—as persuasive in her way as my own mother. If your obedience went so counter to your own inclinations, however, your agreement, though admirable, was perhaps unwise."

Pearl blinked at him in surprise. Was he attempting to be humorous? But no, he appeared completely serious.

"Yes, I know that now," she admitted with equal seriousness. "Once I learned that Lord Hardwyck did indeed return my affection, I realize, I should have cried off at once. I will do so now, of course. Then you need not fight him."

She expected him to exhibit relief, but instead he rose and began to pace. "It is too late for that, I fear. Everything is arranged." After another moment, he turned to face her. "He has duped you, my lady, as he has duped us all. I had hoped not to be the one to tell you this, but Lord Hardwyck has been involved in . . . illegal activities."

Pearl faced him steadily. "I know," she said quietly.

He stared. "You know? And yet you claim to love the fellow?"

"He has reformed." She spoke earnestly, determined to convince him. "He made some unwise choices, yes, but purely from necessity. Now he has no further need to do so. He was only forced into such circumstances through his uncle's villainy."

Bellowsworth started. "His uncle?"

"It is not generally known, but the man we all knew as Lord Hardwyck achieved that title through the murder of his brother and the attempted murder of his nephew—the present Lord Hardwyck. Only through the cleverness of his mother did he escape into hiding."

Horror replaced surprise. "Surely not, my lady! The man who moved among us for so many years, a pillar of Society, a murderer? If true, how could such a thing have been kept quiet?"

"The Prince Regent wished it," she responded. "You may ask my father about the truth of it, however, for he is familiar with all of the particulars, as am I."

Now Bellowsworth began to pace again. "Oh, my. Oh, dear. This is dreadful news, simply dreadful. I should have known something was wrong. And now you say you love the fellow." As she watched, he grew more and more agitated, muttering to himself and wringing his hands.

"My lord, what are you going on about? Why is this news so particularly dreadful now? It all happened more than twenty years ago."

He stopped then and met her eyes, his own filled with misery. "Knox—Lord Hardwyck's uncle—is here in Town. It . . . it is he who told me Lord Hardwyck was a thief—in fact, the notorious Saint of Seven Dials."

Pearl felt a cold knot begin to form in her stomach, but retained enough of her wits to say, "How preposterous! But you say he is in Town? Now?" That explained Flute's arrest, and the trap laid for Luke, she had no doubt. Bellowsworth's next words confirmed her suspicion.

"He meant to have him arrested before the duel—that is why the meeting was not scheduled until tomorrow. But he now has told me that I must meet him after all. That he has an alternate plan to bring him to justice." He began wringing his hands again.

"What plan? Tell me, my lord, quickly."

Her urgency seemed to help him to focus. Seating himself again, he explained. "He . . . he told me that I need merely make it look good—that I should aim at him, but miss my shot. Not that that will be difficult, as I have never been much of a marksman."

"But he has promised you that Luke . . . Lord Hardwyck will not shoot you?" Pearl had to fight the urge to run to Luke instantly to warn him—but first she needed to know all.

"Yes. He said his pistol would be rendered inoperable. That is to be merely a safeguard, however, for he expects that the authorities will arrive to take him into custody before either of us can fire."

Pearl frowned. "Did he say how he intended to tamper with Lord Hardwyck's pistol?"

"No. But as I said, he claimed it would not matter—that things would not get that far. Do . . . do you think he has not told me all?"

"I think it distinctly likely that he has not told you all," she said, "but I thank you for telling me what you have. I hope to be able to use the information to avert a tragedy."

She rose abruptly. "I will tell my father that our betrothal is at an end, my lord, as I have promised." Her mind, however, was focused on Luke and how she might warn him.

"Of . . . of course, my lady," he said, standing hastily. "Mother will be pleased—er, that is . . . If there is anything—"

Pearl managed a smile of reasonable sincerity.

"Thank you, but I believe I can handle it myself. I give you good day, my lord."

Leaving him to find his own way out, she walked quickly back into the house and directly up to her own chambers. Ringing for Hettie, she sat down to compose a letter to Luke. Hettie appeared, and Pearl motioned her to wait while she continued writing. A few moments later, she sanded and sealed the letter and handed it to her maid.

"See that Lord Hardwyck receives this," she said. "It is to be delivered into his own hand and none other. I wish to be informed as soon as it is accomplished, and to be brought any reply he may wish to send."

"Yes, my lady." Hettie took the letter and hurried out. Five minutes later she returned to say that John had left with the letter and would report back directly.

"Thank you, Hettie. Is my father at home?" Now that the most pressing task was done, she might as well fulfill her promise to Bellowsworth and officially end their betrothal.

"I don't believe so, my lady, but I will inquire." When she returned again, it was with the news that the Duke was from home.

Pearl preferred to present her broken betrothal to her stepmother as an accomplished fact once she had spoken with her father, so she settled down with a book to await both the Duke's return and Luke's reply to her warning.

"You should be safe enough here," Luke informed Flute as they drove up to the door of Knoll Grange, one of the smaller Hardwyck properties, only two hours' drive from London. "I may as well introduce myself to the staff here, in any event."

Flute clambered out of the carriage and looked around with wide eyes. "Is this the only house hereabouts, sir?"

"For a mile or more, yes, unless you count the farm buildings," said Luke with a smile. "Down you come, Argos! You should enjoy all of this space, even if Flute finds it oppressive."

"Op . . . If that's a bad thing, then no, I don't, sir. I've just never seen so much of it in one place before, is all."

Luke stepped up to the door, but before he could knock it was opened by a stout, motherly-looking woman in a cap and apron. "Mrs. Meecham?" he guessed, remembering the name of the housekeeper for the grange.

"Aye," she responded in a thick Scottish brogue, her eyes shrewd and appraising. "Be you the new master? I see the Hardwyck crest on your carriage. I dinna know you were coming, or I'd have prepared rooms and ordered up a fowl or two for dinner."

"No need, nor any apologies necessary. I won't be staying. However, this lad will. His name is Flute, and I'd like you to create a position for him here. He's been training as my valet in Town, but he's up to most tasks, I've found."

She regarded the boy appraisingly, a smile beginning to soften the severe line of her mouth. "Aye, we can find summat for him to do, milord. Come in, come in, both of ye." Gray eyes now twinkling, she swung the door wide for them to enter.

His uncle, Luke soon discovered, had rarely visited this property, spending most of his time in London or at the main Hardwyck estate in the north. The staff was therefore small, consisting only of the housekeeper, two maids, a cook, and one manservant.

The house, as its name implied, sat atop a small hill, with a pleasant prospect of the surrounding countryside. Luke could not imagine preferring the crowds and fogs of London to this, now that he'd seen it. What must Knox Abbey be like? He would find out as soon as everything was settled, he decided.

He spent an hour or two touring the house and surrounding farms, saw Flute installed in a comfortable room and Argos happily tussling with the farm dogs, then had a quick supper before heading back to Town.

"I'll return when I can," he promised his erstwhile valet. "If all goes as I hope, I'll be able to bring you back with me before long."

"No hurry, my lord," replied Flute with a grin, mopping up the last drops of a bowl of hearty country stew with a slice of the cook's delicious brown bread. "I'll be fine here."

Secure in the knowledge that Flute would be safe—and well fed—Luke headed back to London, his heart lighter than it had been in days, despite the fact that he still faced pistols at dawn. It was nearly midnight when he reached the city, but he directed his coachman to stop at Lord Marcus's residence before returning to Hardwyck Hall.

Marcus greeted him in the hall, having but that moment arrived home from a series of social engagements. "Good you stopped by, Luke. We haven't yet discussed the details for the morning. Still six o'clock at Primrose Hill, is it?"

"Unless you've heard again from Bellowsworth's second," Luke said, helping himself to a dollop of brandy from the sideboard in Marcus's library.

"Haven't heard a word since Ribbleton called on me Wednesday evening. I've still got to say this was a damned poor idea, even if you don't mean to kill him."

Luke shrugged. "Tempting as killing him is, I've given my word. And I suspect the experience will do the fellow good—providing he doesn't bring his mother along."

They both chuckled at that, then Marcus said, "Say, why don't you stay here tonight? We can jaw a bit before bed, have a bite in the morning, and ride over to Primrose Hill together."

As he had nothing in particular to return to at Hardwyck Hall, especially with Flute in the country, Luke readily agreed. They spent a pleasant hour over brandy, discussing various duels remembered and rumored, then began reminiscing about their time at Oxford.

"I envied you, did you know that?" Marcus asked at one point. "You never seemed the least bit worried about what would happen if we were caught climbing out of a window or picking a lock, while all I could think of was what my father would say if he knew. It must have been nice to have your family so comfortably remote."

Luke regarded his friend thoughtfully. He fully expected tomorrow's duel to come to nothing, but one never knew for certain how such things would go. This might be their last conversation.

"More remote than you knew," he said. "In truth, I had no family whatsoever—and quite envied you yours, hectoring older brothers and all."

"No family? But your uncle in Italy, your Aunt Lavinia in the country? I admit sometimes I suspected there were things you weren't telling me, but—"

"Quite a few things, in fact," Luke admitted with a rueful smile. "But I want to tell you now." As briefly as possible, he gave his friend a sketch of what his life had really been like.

Far from the censure he had feared, Marcus seemed utterly fascinated, asking question after question.

"So you were never answerable to anyone," he finally said, apparently more envious than ever. "How tame our exploits at Oxford must have seemed after risking life and limb daily on the streets! Even Peter's and Anthony's wartime stories can't compare. And just think what the Saint can do now you have the Hardwyck resources at your disposal!"

But Luke shook his head. "The Saint has retired."

Marcus regarded him knowingly. "The Lady Pearl? Does she know . . . ?"

"She does. And yes, it's for her sake that I've hung up my mask, so to speak—not that I ever actually wore one."

"Pity," said Marcus with a shake of his head. "Makes me more determined than ever that no woman will ever get her hooks in me."

Luke had to grin. "Tempting fate, are you?"

Then, at his friend's comical look of mock alarm, he added, "It's not so bad, I assure you."

Marcus protested such a possibility, and after a few more minutes of such banter, they finally made their way to bed.

Clarence, Marcus's valet, roused Luke before first light. Dressing hastily, he went down to join his friend for coffee and a muffin.

"I must stop by my own house before we go," he commented after draining his cup. "Can't show up with a rumpled coat and cravat, after all—won't inspire the proper dread at all. Would you mind lending me Clarence for half an hour? Flute is unavailable, as I said last night, and I haven't had a chance to look for another valet as yet."

"Certainly. I'll use that half hour to fetch the surgeon. For Bellowsworth, of course." Marcus grinned, but Luke detected a trace of anxiety in his eyes. "Shame the fellow didn't choose swords. Are you still the shot you were at Oxford?"

Luke rose. "We'll know soon enough, won't we?"

Wallis Knox surveyed the trees and shrubbery skirting the field on Primrose Hill in the glimmering predawn light. There. That copse would do nicely. Quickly but cautiously, he crossed the clearing and edged through the thick greenery beneath the trees, then turned and crouched.

Yes, he had a clear view of the field here, and should be invisible himself to all but the most discerning eye—not that anyone would be looking for him. He pulled out a gleaming pistol and checked it one more time. He'd had no opportunity to tamper with his nephew's pistol, but no matter. In an hour, if all went as planned, his lands and title would be restored to him.

Shifting to a more comfortable position, he settled down to wait.

Urging her mare faster, Pearl watched with growing alarm the pink and lavender of dawn spreading across the sky. She simply *must* arrive in time!

"How much farther?" she asked John Marley, riding by her side.

"Half a mile, my lady. No more." His voice gave no indication of whether he shared Hettie's disapproval of her desperate venture—nor did she care.

Finally, after what seemed like an hour but could only have been minutes, Primrose Hill came into view. They climbed the rise, and at first she saw no sign of anyone. Had she mistaken the time? The day? The place? But then she saw Luke's black gelding tethered to a tree at one end of the field, with two other horses beyond it. Was she too late? She spurred her mount forward.

"My lady," John called urgently, pacing her. "You cannot ride onto the field. It isn't done, and could put Lord Hardwyck at additional risk if you distract him."

Though every nerve screamed at her to hurry, she slowed her mount to a walk, then halted, still some distance from the field. John was right. And if some dastardly plot was afoot, as she suspected, she had more chance of discovering it by stealth than by charging ahead blindly. Such a distraction might provide Luke's enemy just the opportunity he needed.

Pearl slid from the saddle and continued on foot,

glad she'd had the foresight to wear her dark green habit. The trees screened her view of the field until she was quite near. Circling around to one side, she found a spot where she could see the figures taking their places.

So far, all looked as it should, or so she assumed from what she had read of duels. The seconds were pacing off the distance, and a moment later Luke and Lord Bellowsworth faced each other across twenty paces of lawn. The former appeared completely at his ease, the latter pale and trembling. She experienced a moment of pity for poor Bellowsworth, but reminded herself that Luke had promised not to kill him.

Off to the side stood Lord Marcus Northrup and Lord Ribbleton, who must be acting as Lord Bellowsworth's second. Behind them stood another man holding the black satchel that proclaimed him a surgeon. His presence drove home the seriousness of the situation. How good a shot was Bellowsworth? Or Luke, for that matter?

Recalling what Bellowsworth had told her of Wallis Knox, Pearl scanned the periphery of the field, but saw nothing.

"Positions, gentlemen," called Lord Marcus. The two principals came to attention and raised their pistols.

Just then, Pearl noticed a rustling in the shrubbery, not twenty feet from where she stood. She started forward, with a sharp cry, to investigate, and then several things happened almost at once.

Lord Marcus gave the command to fire, and a shot rang out across the field. Pearl whirled to see Bellowsworth's pistol falling to the ground unfired, his right sleeve torn between elbow and wrist. With a cry, he sank to his knees, clutching his injured arm, and at the same moment she heard, closer at hand, a muffled curse.

Luke still stood at his ease, a thin curl of smoke from his pistol the only evidence that he had moved at all.

The danger from Bellowsworth averted, Pearl focused on the hidden threat. Without stopping to consider, she plunged in the direction of that muffled curse, only to find herself facing the barrel of another pistol, this one held firmly in the grip of Wallis Knox, the man she had known for years as Lord Hardwyck.

"So, my lady," he hissed, all trace of urbanity erased from his manner. "You continue your penchant for interference. I understand I have you to thank for my present state, as my nephew would never have discovered his connection to me unaided. It seems I have a score to settle with you, as well as with him."

Her heart in her throat, Pearl forced herself to speak calmly. The others, tending to Lord Bellowsworth, had not yet noticed the drama unfolding in the bushes.

"I should think it is your own conscience with which you need to settle, sir," she said. "That you are still free and in England at all is a blessing you do not deserve, after the crimes you have committed."

With a snarl, he lunged forward and grabbed her by the arm, thrusting the pistol against her side. "Always so very clever, my lady—or perhaps not.

Come." Holding her arm in a bruising grip, he walked her onto the field.

Lord Marcus was the first to notice them, and at his startled movement, the others looked up. Luke, crouched by Bellowsworth's side, rose and stepped forward with an oath. Then, abruptly, he halted, his glance falling to the pistol Knox held, still pressed firmly against Pearl's ribs.

"So we meet at last by light of day, *Lord Hardwyck*," Knox said mockingly. "But this time I seem to have the advantage. I mean to use it to repay you for what you have made me suffer."

Chapter 22

Luke paused for a long moment, sizing up the situation, then slowly took one more step toward Knox. Pearl, alert to his every nuance, noticed that he kept his right hand behind him, out of sight.

"I believe your accounting is in error, dear Uncle." Luke's voice was calm—deceptively calm, she thought. "You are the one with a debt only partially paid. I confess I was most disappointed when you chose not to contest my claim."

"I was given little choice in the matter, but I am here to contest it now." Knox swept the small group with a glance, his eye lingering on Bellowsworth. "I knew I could not safely delegate such an important matter to a lily-livered poltroon like you."

Luke took another cautious step forward. "A curious epithet, coming from a man who uses a lady as a shield," he commented lightly. "One, in addition, who was not above murdering women and children in their beds."

A chorus of muttered exclamations broke out from the group behind him at these words, and Knox scowled. "If you value this woman's life, you'll say no more on that subject."

With her eyes, Pearl tried to convey to Luke that he was not to worry about her, but he did not even look at her, keeping his eyes on her captor's, gauging his mood.

"What will it profit you to harm her?" asked Luke reasonably. He was walking a fine line, trying to unsettle the man without goading him into unreasoning fury. All for her sake.

"It is I who stand in the way of all you want," he continued. "I who stripped you of your lands, title, power. If you have but one shot to use, would it not be better spent on me?"

The pistol in her side shifted slightly, and Pearl, fearing that Knox meant to fire on Luke instead, twisted suddenly in his grasp. "No!" she cried, heedless of the risk to herself. "Luke, don't!"

With a vicious curse, Knox thrust her away from him. Pearl fell to her hands and knees, then looked up to see him bringing the pistol to bear upon Luke. Dodging to one side, Luke whipped another weapon from behind him—Bellowsworth's, which he must have retrieved from the ground before approaching his uncle.

Pearl let out a scream at the report of Knox's pistol, but the ball whizzed harmlessly past Luke's ear. Falling to one knee, Luke himself took aim and pulled the trigger.

Nothing happened.

"What the devil . . . ?" He glanced questioningly over his shoulder at Bellowsworth, whose color was gradually returning.

"I . . . I unloaded it," his erstwhile opponent stammered. "Knox said that your pistol would be rendered useless, so after what Lady Pearl told me, I thought that if neither of us could fire . . ."

With another oath, Knox tossed aside his spent weapon, and now Luke did the same as the older man advanced on him, his face suffused with a rage that bordered on madness.

"You're all in league!" he shouted. "But I'll have what's mine again. I won't be made a fool of by anyone."

Luke stood his ground, his own anger seeming to turn cold and dangerous as his uncle's burned the hotter.

Pearl turned to Lord Marcus and Lord Ribbleton, who both seemed frozen in surprise. "Do something!" she cried. "You must stop this."

Thus summoned to action, they stepped forward to intervene before Knox and Luke could come to blows, but Luke spoke sharply, halting them.

"No," he said. "This reckoning is past due. I've a score of my own to settle, and now seems as good a time as any."

"With fisticuffs?" asked Pearl, aghast. Luke was taller than his uncle, but the older man was both broader and heavier—and angrier. She doubted Knox would fight fairly, in any event.

Luke did not even glance at her. "Did you not say you were here to challenge my claim?" he asked his uncle.

A slow smile spread across Knox's face, though the fury in his eyes did not lessen. "I did. Name your weapons, Nephew."

Pearl thought she saw a glimmer of satisfaction in Luke's eyes. "As pistols have proven singularly unproductive this morning, I'll choose the swords." He motioned to Lord Marcus, who, after a moment's hesitation, strode to the edge of the field and returned carrying a long wooden case.

"On a whim, and warned by a note I received this morning"—he glanced at Pearl with a smile—"I thought to bring these along. A good thing, as it turns out, is it not, Uncle?" Luke asked almost pleasantly, taking the case from Marcus and opening it to reveal a pair of antique duelling rapiers.

"Indeed. I've always been a traditionalist—it's why you found these at Hardwyck Hall. A pity your generation no longer trains with the sword as a matter of course." Knox seized one of the rapiers and swung it expertly over his head, then practiced a few feints.

Luke's dangerous smile never wavered as he picked up the other sword. "Perhaps that advantage will help to compensate for your advanced years— the years you denied my father."

Pearl watched the proceedings with growing horror, sorry she had spoken before. A fistfight would have been far preferable to this! "Luke, please." Somehow she had to stop this.

"I'm sorry, Pearl," Luke said, never taking his eyes from his adversary. "This is something I have to do. One way or another, the past must be put to rest."

Lord Marcus closed the sword case and stepped

back. At his word, the two antagonists saluted each other with their weapons, and then the fight began. Not a person there doubted that it would be to the death, could either of them achieve that end—though Pearl was the only spectator who fully understood why.

The two men circled each other slowly, each feeling out the other's defenses, taking the time to prepare a strategy.

"Even if you best me, Uncle, you won't regain the earldom, you know," said Luke conversationally, feinting to the left, then the right, watching how the other man parried. "The Duke of Oakshire knows of your crimes, as does the Prince Regent. To allow you to profit might encourage other ambitious younger brothers."

Knox parried again, then thrust low—an illegal stroke, but one that Luke easily diverted with his own rapier. "If I cannot profit, neither shall you," he said. "Robbery sets a poor example as well, wouldn't you say, Saint?"

If he expected the accusation to startle Luke into a mistake, he was disappointed. Luke waited for his chance, then thrust high, forcing Knox back a pace as he parried.

"Who is the more guilty?" Luke asked musingly. "A man who steals, or the murderer who drives him to it?" He was watching Knox's eyes now, as well as his chest. Both telegraphed his next move, a vicious lunge that would have impaled Luke through the heart had he not stepped aside at the last moment.

"So you admit your guilt?" Knox demanded, his exertions now limiting him to shorter sentences.

Luke was quick to take advantage of the older

man's inferior conditioning. "I admit nothing," he replied, circling and feinting, forcing Knox to move more and more rapidly to avoid the tip of his blade. "However, it ill behooves a man who kills his brother and leaves his brother's wife and child for dead to show such belated concern for how that child made his way in an unfriendly world."

"Concern? Hardly that." Knox was breathing heavily now, beads of sweat tricking down his brow. He attempted another vicious thrust, this time at Luke's throat, as his temper overcame his judgment.

Luke brought his own blade across and down, nearly snapping the tip of Knox's sword as he forced it toward the ground. "No concern from my nearest relative? Uncle, you wound me."

"I'll wound you and more." Knox took a pace back, then lunged forward, madness again raging in his eyes. "I spent twenty years and more building the name and fortune of Hardwyck to what it is now. No upstart street thief is going to destroy that."

As he spoke, he drove his rapier straight at Luke's chest, ignoring everything else in his determination to kill the man he blamed for his humiliation. Unable to dodge, Luke brought his blade up, deflecting the deadly thrust even as Knox's own momentum drove Luke's sword home.

Knox stared down in shock for a moment at the crimson stain spreading across his white shirt and embroidered waistcoat, then dropped to his knees. "Damn you, and damn your father before you," he gasped. "You're not worthy of the Hardwyck name."

Luke withdrew his blade and watched impassively as his uncle crumpled to the ground. "No, you have damned yourself. My father and mother are finally avenged. I may not be worthy, but I am Hardwyck, and I will uphold the honor of that name for as long as I live." He spoke it as a vow, and was stunned to realize he meant every word.

The surgeon hurried forward now, and Luke stepped back to allow him to do what he could. Marcus handed him a handkerchief, and he used it to wipe first his brow, then his blade. Finally he turned to Pearl, who still stood with one hand at her throat, so pale that he thought she might faint.

"He's dead, my lords," the surgeon announced.

"Is it true?" Marcus asked, glancing down at the fallen Knox, then back to Luke. "Did he actually kill your father?"

Slowly, Luke nodded. "He did. And as you can see, he was unrepentant to the last."

Marcus, of course, did not mention Knox's own accusations—nor did the others, to Luke's relief.

"We'll have to notify someone, I suppose." Now that it was all over, Luke felt a wave of weariness wash over him, weighing his limbs and numbing his brain. He swayed, but Pearl was suddenly at his side, supporting him.

"We'll go to my father," she suggested. "He will know what steps must be taken."

No one had any objection to this plan, so, leaving the surgeon to tend to the body and Lord Ribbleton to tend to Bellowsworth, Luke followed Pearl and Marcus to the horses.

"Can you ride?" asked Pearl in obvious concern when they reached their mounts.

Shaking off his weariness with an effort, Luke nodded. "I am unhurt. I won't deny that it has been a long morning, however." Nor was it over, by any means. The full implications of what had happened here had yet to be sorted out.

Pearl smiled up at him, and he felt his strength returning. "Come, then. Let's go home."

Riding back to Oakshire House, Pearl watched Luke anxiously. Whatever life he had led, whatever duels he had fought in the past, killing his own uncle must have affected him profoundly. She had never seen him look so weary as he had when the surgeon pronounced Knox dead.

Now, however, he sat his horse well, handling the reins with perfect competence. By the time they halted, his color had returned and he looked much as he always did, if rather more serious than usual.

The Duke was at home, to Pearl's relief. She had not had a chance to speak with him yet, as he had returned too late last night for an audience with her. This promised to be a lengthy interview—and a startling one, for her father. She hoped he would not be too upset.

"Now, what is all this?" the Duke asked, joining them in the library after only a few minutes. "Upwood gave me to understand that there was a matter of some urgency?" He pinned Luke, Lord Marcus, and Pearl alternately with his keen gray eyes.

"Yes, Father, it's—" Pearl began, but Luke stood and silenced her with an upraised hand.

"Your Grace, I have just killed the man who previously styled himself Lord Hardwyck—my uncle."

His voice was nearly emotionless, but Pearl, alert to his every nuance, could hear an undercurrent of sadness and resignation.

"Indeed!" the Duke exclaimed. "Are you confessing to a murder, lad?"

Pearl started to her feet, but again Luke waved her to silence. "There was a duel, Your Grace, and though its beginning was somewhat unconventional, it was conducted before the usual witnesses. Whether or not the circumstances exonerate me, I will leave it to you—and perhaps a jury—to decide."

The Duke now turned his eye on Lord Marcus. "You were his second?" he asked.

Marcus nodded. "I was, Your Grace, and I can state unequivocally that Knox gave Luke—Lord Hardwyck—no choice in the matter. He had already attempted murder on his own account, and threatened your daughter, the Lady Pearl, as well. Lord Hardwyck acted from the highest motives, to protect her as well as himself."

"Is this true?" Her father regarded Pearl in obvious alarm. "Knox involved you in this?"

"Yes, Father." She tried to speak calmly, but her voice trembled at the memory of those few terrifying moments. "Mr. Knox held me hostage with a pistol in an attempt to lure Luke close enough to murder him. Luke—Lord Hardwyck—goaded him into a challenge to induce him to release me unharmed."

The Duke turned back to Luke. "Then I have much to thank you for, it appears. Not only have you rid the land of a dangerous criminal, something

I'd have preferred to have done when the truth first came to light, but you have kept my most precious possession from harm. You have my gratitude, Lord Hardwyck, and I will do everything in my power for you."

Luke still stood, facing him. "Everything, Your Grace?"

"I have said so. What is it you wish me to do?"

"Grant me your daughter's hand in marriage," he replied without hesitation, "should this current matter be settled to your satisfaction."

The Duke blinked, looking from Luke to Pearl and back. "You have discussed this with her, I presume?"

Though nearly as startled as the Duke, Pearl rose to stand beside Luke, placing her hand in his. "Yes, Father. It is my dearest wish as well."

"I won't deny I have suspected a partiality for some time," the Duke conceded. "But what of Bellowsworth?"

"He has relinquished his claim on my hand," Pearl replied. "He has no wish to make me unhappy by persisting in his suit. I know it will occasion some trouble, as well as much talk, as the papers have been drawn up and announcements published, but—"

Her father waved that aside with one large hand. "Paperwork and gossip are of no consequence if your happiness is at stake, my dear. I only wish to be certain that it is what you really want."

"It is," she assured him fervently. She squeezed Luke's hand, and he returned the pressure, sending a wave of warmth and security through her.

"Then let's settle this other matter as expeditiously as may be, so that we can move on to more cheerful concerns. Who were the other witnesses?"

Luke replied, "In addition to Lord Marcus and Lady Pearl, there was a surgeon, Mr. Carter, as well as Lord Bellowsworth and Lord Ribbleton, who acted as his second."

The Duke's heavy brows rose. "There is quite a tale connected with this, I perceive. Tell me all, from the beginning, and then we will summon the others to corroborate your story. If they are able to do so, I see no need to bring this before the magistrate.

Luke and Pearl took their seats, and Luke proceeded to recount the chain of events leading up to Knox's death. He omitted only the circumstances that had led to his challenge of Bellowsworth, instead implying that his emotions had bested his judgment during an argument.

By the end of the day, all was settled. Bellowsworth, who had suffered a mere scratch on his forearm, formally renounced his claims and fully corroborated Lord Hardwyck's story, as did the other witnesses. The Duke wrote everything down, including his opinion that the matter be considered closed.

Before Luke took his leave late that afternoon, Pearl led him out into the garden for a few private words, though the day had become overcast.

"A fit setting," Luke commented, looking around him at the roses. Then he took Pearl by the hand, his expression serious. "Well, my love, save for the formalities, it appears our future is all but assured. If you are having second thoughts about wedding a man with my history, now is the time to express them."

"No second thoughts," she replied with a smile. "Unless, of course, you are only marrying me to buy my silence? Now that the others have given their statements, it appears I am the only one you need fear might identify you as the notorious Saint of Seven Dials." Though she spoke playfully, a tiny doubt, a remnant of earlier fears, arose as she spoke.

It appeared he was aware of it. "I would turn myself in at once rather than risk you believing that, Pearl. Would you like me to confess it to your father?"

His seriousness alarmed her. "No! Of course not." Not caring how brazen she appeared, she moved closer, putting her hands on his shoulders, tilting her face up to invite his kiss. "I know I have always sought to control everything in my sphere, to include you, Luke. But I want you to know that I am trying to reform. My recent attempts at control have had some rather disastrous consequences, after all."

He lowered his lips to hers for a lingering kiss that promised a lifetime of delights. "And some rather charming ones, as well," he reminded her a moment later. "I have no wish to change you, Pearl. Your strength of will and your quick mind are among the things I admire most about you."

"How curious. I was about to say the same thing of you."

Now he grinned. "As long as we share common goals, we should deal very well indeed, don't you think?"

"I do. Right now, my goal is to be wed as soon as

may be, so that we can pursue other, ah, goals freely. Dare I hope you share it?"

He answered her with another kiss, demonstrating his desire in the only way he could, given their surroundings.

Nearly three weeks passed before Pearl and Luke exchanged vows in the ivy-covered chapel at Oakshire—the day after her twenty-first birthday. In drawing up the marriage settlements, Luke himself had insisted on the date, to safeguard Pearl's holdings. The Duke had been surprised at a second request he had made, but had agreed readily enough.

Emerging from the chapel along a path strewn with rose petals, Pearl smiled up at Luke as he held her hand, encased in a white lace glove, close to his heart. A carriage, bedecked with flowers and greenery, waited to convey them back to the enormous manor house for a lavish wedding breakfast, but they paused before entering it to exchange a few words, first with Lord Marcus, and then with the Duke and Duchess of Oakshire.

"Thank you, Father, for everything," said Pearl, kissing the Duke on the cheek. Then she turned to the Duchess, to kiss her as well. "And thank you too . . . Mother."

The Duchess's eyes widened for a moment, but then she smiled. "I have always tried to do my best by you, Pearl, though I know we have had our differences. Perhaps we shall have a chance to become friends, now that we will not be under the same roof."

"I do hope so." Pearl spoke with complete sincerity, whether she believed such an outcome likely or not.

Luke now bent down to lift up the little boy standing next to the Duchess. "So, young Edward, have you given any thought to the succession as yet? You'll be choosing a wife for yourself before you know it."

The child grinned at him and giggled, then glanced at his mother and sobered slightly. "Mother says people are supposed to call me Lord Morehaven—but you can call me Edward. We're brothers now, aren't we?"

Luke tousled his hair before setting him back on his feet, ignoring the way the Duchess's mouth primmed at the exchange. "We are indeed, and I must say, I've always wanted a brother. I hope we'll have some capital times together."

Finally, Luke handed Pearl into their carriage. Once the door was closed and the gravel was crunching beneath their wheels as they made their way up the path, he turned to her.

"Now that I have you secure, there is something you need to know," he told her ominously.

Her eyes widened, though the love shining out of them never wavered. "More secrets? I thought we had done with those."

"This will be the last, I promise you."

Reaching inside his coat, he pulled out the document giving her complete control over Fairbourne. In it, he relinquished a husband's usual claim over a wife's property, ceding to her the management and ultimate disposition of the estate.

She read through the paper, her mouth a small O of surprise, then gazed up at him, her eyes shining. "What a perfect wedding gift!" she exclaimed.

He grinned down at her. "I thought if you had an estate to manage, you'd be less tempted to manage me."

"That reminds me," Pearl said then, with a rather mischievous grin. "I have a gift for you, as well." From her reticule, she drew out a small stack of calling cards inked with a curious design: a number seven, capped by an oval halo. Luke recognized it at once.

"I made them myself," she explained. "Should you choose to continue as the Saint of Seven Dials, I knew you would wish to leave these behind to, ah, tweak the conscience of Society."

Luke chuckled. "And continue to set the *ton* on its collective ear!" Sobering, he met her eyes and saw the vague anxiety there, though she was clearly striving to hide it. She was making a great sacrifice under the guise of a jest—one he was glad would be unnecessary.

"No, my sweet, you need not worry. My thieving days are over. We'll find other ways to help the poor unfortunates of Seven Dials. Thank you for the gift, however—and even more for the thought behind it." He tucked the cards in his pocket. Perhaps he would slip some of them to Marcus later, to see what use he might make of them.

Pearl's anxiety vanished, though her smile held a trace of wistfulness. "I believe I may miss my roguish thief. He brought such excitement to my staid life."

"I never promised to leave *all* wickedness behind," he said, stripping off one of her lace mittens, then one of his own kidskin gloves, to clasp her hand, flesh to flesh. "I intend to prove quite the opposite tonight."

Her blue-violet eyes grew smoky with desire. "I can scarcely wait."

To the delight of the onlookers running alongside the carriage, he took her in his arms. She responded eagerly to his kiss—so eagerly that they were both flushed with passion when the carriage finally rolled to a stop before the great house.

"I will accept that as a down payment of your pledge," Pearl murmured as a footman opened the carriage door. "But I expect payment in full tonight."

"And you shall have it," Luke promised, drinking in the sight and scent of her, this woman he loved with every fiber of his being. "I swear it, on my honor as a rogue."